REUNITED

"*Nothing's* happened." She looked into his face, felt a clamping sensation around her heart, then looked away. "A kiss. We're two adults. There's no reason to make a big deal out of such a little thing."

"We're not just any two adults, Jane. We were in love."

"When we were seventeen to twenty-two. Practically children. People that age fall in and out of love all the time, Roy. They—"

"You didn't," he said. "I didn't," he added, pulling her to him.

It would be so easy to throw herself into his arms, to lose herself there. Instead, she planted her hands against his chest. "But we drifted apart for a reason."

"What was the reason?"

Before she could answer, he bent down and nuzzled her ear. A gasp escaped her lips, and her mind blanked for a moment before rational thought broke the surface again. "We went our separate ways," she said.

"And now our paths have crossed again," he murmured before brushing his lips against hers.

Once their mouths touched, pulling apart was impossible . . .

Published by Kensington Publishing Corporation

You're Still The One

JANET DAILEY

Cathy Lamb • Mary Carter
Elizabeth Bass

ZEBRA BOOKS
KENSINGTON PUBLISHING CORP.
http://www.kensingtonbooks.com

ZEBRA BOOKS are published by

Kensington Publishing Corp.
119 West 40th Street
New York, NY 10018

All Kensington titles, imprints, and distributed lines are available at special quantity discounts for bulk purchases for sales promotion, premiums, fund-raising, educational, or institutional use.

Special book excerpts or customized printings can also be created to fit specific needs. For details, write or phone the office of the Kensington Special Sales Manager: Attn. Special Sales Department. Kensington Publishing Corp., 119 West 40th Street, New York, NY 10018. Phone: 1-800-221-2647.

Zebra and the Z logo Reg. U.S. Pat. & TM Off.

ISBN-13: 978-1-4201-2419-4
ISBN-10: 1-4201-2419-6

First Printing: March 2013

10 9 8 7 6 5 4 3 2 1

Printed in the United States of America

Contents

THE APPLE ORCHARD

Cathy Lamb

Prologue

For most of my childhood I was poor.

I spent years living in a dismal trailer next to an apple orchard. I have spent years trying to forget those years.

My mother died the day after we made an apple pie.

I left home at sixteen.

I fell in love with a man I met at a waterfall. Something very sad happened.

We broke up. I have never stopped missing him.

I bought used clothing until I was twenty-two.

After college I worked for a high-end retail corporation. My fancy outfits helped me to hide my past from myself. I ended up vice president.

I saved money. When you grow up poor, you fight hard to leave poverty far behind.

I was fired when I told my boss off. She threw her Manolo Blahniks at me.

My dad died an hour after I was fired. We hadn't spoken in years because he was both scary and abusive. He left me an apple orchard.

It's hurtful that he chose to leave me apples.

I am using an urn, filled with his ashes, as a doorstop.

My name is Allie Pelletier and that's the summation of my life.

Chapter One

"The doctor will be with you in about ten minutes."

"Thank you." I smiled through gritted teeth, blood gushing down my leg.

The nurse, over six feet tall with curly gray hair, pressed a cloth to my wound, peering at it through his black-rimmed glasses. "You've got Dr. Rios. He recently moved here from New York. Excellent doctor. We were lucky to get him. You're traumatized? He'll untraumatize you—that's what we say here in Portland's greatest emergency room."

The nurse, whose name was Kevin, did not notice the blood instantly draining from my face, as he was busy tending to the blood draining from my thigh.

I swayed on the bed, gripped the handles, and took a deep breath. "It's not . . ." I struggled to breathe, the pain from my gaping gash suddenly gone, lost in my sheer panic. "It's not *Jace* Rios?"

"Yep, you got it. The one and the same. Not surprised you've heard of him. He has an amazing reputation. He's been featured in newspapers and medical journals. He's written articles and done extensive research on best medical practices for all sorts of life-threatening events. You bust it up, he'll fix you up. You're busted up, Miss Pelletier, and he's gonna fix you up."

I swayed again.

Kevin stood, winked at me, then noticed my rapidly declining state. "You're not looking too good. Here, how about you lie down for me, close your eyes, think about being on an island with a pretty drink . . ."

I flopped straight back on the bed, the room spinning, as he took my pulse.

"Your pulse is higher than it was . . . blood pressure is, too," he mused, a bit confused. "Okay, Miss Pelletier, I want you to take some deep, calming breaths. You'll be sewn up like a quilt in no time, by the master quilter himself . . ."

A man's face, Jace's face, floated in front of my eyes. Straight, thick black hair, longer in the back—not long, exactly, but enough to run my fingers through. Dark eyes, high cheekbones. He had a face that was tough, a don't-mess-with-me kind of face, lined from hours of being outside and from a chaotic childhood.

He had a face you wouldn't want to meet up with in a dark, back alley, but once you knew him, knew his kindness, his openness, you knew his innate goodness. If he was in a dark, back alley, it was because he was administering medical care.

"I can't believe this."

"Believe it! You're going to have to be more careful around horses in future," Kevin said, chuckling. "Ya gotta get out of their way when those hooves come up and kickin' . . ."

It had been a horrible summer. Everything, all at once. I was fired from my job after telling my boss exactly what I thought of her, my rougher upbringing coming out in my language. After she threw her Manolo Blahniks at me, I picked them up, waved good-bye, sold them online, and donated the money to a kids' hospital in her name.

Then I received that phone call which, surprisingly, knocked me over. I decided to sell my condo because I didn't like it anymore anyhow. I moved. And, once again, I was dealing with the bitter loss and raging anger that I had stomped down hard over the years. Now this.

Jace.

I had to get out of the hospital. This was not going to work. I struggled up, feeling nauseous.

"No, now don't try to get up, Miss Pelletier. You're pale as a flying ghost. Here, let me take some of that hay out of your hair. What's this? You have a couple of branches in there, too. Ah well, all that brown hair ya got, things are bound to get lost in there. I'll get a cloth for the dirt on your face; you'll be feeling better in a one, two, three . . ."

I have to get away from Jace.

"You know," Kevin said, almost to himself, "I'm going to see if I can get Dr. Rios in here pronto. Your eyes seem a bit vague and unfocused. You're not cooperating real well, either."

"I'm fine, quite fine. In fact, I think I'll bandage this up myself." I pulled on the collar of my light green hospital gown, open at the back. Gall. If I stood up, my white butt would be hanging out the back. And my underwear. Oh, groan. I'd worn my old beige *grandma* pair. I think there was a rip on the side . . .

The nurse chuckled. "No, ma'am. You are not going to be able to bandage this up on your own."

"I'll duct tape and staple it then." I envisioned myself sneaking around hospital corners and furtively limping down the hallways. I would drive to another hospital. I could not see Jace now. I could not see Jace *at all.*

"Duct tape and staples, ha! Hang on now, I'll let the good Dr. Rios know we're ready. Don't you wiggle on out! Promise me you'll stay right here? No hopping up on the saddle, if you know what I mean, and galloping back into the country." His eyes twinkled. "I can't leave till you give me your word."

"Sure will. I'll stay." I sure as hell would *not.* The nurse left and as soon as he was gone, I sat up and swung my legs over the bed, the paper crackling beneath my butt and my grandma underwear.

"Holy hell," I muttered. My head felt fuzzy. My thigh sent up lightning flames of pain. I felt ill with panic and the desire to escape. I lay back down. "Slower, Allie. Take it slow and easy."

I thought of Jace again, smiling, friendly, his hand in mine, pulling me closer to him, both of us in bathing suits in the lake, his leg between mine . . . then the tears that followed the disaster. That wretched disaster. He didn't even know about it. I hadn't told him. The first disaster had led to the second disaster, so nothing needed to be told.

I heard that other voice in my head, the harsh words, the accusation. *My fault, my fault, all my fault.*

I yanked myself up again, gripping the silver bed rails with both hands, and tried to breathe right. Across the room was a mirror. I gaped at it, my mouth dropping open. "That cannot be me. It *cannot.*"

My brown hair, about the color of dark chocolate, was a mess. It had fallen halfway out of the ponytail I'd pulled it into for the usual morning chores on the farm, which I was terrible at. I had hay sticking out in several places. No makeup, of course, and dirt on both cheeks. I had bags under my golden-ish eyes because I was regularly up until two in the morning, often striding through the apple trees my dad left me, hoping to walk myself into exhaustion.

I was too thin. Not because I wanted to be, but because food doesn't taste good when you're spiraling into one of life's pits.

I groaned at my gross face, hopped to the floor on one foot, wobbled, then shakily pulled off the light green hospital gown. I pulled on my jeans, ignoring the blood still zipping down my leg. The duct tape and stapler thing wasn't going to work. I shoved my feet back into my knee-high black farm boots.

I scrambled into my red push-up bra and oversized plaid shirt. The top button was missing. Too much cleavage showed, but I had not dressed to go to the hospital and see *him*; I had dressed to feed horses, chickens, dogs, and cats, none of whom cared about cleavage. I would have worn one of my exercise bras, but both were in the wash. Hence, red lace push-up and a farm shirt.

I took my first step, which was unbalanced. Then I took my second one. More wobble, more pain, screeching pain. I winced, clenching my teeth. *Go, Allie, Go! Start sneaking around those corridors!*

At the third wobbly movement the curtain opened and there he was.

Yes, Jace Rios.

All six-foot-four inches of muscle. Shoulders like a truck. He still had that head of thick black hair, courtesy of a Mexican grandfather. He wore the white coat well. I felt tears burning my eyes. Yes, he looked good in that white coat. He had become who he was destined to become, who he dreamed of becoming.

Jace Rios. Extraordinary doctor.

His head was down, studying my chart, and I saw him freeze for a second.

I knew he'd seen my name.

His head snapped up. He still had that intense, dark gaze—a man who really looked at you, who was truly interested in what you said and didn't say. A man who was interested in who you are, way down deep—not the shallow stuff we show the world, but who we are when all the layers are pulled back and only raw honesty is left. I tried to get air in, couldn't, and squeaked out, with all that I had left, "Hi, Jace. Good to see you again."

Then I passed out.

Chapter Two

"Breathe in, Allie," Jace said, holding an oxygen mask over my face.

That *voice*. That low, gravelly voice I had heard in my head every day for years. The pain came rolling on in, crashing against my insides. It was not pain from my leg.

It was pain from a long time ago; it should have been long gone. Tears filled my eyes, so for long seconds I left them closed, blocking out that face I knew so well, until I could gather my strength enough to open them.

When I did, I saw Jace and nurses, including Kevin, hovering around me.

"And hello again to our horse-loving friend who tried to escape the hospital," Kevin said, clucking his tongue in admonishment. "I told you not to gallop off!"

Jace's eyes were on mine and I could not look away.

I bet he thought the hay in my hair was attractive. Probably liked the circles under my eyes, too. I might well smell like a horse or a dog or both—a hordog. Why could I not have seen Jace again while wearing something silky and sweet, not bleeding and dirt covered?

"How are you feeling, Allie?"

I nodded, then took off the oxygen mask. His hand closed over mine over the mask, his fingers warm.

"I'm just dandy."

I saw his eyes crinkle in the corners.

Sarcasm is my specialty. I used it to get through my childhood.

"Dandy, huh?" he said. "That's why you passed out?"

"Yes. It was a swoon. Not a pass-out."

The nurses laughed. I saw Jace's mouth, that mouth I'd kissed a thousand times, turn upward the slightest bit. The smile, however, did not match the seriousness I saw in his expression. He knew why I had tried to leave.

"She swooned gracefully," Kevin said. "There was definitely some elegance there."

Jace seemed older, more experienced, the lines on his face more finely drawn. But—ah, shoot—sexier than ever. "Thank you, Kevin."

"You'd call that a swoon?" Jace asked. "Didn't look like much fun. You went white and then crumpled. I caught you before you crashed to the floor. Now you get to have your leg sewn up. More fun. A horse kicked you?"

I needed to mask what I was feeling, darn quick. Humor might work. I'd be humiliated if he knew what I was thinking, how crushed I felt looking at him. "She's in menopause."

"I'm sorry?" Jace said.

"I think she's in menopause."

"The horse is in menopause?"

I nodded. The nurses laughed.

"Spunky Joy appears to be having some emotional mood swings. She doesn't like male horses." I wondered if he was married. He didn't have a wedding ring on, but that didn't mean anything. Emergency room doctors who perform surgeries wouldn't wear rings.

"No male horses?" Jace asked.

"No. She's off men. She wants them to stay away." I wondered if he had kids.

Something flickered in his eyes and I knew he was relating that statement to us. I wanted to tie my tongue into a knot.

"Her horse boyfriend, Leroy, entered the barn, and Spunky Joy backed right into me, then kicked. I figure she is either madly in love with Leroy or they've had a bit of a spat." I bet Jace loved his wife and kids dearly. He had always wanted a family; he had been clear on that. He would be an outstanding dad. I wanted to pull that silly hospital blanket over my head and sob my brains out.

Jace's face finally started to relax, and he chuckled. It had been tight, focused, the second he saw me. "I'll fix up your menopause wound and you'll be good to go. You're going to have to take off your pants."

I sucked in my breath.

Something flashed in his eyes and this sizzle—yep, it was a sizzle—shook between us.

"I'll leave, don't worry. But don't try to escape again, or we'll have to track you down. You need to be sewn up." He left and the nurses helped me get my pants off, then Jace was back in.

While he stitched me up I could not look away from him. The nurses stayed for a bit, then left to tend to other patients.

"Whose horse was it, Allie?"

"My dad's."

I saw his jaw tighten, his gaze sharp on mine.

"My dad died. He lived in the country."

"I'm sorry."

"Thank you, but it's okay."

"When we were in Yellowstone, you told me you didn't get along with him, but you never told me anything else. I remember we talked about your not wanting to discuss your past."

"It was a messy past." I had told him few details about my dad. He had gently asked more, and I had given him, deliberately, the impression that my dad and I were temporarily not getting along. I didn't go anywhere near the depth of our estrangement.

"What happened?" he asked.

"Heart attack." I waved my hand. "I still don't want to talk about him."

"Okay." His eyes gentled, his hand warm on my leg. He went back to stitching me up. "You live in Portland, right?"

He knew I lived in Portland! Had he checked on me, as I had him? I had followed Jace's career online. I had felt like a stalker, but I did it anyhow. "I did. I moved recently to the country. My dad left me his house and an apple orchard."

"I remember you loved apples. You made apple pies."

"Yes, I did."

"Now and then, over the years, I've had apple pies, but they're never as good as yours."

"Really?" I was so pleased, I could feel myself blushing. "I still love apples, and now, I suppose, I have all the apples I need in that orchard."

"Sounds beautiful."

"It is. Sort of." That orchard was bringing back all sorts of harsh memories I didn't want to deal with.

"I'll take one of your apple pies."

I instantly envisioned me bringing him an apple pie, *naked*.

Stop it, Allie.

"I . . . uh . . . you want one of my apple pies?"

"Sure. Anytime. How about tomorrow?"

He smiled. So many times I had smiled back. Kissed those lips, held his face in my hands, pulled him down to me . . .

"I . . . uh . . . tomorrow? For a pie?"

"Sure. It'll be Wednesday. Wednesday is always a good time for apple pie. As are Tuesday and Friday . . . Monday isn't bad. I'll even take one on Sunday."

"You forgot Saturday."

"I'll have one then, too."

My leg was being sewn right up, his hands competent and efficient, comforting. It was like watching a seamstress.

The seamstress was turning me on and rebreaking my heart.

He stopped sewing and looked at me—serious, contemplative, flirty—daring me. For a second his eyes dropped to my shirt. I knew it was gaping. I looked down. That red push-up bra was doing what I paid it to do to my boobs.

It was all still there between us. That instant, intense, electric connection. How ridiculous that sounds; how true it was.

In those dark eyes I saw everything that I was feeling. I felt that . . . magnetism . . . what a dumb word. Electricity. Sparks. More silly words to describe my feelings toward Jace, but there it was.

He remembered.

He remembered everything.

He hadn't forgotten a thing.

Neither had I.

Not forgetting had been excruciatingly painful.

Chapter Three

Apple trees have been around forever.

They have an interesting history. Eve and her apple eating—naughty lady. Johnny Appleseed. Sir Isaac Newton and the apple. Apple pies.

On my dad's property in Schollton there are Jonagold, Gala, Honeycrisp, and Granny Smith apple trees. When I arrived five weeks ago, suitcases in hand, it hurt to see them. Yes, it *hurt* to see the apple trees.

How could he? I thought, stomping through the orchard west of his hundred-year-old, two-story, white, run-down home the first day I explored the property. There were two bullet holes in the house. One in the floor, one in the wall. I wasn't surprised. He probably put them there in a blast of self-righteous anger.

I zipped up one row and down the next, steaming mad. Why would he buy a dilapidated house and land with an apple orchard and leave it to me? Was he mocking me to the very end? He knew I loved apples. He had seen me eat them by the dozen. He knew why I ate them by the dozen.

"Spike me in the heart and twist it, Dad," I whispered into the orchard. Then I decided not to whisper. I would not let him smother my voice any longer. I picked up one apple after another and pelted them through the rows, swearing every single time an apple hit a tree. "You jerk . . . you were never a dad . . . you were horrible to Mom . . . you never even hugged me . . . and now you have an apple orchard? Really? An apple orchard?"

I threw those dead apples until I was sweating, my hair falling all over my face, my chest heaving. I started kicking the apples on the ground, sending them flying. When I was totally exhausted I collapsed against a tree, an *apple* tree from my stupid dad, and sobbed.

I sobbed for him, for us, for what he'd done to our family. I sobbed because I was so angry. So frustrated and resentful. And *guilty.* I felt guilt. He didn't deserve for me to feel guilty, but I did.

I composed the letter later that night.
I sent it to the top of the ladder.
Hopefully a wrong would be righted.
She shouldn't be allowed to give people nervous breakdowns.

At dusk, my bandages tight on my thigh, I limped out to my dad's creaking deck and stared at the orchard as the sun sank down over the blue-gray hills in the distance. Margaret and Bob, my dad's brown and white furry mutts, played together in the grass. Marvin, a gold cat, and Spot the Cat, a black cat who had no spots, perched on the rail of the deck, side by side. I saw Spunky Joy the horse in the field, she neighed at me, and I rolled my eyes.

"Hey you, menopause horse!" She swished her tail. "You gave me a bunch of stitches. Do you know that? Cool it with the hormonal swings and we'll get along better."

She neighed again.

"I don't like men, either, Spunky Joy, but that's no excuse for your hoof coming up and kicking me in the thigh."

She neighed.

"Yep. Women are better on their own, I agree with you there." I shook my head at the irony here. From retail executive supervising hundreds of employees, wearing outfits that cost hundreds of dollars and heels so high I could have broken an ankle if I fell, to an apple orchard, farm animals, and a sagging house where I sat on a deck and talked back to a horse.

The sky was a painting full of shining colors folding over the mountains. I swallowed more pain-reliever pills. I hate taking medicine, but I did it anyhow. Without it my bruised and cut leg would be throbbing.

I thought of seeing Jace at the hospital, letting him handle my thigh, talking to him again . . . and I smiled. Then I cried, some of the tears I'd dammed up forever spilling over. I cried as other memories slipped back in about a trailer awash in fear and domination and a young man in a lake who hugged me close.

Next I thought of the deranged man who had burst through the emergency room doors wielding a ferocious temper.

"I thought you were working for Mackie's Designs, Allie." Jace made a couple of final stitches, his hands sure, capable.

"I was. I was fired."

Jace's eyebrows rose. "You're kidding."

"No." Fired and my dad died. In one day.

"Why were you fired?"

"My boss pushed me to the edge of the cliff and I decided to jump instead of continuing to work for her. I told her what I thought of her and the way she treated other people. She didn't appear to like my input, and I left with a pair of designer heels."

"How did she treat people?"

"Worse than cattle. If she'd had a cattle prod and a red-hot branding iron, she would have used it."

He asked more questions. Jace was always curious, always wanted to know more about me, what I thought, my life. Most people don't. Bare essentials are enough for them.

"Way to go out in a blaze of glory, Allie." Those dark eyes said it all. He respected my decision. "Good for you. What do you want to do next?"

"I don't know. It hasn't been that long, but it feels like that person, who I was, is a strange and mysterious creature; and who I'll be in the future is also a strange and mysterious creature."

"Do you want to go back to retail management, back to being a VP?"

Aha! He knew that about me, too! I felt a bit giddy. "No, I don't want to." I thought of my bank account. I could not be poor again—could not. "If I *had* to go back to being an exec, I would. The thought makes me feel ill. I was not happy."

"Why weren't you happy?"

"Besides my boss, who arrived on a chariot from hell with a whip, my whole life was marketing and selling clothes. Choosing lines. Working with designers, public relations, managers, traveling. I love clothes, I love style." At least I used to love style. Wearing the latest fashions and four-inch heels allowed me to hide the "trailer trash" girl my father always told me I was. "Yet there was no substance to my job. There was nothing of value. I figured out how to sell expensive clothes to expensive people. I was exhausted all the time and I didn't have a life." I stopped. "Why am I telling you all this?"

"Because I asked."

"I know, but I haven't seen you in years and here I am, yammering on."

"We've always yammered on together." He smiled, and I saw sadness in his eyes, probably the same sadness that lived in my eyes. "If you could do anything, what would you do?"

"Bake pies. All day. I'd bake pies." I laughed and pushed a strand of hair back behind my ear. How I wished I'd washed my hair in the last three days, but I hadn't. Turmoil does that to a woman. "I've hardly baked pies at all for years, but I used to love it."

"They were delicious."

"Thank you." I blushed *again*. "My whole life needs a reset. After I was fired and my dad died, I decided to move out to his house in the country. My condo sold really fast. I don't know how to take care of apple trees and I now have two dogs, Bob and Margaret. Bob thinks squirrels are his sworn enemies and Margaret has to sleep with a stuffed pink bear in her paws or she won't sleep at all. I was up for thirty minutes the other night looking for that dumb pink bear."

We both laughed, and as we talked I continued to pretend I was confident. I pretended I was brave. I pretended I was in control, amusing. And I pretended I wasn't completely spun up about seeing him; that my insides weren't shaking.

"I'm so glad you're a doctor, Jace. I really am. Congratulations."

He looked at the floor for a second, then met my gaze. "Thank you."

"Tell me about medical school, where you did your residency, everything."

He smiled and told me about medical school. He made it short; he didn't talk about the newspaper articles that had been written about him, humble as always. I wanted to hug him. I wanted to cry on his shoulder. I wanted to tell him all my worries and problems. I was with the very best friend I had ever had in my life.

Only he was so much more than my best friend, because I

wanted to climb into a naked hug with him. I actually envisioned that, and could feel my face getting hot. I tried not to stare at his mouth. Tried not to remember kissing him, holding him close as I lay down and he lay on top of me in a tent, or by a river, or in a field on a blanket. I tried not to remember what that black hair felt like running through my fingers, and how that slight razor stubble would grate against my cheek in a way that turned me on even more.

I tried not to remember what those hands had done to me, what he'd said to me, how there had been this huge fire blazing between us.

I tried not to remember *us*. I tried hard.

In the end, before the deranged man walked in, it came out in my tears, which he gently, sweetly wiped away. I saw tears in his eyes, too.

We smiled at each other, one of his hands resting on my thigh where he'd fixed me up, burning me through, but comforting at the same time. Then all hell broke loose in the corridor. Instantly, Jace whipped around, threw open the curtain, and was gone. I heard yelling, swearing, and a man's voice bellowing, "Let me go and be free," and "You can't make me go in this prison," and "Shut up, weasels."

I followed Jace, worried about him, about what was going on, when I saw a young man being restrained by two medical personnel. He was thrashing about, head back, eyes wild.

Jace walked right up, his white doctor's coat billowing out behind him, and put a hand on the young man's shoulder. Behind the young man I could see two people who were clearly his distraught parents.

"Hello, I'm Dr. Rios."

The young man swore at him, stumbled a bit, then said, "I don't want to be here!"

"I hear you, man," Jace said. "A lot of people get the sweats walking into hospitals. I'm here because they pay me to be here. If there wasn't a paycheck involved, I'd never set foot in this place. Never."

I chuckled. I wasn't surprised by what Jace was saying. He was always so quick on his feet, so entertaining.

"Everything's white and sterile," Jacc went on calmly, as if he was conversing over a steak dinner. "There are shots here, bad-tasting medicines, all kinds of beeping machines, people in white coats rushing about who want to poke and prod you. No, I'd rather be biking."

"Yeah?" the young man yelled, still belligerent, still being restrained but slightly calmer. "I don't like it here. Yeah!"

"Yeah," Jace said. "Biking or fishing for me, that would be a better place to be. What would you rather be doing?"

The young man looked confused. "I dunno, man! Maybe fishing for a shark. I know I shouldn't be here. I didn't mean to do that much of that white powder, and I only needed to chill out, you know, kick back? The whole thing messed with my brain and I don't like it here."

"I know, friend." Jace patted the young man on the shoulder. "How about if you and I sit down and I'll make sure you're doing all right, and then we'll send you back out and you can go fishing for a shark. How's that sound?"

The young man struggled again, still confused, still fighting but halfheartedly. "Okay, but I'm not stayin' in a hospital. No way. You can't make me."

"That's right. I can't." Jace nodded. "It's a free country, buddy, and you can make your own choices. But you look like someone I can sit down and talk to, and I need a break. I need to sit down, rest my feet. It's been a busy night—a lady got kicked by a horse—so come on in this room and we'll get things figured out."

"Nah. No. I don't want to go in a room. You might lock me up. Leave me there. I'd be alone. I gotta take off my clothes and my head is all screwed up and I itch and I'm seeing weird stuff in front of my eyes. Is there an elephant in that corner?"

"No. No elephant. We got rid of the elephants last week." Jace put his hands out. "They took up too much room. But look here. There's not even a door on this room. Only a curtain. You want out, you're out. Come on in. Let's talk. Five minutes. I know you're busy."

"I'll give you five minutes," the young man insisted, holding seven fingers up. "Five. I got things to do and my guitar is talking to me and I gotta get some Jell-O. I need Jell-O."

"We have Jell-O here. I think it's red. Or green. Can't remember. We've got chocolate chip cookies, too, I think. I like those. Not as much as apple pie. Allie's apple pie."

I froze on my good leg as Jace turned toward me for a millisecond and grinned.

"Anyhow, I'll have someone bring the Jell-O up. Come on in and hang with me for a minute."

"Okay, doctor dude. I'll do it. Let's go, Mom."

The young man's parents, already limp with stress, sagged in relief when their son stopped fighting.

I didn't want to stay in the hospital any longer, either. Hospitals make me nervous, too. All those shots, machines, scary things happening. But there was Jace. Gorgeous and kind. He was one reason to stay, but I knew I wouldn't.

I limped out. As I passed, I listened to Jace speaking calmly to the young man, figuring out what drugs he'd taken; so soothing, so in control. I glimpsed the back of his head, that black hair I used to love to touch.

I started crying even before I walked through the hospital's exit door. My tears lasted all the way down the highway, back into the country, by the vineyards and farms, and up to the seriously-needing-work white house my dad had left to me. Probably the only thing he had ever given to me.

My leg burned as I went up the stairs of the deck. I sank onto a couch in the family room, stunned. Seeing Jace again had knocked me down like a pitchfork to my heart. The pain was as raw and as fresh as the day we broke up.

Margaret and Bob put their heads in my lap and I petted them. Margaret whined. She'd lost her stuffed pink bear again. I got up to find it.

I didn't think I'd see Jace again in my entire life.

Now he was back. Less than half an hour away, living here.

I wanted to hold that man, but it wouldn't work. For many reasons, it wouldn't work. I had done the unforgivable. Jace would not like me if he ever found out.

I stared at my dad's urn. I could hardly believe it when the attorney my dad hired to handle his estate and cremation called me about his death. I was so angry.

So, so angry.

I ride my bike to get rid of some of that anger. I have a really cool bike. It was expensive. I have cool bike clothes, too, also expensive. I am not trying to show off; I'm trying to outride being poor and desperate. My mother bought me a pink bike with a basket, which I rode in Montana. I loved it. My dad wouldn't allow me to bring it back to Oregon.

When I was twelve, I rode a used bike that a neighbor in the next-door trailer gave me. She had been in jail for ten years for a robbery she committed with an ex-boyfriend. Glenda was a very nice woman who told me she had been "as crazy as a cat in heat, and I made some crazy mistakes."

That bike was crucial to me. I had to ride that bike to school and to the grocery store. I rode it when I could no longer stand another minute with my dad or when I thought of my mother. I rode hundreds of miles on that old bike, and when kids made fun of it, I literally tried to run them down. They shut up after that.

When that bike finally broke when I was a teenager, it made my life truly hard, until the teachers at my high school gave me another one. I loved it because it took me to school, then to my job.

Because I had a job, that meant I had money, which meant I could buy food.

Because I had a job, that meant I could save money and leave home at sixteen as an emancipated minor.

When I got my job after college, I saved every penny so I could buy my condo and feel like I had my own, safe home with a door lock, something that was mine that he couldn't enter and ruin. After I had a savings account, which brought peace to my mind, I bought my first cool bike.

The racing bike I have now reminds me of who I was and who I am now. It reminds me that now I bike by choice, not because I'm desperate. The sleekness of my cool bike reminds me that when I bike to the store, it's to buy blackberries or ice cream, not to buy noodles and sauce that will take all the money I have in my pocket, even with carefully saved coupons.

When I ride in the country, I ride because I love to see the leaves change, or flowers in spring, or geese flying overhead, or a sparkling lake. I'm not riding because I'm trying to escape my dad's triggered temper.

My bike is an accomplishment to me. It lets me outride my pain until it's behind me. My bike lets me be me—the new me, not the scared, trembling, deeply saddened, lonely girl I used to be.

Two days after I left the hospital and Jace, I drove to the store. In the curve of the road there was a huge steel goat that made me smile every time I passed it. It was an awesome piece of art. I'd heard that an artist lived in the house behind it.

A little way farther I saw a sign outside a red barn. It said BARN DANCE and gave the date and time.

That was sweet.

But I don't dance anymore.

And who would I dance with anyhow?

My phone rang at ten o'clock the next morning.

"Allie."

I knew that voice so well. It rumbled through me—warm, soft, and strong.

"Hello, Jace." I didn't need to ask how he got my phone number. It was in my medical records.

I had been up for three hours. The horses on the farm, Leroy and Spunky Joy, did not seem to think that I needed rest. They liked their food on time, and they liked their servant, me, to bring it to them, no matter how mottled her thigh was from the menopausal horse's attack. The rooster, Mr. Jezebel Rooster, cock-a-doodled appallingly early. I thought it was strange he had a witchly, female name. If I could I would eat him.

"How are you doing?" Jace asked.

"Fine. I'm doing well." That was a lie. My heart felt like it had been stepped on by a gang of stampeding horses. I sank into a dusty blue chair in the corner. I didn't like the chair. It reminded me of my dad. Old, uncomfortable, hard. I didn't like the inside of his house, either. It was crowded with stuff; it was dreary and depressing. I simply hadn't had the emotional energy to take care of it yet.

"Really?"

"Yes." Bob jumped up and sat on me. Margaret squished in, too. I was covered by dog. I heard a long pause, and I knew Jace didn't believe me.

"I don't believe you."

"What are you, psychic?"

He chuckled, and that chuckle zipped all around and through me.

"Not psychic, but I do know how much your leg must be hurting right now, Allie. Make sure you're taking that medicine I prescribed. No sign of infection? Red lines? Good. I'm sorry it happened, but it was . . ."—he paused, and I heard a quick intake of breath—"I really liked seeing you."

I closed my eyes, a flood of utter anguish seeping into every inch of my body. "It was good to see you, too."

"Why did you leave? I wanted to check on you again."

"I left because I have hungry animals at home who get annoyed when they're not fed on time, and I had to pick apples."

"For my apple pie that I'm getting soon?"

"Your apple pie?" *I've missed you. I've missed eating apple pies with you.*

"I'd like to bring you lunch, then we can eat the pie together."

"What?" I feigned outrage, though my hands started to shake as I petted the dogs. "You can't see a patient outside of the hospital. It's against the rules!"

"You're not my patient anymore, and I like to break rules. Where are you?"

"I'm at . . . I'm at my dad's home in the country."

"Can I come over?"

"No." *Oh yes. Please come over. I want to hug you. I want to be with you. I want to make love among the apple trees.*

"Why not?" Jace was a forceful, take-charge sort of guy.

"Because, I think . . . I think it's better that way."

"Better for us not to see each other?"

"Yes. It's . . . it's too complicated . . ."

"It was a long time ago, Allie."

"I know. But, but why . . . why see each other?"

"Because I'd like to see you again. How's that for honesty?"

It had always been like this between us. Raw, amazing honesty. Unless it was about my childhood or my father. Those parts I hid. I held my head in my hands.

"It's lunch, Allie—only lunch."

"I can't, Jace. I can't do it."

I heard that zinging silence.

"Are you seeing someone?"

"What? No. No, I'm not seeing anyone. Just because I'm saying no, it doesn't mean that I'm seeing someone." I paused. "Are you?"

"No, I'm not. If I was seeing someone, I would not be

asking to bring you lunch. Or dinner. Or to walk through your apple orchard with you to pick apples for my pie."

Loneliness radiated from my heart. Without sounding whiny and pathetic, that loneliness has been lodged there for so many years. "I would have thought you would be married by now."

"I would have thought so, too. I wanted to be married with loud, rowdy kids running around, but it didn't work out that way."

I didn't respond to that one; I couldn't. My voice would have been all trembly and emotional and he would have known I was crying.

"I thought you would have married Zack, Allie."

"Who?" Who was Zack?

"Zack."

My mind raced. Oh my gosh. *That Zack.* "Uh. No. I didn't marry him."

"Why?"

"Uh . . . it's a long story."

"I'd like to hear it."

"It's boring, too." I covered my mouth before a sob escaped, then I rushed to change the subject. "When did you move here, Jace?"

"About three weeks ago."

"Why? Why here?" I actually patted my heart because it started to race.

"I like Oregon. I like the hiking, the fishing, the biking, the city. I got a great offer from the hospital."

"Well, congratulations. You'll like Oregon. Okay, Jace, I have to go." I put my hand over the phone so he wouldn't hear me make a fool of myself. I am not a quiet crier and I was beginning to sound like a drowning hippo.

"Why? Where are you going? Can't we talk?"

I tried to get myself under control so I could answer him. I bit down hard on my lip. "No. No, Jace. No."

"Allie—" His voice softened, so gentle.

I hung up. I felt terrible for hanging up. But he would persist, and I wanted to see him again; and that I shouldn't do.

That I *couldn't* do.

I thought the pain of seeing and leaving Jace was going to kill me again, and since I hate being pathetic, I decided to get something done around my dad's house and keep my hands busy.

The walls and ceiling were painted white, which helped. The wood floors were solid but scuffed. The only thing new was his bed; everything else was old, and the place was cluttered.

The whole house had to be cleared out. I'd cleaned it some when I arrived, because I couldn't stand to live in it as it was, but now I had to get rid of stuff. I would sell the home, and the sooner it was cleaned out the sooner a Realtor could list it—and the sooner I could put miles between Jace and me.

For the next three days, being careful not to bust my stitches, I packed up plastic bags full of my father's clothes, shoes, pillows and bedspreads, sheets, old lamps, chipped dishes, and two worn-out rugs. I hauled out old furniture to clear up the space, then his hunting gear, then his fishing gear. I kept one fishing pole, the one I used when I was a kid to literally catch dinner for us. I don't know why. Why keep a memento of poverty?

When I saw an old blue cardboard box in a closet, my hands started to shake and I pushed it back into a corner to deal with another day. Some things are best handled when you are not feeling like an emotional, ragged mop head.

I filled up my entire car with his stuff. I could hardly see around the junk in the back when I checked the rearview mirror as I drove to Goodwill. I dumped that load off, then took more stuff to Goodwill in two more trips. When I came back I threw out another eight bags of trash and arranged for them to be picked up, and the next day drove a separate load to a company that shreds paper. I passed the giant steel goat statue in the curve of the road. I liked that goat, and it gave me my only smile that day.

When I came back, I cleaned. As I cleaned, I cried.

I hadn't seen my dad in years. He was a tall, beefy man with black hair, and my mom said he used to be handsome. They had met, ironically enough, when she was in college on spring break in Florida. He was a bartender. She said she was bowled over by his tough-guy demeanor. He had scars on his forehead, left cheek, and chin. He was also charming, which soon faded, and aggressive. My guess is that she was a young, impressionable, innocent girl having a wild spring break and became pregnant. She was from a conservative family, was humiliated and scared, and married him. Her parents were livid about the marriage.

My dad tried to contact me a few times in past years— sadly enough, on my birthday and my mom's birthday—but I did not return his calls because I refused to be terrorized by him for one more day.

In the last six months, he called several times and left messages, asking me to call him. On one of the messages he said he loved me. It was the first time in my life that my dad told me he loved me. I did not return that call, either. The "I love you" part should have come years ago, minus the back-handed slaps to my face and the total neglect.

Now I was in his house, next to an apple orchard that he had bought with an inheritance from his wretched father, a man exactly like his son in personality and temperament. I remembered Grandpa Tad. He was hell on wheels, too.

I scrubbed the bathroom and thought of the tiny bath-room in our trailer, how it smelled of my dad: beer and alcohol and unwashed man.

I scrubbed the kitchen sink and thought of all the times I'd spent at the sink in our trailer, trying to cook with whatever we had in the refrigerator, which was usually next to nothing. He'd come home drunk and scathing when I didn't have dinner ready. Without money, it was hard to buy food.

When I swept the floors I cried again. I could never sweep that trailer clean enough for him.

While I scrubbed the floors, I thought of how dirty the floor of our trailer would get each day, how he would yell if it wasn't clean enough, but he always dragged in mud.

I washed the windows. I stripped all the droopy curtains and put them in trash bags. I dusted.

On the third day, when I was finally done, it was a whole new house, open, white, and clean. I left only a table and chairs, shelves, a couch and two chairs in the family room. Much better.

I found the red-and-white flowered quilt in a closet. It had been my mother's. I remember being on that quilt with her while she read books to me. I took the quilt out of its zippered plastic bag, shocked that my dad still had it, fluffed it out outside, and laid it over the couch. I sat on the couch and shook.

Bob and Margaret climbed into my lap. Margaret whined at me until I found her stuffed pink bear, which was under the couch. The cat, Marvin, climbed on, too, and settled on the pillow next to mine. He meowed at me; I meowed back.

My dad's urn was propping open a bedroom door.

I ran my hand over the quilt. So much had died with my mother.

I blamed him.

Chapter Four

On Tuesday morning—well, *barely* morning—Mr. Jezebel Rooster cock-a-doodle-doo'd again and I'd had it. I whipped on my black farm boots over my flannel pajama pants and stomped out toward that pesky rooster sitting on the top of a fence post screeching so proudly.

"I am not a country girl, you stupid rooster, and I don't want to be up this early!" I knew that my annoyance was totally irrational and ridiculous. He tipped his head and stared at me as if I were beneath him. "Stop it! Stop your stupid cock-a-doodle-doodling!"

He was silent for a minute, then thrust his neck back and announced, "Cock-a-doodle-doo!"

"No." I pointed my finger at him, stalking closer. "No!"

He was quiet again, but I could tell he had an attitude about it all.

It was dark outside, with blues, pinks, and yellows skittering across the sky, and still and silent except for my ranting.

I hardly knew what to do with this silence after living in the city for so long. I hardly knew what to do with the cooing of pigeons and the wind hugging the leaves of the apple trees. When Marvin the cat meowed behind me, I about jumped out of my skin.

I had always slept like a dead woman through this part of the morning. When I did get up, mornings were stressful for me, putting together some couture outfit so I could "look the part," commuting to work, planning my day, all the relentlessness of work ahead of me. I was on full blast.

But this tranquility, the hills golden in the distance, the mountains purple to the west, a vineyard east of me—it was truly serene, like silk and a kaleidoscope mixed together. The country calmed me down. It made me see and hear things I had not seen and heard before.

I noticed that the lights were on in a Craftsman-style home with a huge deck on top of the hill. I'd seen a moving van up there a few weeks ago.

Mr. Jezebel Rooster cock-a-doodle-doo'd again.

"Shush!" I hissed. "Oh, shush."

When I was at my door, that rebel rooster cock-a-doodled again, and I finally laughed.

Yes indeed, I laughed.

But this I knew: You won't win against roosters. Especially when they're named Mr. Jezebel Rooster.

I went back to sleep, then later pulled on my boots and started hobbling around the property.

A red barn, in fairly good shape, squatted about a hundred yards from the house. I thought of it as Spunky Joy and Leroy's home. I fed them their hay and grain, and gave them fresh water. They seemed excited to see me—they neighed, swung their heads, pranced about. A helpful neighbor, Rita Morgan, a retired FBI agent, had shown me how to saddle and how to ride and I rode them most days on a nearby horse trail, which they loved.

The barn had a hayloft and I climbed the adjacent ladder, about twelve steps, to peer into it. I had not yet done so, and I was curious.

This did not prove to be a good idea.

I heard the splintering, I heard the first crack, then the second, third, fourth, as all the rungs broke straight through and I tumbled right down, then through the air, my ankle twisting on the last remaining rung as I landed on my back.

"Oof," I said, then let fly a few bad words, crackling pain ripping through my body.

Spot the Cat, the cat with no spots, wandered over. My leg with the purple and green bruising and the stitches had been feeling much better. My left ankle was now killing me.

I groaned and pulled up my pant leg. There were splinters everywhere and my ankle was swelling rapidly.

"Help me, Spot the Cat," I muttered.

I felt faint for a moment, that breathless feeling you get when pain makes you sick, then I lay back down in the hay, staring at the rafters. Two pigeons and Spot the Cat peered down at me. Hay from the hayloft drifted down. What on earth was I doing on a farm? Why was I on my back in a pile of hay? Mr. Jezebel Rooster cock-a-doodled on his fence post. He gets his times messed up.

I shook off the pain and told myself to buck up and go to the hospital. I lay still for another fifteen minutes or so, Spot the Cat licking my face, sitting right by me like a true friend.

I half limped, half crawled back to the house, grabbed my purse and keys, and headed to my car. I told myself in my foggy haze of excruciating pain that Jace probably wasn't even working. The last time I'd been there was six days ago. He worked twenty-four-hour shifts, then forty-eight hours off. It would be another shift of doctors, right? I couldn't think.

I pulled into the hospital parking lot and sat panting in my car, hands to my spinning head, both legs throbbing. I gathered my bearings, caught my breath, shook my head again to clear the awful nausea, and carefully swayed back into the hospital.

The first person I saw . . .

Dr. Jace Rios.

*   *   *

When Jace saw me, he instantly smiled, gently, welcoming, and I was so touched my breath became stuck in my throat. I wanted to pirouette right into that man's arms and rip off his white coat. I must have looked frightful, though, because his expression instantly turned to deep concern. He ran over to me.

"What happened?" His voice was sharp and he put an arm around my waist as I teetered like a drunken sailor, the floor rollicking.

I leaned heavily against him and shut my eyes against another swell of pain. "I can't believe it. I was up on the ladder to get into the hayloft . . ."

"You were *what*?" He shook his head in disbelief. "Why were you on a *ladder*? You have stitches in your leg."

"I wanted to see the hayloft, and the ladder broke—" I winced. "I believe that I won the fight with the ladder. The ladder is now destroyed."

"And your leg?"

"Part of the battlefield. The bruises on my ankle will soon be as lovely as the bruises on my thigh. I'm looking forward to an exciting blend of colors."

"You'll match. Right and left legs, both in various shades of blue, purple, and green, with some red thrown in. Perhaps you should stay off ladders and away from horses."

"Perhaps. Maybe I'll take up knitting."

"If you can keep the needles from poking you, it might work." He shook his head at me, those intelligent, intense eyes looking deep. "Let's go, Allie."

I was in the hospital room a long time. Jace took out every one of the splinters imbedded in my leg. The X-ray showed that my ankle was not broken. It was badly bruised, swollen, and truly ugly.

The X-ray did not show anything about my heart because my heart didn't get X-rayed. I am sure it would have shown it was broken, though, yes, I am. Even after all these years . . .

* * *

"Here's your coffee. I poured whipped cream in." Jace handed me a chipped coffee mug, then sat down about two feet away from me on my dad's worn gray couch, my mother's red-and-white flowered quilt beneath us. I made a note to buy myself mugs without chips.

"Thank you."

"You're welcome." He smiled, and I couldn't move, those dark eyes straight on me, intense but cheerful, happy, as if he was glad to be here. Glad to be with me.

It was late morning, Jace had finished his shift at the hospital. He'd asked me, while holding my swollen ankle on his lap, plucking out splinters, if he could come over and check on me later in the day. I had resisted, then I'd melted. I needed him out of my life because our past was an alarming mess, *I* was a mess and my grief over my dad made me messier, and somehow my dad's death was bringing up my mom's death, making me a black cauldron of confusion and not a little anger.

But I wanted him. I wanted to talk to him. I knew it would get my heart even more bent out of shape, but I said yes. I told myself I would talk to him, this one time, and that would be that.

He had helped me out to my car at the hospital; I leaned on his arm, and he strapped me in. I had refused a taxi that he offered to pay for. When I got home I showered, washed my hair, and put on clean jeans, a pink push-up bra, a white lacy camisole, and a white sweater with a deep V. I put on silver hoop earrings, silver bracelets, and perfume that smelled like roses and vanilla. He had seen me, not once but twice, looking as if I'd rolled through hay and taken a dive into a pig's trough. This time would be different.

Jace had arrived with flowers, a bag of coffee beans, and whipped cream. He looked so darn cute holding those flowers, I couldn't stop smiling. Ah, Jace.

I smiled into the chipped blue ceramic coffee cup. "I'll

admit to being a tad embarrassed about drinking whipped cream in my coffee."

"Why be embarrassed? You like whipped cream in your coffee. You like swimming in lakes at night, biking for hours, Jane Austen and crime thrillers—which you sometimes read concurrently—locating the constellations at night, and puzzles."

I laughed, although I didn't do puzzles anymore. That's what Jace and I did together. Too painful to do on my own. "You remember."

"Yes, I do."

"And I remember that you also like swimming at night, biking for hours, and crime thrillers. Not so hot on Jane Austen. I remember that you like reading medical textbooks for fun, hiking, and photography—especially of wild animals in Yellowstone that you got too close to."

He laughed, low and rumbly. "Remember that grizzly bear . . ."

And we were off and chatting, all about the summer we worked at Yellowstone. The animals, geysers, waterfalls, hiking trails, Mammoth Hot Springs, camping. Darn. Why was he so charming?

While we were talking he examined both my legs again, then made us scrambled eggs and toast. "Have you spent a lot of time outdoors in the last years?" he asked.

"No. Mainly I've worked. I do bike." I could never give up biking. Biking leaves my problems in the dust, at least temporarily.

"That's funny. It's the one thing I do still, too."

"It's traveling on two wheels," I said.

"A mini vacation."

"The way to see details in nature. You can't get that in a car."

"The air smells better when you're on a bike."

I tried not to stare at him, but he was all man. Huggable shoulders, lean but not skinny, rangy and muscled. It was almost surreal that he was here. Before all of the other stuff happened, we never would have sat apart on a couch. We would have been together, close, soon naked. Loving and laughing. We would have been threading our fingers together. Kissing all the time, a roll here and there, Jace's muscular arms picking me up and putting me exactly where he wanted.

I felt old all of a sudden. Old, as if joy had passed me by, love had passed me by, chance and luck had passed me by.

"So, this is your dad's place."

"Yes. I recently cleared out a houseful of junk."

"What are your plans for the house, then?"

"I'll sell it. But currently I have no job. I had a condo in the city, but my agent listed it, we had a cash offer, and everything went really fast. I sold the furniture to the new owners and packed up." I hadn't liked the furniture. It was cold, modern, and hard edged. I think I used it to hide behind, too, as I did with my fancy-schmancy clothes. The better the furniture, the farther I would be from our trailer.

"I thought I would come here until I get my life figured out, and get a new job. Plus, there are animals all over that I have apparently inherited. Two dogs, as you can see"—Bob and Margaret were at our feet, snoring—"two cats, two horses, and a rooster that is stubborn and fearless."

"It's beautiful out here."

"It is. It's serenity and peace, all mixed up between the hills and mountains. I even have a little stream out back that runs behind my apple orchard. I can hear birds. I can hear the horses neigh. I can hear the wind and the raindrops. I can hear silence."

"It rests my brain."

I laughed. "Yes, it rests my brain, too. You moved from New York, then?" I knew he had.

"Yes."

"How do you like living here in Oregon?"

"I love it."

"Are you planning on staying?"

"Yes."

I nodded my head. "Have you found a place to live?"

"Yes."

"A house?"

"Yes, on land in the country. No red barn, though, like yours."

"That's great, it really is. You always wanted to live in the country." He had talked about it at length. He wanted to get married, have kids, be a doctor, and live in the country. He had never wavered.

I wanted an education and a pile of money in savings so I would never again have to worry about whether or not I had enough cash and a big-enough coupon to buy macaroni and cheese. I wanted to become someone who didn't have to fake being courageous and strong. I wanted to become someone who didn't come from a scary trailer and had to hide in an apple orchard.

But I had wanted Jace most of all.

"I like having land to walk on." His fingers, those capable fingers that took care of countless people, in countless critical situations, tapped his coffee cup. "After I operate during the day, or sew someone up, get someone through a traumatic event, I always thought it would be good to come home to a place in the country where there are sunrises and sunsets you can see, uninterrupted land in every direction, nature, animals, and a close-up view of the seasons."

"It's ironic, isn't it? Here we are, in the country, years after we first met, sitting in a house my dad owned."

"I like this." He smiled.

"You like it?" I chuckled.

"I do. I like that we've met up again, Allie."

I did, too. Even though nothing would, or could, come of it. "It's odd that we're talking like we've been together . . ." I stopped and choked back those years and tears. "I mean, not that we're together, together as in a couple"—*oh, be quiet—*

"I mean, we're talking as we've always talked, and that's . . . surprising."

He leaned forward, so close, too close, his elbows on his knees, and my breath caught. "It's always been like this between us. Why would it be different now?"

"Because—" I pulled back my hair, my hands jittery. "Because we're not who we used to be. We're not us."

"We are us. We're different people than who we were. But that doesn't mean that our basic personalities have changed. You've recently been kicked by a menopausal horse and you fall through ladders, and I deal with a lot of blood and guts, but it's still us."

He smiled, a relaxed smile, his face so lovable to me, so familiar and yet different. The years had made him even more appealing, and I wanted to kiss him. I wanted to wrap my arms around him and kiss him that first day in the hospital, and I still did, preferably with my heels hooked around his back . . .

"I'm still Jace, you're still Allie."

"Yes, you're the Jace who can talk a young man who is high on something into getting care and help, who can handle any emergency, and look good doing it." I blushed. I had not meant to let that last part pop out.

He grinned. "Well, being handsome is the most important thing when I've got my hands in someone's chest cavity. I'm sure it's most important to the patient, too. Whenever someone's been in an accident, the first thing they yell is, 'Get me the best-looking doctor you can.' "

Jace had always had a wicked sense of humor. Tough face, and then he'd crack a joke. "I'm sure your handsomeness is what you think of every minute when you're sticking a tube down someone's throat."

"Oh yes," he said, his voice deep. "My rampant beauty. Is my hair brushed? What about my shirt? Is it ironed perfectly?"

We laughed together. Jace was the least vain person I'd

ever met. He'd shower, dry his black hair with a towel, and
he was done. We talked and chatted, drank more coffee. I
pushed out all of the trepidation I had felt about seeing him,
and I enjoyed him, every single minute of it.

"One more thing, Allie."

"Oh no. What is it? You have a harem. You've grown a
tail. You're moving to Swaziland to learn a new language."

"No harem. One woman is perfect for me. I don't think I
have a tail. No move to Swaziland." He smiled again, and I
could not look away from him. We sat where we were, everything else gone, the old house receding, the bad memories,
my rage at my dad . . . and I tried to restrain myself from
jumping on him.

"I told you that I bought a place."

"Oh yes." I shook my head and tried to cool my lusty
thoughts. "Where did you buy your home?"

"I bought thirty acres and a house."

"Wow." I smiled. "Congratulations. That's incredible.
Good for you. You have what you've always wanted, then.
Did it come with cats, dogs, horses, and an obnoxious
rooster? Would you like my dogs, cats, and horses? Please
take the rooster. I beg you."

"I'll take them. My house didn't come with any animals.
There's a bridge over a stream, the house has a hot tub, and
there's also part of an apple orchard on it, just like here."

"Maybe you can teach me about apple trees, then."

"I'll learn and let you know."

"Where is it?"

He clasped his hands together, his gaze not wavering.
"Allie, I knew you were in Portland when I applied for the
job here, then moved from New York. It was why I wanted to
be here. I wanted to see you again. I was going to call you,
but I've only been here a few weeks, and I wanted to move
into my house and get settled before I did. I wanted to show
you what kind of life I had, but honestly, I didn't know that
you were here in Schollton."

"How could you? My dad only recently died. The property is in his name. He only bought it five years ago." And why was it an issue?

"I didn't research the property owners around me before I bought my land, I promise you that."

"Of course you didn't. Who does that? But what are you talking about?" My hands started to get cold.

"I looked around for quite a while, but then when I saw what it looked like out here, when I found the house, it was perfect, and I bought it."

"Jace, where is your place?" My knees started to shake.

"Look out those windows."

I looked out my front windows.

"Do you see that house on the hill?"

I nodded. The Craftsman-style home with the decks. Gorgeous architecture.

"That's mine."

Chapter Five

I stared at the urn, filled with my dad, functioning as a doorstop.

That probably wasn't a respectful way to use my dad, but I needed to prop the door open in the second bedroom, and the urn was doing the job. In essence, then, my dad was currently opening a door. He had opened so few for me over the course of my life, so perhaps it was fitting that he do so now.

Anger and bitterness started creeping on in, so I put my hands on my legs and stood up—gingerly. My legs were still a bruised mess.

I took Bob and Margaret outside for a walk. Bob took off after a dastardly squirrel and Margaret followed, tongue wagging.

Spot the Cat and Marvin walked along the fence line together. They were friends. I would have to find them good homes. I would have to stop getting attached to all of them. That was hard when Bob and Margaret slept with me on the bed and both cats meowed at me as if we were friends having a normal conversation. When I meowed back, I knew I was losing it.

And what about Mr. Jezebel Rooster?

I took a deep breath. My dad's animals sure were cute, even if he sure wasn't.

My father had never liked animals. I had seen him kick two dogs. Yet these animals were obviously well cared for and personable. I didn't get it.

I headed into the apple orchard and wandered among the trees. I wondered which tree it was that my dad had leaned against as he'd had his heart attack. I wondered how he'd felt. Was it instant? Did it take awhile to die? What did he think, staring up into those apple trees? Did he have regrets?

When I was a girl I used to steal apples out of an orchard near our trailer because there was often no food at home. I'd take some for dinner, for snacks, and to pack in my lunch bag. I brought two apples to school so my lunch bag would look as full as the other kids' sacks. They would take out their sandwiches wrapped in plastic bags, fruit, two types of chips, cookies. Clearly their parents had lovingly packed their lunches.

I would take out two slices of bread with a thin layer of peanut butter *or* jelly—rarely did we have both at the same time—two apples, and crackers, if we had them. I looked forward to class holiday parties like other kids looked forward to Christmas, because of the cookies and cupcakes.

I knew there were free lunches at school for poor kids, but that would have required my dad to fill out paperwork, and he had refused to do it, yelling, "I am not going to take charity, you stupid girl. We don't need it—now shut up!"

I was often hungry, but I didn't want the other kids to know we were poor, either. He had rammed it into me that I was part of the problem of him not having money. He had rammed it into me that I was a burden, difficult, stupid, unwanted, and part of the conspiracy my mother had waged against him.

My dad always laughed at how many apples I could eat, but his laughter ridiculed me. I didn't find it funny. Being hungry is never funny. He told me my face looked like the core of an apple. *Hello, apple-core face*. I never forgot that. He also said to me, *Your brain is about the size of apple seeds*.

I often went to sleep by myself in our trailer. My dad always said he was *Going out for a short while, be back before a bullet could pierce that there tree*. That meant he was going out drinking. He did that all the time. Money for beer, no money for food. The dark outside scared me, and I was usually freezing cold and hungry. I would grab my two blankets and settle in on the skinny bench in our trailer that served as my bed.

The outside noises—the rustling of an animal under our trailer, probably a raccoon, terrified me. Sometimes I'd hear people yelling at each other in other trailers. Cars backfired. People came in and out at odd hours. I always pulled the brown-haired doll with the yellow dress my mother made me close to my chest and went to sleep.

I moved back in with him when I was eleven, after my mom died, and he forgot my twelfth birthday. When I got home from school he was passed out on his bed, black hair back, scars prominent. I asked him where he got the scars one time and he shook me hard and told me never to ask again.

I made a "cake" for myself by slicing up apples in the orchard and piling them together on a paper plate like a layer cake. I sang myself "Happy Birthday," thought of my mother, and cried the whole way through eating my cake. I was so lonely I couldn't keep the apples down that day.

My dad sporadically remembered my other birthdays. One time he gave me a box of chocolates. He'd already eaten half of them.

If my dad had any loud and obnoxious friends over, I used to go to the orchard and carve the skins off apples to see how long a train I could make. I would hide in the apple trees if he was in a bad mood—cursing, lashing out at me—or if I needed to cry for my mother. I would carve faces into the apples—or boats, or dogs and cats. Apples entertained me.

I should have hated apples because of what they reminded me of, but I didn't. They saved me. I ate them, I juggled them, and used them for throwing away my rage.

I reached up a hand and brushed the leaves of an apple tree on my dad's property. The apples were beautiful—red, golden, light green.

I would miss them when I left.

My letter would have arrived.

She was a viper. She took advantage of her position. Seduction should not be a part of promotions.

The you-know-what would be hitting the fan.

It almost made me laugh.

"No, I will not go out to dinner with you tonight."

Jace stood on my porch wearing a white shirt, jeans, and cowboy boots. He could not have looked hotter if he set himself on fire.

"Why not, Allie?" He smiled. If it were possible, I would have melted into goo.

"Because I don't want to and I want to and I won't go." I slammed my teeth together. "That didn't make sense."

"Not much. Come out to dinner with me tonight and we'll talk about it."

"I'm your patient. Aren't you supposed to keep a professional distance?"

"You're my ex-girlfriend, and that overrides the patient-doctor relationship. Besides, our relationship, professionally speaking, is over because I've already sewn you up, plucked splinters out of your skin, and wrapped your ankle."

His ex-girlfriend. That I was. Even the word *girlfriend* gave my heart a wallop.

It was about eleven in the morning. I had hobbled around to feed and take care of the horses. Bob chased his enemies, the squirrels, barking, and Margaret followed him as usual, tongue hanging out. Spot the Cat, came up and meowed at me and I meowed back like a fool. Spunky Joy's head hung over Leroy's neck and they were both happy to see their servant, me.

I had not gotten hit by a horse's hoof. I had not fallen through a ladder. The day was young, but so far, so good. I had not showered yet, so had not gotten to the makeup point, and was wearing old jeans and a flannel shirt, my usual chic and glamorous attire, so different from who and what I used to be. Then Jace arrived at my door.

"Why can't you show up in my life when I'm wearing something other than raggedy clothes and have brushed my hair?"

He smiled, rocking back on his heels. He was huge and huggable, darn him. "You look good to me."

"I don't look good to me. I think I smell like a horse. I need to check the lovely colors of various bruises on my body. Bruising adds a special shade of beauty."

"I'll take a look at your bruising."

"You will not."

I remembered Jace's hands on both of my legs at the hospital. He was completely professional, but I thought I was going to burst into a ball of desire. His hands could still do that to me, after all these years. Still.

He smiled. "Ma'am, I think I should check out your legs."

"Very funny, Jace."

"Drop your pants."

I laughed, despite my rebellious hair, despite my bruises and my stitches. "Don't make me laugh. For some reason it makes my legs hurt."

"If not dinner, how about breakfast?"

"No." I grinned.

"We could sit at separate tables in a café."

"No, again." Oh, he was lovely.

"We could sit at separate ends of the café, and I won't look at you."

"No, a third time." He reminded me of one of those he-man warriors in movies. "I'm going to read a Jane Austen book."

"Bring it with you."

"No."

"Okay, then we'll do it the other way."

"What other way?" He smelled luscious, too.

"We'll have breakfast at my house."

He took a few steps forward, then lifted me up into his arms and started walking out to his truck. "Just keep still, ma'am, and I'll have you fed and watered in no time."

"You can't do this!" I laughed, my arm looped around his neck, our faces inches apart.

"Looks like I am, darlin'."

I kicked my legs but it hurt. "Shoot. I can't even kick you or my stitches will bust and my bruises will turn more purple or yucky green."

"Hang tight, apple-lover lady."

"I am an apple-lover lady. I think I'll use it for my next résumé . . ." I gave up. I wanted to give up, I knew that. I was having a hard time resisting him. The man is a force of nature. What he wants, he goes after.

"Don't move your legs, and close your mouth so no more refusals come out. Bacon and eggs makes everything better."

He put me in his truck, corralled the dogs back in the house, shut the door, and away we went.

I knew I should have gotten out of the truck.

I knew I should have protested.

Getting involved with Jace would end in no place right or good or happy. It would end in tears and loss, and Jace would get hurt if he knew the truth. I did not want to hurt Jace.

I went anyhow and I felt selfish for doing it.

I told myself to enjoy him for one more day.

One more day only.

I would get a job and move and he'd never have to know anything else, anyhow.

Chapter Six

"You're even more beautiful now than you were years ago, Allie."

Whew! "Don't say that."

"Why not?" Jace leaned back in his chair on the deck, watching me carefully, the picnic table between us. "I've missed those gold eyes of yours, all that hair, your smile . . ."

I fixed my gaze down the hill on my dad's run-down home, sagging and sad in the distance. In contrast, Jace's home was an architectural delight, modern but log cabin-y, too. That's the only way I could describe it. The great room had high ceilings, the wooden rafters exposed. There were wood floors, a two-story rock fireplace, leather furniture, and windows that invited in the expansive view of mountains, hills, vineyards, orchards, and farmland from all corners of the home.

His deck, where we sat, wrapped around most of the house. As he said, "I can see the sun come up and the sun go down. It's like watching the world move."

When we arrived at Jace's house, I actually took a shower. It was embarrassing to ask, but I had to. I was sure I smelled Spunky Joy on me, and both dogs, dear as they were. He had jokingly said in a singsong, "Sure. I'll be in there in a minute, honey," and I had said, "The door is locked; don't you dare."

I drummed my fingers on the arm of my chair. "Don't say that I'm more beautiful now, because I don't want to hear it."

"Why?"

I was trying real hard not to get sucked in by him and his engaging, masculine, he-man, most alluring personality. He was danger on wheels, and I knew it. "Because I'm not ready for it."

He nodded, and I knew he got it. "When *will* you be ready for it?"

"I don't know, Jace." I rubbed a hand over my forehead. "I'm still the same head case you knew before, only older."

"You were never a head case, Allie."

"Yes, I was. I hid it. I pretended things were better than they were. I pretended I had confidence, that I knew what I was doing, but I didn't." Childhood scars have a way of wrapping around your whole soul. They weave in and out and grip you tight.

"You were independent—still are, I can see that. You're outrageously intelligent. And funny. Very funny. You kissed incredibly well, I remember that most of all. Hugged well, too, and—"

"Stop that, too. No flirting." I tried to smother a smile. It was hard.

"Why?"

"I appreciate the breakfast. I appreciate you sewing me up, bandaging me up, and taking out my splinters. I appreciate all of it, but we can't . . . we can't . . . see each other again."

Those dark eyes flashed and his face stilled. "Why not?"

I ran my hands over my hair. I needed a haircut. I needed makeup. I needed a decent outfit on. "We were . . . in the past. And the past is over, and we're over . . ." *and I am so attracted to you still.*

"We did have a past. And now we have now." His eyes sharpened up. He was a very bright, perceptive man.

"What's *now*, Jace? I'm not staying here. I'm moving. I have to get a job. I mentioned I'm unemployed? I don't want to be in my dad's house."

"I understand completely. What does that have to do with us not talking again?"

"I don't think we need to talk again, after today." A shooting pain blasted through my heart.

He leaned forward, broad shoulders and all. "I think we should."

And there it was. That tone, that intensity, that will.

Jace could be seen as an easygoing man. Watching him in action at the hospital only reinforced what a talented doctor he was, with his calm and calming bedside manner. He cared about all his patients. But Jace was no pushover. He was strong willed, like me; independent because he'd had to be, like me; and he had a tough side, like me. He was a wall of steel, a man in the fullest sense of the word, one who did not back down, and anyone who overlooked that part of him was a fool.

"No, Jace." I studied the scenery and wrapped my arms around my body. My brain said no to him, but my body said, *Heck yeah!*

"Allie, we were together a long time ago. We broke up under really sad circumstances, which I still don't understand."

"And I don't want to talk about those circumstances."

"I do. And we will. Someday soon. I want to know what happened. I know what you told me, but I didn't believe you. There was something else you weren't telling me and then you cut off contact; so I deserve to know what happened, but I won't push you on it yet." He spread his hands out. "But we can be friends again, Allie."

"Friends?" I laughed, but it wasn't a funny laugh; it was more bitterness running through a scoff. "Do you honestly think that it's possible for us to be just *friends*?" I took in that black hair, that hard jaw, the steely personality behind it all that was born in his rocky childhood. Two people, both with troubled childhoods. One more thing in common.

"Sure. Close friends. Best friends." He winked at me.

I tilted my head in challenge. He knew what I was saying. The desire between us was there and leaping.

"For example, Allie, we can walk around my property as friends, and when you want me to kiss you, tell me and I'll oblige."

"That's what I'm talking about."

"What?"

"This . . ." I waved a hand between us.

He smiled, slow, seductive, absolutely firm in his belief that we could be together. "I like *this*. It's still there. Can't deny that. When I held your thigh in my hand at the hospital, it all came back. And I like you. Still do. Always have."

"You don't know me anymore."

"I know that you're still brave and funny. You didn't even cry when you came into the hospital. You downplayed your injuries. You talked about the menopausal horse and beating the battle with the ladder. I like how you're kind to the animals at your place. You have integrity, Allie; you always have. We laugh at the same things. Our conversation is quick, you're witty as hell, and we talk about everything. We flow. I'll bet you're still good at puzzles. I've missed your smile and your laugh. I like your lips a lot. *A lot.* Can I check out your lips with my lips?"

I bent my head, trying to get control of emotions that were already on high, then rolled my eyes at him. "You are a force like a brick wall—did you know that, Jace Rios?"

"I like brick walls. They add architectural interest."

"You're like a kind and funny hurricane."

"I don't like hurricanes. I'll take the kind and funny part." He put his palms up. "Look, Allie. I'll try to take it slow. I'll try not to hug you or kiss you or ask you to get into my hot tub naked. Don't shut down on us."

"Jace, I don't want to be involved with anyone. I like being on my own." That was a lie. I had been achingly lonely for years. "I like my own company." That was a lie, too. I preferred his company. It was my own company, my own memories, that made me nervous and angry.

"Let's not call it getting involved. Let's call it . . ." He ran a hand through that thick hair. "Hanging out in the country."

Hanging out in the country naked.

Hanging out in the country in bed with naked Jace.

Hanging out in the country at night in a hot tub with Jace.

One graphic vision after another danced in front of my eyes. He was all man. He had shoulders to grip and a chest to lie on. He had legs that were hard and strong and a back full of muscles. "You are fire on wheels and you always make me lose my head, but I can't this time."

"Well, you have a very pretty head, and your gold eyes have haunted me for years, so please don't lose it. We're older now. We had an incredible relationship last time. I thought it would end in a different place than it did. But it doesn't mean we can't try again."

He didn't even know what I'd done. If we were involved, I'd have to tell him. When he knew, I couldn't imagine he'd want to be with me anymore. He would lose all respect and find me dishonest and secretive. I didn't want to talk about it. I didn't want to deal with it. I was still steaming about my dad's death, too, and I could feel myself coming apart. I don't know why Jace and my dad are somehow connected, but they are.

"No." I shook my head. "No. I'm going, Jace."

"What? What are you talking about?"

"I can't." I felt the tears fill my eyes. "We were together once." He was my best friend, my boyfriend, everything. "And it was so hard . . . so hard to have it end, and I'm not up for it again. I can't do it."

"Who said it has to end? I'm not even talking about it ending; I'm talking about it starting. Allie, don't go."

"Good-bye, Jace. I'm glad you're well. You look amazing. I'm glad you're a doctor. I know I already said this, but you're really good at it. So incredibly talented."

"Please, Allie, come on."

He stood in front of me and I pushed by him. He gently grabbed my arm; I pulled away. He asked me to stay; I declined. He said he would drive me home, but I ignored it.

He followed me out, telling me again he wanted to talk, that we could talk about something else, but I started hobbling down his hill.

He climbed in his truck, pulled up beside me, and insisted I get in. I refused, and he actually got out, picked me up again, and put me in the cab. "You've got a bruised ankle and stitches. I am driving you home. If you want to fight with me on this, I'll win, Allie. Stay in the truck."

He was angry, he was stony. He was ticked off, and I didn't blame him. We didn't say another word.

When he dropped me off at home and drove away, I grabbed my keys, drove to the store, and bought a pint of chocolate chip ice cream and three romantic movies. I got in my sweats and an old yellow robe and watched TV while I cried. I read a Jane Austen novel, thought of my mother who had loved Jane, too, then I read a crime thriller. I couldn't sleep that night.

The lights in his house were still on.

Chapter Seven

I could not stand living without color in my dad's house. It reminded me of our dull, dreary trailer, and almost made me ill. I knew I would list the house and land for sale as soon as I had a job and knew where I would live, but I couldn't stand to live in the bleakness anymore.

I went shopping and bought blue-and-white flowered slipcovers for two chairs, and a blue slipcover for the sofa I had covered with my mother's red-and-white flowered quilt. I bought throw pillows with designs in red, blue, and yellow. I also bought two pillows with apples on them, one with a hummingbird.

I bought bright woven rugs for the family room, kitchen, and my bedroom. I bought two floor lamps and three table lamps with flowered and striped shades to bring light in. I bought two plaid tablecloths, and red cushions for the kitchen chairs. I bought a new bedspread in bright yellow with a swirling design, and four huge yellow pillows. I bought white towels and white bath mats and thick red ceramic dishes and mugs.

I bought two pots of chrysanthemums for the deck. I

bought scented candles. I bought three vases to display wild-flowers in my bedroom, on the kitchen table, and in the bath-room. I hung up photos of my mom and I in Bigfork, kissed my finger and brought it to her smiling face.

My dad's place had been transformed.

There was life in it.

Cheerful, bright life.

The clinging, dirty, dangerous trailer feel started to re-cede, along with that sick power my dad had had over me.

I took the dogs for a walk.

The squirrels taunted Bob.

Later that evening I turned on the oven, found a cutting board, then settled down at the table to chop the apples I'd picked from the orchard to make an apple pie, my first in a long time.

My mother and I made apple pies here in Oregon when I was younger, and later when we moved to Montana. We made one the day before she was killed in an avalanche in Montana when I was eleven years old.

She was skiing with two friends. Ironically, it was the first time we'd ever been away from each other. One of the hus-bands offered to babysit the kids of all three mothers. We had so much fun until that terrible news stalked us down.

My mother, MaeLynn, was a pretty woman with wavy, long brown hair, like mine. I inherited her golden eyes, tipped a bit in the corners. The resemblance between us was startling. After we escaped from my dad, we lived in a blue, two-story house in Bigfork, Montana, and I loved it because for the first time I wasn't living in an unpredictable war zone.

She worked as a waitress, and after rent was paid we did not have much money, but she showed me how to make used clothing, bought from Goodwill or garage sales, look mod-ern and stylish.

My mother encouraged me to *Show your Montana style!* Looking back, I realize she was simply trying to charge me up and make me feel more confident about looking different from the other kids because we couldn't afford new clothes.

We sewed on lace, ruffles, and satin to make boring shirts or skirts fun. We made earrings, necklaces, pins, and bracelets out of beads, crystals, and charms she found at garage sales. Other kids loved them and wanted to come over and make them, too.

We sewed on fancy patches to hide the holes in my jeans. I wore cool belts made out of rope or leather, fastened up with buckles wrapped in glass beads. I wore embroidered headbands and wristbands and ribbons that matched my outfits. We even added silk flowers or ribbons to hats, and I'd wear those to school, too.

My mother knew how to make regular clothes original, and she taught me everything she knew. Most especially she taught me how to keep my chin up. *We may be temporarily poor, honey, but hard work will change that. Chin up, shoulders back. We'll show the world who we are!*

After her parents died in a car accident, she found out they had left her enough money in their estate to go back to school. They had disowned her when she married my dad, hoping the pressure would make her walk out of the marriage. She went back to school while waitressing full-time, earned her teaching degree, and taught second grade at my school.

My mother had been the principal's favorite waitress: *She knew how to make her customers feel cared about, so I knew MaeLynn would do that for the kids, too,* he'd told me.

I remembered how scared she was with my dad, how she cowered in corners, how he intimidated and insulted her, called her stupid and worthless, backhanded and shoved her. She was never allowed money and he accused her of having boyfriends, yelling right in her face. He wouldn't let her go anywhere; she could not drive his truck. Looking back now, she was incredibly brave to leave and take me with her, because he had crushed her spirit and her will.

I remembered how he came to see us in Bigfork about two years after we left. My mother had changed her name, so he probably couldn't find us at first, and when he got good and fed up with no one to browbeat, I'm sure he'd had to hire an investigator.

When he landed on our doorstep, my mother took the gun off the top shelf of our bookcase, opened the door, and pointed it at his forehead.

"Get the hell off my property, Ben," she said, real quiet, then cocked the gun. My mother had become a new woman since she'd escaped from his violent clutches.

My dad could not have been more shocked if a monkey had dropped from the sky. "You wouldn't shoot me," he told her.

She shot clean through the deck about two inches from his feet and I saw him jump in shock. She shot a second time when he didn't leave. He swore at her something awful but turned around and backed off. He was running by the time he got to his truck, and she shot two bullets right into the cab.

He didn't come back. She looked at me and said, "I will not let you live with that monster again, my love. I failed you once, but I will not fail you again. Let's make apple muffins, shall we?"

We both trembled that day, making the apple muffins, but she was taking no more crap. Hence the gun, to help alleviate the crap.

After that avalanche everything changed. My dad came to get me. I stayed with a neighbor until he arrived. Her name was Mrs. Ashley. She cried over me many times and told me, "What a wonderful mother you had . . . we'll all miss her, honey. Tragedy for you, for everyone here . . . all her students crying . . . heavens to Betsy, why did this have to happen?"

My dad drove up, engine growling. He hardly glanced at

Mrs. Ashley, slammed the door to his truck, which still had the bullet holes in it, and snapped, "Let's go, Allie. Move your butt. I drove all the way out here to get you and I don't got time to waste."

Mrs. Ashley and her husband were appalled. Mr. Ashley said to my dad, "Now, maybe we should talk for a sec . . ."

"Who the hell are you? There ain't nothing to talk about," my dad said, his face scrunched up and angry, his scars so prominent. I didn't know why he was angry at Mr. and Mrs. Ashley. "This is a big inconvenience to me, coming to get this kid."

"Her mother just died—" Mrs. Ashley had one hand to her heart and the other on my shoulder.

"How about if you leave Allie with us for the school year," Mr. Ashley said, adding his hand to my other shoulder.

"No. That ain't happening. Her whore of a mother kidnapped her and now she's coming with me."

"How about another month —" Mrs. Ashley said.

"I said no." My dad's hands clenched into fists.

"Can she come and visit this summer?"

"What are you, deaf?" my dad shouted, chest puffed out. "She's not coming back."

He gave me time to pack: "Five minutes and not a minute more, apple-core face." I cringed hearing that name.

Mrs. Ashley raced to help me. She gave me one of her suitcases, and while she packed my clothes, I packed things from my mother in my backpack: a locket from her deceased mother and a harmonica from her deceased father, whom she never stopped missing; her favorite books; two china plates with tiny purple flowers that we loved to eat pie off of; three dessert cookbooks; and two aprons with apples, one for her, one for me. I grabbed three photos of us together in Montana. There was no time to get anything else as my dad was already shouting from outside to "Move, Allie, move!"

I looked longingly at my picture frames with the pink ballerinas, my mother's tablecloth with the yellow tulips, her perfume bottles, the tiny mirror with the ornate gold frame, her photograph of an apple orchard bathed in sunlight.

My dad's horn honked incessantly. "Get out here right now, Allie. Don't piss me off!"

Scared to death, I went tumbling out of the house with my backpack, Mrs. Ashley following behind with the suitcase, swearing at my dad. She called him many bad names, I remember that, and my mother had always said she was a God-fearing woman.

We went speeding down the road, me waving and crying out the window, our blue house fading in the distance. I would not see my swing set again, my bedroom with the yellow walls, the kitchen wall where my mother had painted a mural of a tulip field. I had helped paint the tulips.

My dad told me to "Sit down, strap up, and shut up," and that's what I'd done. He then grilled me the whole way about my mother and her "harem of boyfriends," and said terrible things about her. "I hope you're not like your mother. I won't tolerate you being like her—loose, wild, slutty."

I told him she wasn't like that at all and he punched my face, loosening a tooth. I turned toward the window and willed myself not to cry.

That was a microcosm of what happened for the next five years. I willed myself not to cry in front of him and stuffed my emotions down, hard as I could, until I was on autopilot, hands over my head, cowering, but somehow also fighting to live.

I rolled out the crust on the counter, my hands trembling.

After I made that apple pie, I made another one, then another.

It was apple pie therapy. I realized how much I'd missed making pies.

Why had my dad been so horrible? Why hadn't he had any redeeming qualities? Why had he been so unkind to his wife and to me, a little girl who had lost her mother?

I was so angry at him. I often thought I hated him. The hate was hurting *me*, though, not him.

I would have to figure out who to give the apple pies to.

I had apple pie for dinner that night.

I did not look up at Jace's house.

But I did hear my dad's voice in my head. *You will always be a no one, Allie. Like your mother. You're trailer trash. I'm trailer trash. You think that doctor's ever gonna marry you? Yep. You do. Can ya hear me laughing? You're not good enough for him and you're stupider than I thought.*

Mr. Jezebel Rooster woke me again when the sky was still black, the morning still sleeping. I stomped outside, I don't know why. It's not like the rooster speaks English and would understand my swear words or that he would enter into some sort of mediation with me on how we could resolve our conflict.

When he saw me he cock-a-doodle-doo'd again. I yelled at him to stop it. He did.

I turned away. He cock-a-doodled.

This went on twice more. The second time I turned and saw the lights of Jace's truck coming down his driveway, toward the road. He would be leaving for the hospital. Through the darkness I saw him get out of the car and wave. He must have seen me in those headlights, railing against a rooster.

"Good morning, Allie."

"It's not a good morning," I yelled back at him. "It's too early. Come and get this rooster."

"I think I'll do that soon."

I heard him laugh as I stomped back into my house.

Jezebel Rooster cock-a-doodle-doo'd again.

I missed Jace.

* * *

That afternoon, I went on a careful, slow bike ride on my fancy bike in my fancy bike clothes.

It reminded me that I'm not poor.

It reminded me that Jace and I used to love to bike together around Yellowstone.

It reminded me that we would not ride together again.

I pedaled faster.

Chapter Eight

The storm hit unexpectedly and took out the electricity two evenings later.

My cell phone rang as a blast of rain smacked my windows. I picked it up and said hello without looking at the name.

"Hi, Allie."

"Jace." My voice squeaked.

"How about if I come down and get you? No one on your side of the road has electricity."

"No, I'm fine."

In the distance I heard an earsplitting crack, like a lightning bolt, and I jumped. The lightning bolt kept crackling. "Hang on." I kept the cell phone in my hand and ran to my window in time to see one of the giant trees behind my dad's house crash down about six feet from the window.

I screamed, then yelled, "Oh my gosh!"

"What is it? What happened?" Jace shouted. "Allie!"

"A tree crashed down right by the house. It was so close." I heard another earsplitting crack and I cupped my hand to the window only to see a second tree fall.

"I heard that," Jace said. "I am coming to get you. Try not

to argue much or I will have to pick you up, throw you over
my shoulder like a knight in shining armor, and shove you
onto my horse. Don't think I won't do it."

"I can go to a hotel."

"You can go to Hotel Jace. It's close by, it's cheap, and I
don't have to work tomorrow, so I'll make you breakfast."

Trouble. Oh, that was trouble. He was trouble. "I need a
room for one."

"You'll have it."

"With a lock."

"I don't have any locks on my doors."

"That figures."

"You can have your room for one, though."

I felt like I'd been in a room for one my whole life.

"You can come in my room and tell me good night, Allie,
then go to your room for one. I'll be there in three minutes."

"Storms are great as long as they stay outside," I drawled,
sitting in front of Jace's stone fireplace holding a huge mug
of hot chocolate. He had even added marshmallows. He
knew I loved marshmallows. He did not have towering trees
around his home, and I was grateful for it.

Beside me on the couch, he nodded. "I agree. I do not
want to see wind, rain, thunder, or lightning in my living
room. But I do like storms, like you. Remember that one in
Yellowstone . . ."

"We were in that tent that wouldn't stay up, and the thunder and lightning were right overhead, the rain poured down
like a river, we were soaked . . ."

"And laughing . . ."

We chatted on, as if all was well between us, as if I hadn't
darted out like my hair was on fire the other day, telling him
we couldn't see each other, and he hadn't manhandled me
into his truck. I'd even snatched up two of my apple pies
when Jace came to pick me up. When I saw the smile on his

face as he took them, it about melted my heart into a puddle. "Thanks, hon—" He stopped, his eyes crinkling in the corners. "Thanks, Allie. These are going to be delicious. I've missed your apple pies."

We drove through the pounding rain and buffeting winds, another lightning strike making the sky glow, and arrived three minutes later at his house. He put the pies on the counter. I cut one into slices, he got the plates, I got the forks, and he started a pot of coffee. We worked in familiar, happy tandem. I squashed down how much I liked the domesticity part of it.

I heard about his day, and was fascinated by all he'd done in the emergency room, the people he'd met and helped, his compassion and empathy for them. He heard about mine. He asked questions about my past job, what I was thinking for the future. I told him about my latest crime thriller. He told me about a medical journal article he read. I told him about my short and careful bike ride. He told me to stay off my bike until I was healed, then he told me about a ride he'd been on. It was normal husband-wife talk. The comforting, familiar, happy sort.

Sitting on the leather couch, about a foot away from Jace, the storm thundering, the fire burning, I knew I was in dangerous territory. Dangerous and lusty.

Why had I agreed to come to his house when I could have climbed into my car and zipped to a hotel for fear of falling trees? Clearly I am a woman who likes emotional torture and invites sexual frustration into her life.

I stared into the flames of the fire and tried to distract my traitorous heart, but it would not be tamed or lassoed up. Sex with Jace was like falling into heaven on a feather bed with candles all around . . .

We were laughing about something and then . . . I don't know who moved first. I may have been the guilty party. I probably was. In fact, it's likely that it was me, sexually frustrated woman. When his lips came down on mine, I relaxed into him as if I'd kissed him an hour before and had been kissing him for years. His arms came around me and my arms linked around his neck and that kiss was . . . deep and delicious.

It was exactly as it had been before, that blazing passion back, all consuming.

It was the same as when we were in the lake at Yellowstone, body to body, magical and seductive, the constellations overhead.

It was the same as when we held each other through long nights, talking and laughing inches apart, camping near a river.

It was the same as when we kissed near a waterfall . . .

But it was different, too. The years had passed, I had missed him to the core of who I am, and sheer, throbbing pain had come between us, which simply seemed to make things . . .

. . . absolutely, positively out of control.

I could not get enough of that man's kisses. I could not stop my hands from wandering over familiar territory. Jace was thicker now, more muscled, all man. When he flipped me over onto the couch and came down between my legs, I wrapped them around his waist and tilted my head back so he could kiss my neck—and lower.

We fell into our rhythm, our beat, as if the rhythm had never been lost, the beats never gone. I arched into his hips, his fingers undid my pink blouse, I ran my hands down his back and up his shirt, feeling that tight, warm muscle, his hands molding me to him. Both of us were breathing hard, panting, a moan here, a groan there . . .

I could think of nothing but him, nothing but my own passion for him, for Jace. Lust kills brain cells and mine were clearly dead as I unbuttoned his shirt, my hands flying, my mouth to his . . . utterly lost.

It was when his hands were so adeptly unbuttoning my

jeans that I pulled away, pushed at his chest, and said, "Oh no. Not again," and "Please stop."

He stopped. We were both out of breath, both in the midst of some really excellent arousal, and yet . . . I could not go there again with him.

"Stop, please." I hadn't needed to say it again, though. He had already stopped, his face tight with frustration and disbelief.

"What? Why, honey?"

"See, Jace," I said, my words harsh. "This is why you and I cannot be friends." I tried to get my breath back, tried not to cry. "We're not friend material. We never will be."

"What are you talking about? We are friends, Allie. We were best friends, and we have this, too, the passion—"

"No, no, we don't have this. No passion. *No* to passion. Get off of me."

"Allie—" I saw the hurt in his eyes; I heard the rawness of his voice.

"Get off."

He put his forehead to mine for a long second, his chest heaving, my chest heaving, and he whispered, "Oh my God." Then he got off and I scrambled away from that couch, my pink blouse fully open, my white lace bra unsnapped, my jeans unbuttoned, my hair all over the place. His shirt was open, too, all the way, and I tried to ignore that he is a smolderingly hot man.

I tried to snap my bra, but my fingers would not work.

He stood up, towering over me, warm and soft and huggable. Damn.

"What the hell is going on, Allie?"

I was breathing so hard I might have been embarrassed, but he was, too. My whole body was tingling. I had to look away before his body tantalized me way too much and I gave in. "Damn, Jace. Turn around or something."

"Why? I think I've seen everything."

I inhaled to steady my racing heart. "You look way too sexy after we've been messing around, and I don't want to jump back on that couch with you."

"I'd like you to jump back on the couch with me." His tone was edgy, angry. "Why are you pulling away?"

"Because I'm a wreck." I wanted to get back on that couch so much I ached.

"You are not a wreck," he said, his voice sharp and frustrated. I didn't blame him. "Why do you say that?"

"Look, Jace, I have no idea what I'm doing next, where I'm going in my life. You're all set. You have what you wanted. And I have . . ." My fingers fumbled on my buttons. "I have a rooster that wakes me up too early, an old house, two dogs who insist on sleeping with me, cats I meow back at, and an apple orchard from my dad, who knew I loved apples, but I don't think he meant the apples as a gift. You and I ended a long time ago, and I can't get any more emotional or crazy than I already am." I put my hands to my face, a vision of a run and a fall and a rock and a secret barreling into my brain. "We're too late, Jace."

"We're not too late at all." His eyes showed his deep pain and utter bafflement. "Not at all."

And now I would lie. I'd done it before. "I don't want to be with you, Jace. It's that simple."

His head actually moved back, as if I had slapped him.

"I don't want *us* again, Jace. We were an *us*, but we're not going to be an *us* again."

"Why?" I heard that simmering anger. Jace never lost it, was never like my dad, but he wasn't a saint. He swore and said, "I don't understand you, or this, at all. I'm sorry if I moved too fast—I am. I'll slow down. We'll slow this down—"

"You don't need to, Jace. I said no, so it's no."

"Then that's it?" He put his hands out, his anger up another notch. He was huge and so unhappy. "We have everything we did before, Allie—friendship, we talk all the time, we laugh—"

It would be so easy to give in, to walk back into his arms. I burst into tears, those racking, embarrassing type of tears.

"Oh, honey," Jace said, his anger spiking all the way back down as he tried to hug me.

I pushed him away, my hands against his warm and lovely chest. "Don't hug me, Jace."

"You're making me sad watching you cry."

"And I'm sad crying. It's not like I want to be a sniffling mess. Where's my room?"

"Let's talk this out—"

"I'm not talking this out."

"Then let's sit in front of the fireplace—"

"No. You'll talk me into this, I know you and I can't resist you, and you are too much for me, and this is not right for us." *It's not right for you, Jace, trust me on that.*

He argued, I argued, I cried more, I saw tears in Jace's dark eyes, too, then I stalked off, found a bedroom with a bed in it, and slammed the door after telling him, "Stay the hell out."

My body was strung out, wanting Jace, my mind frazzled. I crawled under the covers and cried myself to sleep, by myself, my body rocking back and forth.

At five o'clock in the morning, I tried to sneak out the door. Through the French doors I saw Jace sitting on his deck, the sun rising like a golden ball pulled by an invisible chain from the clouds. I didn't join him. I knew he would see me hurrying down his road to my house, but I didn't bother to turn and wave, and he didn't bother to call me back.

The next day I stopped by a local artist's home studio. She lived about a mile down the road in a blue house with white trim, and had a sign out in gold lettering that said PEARL'S MOSAICS AND PAINTINGS.

When I walked in, bells chiming on the door, a woman in the other room called out, "I'll be right with ya!"

There were paintings and mosaics, all bright, bold, flowing, and magical. One painting, about four feet tall and three feet wide, caught my eye. It was an apple tree, but tucked among the branches was a village with miniature houses and thatched roofs. Swinging wooden bridges attached one house to another. Tiny people, in traditional dress from countries all over the world, gathered under the leaves for picnics, sing-alongs, or holding hands. One boy chased a blue balloon.

The details were pure fantasy. The fall leaves on a Japanese woman's purple kimono glowed. An Indian woman's pink sari with gold trim floated in the wind. The plaid of three men's Scottish kilts dropped exactly to their knees. The apple tree was a living, breathing, utopian place with stairs at the bottom of the trunk winding to a gazebo at the top, which was hung with bright white lights. A chief with a feathered headdress and moccasins played the piano.

A woman entered the studio. She had lush, thick white hair in a loose bun and a welcoming smile. Her white shirt and jeans were both covered in paint. She was beautiful. "Now, heck, you're Ben's daughter, Allie, aren't you?"

"Yes, yes, I am." I shook her hand, surprised. I shouldn't be surprised—this home was five minutes from my dad's, so they were neighbors—but I was. My dad did not socialize. He did not like people. He called them *stupid beings posing as humans, with cardboard brains*.

"I'm sorry about your dad."

"Thank you." I tensed up.

"Your father pushed it, by hell he did."

I felt my mouth drop. "I'm sorry?"

"Your father, and I told him many times." She swung a finger through the air. "He didn't act like a father. He was a drunk pig in mud when I first met him. He was a bull with his horns down. He should have been born a slug because that's how he was as a father, and I told him so, especially after he told me about himself in his parenting years. Inexcusable and sluggish. He was a slug."

"Uh . . ."

"When he quit drinking the last three years, he started to talk about what a lousy father he was and he told me he didn't think there was a worse husband on the planet."

I felt like I'd been struck in the face with a handful of paintbrushes.

"He talked to his AA group about it, too."

His AA group? Darned if my jaw wasn't almost on the floor. My dad had actually admitted he was an alcoholic? He went to AA?

"I tried to get him to shape up that butt of his. I even prodded him with a pitchfork one time. Truly, I poked him in the butt, and I told him, 'See, even when I prod your butt, Ben, you still won't move to make amends for your cruel behavior to your daughter.' I didn't understand it. I've got six kids and fourteen grandkids and they're over all the time, and I could not understand why he did not apologize to you and do whatever it took to make amends."

"You knew him—"

"You bet I did, although the first two years he lived here we didn't talk. I met him once the first year—he was a mean, slobbering, warthog drunk. He called me an old witch. We didn't get along. But eventually I knew him backwards and forwards and inside out." She tapped her boot. "I got him cleaned up three years ago. Told him he was an alcoholic. He argued, threw that temper tantrum of his. By golly, it didn't scare me at all—they're all in denial, but he had his accident, you know—"

"No, what accident?"

"Oh, that's right. You didn't know because he was a crappy father and out of your life. Flipped his truck late one night. He was stuck upside down like a pig hung out to slaughter. It happened right down the road in the curve where that steel goat statue stands in front of Shelby's house. He's a steel artist.

"Anyhow, I galloped my horse, Give Me A Shiner—that's her name—pretty darn fast when I heard the crash, but when I saw that it was him and I smelled liquor I peered in and said to him, 'Hello and good-bye, you pathetic drunk. You could have killed someone or knocked over a cow.' He was trapped, hanging upside down, and I galloped away. He yelled and slurred and swore and, by God, I left him there after I told him, 'Tonight I'm going to pray to the good Lord that wisdom will be forced into your dense head.' "

I scrambled to keep up with her. "You left my dad upside-down, drunk, in his truck all night?"

"Sure I did. Although I think he was able to unstrap himself later. He was still flattened out, though, stuck in that crushed truck of his."

I almost laughed. I have a mean streak when it comes to my dad.

"You gotta let drunks hit the very bottom rung of their lives, or they're not getting better. By the time I rode back out about eight hours later, after my morning coffee, he'd made a mess all over himself in each direction. Lucky it was summer so he didn't freeze, but he was still cold. Hungover and screwed up—that gave him a God moment, I think. Can you get much lower?"

"That's pretty low." I stood and marveled. I was totally amused at the thought of Dad upside-down. That's what a drunken parent who calls you apple-core face does to you. They warp your sense of humor.

"I peered into the window and said, 'You ready to change now, you donkey's ass?' He was crying. Broken. Like a bird with all the bones shattered here and there, the feathers of his wings all falling off. I hate to see a man crumble down to nothing, but he had to have that sweet meltdown. He nodded his head and vomited, so I called the police and a tow truck. They came. Ambulance took him to the hospital. I wasn't going to take him smelling to the high heavens like that. He had to stay there for three nights."

"What were his injuries?"

"Oh, a bunch of 'em. Self-deserved, by golly. Broken leg, broken arm, concussion. Dehydration. He'd tossed his cookies. Bruises. Bumps on his noggin. Truck was totaled. He remembered seeing me the night before, but I told him he wasn't ready to join the civilized world because he was a menace to the rest of us on the road, so I'd left him."

"What did he say?"

"He told me later that he was grateful every day he didn't hurt anyone else and he deserved to be left there."

I had to take a moment to process that one. My dad never took responsibility and was never concerned about anyone else. *Never.*

Pearl pointed her finger. "That man was so destroyed from what he thought was going to be his certain death, he didn't even get mad at me. He had trouble breathing in there, he told me later. He'd had two heart attacks in his life and he thought the big one was coming and he was going to die upside down in his truck—"

"Two?" I knew about the one. "How . . ." I choked back a wall of emotion that unexpectedly sprung up in my throat. "How was he after that?"

"Didn't touch a drop."

"He stopped drinking? On his own?"

"Nah. That would have been impossible—he was too much of a lush, total crackpot. A bunch of the neighbors had one of those interventions. We went over to his house and told him he was the worst son of a you-know-what when he was drinkin'. We told him he was goin' to rehabilitation. He refused, said he could do it on his own, so Tally raised his gun and shot a hole through the floor."

I hooted. "I saw that bullet hole, and there's another one in the wall."

"The one in the wall is from Larry Dave. He said, 'Donkey's butt, you're going to rehab because if you don't, I'm going to burn your house down so you'll move. We can't have hammered drunks driving here—there's kids on bikes who could get hurt, and you have tried our patience to the limit.' Your dad gave some more push-back, his face all bruised and busted, bandages everywhere, and Larry Dave shot the gun again. That was about it. Your dad almost pissed himself.

"We shoved him in Bryan B's truck—he's got his guns on a rack there. You know Bryan B yet? He owns a high-tech business. Anyhow, he and William took him in. William's an ears, nose, and throat specialist and his brother is a doctor in one of the rehab places, so we were able to smooth things along."

"How long was he there?"

"Six months—can you believe it? He was a bad case. He didn't have any of the animals then, so we checked on the house, made sure the pipes didn't freeze and bust."

Six months in rehab would have cost a fortune. I thought of my ball-breaking Grandpa Tad. He'd owned a chain of liquor stores and had made a bundle, although he lived like a pauper. That was where the rest of my dad's inheritance went. Rehab and the house and orchard.

"They cleaned him up and started him thinking like a normal man, they did," Pearl said.

I tried to squish down my roaring anger with my dad. Finally, *finally*, at the end of his life he gets sober? What about *me*? What about *my mother*? Why couldn't he have gotten sober for us? His lack of sobriety cost my mother her life. "How was he after rehab?"

"New man, sweetie. New man. Humbled down to nothing. Went to AA every day. Kind, gentle, started talking a lot about you and your mom." Pearl's eyes got watery. "He knew he'd blown it. It was one of the reasons he'd kept drinking. Said he'd been a terrible husband. He blamed himself for your mom's death. Said if he hadn't been a jerk, she wouldn't have left, wouldn't have been killed in the avalanche. Hadn't talked to you in years and said he missed you like the dickens, but said he didn't do a good job."

"He didn't do a good job? He did a *horrendous* job. I moved out when I was sixteen because I couldn't stand him. Couldn't take being called useless, dumb, weird eyes like a cat, sneaky, loose . . ." I could hardly say the words, and I had no idea why I was sharing them with her. Maybe it was Pearl's kind eyes; maybe it was because she had known my dad but had a clear view of his vile personality.

I deliberately tamped down my rising temper. Why did I let the memory of him still yank my emotions around? Why did I let him have that control over me? "Were you friends with him then?"

"We were more than friends, sugar. After about a year of him being sober, we became a couple. He had a lot of edges that I had to smooth down with a sandblaster and a pickax. I let him have it a number of times, and sometimes I wouldn't even speak to him and he wasn't allowed to cross my doorway. See, I think the alcohol stunted his emotional growth and maturity, and I had to play catch-up with him, beat him into human form and release the caveman within."

"How'd he do?"

"By the end he was a good man, Allie. He even adopted the animals, all of them strays or rescues, to keep him company, and he spoiled all of them. He trained as a carpenter and actually did good work. See all my shelving? He did that for me."

I choked down a sob and put my hands to my face.

"I'm sorry, honey. I know that's gotta hurt to the core. He was good for me but not good for you and your momma, who deserved it. I get it. Man, that chicken-crap man! It makes me burn to think about it. You and your poor mother. That scarecrow creep. I'm telling you, I told him to call you and he said he did, but you didn't call back, and I said to him, 'What did you expect?' He knew—he knew, Allie—that he didn't deserve you. He cried over it."

"You must be joking."

"Not at all. Bawled like a baby. Many times. He had your photos in his wallet, along with your momma's, and I saw him staring at them time and time again."

The tears welled out of my eyes. I was touched by what she said about my dad, but I was red-hot mad. He found love for us at the end of his *life*?

"This painting—" I changed the subject. I'd had enough. I was going to explode. "I'd like to buy it."

"Let me wrap it up for you, honey."

"You're a talented artist, Pearl."

"Thank you." She paused. "Perhaps . . . perhaps we could have lunch one day? You could come over here. I'll kill one of the chickens and we'll have avocado pesto chicken sandwiches and lemonade."

I blinked, surprised. I had lived in the city a long time. I wasn't used to such outward friendliness or having someone offer to twist a chicken's neck for me. "Yes, yes, I would like that. Thank you." Looking into her kind eyes, I realized that I would.

"We can talk about your dad if you want. Or we can leave the ole saddle-buster out of the whole thing."

"I . . . I don't know what I want. I don't know if I want to hear about it . . . I think I do, maybe not . . ."

She put her hands on my shoulders. "Don't make a decision now, sweetie. We'll start as girlfriends."

"Thank you." I gave her my debit card to pay for the apple-tree painting with the amazing details.

"I refuse," Pearl said. "It's my gift to you, Allie. I know that your dad would want you to have it, too. I'm sorry about your daddy, sweetheart." She gave me a hug. "He was sorry, too." She gave me another hug. "You know there's a barn dance coming up, right, sugar?"

*   *   *

I found a hammer and nails in the garage and I hung up Pearl's painting over the fireplace. It added life, color, fantasy, and imagination.

I sat down on the couch with my mother's red-and-white flowered quilt, took a peek at my dad holding open the bedroom door in his urn, and wrapped my arms tight around myself.

He had become a good man too late.

Way too late.

I read Jane Austen that night, lying under my yellow bedspread, then a crime thriller, and back to Jane. My strawberry-scented candle flickered on the nightstand. I couldn't sleep and ended up pacing through the orchard, Bob and Margaret running around me in circles. I studied the constellations. I found no peace in them.

Chapter Nine

I recognized him immediately.

Jace was clad in a bike helmet and dark glasses hunched over his racing bike, making the bike look small. We were about to pass each other in the middle of a quiet, winding road, a vineyard to one side, a farm on the other, the morning sun warm, a bunch of birds peeping.

I kept biking. Maybe he wouldn't recognize me. I was pedaling slowly because my ankle and leg were still tender, but I crossed to the other side of the street and turned my head away to hide my face. I, too, had on a helmet and dark glasses.

We passed. I exhaled with deep relief, before the choking sadness that has chased me around since I lost Jace years ago came roaring back, like grief on wheels. I put my head down and pedaled as hard as I could without splitting my leg open, as I'd always done to outride what I didn't want to think about.

"Good to see you on your bike, Allie."

I turned my head. He was right next to me, smiling. Handsome. Overpoweringly manly and muscled and huge.

"I can't believe this," I muttered.

"Where are you riding to?"

"I think I'm riding away from you. You go that way, I'll go this way." I tugged on the strap of my helmet as we pedaled beside each other.

"I was just thinking that I wanted to backtrack."

"You never backtrack."

"I can think of a lot of backtracking I'd like to do."

"Then think of it while you're pedaling north."

"Will you bike with me?"

"No, I won't."

"Can I bike with you?"

"No, same thing."

"Why not?"

"Because . . ." I struggled to find the right words, finally settling on honesty. "I don't want to get wrapped up in you again because then I can't think like a normal person." And yet . . . I so wanted to do that. I trusted Jace enough to lose my mind around him, I did.

"I cannot understand why."

I did not miss the sharp edge in his tone. Jace was no sap.

"If you'll let this work between us, Allie, it could have a different ending than it did before."

"I'll be leaving soon, so what's the point? I'm going back to the city. I was invited for interviews in Boston, Seattle, and Houston."

He was quiet for a second. "And when you get a job, that's it. You'll be gone?"

"Yes." My voice was soft. I ignored the way that traitorous heart of mine screamed in protest.

"Why? Why would you leave so soon?"

"Why? Because I need a job. And why would I stay?"

He shook his head a little and I knew I'd hurt him.

"Stay for us. Or stay because we're living in the country with a stream running through our properties and apple orchards. Stay because you have a home here and a bunch of animals who like you. Stay because you can find a job here."

"The jobs I applied for start immediately." *And if I stay here longer, it will kill me to leave you, Jace. You deserve more. More than me.* I kept pedaling. "I am not used to not working. I need to work. It fills up the time."

"Other things can fill up time, too."

"Not in my life, Jace. Working is part of me. I've worked since I was sixteen, and from that moment on, the independence it brought me, the financial security . . . I can't *not* work."

"I'll pay you to stay here."

I laughed; he didn't. He was serious, I knew that. Jace was the most generous, protective person I knew. Yellowstone showed me that. "No. I would never accept money from you."

His jaw tightened and I could tell my quick rejection hurt him.

"You're running from here as fast as you can. I can see that. You like to run, don't you? When things get to a place that you don't like, you shut down and you cut out."

"That's not true." I bit my lip to keep a flood of emotions under control. "Maybe I am running. Okay, I think you're right. I am running."

"Why? Why are you running *again*?"

"My dad's house is a reminder of him. We didn't get along, so I need to move. I hardly know anything about horses or how to take care of an apple orchard or all that property." I stopped my bike because my eyes were filling up behind my sunglasses and I couldn't see. We were up on a hill, the land stretching out in front of us like a quilt, sections here and there for fields, farms, orchards, vineyards. "You're here and you're kind and fun and interesting, like before, and I feel us falling into *us* again, and I can't have that."

He stopped next to me. "For God's sakes," he swore, his voice raised. "Why do you keep pulling away? Why won't you give us a chance?"

I could only give him a partial truth. "I can't do relationships, Jace. I can't get that close to anyone. I don't trust men; I hardly trust women. You were the first person, outside of my mother, that I trusted."

"Doesn't that say something about us, then?" He pulled off his sunglasses with a little too much force. "About the quality of our relationship, our future?"

"We don't have a future. You are looking for a wife, we both know that. I don't want to be a wife, and I'm not presuming that you would want me to be your wife, but I don't want to . . . to . . ." I waved my hand in the air.

"You don't even want to try to be together? Get naked in my hot tub or wake up every Saturday morning and have French toast? Bike? Travel?" He moved his bike so our legs were touching. "Work on puzzles? Hike? Study the stars on our backs? Talk?"

"Right. No. I don't want to do that." *Oh yes, I do!*

"No commitment then?"

"No." *Yes!*

"Why are you so averse to commitment?" He put his palms up, those muscles flexing in his arms. "What could possibly be wrong with being committed to someone you love for the rest of your life? What could be better than that?"

Nothing. Nothing would be better. "I'm better on my own. I didn't have a good example of a marriage growing up." That was minimizing it. "You almost have it all, Jace. Everything you wanted. You have the house in the country, you're a doctor—"

"I don't have it all. I have the job, I have the house in the country, but I don't have a wife or kids."

"Then go find her, Jace. It's not going to be me. And I don't want children." That wasn't true. I choked back tears. I did want kids. I wanted kids so much I ached. But that wasn't going to happen because of a tragedy on an inky-black night.

His face registered shock. "Why? Why would you not want children? We talked about kids before. I thought you wanted four, at least. Remember we joked and said we were going to name our kids Grizzly Bear, Waterfall, Fishing Stream, and Geyser because of Yellowstone." He shook his head. "What changed your mind?"

"Life did."

"What do you mean by that? You would make a great mother, Allie. An *outstanding* mother."

I didn't know about that. "I have no desire to get involved with you, to get close to you, only to walk away. What's the point? We'd both get hurt."

"Maybe you won't walk away."

"I will walk away, Jace. I can assure you of that." I would walk. I would save him from me, as utterly and ridiculously melodramatic as that sounded. I didn't want to hurt him by telling him the truth and I didn't want him to feel obligated toward me in any way. But he would not want a life with me once he knew. I knew him, and I knew what he most wanted.

He studied me for a minute and I could tell that his fast, capable brain was working at a zillion miles an hour. Jace was a keenly intelligent, perceptive man, who listened carefully. I tried not to think about how much I loved that brain.

All around us the country danced, birds chirped, a cow mooed, wind puffed up the tree leaves, and the country quilt in front of us shifted square to square in a plethora of colors.

"Around the corner is the most amazing view of Mt. Hood," Jace said finally, his voice kind. "Let's go look at it. Then we can bike back and I'll take you to lunch at Abigail's Café. It used to be a house of ill repute, then a saloon, then a gas station. Now it's a café, and they serve soup and sandwiches. I know you love soup."

"Did you not hear me, Jace?"

He leaned in close, inches from my face. I wanted to cup his head with my hands and kiss him until we both dropped into that familiar, out-of-control passion. He smelled like pine and the woods and man and musk. I liked his razor stubble and knew how it would feel. My gaze dropped to those lips that were truly creative in terms of turning me to mush, to say nothing of what those talented hands had done to me each and every time we'd gotten naked.

"I heard every word. So, here are my words to you. I don't want you to go to Boston. I don't want you to go to Houston or to Seattle. I want you to stay here. I want you to reach up and kiss me."

"I'm not going to reach up and kiss you." Oh, but I wanted to.

He studied me, and I raised my eyebrows in challenge. He was a strong-willed man, and I was a strong-willed woman. Those characteristics sometimes clashed.

"Okay, Allie. We have no choice but to base our relationship on our mutual lust and attraction and go from there."

"You don't get it. There's no going *from there*." But that sounded delicious.

He grinned. "Then I'll take the mutual lust and attraction part."

He leaned in, looped an arm around my waist, tilted his head so our bike helmets didn't smack together, and kissed me. I automatically closed my eyes and savored that kiss. He pulled away after long, yummy seconds, but only by an inch.

"Kiss me, Allie," he murmured. "One kiss."

I tingled up one side and down the other. My body heat notched up a hundred degrees. I could not resist. I put my hand on his shoulder, drawing him closer, and he kissed me again, and again, and again, both arms around me, holding me as close as he could with our bikes between us.

When I was good and steamed up, almost panting, totally not thinking anymore, and sunk way down deep in that erotic passion he engendered in me, he pulled away, smiled at me in a friendly and sexy way, and climbed on his bike.

He put out his hand to pull me along.

I swore again that he was trouble in the first degree and that this would lead to nothing but searing heartache for me, and him, but I put out my hand, he grabbed it, I climbed on my bike, and we pedaled up the hill to see a stunning view of Mt. Hood. We held hands halfway up.

At the top, we stood and stared at each other. He smiled at me again, our legs touching, and I could feel his happiness: his happiness that we were together, that I'd kissed him, that I'd agreed to bike with him.

I felt him, as I always had. I felt his friendship and kindness, his deep attraction to me, his sadness that I kept scrambling away from him.

In my head—not out loud—at the top of that hill, the serenity of the sweet countryside all around, I heard the words I'd said thousands of times before. *I love you, Jace. I love you, I love you. I will always love you.*

He kissed me again, hugging me close, and I kissed him back, sinking right on in.

Chapter Ten

I had an interview in Boston. I went from there to an interview in Houston, then up to Seattle.

I practiced my confident act. Breezy and smart, ultrastylish and competent. I could manage people, keep up with fashion trends, work with designers and other creative types, improve sales. My feet hurt in their four-inch heels.

Each interview made me feel sicker, as if I were wandering around lost, entering enemy territory where everyone was living a life that I didn't want to live anymore, complete with spears, dead animals around their necks, and warring factions. I watched people scurrying about, stressed to the ceiling, faces tight. I saw the piled-up folders, the fashion photos, the couture clothes, the intense conversations among Type A people who thought a lot of themselves. I could *feel* the competition there. I didn't think I could do it anymore.

The whole time, I imagined Jace beside me, smiling gently, in every interview. I saw him on his bike. I saw him relaxed at his home, on the deck. I saw him bandaging my ankle and my leg. I felt him kissing me, holding me.

I asked for an outlandish sum of money for my salary, to

which the executives I was talking with nodded their acquiescence and told me about the other benefits I would receive.

I teetered out of each interview on my sweet designer heels, feeling skittish. Unhappy. Filled with dread.

My fancy clothes were suddenly so uncomfortable.

I had been living a whirling, hard-charging, fashion-centered life for years.

I no longer wanted to do that. It was nothing to me.

What did I want to do?

What appealed?

What did I like to do?

I started doing math problems in my head. How cheap could I live until I could figure this out? The house was free, there were taxes, though . . .

My time in poverty in the trailer park told me that I could not use much of my savings or I'd start to feel the three S's: sick, scared, and sliding. As in sliding back into being poor.

But it was abundantly apparent that I needed to do something different with my life, workwise.

What could I do . . .

I wondered what the letter I'd sent was doing in my former company.

She would have hit the roof, stayed on the roof, and thrown her designer heels at everyone while cursing me.

The farther I got away from her, the better I felt.

I laughed.

When I was in Seattle for my interview, Jace called me. I was strolling through Pike Place Market, which overlooks the waterfront in Seattle, surrounded by wildflower bouquets, spices, fresh vegetables of all colors, and fish being thrown by fish sellers. I had bought a six-foot-long woven tapestry of red poppies for the house; not that I was staying in Schollton.

"Hey, Allie."

"Hi, Jace." I ducked into a quieter corner.

"How are you?"

"Fine."

"How were the interviews?"

"My feet hurt."

He laughed. "If you were wearing boots and walking through your apple orchard, your feet wouldn't hurt."

"That's true."

"How about coming with me to the barn dance?"

"I'm not going to the barn dance."

"Why not?"

"I don't dance."

"Yes, you do. We danced in Yellowstone all the time. By the lake, in that field, camping at night with friends . . . near the elk that one time, after we got past that black bear . . ."

"That was different."

"How so?"

"It just was. Let's say there was magic in the lake or in the waterfalls or something."

"Huh. Well, there's magic here in the apple orchards."

"Haven't seen it."

"You will. We'll dance at the barn dance and you'll know those apples have something special in them."

"Apples are for apple pies, not dancing."

"Bake us an apple pie and then we'll go dancing in a barn. If you moved away, you would miss next year's barn dance and that would be bad. Plus, I would miss you."

"You would?" I loved Jace's voice. The deepness of it, the totally masculine tone.

"Yes. I've always missed you. Come home, Allie. Please?"

"I can't." I watched another fish go flying through the air. "I can't."

My heart was cracking like a melon split in two by a hatchet. Ten feet away from me a man with a violin started playing a poignant love song, and I teared up.

"Well, if you can't come home for me, come home for Margaret and Bob, Spot the Cat and Marvin, Spunky Joy and Leroy. They told me yesterday, when I was visiting and feeding them, that they missed you. What about Mr. Jezebel Rooster? What would he do without you? He so enjoys seeing you first thing in the morning. He's lonely. He's lost without you. He'll never be happy without you."

I wiped my tears. "I don't want Mr. Jezebel to be unhappy and lonely."

"Neither do I, Allie," Jace said softly. "I don't want that at all."

When I hung up the phone I realized that Jace was still pursuing me, even though I told him I didn't want kids. I assumed he assumed I would change my mind. The tears kept falling.

I left my dad's dark, decrepit trailer when I was sixteen. Almost panting with fear, I hastily packed a bag of clothes and everything I had brought with me from Montana that had been my mother's.

I recognized, somewhere in that firestorm of turmoil, in the hail of verbal attacks and neglect from my dad, that if I didn't leave, I would permanently succumb to my pervasive depression and probably self-destruct.

I had almost no will to live. I missed my loving, kind mother, and my grief had only deepened for her until it was a rock in my soul. I missed the mountains of Montana, and Flathead Lake, and our blue house. I missed feeling safe, feeling loved. My dad told me I was no one—a poor and ugly kid with odd gold eyes—and I believed it.

There was one tiny and shiny spark, however, down deep

in my heart, that hoped things would be better, that believed things *could* be better, and it pushed me out the door. I am sure that spark was my mother's love. I remembered how often she had told me that she loved me, that I was a lovely person and showed my "Montana style" with flair and fashion.

My dad worked factory-type jobs until he was fired. Most nights he came home drunk, or he would come home and start slugging it down. Until I was old enough to get a job, I did anything I could to avoid going home after school. I joined sports and arts programs and helped teachers. One of my teachers actually had a sewing machine in her room, and I spent a lot of time making my used clothing look individualistic and modern, with lace, silk, beads, even leather, like my mother taught me. I was desperate for cool clothes so people wouldn't know the truth. Kids actually called me "Model Allie," and thought I was a trendsetter because of my outfits. They had no idea the dire straits I lived in—my clothes kept that hidden from them.

I would leave if he was home, pretending I was going to do homework at someone's house. In reality, I would go hide outside somewhere, usually in the orchard, but I would also sometimes bike to a forest near our home and hike around, sit on a rock and fall apart, watch the leaves change color, or follow a squirrel. It's where my love of nature started.

Nature didn't judge, it didn't hit, it didn't scream and intimidate, it didn't make me feel bad about myself. Nature was always changing, comforting, soothing. There was originality and beauty in every leaf, flower, and tree. Nature was a friend who gave back without words. I lived half of my childhood in nature.

But I couldn't avoid my dad all the time.

"Don't wear that T-shirt. You look like a whore . . . You better be home when I get home, Allie . . . If I find you with a boy, I'm coming after you and I'm bringing my gun. I'm not raising no slut . . . You got all A's on your report card?

Must be an easy school . . . What's wrong with that mud-brown hair of yours? Don't you brush it? . . . Where did you get those clothes? Think you're a model or something? Your mom was like that, too, always trying to dress higher than she was, always looking for better. She wanted a rich man. She never thought I was good enough. I know she cheated on me . . . then she took off, damn her . . ."

He was constantly angry, and his scars made him look even more threatening and dangerous. He threw my mother's purple-flowered china plates and broke them one night, though he knew I used them to cut up apples. When he wasn't looking, I picked up the pieces and put them in a bag, hating him. I still have them. He stomped through the trailer. He swore. I don't remember him ever hugging me or telling me he loved me.

One night his rage, blowing at full volume, was too much. "You look like your damn mother! You got the same golden eyes, same brown hair. She kept secrets. What kind of secrets are you hiding from me? Sixteen years old and you think you know everything?" He towered over me, chest puffed out.

I assured him, shaking, that I didn't.

"You think you're better than me?" With one fell swoop he dumped my homework off the table.

I assured him I didn't, feeling nauseous.

He threw a coffee mug and it shattered the window. I remember my stomach sinking. The window was right above the bench that I slept on. It was winter. I would freeze.

"I thought you had a job, but maybe a man's giving you money."

I told him there was no man. I didn't tell him my clothes were bought used, for quarters, because my knees started to knock.

"Don't be smart with me, apple-core face."

He was huge, a thundering monster. He picked up apples that I'd taken from the orchard for dinner that night and smashed them together in his beefy hands. "Guess you lost dinner, Allie." He pelted an apple through the shattered window, then the next apple. He pointed to the floor, then swayed. He reeked of alcohol. "Pick that mess up."

I grabbed paper towels and picked up the smashed apples off the floor, my hands trembling, my mind rebelling, hating him.

"Wipe my boots."

I wiped off his boots. Black misery wrapped around me tight.

He smashed two more apples when I was on my knees. The apple pieces got in my hair. I started to cry.

"Clean those up, too, and quit crying, you baby. Your mom used to cry, too."

I waited for him to backhand me. That's how he really showed me I was nothing.

I cleaned everything up, my stomach growling. It was dark. I didn't want to go back to the orchard that night, but I was starving.

I threw out the paper towels and apple pieces, his mean stare glaring right through me. "Tell me about your mother's boyfriends."

I sagged, completely defeated. I hated this topic. My mother didn't have a boyfriend when she was married to my dad. I was with her all the time. I remembered no man. She didn't even have a boyfriend in Montana. She had me. I had her. Like she said, *I had a man and that was a nightmare. No more men for me*.

My dad bullied me, his face an inch from mine, his hand up in the air, ready to strike if I denied she had a boyfriend, ready to strike if I lied and said she did have a boyfriend. It was at that second that I finally brought my chin up, defeated but not dead, and said, my voice strong, "I hate you."

Those three words stopped him. His open palm froze in the air, his eyes widened, and the color drained from his flushed face, red with broken blood vessels.

"I hate you, Ben." I didn't call him Dad. He wasn't a dad. He was a monster.

Something flashed in those narrowed eyes—hurt, anguish, I don't know, but he lowered his hand, he bent his bull-sized head, and his heavy shoulders dipped.

He swore softly, then said, his voice breaking, "Your mother hated me, too."

He turned and I saw him wipe his cheeks before he lumbered back to his bedroom and shut the door.

That night I scrambled out to the orchard and picked six apples and ate them. I was scared by a raccoon and a distant gunshot. I thought I heard someone else running through the orchard, gasping, as if he was being chased. The night was black except for a moon that kept hiding behind the clouds. It started to rain and I was soaked, hungry, and freezing.

I sat against a tree trunk, scared of the shadows and creepy noises, rain dripping off my face. But it was there, under the leaves of the apple tree, that I knew I was done. The unknowns in the apple orchard were less scary to me than the knowns of being in the trailer with my dad. I could not live like that anymore. I thought of my mother and her love and her hugs, how we made apple pies together, along with peach, blackberry, rhubarb, lemon meringue, and dark chocolate pies with whipped cream. She would not want me to live like this.

I had saved money from my job as a retail clerk in a high-end clothing shop and hidden it from my dad. I spent only what I had to on food, I probably should have spent more so I wasn't so hungry, but I wanted money stashed away for safety and for my eventual escape even more than I wanted the food. I was on hourly wage and commission. There is nothing like being hungry to make you sell things well, and quickly, so I made a lot of money for a sixteen-year-old. Plus I understood clothes and style, taught by my mother.

I would use the money I had saved to make a new life.

The next day was Saturday. I sat, frozen to my bones, in the apple orchard until I knew my dad had left for his weekend job hauling rock. Before he left he stood outside the trailer and hollered my name, alternating it with swear words, and "Get the hell home, *now*, Allie!"

I stayed hidden behind the trunks of the apple trees, and after he had shoved his ungainly body into his truck with the bullet holes and sped off, I took a shower, packed a bagful of clothes and the treasures I had from my mother—including the broken china plates, the locket, and the harmonica—and left the trailer.

I went to my favorite teacher, Mr. McRose, so scared I could hardly talk. He was about sixty, his wife was an attorney, and they helped me become an emancipated minor. I had often been an angry student. I had gotten into fights, sometimes even with my fists, with other kids. I had a short fuse. I was taking it on the chin at home, so I wasn't going to take it at school, too.

In some twisted way, it made me popular because it made me intimidating, cold, and tough. A real rebel who had her own cool clothing style and who had affected a swagger. But Mr. McRose reached out a hand to the desperate kid who was faking that swagger.

I lived in the apartment above their home. They insisted I live there for free; I insisted on paying two hundred dollars a month. They only acquiesced when I started to walk away. "I won't take charity. I'll pay you or I'm leaving."

Mr. McRose cried, and his wife led me up the steps. My apartment was bright, yellow, cozy, clean, with lots of windows and a lock to keep my dad out. I loved it. It was the first time since living with my mother that I lived without fear.

My dad threw impressive fits. He even came to school, steaming, blowing smoke, threatening. Twice. The police were called. He went to the McRoses' house, hammered up on alcohol, screaming for me. The police were called again.

I had to take out a restraining order on him after he clocked me in the face and broke a window in my apartment with his fist.

The McRoses, who I'm still close to, helped me. I stayed in school. I worked full-time. I saved everything I could. The teachers adopted me for the next three years at Christmas. I was given boxes full of food and used, but really nice, household furniture. New coats, new boots, new sweaters. I'd never had new clothes. A new red purse, I remember that, from Mrs. McRose. And, most helpful, a new bike. That bike helped hugely because I could bike to work instead of taking the bus or walking, and I could bike away my pain down charming roads in the country. It was my freedom and my survival.

It was the first time I felt cared for. The McRoses liked me. The teachers liked me. I hadn't felt liked in forever. That helped me even more than the gifts. I have never forgotten their kindness.

I nailed the SAT because I was hell bent on going to college and I studied for months. An education was my way out of poverty. I had a 4.0 grade point average. I had excellent recommendations from teachers who were honest about my circumstances and told college counselors that I had persevered against heavy odds.

I got a full-ride scholarship.

I moved on. I moved forward.

I didn't know what else to do.

Chapter Eleven

"Let's talk over dinner, Allie."

I sank onto my dad's couch with my mother's red-and-white flowered quilt on it, my head in one hand, my phone in the other. I had returned late last night from my trip and I knew Jace was not happy. He was a kind man, but he was a proud man, and he was frustrated with me, with us. He did not like getting the runaround. I got it.

"Jace . . ."

"I have calzone and salad and I'm bringing it down to your place."

"Jace—"

"Jace what?" he snapped.

"I'm—"

What to say? *I thought of you my entire trip and I'm wiped out and I have no resistance against you at all . . . I can't wait to see you . . . I can't believe I'm thinking very seriously of moving, because then I would never see you; but it would be another form of hell to stay here and be near you as your life goes on . . . I have missed you since Yellowstone . . . I love you and I want to jump into bed with you more than I've wanted anything.*

"You're what, Allie? No, hold that thought. I'm coming down and you're going to eat Italian with me."

He hung up.

I stared at the phone, then looked up at his architecturally stunning, warm, safe house on the hill. He would do what he wanted to do. He would be here in five minutes.

I ran for my closet and my lipstick.

It is amazing what a woman can do for her looks in five minutes, if pushed.

"How were the interviews?"

"They were fine." *I missed you.* I put down my fork. I love calzone, but I could hardly focus on it with Jace sitting across the kitchen table from me looking all manly, the sun plopping down over the horizon. I had lit my scented candles. He looked even lustier by candlelight, and that beat down my resistance to him even more.

"And? Are you moving?"

"I don't know."

"Were you offered jobs?"

"Yes, two offered me jobs and I received a call this morning from the third." The salaries were impressive. The workload would be incessant, draining, and no Jace.

He nodded, those brown eyes guarded, not happy.

I had a quick vision of me underneath him on his couch the other night . . . how far we'd gone, how yummy and toe-tingling it had felt.

"I would be selling expensive clothes to expensive women again. Traveling, too." How frivolous. How lonely. I was wearing a burgundy sweater with a deep V, jeans, and crystal earrings, my hair up in a loose ponytail. I will not admit that I wore a black push-up bra so my cleavage would be up and out for Jace. I was so much more comfortable without the tottery four-inch heels I wore during the interviews.

"Would you be happy doing that?" he asked.

"No."

He leaned back in his chair. "Do you not like me?"

I like you and I love you. "No. I like you."

"Good. I like you a lot. You're my favorite person. Let's play a game."

"A game?"

He pulled his chair over until our knees were touching. "If you don't kiss me, we don't go to the barn dance together. If you do kiss me, you're my date."

"I'm not going to kiss you."

He grinned.

"For heaven's sakes, Jace."

I stood up, he stood up close to me. I moved to the left, he moved to the right. I moved to the right, he moved to the left.

He knew I was starting to feel waves of luscious desire rolling on through. I could feel my own blush. He knew what he did to me. He bent that dark head, his mouth an inch from mine. He pulled me close, hip to chest.

"That's not fair. You can't touch me." My voice was all whispery, breathless.

"That's not part of the rules."

I took a few steps back. He backed me into the wall. I put my hands on his shoulders and laughed; couldn't help it. Sexual tension did it, I was sure. We were pressed up close to each other. "One kiss, Allie," he murmured. "One."

He pressed up even closer, tight and warm, and I wanted to wrap my legs around his hips. I could smell him. Mint, pine trees, yum. His mouth was inches from mine.

"I missed you," he said. "Missed your smile, your laugh."

My eyes fluttered closed and I breathed in deep. The man was overwhelming.

"I looked down the hill and your lights weren't on. You weren't there."

I was revved up about as high as I could go. I could feel his heart under my hand.

"I thought of you not being there, and I think I'd have to sell my house, honey, if you moved."

Desire zigged and zagged through my body, and I felt weak.

"Maybe we should discuss this kiss in bed, babe?"

"Ahhh . . . not in bed."

"Kiss me, Allie. One kiss. For the barn dance."

I couldn't help it, I was shivering for the man. I put a hand behind his head and brought his lips down to mine.

"Please don't leave, Allie," he said, between marvelous kisses that traveled all over.

My dad kept holding open the door with his urn.

I didn't know what to do with his ashes.

People often spread their loved ones' ashes.

But where would I spread my dad's? He was not a "loved one." He was a scary, manipulative, drunken loser.

Did I even owe it to him to spread them?

Jace came by at seven o'clock the night of the barn dance.

"I told you I'm not going to the barn dance." Heck no. "I don't dance anymore, and you tricked me with those smokin' hot kisses."

He laughed, walked into my house, and shut the door.

I had showered with apple-scented body wash and apple-scented shampoo, not because of the barn dance and Jace, but because I like apples, and for no other reason. Same with the apple-scented lotion I spread all over afterward, too. I also put on a low-cut, lined, white lace shirt; a pretty yellow bra; my tighter blue jeans; cowgirl boots; and lipstick, because I was tired of being frumpy, and surely Margaret and Bob—he who hates squirrels—would appreciate my efforts.

"I don't dance, Jace. I don't need to meet people, I don't

know how to play the fiddle, and Marvin, Bob, and Margaret need my company. They're lonely. And I need to find Margaret's pink stuffed bear. She can't sleep without it." By the time I stepped back from Jace's smokin'-hot kisses that night, all my clothes were on the floor and he was shirtless. Oh, how I loved that sweet man naked . . .

"I'm lonely for you, too, Allie. You kissed me last time, and that makes you my date for the barn dance, per our agreement, and you look . . . you look . . . absolutely gorgeous." Jace's chest heaved up for a second, and his jaw was held pretty tight. "As for the dancing, I know you dance, I've seen you dance, you have perfect rhythm, you don't need to know how to play the fiddle, and the animals have had you all day. Marvin wants me to tell you to go to the barn dance."

I looked at Marvin. He meowed. I refrained from meowing back in front of Jace. Marvin meowed again, irritated with my lack of conversation.

"I'm staying home to embroider."

Jace studied me and I studied him back. He had on jeans, a blue shirt, a cowboy hat, and well-worn cowboy boots. Man, if he was any sexier, I would pass out, I would. I so loved that weathered look he had, too—that tough, rough, I can round up cattle, ride a horse, and sew your leg up if you need stitches look. My heart beat like a fool.

Jace smiled, free and easy, the tough-guy face softened by indulgence and humor. "You're going to stay home to embroider? Well, okay. We'll stay here together. I'll hand you the thread."

"I can't embroider when people are watching."

"You can't embroider at all, Allie." He winked.

"That's true. I think I'm going to dust."

"Looks clean enough in here to me"—he glanced around—"plus housework bores you out of your mind."

"And I'm going to take a toothbrush to the wood floors and clean them."

"I'd like to see that. Maybe you could do it naked."

"I have told you not to make comments like that." *Stop, foolish heart!*

"Okay. Well, you could be naked and so could I. We could clean about a foot of floor and then do something else."

Full-blown, 3-D images of what he and I could do after we cleaned a foot of floor, nude, filled my mind. My gaze went to his chest. Wide, strong, safe. Then his hips. Ah, how they moved. "I'm trying to stay out of trouble with you, Jace."

His face became serious, but I saw the kindness there. "We're not going to get in any trouble together, Allie. We never did, we never would. We'd be together. That's it."

That would not be it. He doesn't know.

He is so irresistible.

Jace wrapped his arms around me. On instinct, I hugged him back, our temples together. That big bazooka then started to dance me around my family room, past the magical apple tree painting, singing a country song. I got that giddy, breathless, smiley feeling and gave in, my feet following his. What else could I do?

I rode the first wave of desire, starting from my brain and heading toward the nether regions. I sucked in my breath and pulled away before I stripped and handed him a toothbrush.

"Okay, Jace." I laughed. "Yes to the barn dance."

He shook his head mockingly. "Shoot. I was thinking it would be better if we stayed home and worked on that embroidery pattern."

"No, oh, whew. No." My whole body was now throbbing, all drummed up. "Can't do that." I turned and grabbed my keys. "Let's go, cowboy."

He chuckled, deep and sweet, but I didn't stop to catch that inviting gaze again. I couldn't.

I might turn around and head for the bedroom.

* * *

The red barn was decked out in white twinkly lights, hay bales, and a few chickens who wandered in and out. An amazingly good honky-tonk band belted out one country song after another on a stage. The barn was jammed with people in jeans, cowboy hats, and boots, and rows of tables holding traditional American barn-dance types of food— fried chicken, baked beans, chili, cornbread, corn, and salads. In typical American fashion, there was also Asian, Mexican, and Italian thrown in.

Jace brought ribs in huge tin pans. "I'm the rib man," he joked.

"I'm the pie woman." I'd baked three apple pies. Not because I'd been planning on going to the barn dance with Jace, oh no.

Later I took tiny slices of different pies: apple, pecan, lemon meringue; then bites of pies called Coconut Devil, Explode Your Taste Buds Chocolate Pie, Bite Me (raspberry-rhubarb), and Sexy As Hell.

Sexy as Hell was my favorite—it was a butterscotch pie.

The pie competition was fierce here, I thought, then laughed.

I met a lot of people. A number of them knew my dad. I was shocked to find that they liked him.

I asked Pearl about this as we shared a slice of pie called Wake Up Your Romantic Life, a three-layer slice of chocolate heaven topped with chocolate chips and whipped cream.

" 'Pearl,' he told me once, 'I hate myself for what I did to Allie and MaeLynn. I hate myself. Hate myself. *Hate myself.*' He said it three times. I told him to stop making life gruesome for everyone else and get out there and be friendly and helpful to atone a little bit for his past."

"Did he do it?"

"He sure did, sugar. That's why these people liked him."

I watched a chicken strut by. Did I still hate my dad? If so, how long was I going to hate him for? How long was I going to let myself be angry at him and the past? The hate was hurting me, not him. How much more of my life was I going to allow him to negatively affect?

"He said he bought the house and apple orchard to make amends to you, Allie."

"I think he bought it to make fun of me and how many apples I used to eat." I heard the bitterness in my voice. "He called me apple-core face. One time he broke my mother's purple-flowered china plates, which I used to cut apples on. I still have the pieces."

"I'm sorry, sweets, about the plates, but he did buy the apple orchard for you as a gift and as an apology."

"You're kidding."

"Not at all. He wanted you to have all the apples you could ever want. He told me that."

All the apples I could ever want. I could hardly wrap my mind around that one. My father had wanted to give me a gift.

"He did love you, Allie, and your mom. He was simply too demented with alcohol to show it."

I sniffled and Pearl squeezed my hand. I saw Jace laughing with some other cowboys. One of the cowboys was the police chief, the other was a lieutenant with the fire department, the third owned property in Hawaii.

Man, he was better-looking now than he was when we were younger.

He was a whole heck of a lot of man. *Real man.*

Not like my dad at all. No, Jace was polar opposite to my dad.

He turned and saw me smiling at him and wandered over, setting his beer down on the way. He put a hand out to me and I grabbed it.

"Now, there's a tall glass of manhood for ya, honey," Pearl drawled. "I'd drink that one up."

Jace swung me into his arms and out onto the dance floor. We danced most of the night: line dancing, the swing, square dancing, the two-step. I found my rhythm with him, my beat. The rhythm and beat I'd always had with him.

The barn dance was, without a doubt, the most fun I'd had in years. Jace swung me around the floor, sat close to me on hay bales while we ate ribs and laughed with others, snuck in more than a few kisses, which tingled those nether regions, and held me close.

When we arrived at his house, well, things got out of control.

Jace kissed me straight out of my mind as we left that red barn, the white lights behind us twinkling through the night.

He kissed me when he opened the driver's side of his truck.

He kissed me when I was sitting beside him in the truck, then pushed me back on the seat and kissed me until I could hardly breathe and I felt like we were teenagers again in Yellowstone.

He kissed me on the drive back to our homes, my arms wrapped around him.

In the middle of the street, where he could turn left to go to my house or right to go up the hill to his house, he stopped. Outside it was quiet, inky dark, the apple orchards dark shadows.

Inside that truck, the windows were steaming up, my white lace shirt was off, and he'd unhooked my pretty yellow lacy bra. My hands were in his black hair, my chest arched against his, those talented hands of his doin' their thing . . .

"Allie," he said, his own voice ragged. "Spend the night with me, please. Please, Allie."

I couldn't even answer. His hands were making mush of my brain, and all I could do was feel and breathe hard, like a locomotive.

"Please, honey, come home with me."

He kissed me again, long and seductive, holding me close. I ran my hands straight up his chest and he groaned, inhaling sharply. Jace was my best friend and the only man I have ever trusted in my life. "I can't resist you for one more day, Jace. Let's go."

He had that truck up the hill in record time and parked in front of his house.

When he parked, he lifted me up and straddled me across his lap, one kiss following another, wild and fun, passionate.

He pulled me out of the truck and scooped me up in his arms, my pretty yellow lacy bra and lace shirt now hanging off my fingers. He opened his front door, then kicked it shut while I kissed his neck and face, and we stumbled up the stairs and onto his bed.

His bed was huge, the blue bedspread cushy, the moon shining through the windows. I let my hands, my mouth, and my whole body do what they had longed to do since the second I'd seen him at the hospital.

I did not look away from him when our eyes met. I matched each kiss, each caress, each arch, each stroke.

I welcomed him, welcomed us, welcomed the love I felt for him.

I didn't fight that love, and in the middle of it all, I cried, and he became teary eyed, and we wiped those tears away, then kissed again, rising and falling with the same passion we'd felt forever.

I woke up in the middle of the night, the moon still glowing, with Jace wrapped around me, his arm over my waist, my fingers entwined with his. I felt his steady breathing behind me. For the first time in so long, I felt at peace, safe, *happy.* Grateful. I closed my eyes and went back to sleep.

I did not allow myself to think about what I'd done.

That would have ruined it all.

* * *

I woke up again to Jace's mouth on my neck when the sun began to rise and I turned to him, our passion burning us up in a whirlwind of incredible lust and love. I felt it in every touch, every kiss, every roll, and I heard it in his voice as he held me close, his voice gruff and raw. "Allie, I love you. I have never stopped loving you, babe."

It wasn't hard to say. It slipped right out, as if I'd been saying it to him for years and years. "I love you, too, Jace. I love you so much."

I smiled at him, and we made love again.

It was so fun.

Chapter Twelve

We fell into a happy rhythm and I ignored the screaming in my head.

I ignored the voice that said I was being deceptive and dishonest, lying by omission.

I ignored my dad's voice, echoing back and forth, telling me I was trailer trash, Jace was too good for me, I wasn't enough, I was stupid.

I ignored the hurt I would cause Jace when he knew the truth, which was the worst thing of all.

I ignored it all. I was inexcusably selfish.

He worked, I took care of the animals, and I actually grew to like my father's home, now that almost everything of his was gone. My mother's flowered quilt was on the couch, Pearl's apple tree hung above the fireplace, and my vases were filled with flowers.

I baked pies for hours.

On a whim I took three to a nearby café and they ordered two dozen.

I was contacted again by the high-end retail stores in Seattle, Boston, and Houston. I put them off, told them I would have an answer for them soon. I did not miss my couture clothes and impossibly high heels at all; jeans and boots were suiting me perfectly fine.

Maybe I didn't need to hide behind my clothes anymore. If so, why was that? What had changed? Was it simply my love for Jace? Was it me coming into myself? Was it my father's death?

I played with those questions for a long time.

When he wasn't working, Jace and I were together.

We hiked, rode bikes, had picnics, and we lay on our backs at night on his deck, or in a field, and located the constellations.

I read Jane Austen and crime thrillers beside him in bed while he read medical journals. We rafted down the Deschutes River one weekend, and drove to the beach and ran through the waves another weekend. We kissed under a waterfall, and it tasted as sweet as before.

He took photos of us and of nature, a hobby he said he had stopped since we broke up. "No time, and no Allie to come with me when I took the photos."

I held his hand. He took a photo of our hands, entwined. Then he kissed each finger, up my arm, across my chest to my lips, and we were soon stripping quickly.

We put together a puzzle of Mammoth Hot Springs in Yellowstone.

"I haven't put together a puzzle since you and I broke up, Allie. Hurt too much."

"Me neither, Jace."

He leaned over to kiss me. I ended up naked on top of the puzzle on the table.

We talked, the flow easy, of the most serious of subjects, and down to the tiniest and most inane detail, like what kind of salad dressing was our current favorite.

We made hot, simmering love all the time, three times under the constellations, as if catching up on what we'd missed out on. We used birth control. I didn't tell him the truth.

It was one more thing that he needed to know, he had a

right to know. I told myself I was selfish and unforgivably hurtful. If he knew the whole truth, he would not only be hurt by what happened, by my secrecy, he would not be rolling around under the covers with me.

I would vow to tell him, and then I'd look at him, at his smile, those gentle eyes, his hardened face that softened up just for me. Soon I'd be in his arms, comfortable and thrilled at the same time, hoping to be naked, laughing and feeling like I was going to cry, all at once.

How I loved Jace.

And every day, when I wasn't lit up by this golden light of love for him, when we weren't together, I fell further and further into a swirling, sad, lonely pit.

I reached for Jace one more time when the sky was still dark. He kissed me before he left for the hospital and drew his finger over my lips. "I love you, babe," he whispered.

"I love you, too, Jace." I brushed my fingers through his black hair, cupped his face.

When his truck was down the hill, I headed home and began packing.

I left the note for him on his kitchen table. I told him I'd be back in a week. I left him an apple pie. I told him I loved him.

He would say I was running away again, and he was right, but I had to do it anyhow.

I had to come to peace with my dad before I could come to peace with Jace and me.

I loaded a suitcase and my dad into the trunk. Yes, my dad, in his urn, was loaded up in my trunk. I didn't miss the symbolism there.

The first place I drove to was my dad's trailer, about an hour away from Schollton. It was clearly abandoned and leaning to one side, the grass grown up around it, the stairs rotted. I opened the unlocked door and peeked inside. The smell almost knocked me over. The scent of cigarette smoke, unwashed people, and stale liquor came at me like a putrid wave. It was battered and broken inside. I held my breath as one appalling memory after another tunneled through me.

I had lived here.

I was from here.

This had been mine and my mother's life.

I pictured my father's looming presence. I saw where I'd slept, the window he had broken now taped over. I saw my mother cowering, beaten. I could smell my own fear, my pervasive loneliness.

It made me sick. I had to lean over in the tall grass when I raced outside.

I stumbled into the apple orchard, sucking in air, surprised it was still there. I hiked up and down every single row, one mind-blowing, soul-kicking memory chasing after another. My nerves rattled remembering how many hours I'd spent there, eating the apples, carving them, throwing them in fits of fury, hiding in the branches when I had to escape the harangues of my dad or I wanted to cry for my dead mother. I felt pity for the lost little girl I used to be.

I dumped some of my dad's ashes on the steps of that trailer, swaying with nausea.

When I was done, I headed to the place where that terrible thing happened. I found the rock. I picked flowers. I left flowers on top of the rock, my tears rolling down onto the petals as I sat there.

In the distance I saw our trailer, a metal coffin for a girl's spirit.

I would not ever return again; I knew that.

I drove to Bigfork, Montana. I took two days to do it, stopping in Coeur d'Alene on the way. It gave me a lot of time to think. Most of the time I thought about how much I loved Jace. I pretended we could be together, daydreaming about it for hours. When the daydreams ended, I'd be back in abject hopelessness.

I stopped by my mother's grave and left a huge bouquet of pink tulips, her favorite. I sat there in that cemetery and cried, then I started talking to her, remembering all the good times, and those cherished memories finally started to squish out the despairing ones.

We had been happy in Bigfork. So happy.

I drove to our old house and climbed out of the car.

"Allie! Is that you?"

I turned. It was Mrs. Ashley, the woman who had begged my dad to let me stay with them.

"Mrs. Ashley!" I ran to her with open arms. She met me halfway.

"I would recognize your mother anywhere. Sweetheart, you are her mirror image, with all that gorgeous hair and the golden eyes."

I had dinner with her and Mr. Ashley. It was such a pleasure, a relief, a *gift*, to be able to talk to someone about my mother. She brought out three huge boxes right away. Inside were all of my mother's things that I'd so wanted to keep— her perfume bottles, her tablecloth with the yellow tulips, the tiny mirror with the ornate gold frame, her picture of an apple orchard bathed in sunlight, my pictures with the pink ballerinas. I pulled out two Jane Austen books and clutched them to me.

"Thank you, Mrs. Ashley," I said.

"Oh, dear. You are so welcome. I loved your mother. She was a good, strong woman. She would be so proud of you. She loved you very much. I wanted to mail these to you sooner but I didn't have your address. Your mother changed her last name when she arrived, didn't she?"

I nodded. "She had been trying to hide."

I left none of my dad's ashes in Montana.

* * *

From Bigfork I went to Yellowstone. I had pretended I was someone I wasn't when I was with Jace. I pretended that my dad's voice, telling me I was ugly, too thin, bony like a skeleton—a weird, dumb kid with a huge mouth, who was addicted to apples—was not ricocheting around in my head.

I'd been in college for three years and Yellowstone's incomparable beauty called to me for the summer. I had checked out a book on Yellowstone as a high schooler, and because I loved being outside, loved the serenity that nature brought to me, Yellowstone seemed like the ultimate heaven of natural wonders.

Jace told me he loved me about three weeks after we'd met by a waterfall that flowed into a stream. I cried. No one had said *I love you* to me since my mother died. Every time he told me he loved me, I became teary, and he wiped away my tears. We talked about *almost* everything. We talked about his childhood, which had been rocky, too. His mother had had four husbands. His father had taken off when Jace was a baby. His mother lived in Florida. He did not see her much. He wanted a family of his own, completely unlike the one he had grown up in.

I almost shared the truth about mine, but I couldn't. I was trying to pretend I wasn't trailer trash, and it had been engrained in me not to talk about being poor.

I was vague, said my mother was dead, my dad wasn't that nice.

We started making love about a month after we met. Our passion was this uncontrollable . . . *force*. We used birth control.

But one time we didn't.

I thought it was an okay time in my cycle.

It was not an okay time.

We both cried when we parted, Jace for medical school and me to finish my senior year of college. He was so masculine, so manly, even then, and there he stood, tears rolling out.

We would write, we would call, we would stay together. He would be eight states away.

I love you, Allie. I will always love you.

I love you, Jace. I love you with all my heart. I miss you already.

We'll be together soon, at Thanksgiving.

I stayed three nights in Yellowstone. I visited all the places Jace and I visited.

The journey had, finally, brought clarity from a morass of colliding emotions. I had been dishonest with Jace years ago. I had denied him the truth of his own life, which was unbelievably wrong of me.

I dumped none of my father's ashes in Yellowstone, either.

ㅤ

I drove back toward my dad's house early the next morning.

When I finally arrived in Schollton, I dumped some of my dad's ashes in the curve of the road near the steel goat, where he'd flipped his truck upside down. I thanked Pearl for taking care of my animals, then asked her if I could dump some of his ashes in her flower bed, because she said my dad had worked with her in her garden.

She picked up a bag of manure, so symbolic for what she said next. "He knew he treated you like crap, but he did love you, dear, make no mistake."

On his property, I dumped the last of his ashes amid the apple trees.

When they were all gone, I tossed the urn outside in the trash.

Had I forgiven him? I don't know. What he did to me, to my mother, was a lot to get over. But was that important? I was moving forward. I was not going to allow him to control my emotions or my life any longer. He was not going to be allowed in my head anymore. My anger had dimmed way down.

I walked into my house and saw Pearl's magical apple tree and my mother's red-and-white flowered quilt and smiled.

Chapter Thirteen

I baked apple pies almost all day.

Bob and Margaret followed me around the kitchen until I took them outside for a walk so Bob could chase his lifelong enemies, the squirrels, with Margaret as his right-hand woman, tongue wagging. Marvin and Spot the Cat meowed at me and I meowed back. I took Leroy and Spunky Joy for a ride on the property.

I dropped off a pie at Pearl's, and a few more at the homes of the other neighbors I'd met at the barn dance, all of whom invited me in for a slice and a chat. I think I had four slices of apple pie that day.

That night I walked up to Jace's house. His lights were on; he was home.

He was home to me.

I figured I would not feel like home to him when I was done.

"I'm sorry for leaving, Jace."

He turned away, running a hand through his black hair in front of his stone fireplace, the glow of the fire making shadows on the wall. He was wearing a sweatshirt and jeans and looked like he'd lost weight since I'd been gone. He was drawn and tense.

"I know you're not happy . . ."

"Not happy?" He whipped around. "Is that how you would describe this, Allie? Not happy? You *left*. You took off. You dropped a note on my table. Hell, does this remind you of what happened between us years ago? I think we're doing great, I'm hoping we can do something normal like have dinner and watch the sun go down when I get home from work, and then I find out you're gone. *You are gone*."

"I know, I'm sorry." I wrung my hands together. I deserved his anger.

He strode over to me and stopped three feet away, his face stormy, jaw tight.

"I didn't . . . I didn't want . . ." I said.

"You didn't want what? You didn't want to have a conversation about why you had to leave? The potential conflict? What does that say about you and what does it say about us? That you're too afraid to speak up? That you can't trust me with something you need to do? That you think I'd try to change your mind? That isn't the case, Allie, and you know it."

"You're right. It isn't." I felt sick, anxious. "I had to go by myself."

"Then fine. Go, but don't shut me out and take off. Damn it, Allie."

"Jace, I'm sorry. I shouldn't have left without telling you—that was awful. I need to tell you a few things. Things that happened years ago, things that happened recently, and then . . . and then you can decide if you even want to be with me again."

"I want to be with you, Allie. I have made that perfectly clear this whole time." He threw up his arms. "That has *never* changed."

"Can we sit down? Please? My legs are about to give out and I'm going to fall into an inglorious heap on the floor."

He held out an arm, frustrated, hurt, baffled, and I sank to the sofa. He sat down beside me and I reached for his hand. Even then I needed his comfort. He automatically held mine, our fingers entwined.

"First, Jace, I'm sorry. I am sorry to the depths of my soul."

"For what?"

I told him everything. I told him about living in a trailer, the abuse from my dad, fleeing to Bigfork with my petrified mother, her death, and back to my dad and the abject loneliness, fear, and poverty. I told him why, as a young, poor girl, I redesigned my used clothes with satin, lace, and beading; how I later hid that young, poor girl behind designer outfits and high heels. I told him why I liked apples.

"My dad had always told me I was trailer trash. He also said I was stupid, useless, worthless, a slut, had a face like an apple core, had strange gold eyes, not good enough for any man . . ."

Jace swore, got up, and started pacing in front of the fire.

"I didn't think I was good enough for you, Jace. I was pretending to be someone I wasn't in Yellowstone. But inside I felt dirty. I felt unworthy. I was ashamed."

"Is that why you broke up with me?"

"Part of it."

"There wasn't a Zack, was there?"

"Of course not. There was never anyone but you. There has never been anyone but you."

He strode back over to me, kneeled, and cupped my face so I couldn't turn away. "Then why? Why did you break up with me?"

"I broke up with you . . ." My eyes filled with tears and I put my hands over his and bent my head. Jace wiped my tears away with his thumbs.

"Why?"

"I broke up with you because I was pregnant."

The words went off like little bombs. "You were *what*?"

"Pregnant."

"But we always used birth control—"

"Not that one time, by the lake, at night . . . remember? We had gone swimming."

"Oh my God." Remembrance dawned and he sank onto the couch next to me, his head in his hands. I put my arm around his broad shoulders.

"What . . ." His voice was strangled. "What happened to the baby?"

I let out a small cry.

"Oh no, Allie, you didn't—" he whispered, eyes anguished.

"No no, I couldn't do that, Jace. Never. I didn't abort it, but I caused the baby's death." I started crying, interspersed with choked, anguished gasps. "It was my fault. All my fault. Sometimes I think I can't live with this—it's haunted me forever, followed me around. I am so sorry, Jace. So sorry."

"What happened?"

I tried to pull myself together, but it didn't work well. "In the fall, after you left for medical school, I found out my dad had had a heart attack. I knew what it would do to me, being back in his trailer after five years, but I thought maybe he had changed, that he would be kinder. He was all I had left. My mother was dead, and I felt guilty and ashamed for not seeing him. I don't know how to explain it, but I wanted . . ." I tripped over my words again. "I wanted my dad to love me. He never had, and I wanted it."

He groaned. "Oh, Allie."

"It was hopeless, I should have known that. I dropped out of school, went home, and stayed in his trailer. I tried to get him healthy again. When I arrived he was in terrible shape, on oxygen, medications. He told me that I was a bad daughter, that I'd abandoned him. From the moment I walked into my dad's trailer I felt like trash again. It was like he took over my mind and I turned into that same kid, lost and lonely, devastated, missing her mom, not knowing what to do. I was young, Jace, only twenty-one . . ."

It was dark and dismal and dirty in my dad's trailer. He was dark and dismal and dirty. He was unemployed. I took care of him. I had always battled low self-esteem, and my dad crushed what I'd managed to build up while I was away. He was demanding and critical, lying there in bed, hardly able to breathe. He'd added about eighty pounds.

"Why did you abandon me? You're exactly like your cheating mother. You lied to those people from children's protection services so you could get yourself emancipated when you were sixteen. Your mother lied to the police about what I did to her when the neighbors called them . . . You're both ungrateful, and look at me now. You caused this heart attack with how much I've worried about you . . . Got your mother's big nose and skinny hips, don't you? Hopefully you don't have her brains, apple-seed brains . . ."

It was ludicrous. It was relentless.

But I didn't leave.

I felt trapped by him again, like a tortured rat, my mind a mental morass of sludge and guilt. He was critically ill and I was afraid if I left he would die and I would be responsible for his death. In fact, he told me that many times. "If you leave, I'll die, so get your butt in here and help me."

I was young, missing Jace, and exhausted from the first day on. Soon I could hardly think, my dad's mind manipulations working so well on me, his medical needs enormous. I went into self-protection mode, duck and dodge, survive. I even started hiding in the apple orchard again, eating apples when I was hungry.

I had morning sickness. I passed it off as the flu at first. My cycle had never been regular, but soon I knew, and so did he. He wasn't that stupid.

"You whore." The scars on his face seemed more pronounced to me. "You're exactly like your mother. She got pregnant before we were married; that's why I had to marry her. What poor sucker are you doing that to? Where is he?"

It went on and on.

"I've got a pregnant, unmarried daughter on my hands. I'm so humiliated."

Three nights later, under constant pressure, I told him I was in love with Jace, that he treated me well and was going to be a doctor.

"A doctor is never going to marry someone like you, trailer park princess," he scoffed, beer heavy on his breath. "You were his summer fun. He'll find a doctor to marry. You're a fool. You're candy to him—that's it."

He threw a beer bottle at me. Then an ashtray. Next a plate came flying at my head like a saucer. I dodged all three, then managed to grab my bag and purse and fight my way out of the trailer. He slung out a thick arm and I hit the side of the trailer and then pushed him away. He kept swearing, calling me all sorts of names.

I shoved my way past his bulky body, tripped off the steps and started running. It was black and moonless, slippery and wet. I sprinted down the road, my dad actually tottering after me, gut over his pants, hollering at me. I thought he would probably die trying to catch me, but I was running for my life. I could hardly see with the tears in my eyes, my breath coming in gasps. All I knew was that I was out of the trailer.

I was out, and so was the baby.

In my blind panic, I did not watch where I was going. I tripped and went flying over a hill, rolled straight down, and landed on my stomach on a rock.

The blood flowed out like a river.

Jace cried; I cried with him.

"I sat in that hospital bed and I cried for the baby. I thought the tears would never stop. That baby has never left my heart, ever. I kept thinking about you, Jace, and how our baby, *our baby*, was gone, because of my recklessness, my stupidity. I never should have gone back to that trailer."

"This didn't happen because of you; it happened because of your father." Jace swore; he was so furious with my dad he was shaking. "You should have told me you were pregnant. I would have come for you."

"I felt awful for not telling you, Jace, but you were in med school and I was afraid that you would leave med school because you would feel obligated to take care of the baby, and I . . . I knew you wanted to be a doctor more than anything. It was your dream." My hands fluttered. "I also worried that you would marry me, but it would be out of obligation. My self-esteem was so low then, it could not have gotten lower if someone had taken a sledgehammer to it, and my dad's words were ping-ponging back and forth in my head: I was nothing, you were a doctor, you would never want me."

"I have always wanted you, Allie, always. I have never wavered. Were you even going to tell me about the baby? Was I going to have a kid in this world and I wouldn't have even known about it?"

I could tell the thought infuriated him. "I was going to tell you after I gave birth to the baby. I thought I'd have the baby, graduate from college, get a job, then tell you, so you wouldn't feel like you had to take care of me; I wouldn't be a burden. I grew up poor, Jace, and being a burden to someone else made me feel ill. My dad had always told me I was a burden, that my mother was a burden, and I could tell he hated me for it. I didn't want you to hate me."

"I would never hate you. Do you honestly think you and our baby would be a burden to me?"

"At that time, in that chaos, yes. I had no money, no degree yet, no job."

We were quiet, my hand in his. He wiped his eyes.

"I'm sorry, Allie," he said gruffly. "I should have delayed medical school to be with you, waited until you graduated, worked where you were going to school, but instead I left you."

"You had to leave. It was a prestigious university, an incredible opportunity."

"I'm so sorry that I wasn't there for you. I am so sorry."

"How could you have been? I broke up with you. You wrote and called—"

"I should have come to see you."

"After I broke up with you, you told me you were coming, Jace, so we could talk. I told you not to, that there was a Zack in my life. I hope you can forgive me, I really do. I have been sorry every single day since it happened—"

"Allie, please, honey, I do forgive you; there's nothing to forgive." He brought my hand to his lips and kissed it. "You were pregnant, you were scared, you were young, I was gone, your dad had a heart attack, and you were trapped in that trailer, being abused. Let go of that guilt. You have to. Your dad was a hateful, dangerous, violent man and you ran from him when he started throwing things at your head." He clenched his fists. "If he were here I would beat him down to nothing."

"I would enjoy watching that."

His expression changed to confusion. "But after you lost the baby, why didn't you call and tell me? I had a right to know. It was my baby, too."

"You did have a right. I knew that losing the baby would hurt you and I thought . . ." I put my hand on his face. "I thought I was protecting you from knowing about that loss."

"But I called you again a couple of months later. I thought you needed space. I was hoping you would break up with Zack, but you never called back. Why? I don't understand, Allie. This whole thing is not making sense. You didn't tell me about the baby because you didn't want me to drop out of school, you didn't want to be a burden, but then you didn't try to contact me again, either, after the baby died."

"I wanted to be with you, Jace." An anguished cry left my

throat. "There's one more thing. One more terrible thing. When I was in the hospital the doctors told my dad, and he told me, that because of the damage I sustained in the fall against the rock . . ." *Oh no, oh no.* I put a hand to my trembling lips. "They told me I wouldn't be able to have kids."

His face paled.

"I think he was happy telling me that." My voice pitched high, my dad's total lack of love and kindness stunning. "He was drunk and he said that no man would want me now, especially not a doctor like you, and I might as well come back home to the trailer with him. Though I never set foot in his trailer again, I thought he was right. I knew you wanted kids, you wanted a family, and I couldn't have any. Depriving you of kids wasn't fair. I knew you would always miss that part of your life, and you would be such a good dad. Since I hadn't told you about the baby, there was no reason to tell you I couldn't have kids, because I knew I wouldn't be your wife anyhow."

He wiped his eyes again and sighed deeply, then picked me up and put me on his lap and leaned back against the couch. "First, Allie, I'm sorry you can't have kids. I truly am, but you made a decision that affected both our lives. You made it by yourself, without me."

"I did, and I am so sorry." The tears rolled off my chin. "I thought it was the best one, at the time. I was so screwed up."

"We lost years together. Years. You decided to act alone. I had no say. I had no say in *our* life." His eyes swam in tears. "Allie, when you broke up with me, everything went black in my life. That's why I worked so hard in medical school, to keep that blackness away. I missed you every single day. Everyone else complained about the long hours at medical school. I was glad of them; they kept me from falling apart."

"I felt that same blackness. It clung to me. I went back to school, graduated, and drowned myself in relentless work so I couldn't think, so I could block out missing you and the baby, and what we could have had."

"Allie, I love you. I want you. If we can't have kids together, that's the way it is. I want us to be together—"

"But, Jace, you will live your whole life without kids if you're with me."

"I'll live it that way, then. Or we'll adopt. From here in America; foster kids; kids from abroad. Families come together in different ways, babe, and you and I are a family, and whoever else we put in our family is part of our family, too."

"But Jace—"

"Allie, we were meant to be together. I knew it when I fell in love with you up at Yellowstone. I know it now. I have had this place in my heart, forever, that has wanted to be with you, that has missed you, that's been lonely for you. Honey, I love you with all that I am. You and I should be together, always. I want to marry you. I would marry you tomorrow if you would agree. Please, Allie."

"Really, Jace? Even without kids?"

"Yes, of course. Say yes, Allie. Say yes to us. I want you to be my wife more than I want anything, more than I will ever want anything."

I felt like the Grinch whose heart grew three sizes. "Yes, Jace. Yes to us." I kissed him, my arms around his neck, his arms holding me tight. "I love you, Jace Rios. I always have, I always will."

We made love on the couch.

Then in the hot tub.

We had tacos for dinner.

It was a most excellent night.

Chapter Fourteen

The next day, I explored the contents of the blue cardboard box. It was the last step for me—then the space my dad occupied in my head was going to be banished forever. What I found shocked me.

Inside were some of my mother's things: A burgundy velvet-covered jewelry box. Her wedding ring with a miniscule diamond that I remembered her leaving when we fled. A brooch with a hummingbird on it. A colorful Mexican fan. A ceramic vase painted with blue flowers.

What shocked me was his note. My dad, my often violent, uncontrollable dad, wrote that he loved me, that he loved my mother, that he was sorry.

That word *sorry* came up at least ten times. He blamed himself and took full responsibility. He blamed himself for my mother's death.

"Without my abusive attitude and behavior, Mae-Lynn would not have high-tailed it for Montana. I take full blame for MaeLynn's death. I loved her, Allie, as I have always loved you, too. I am dying a broken man.

I say this not to make you feel guilty. You were right to walk away from your old man. You had to. I was a mean SOB and a threat to you.

"*Your Grandpa Tad left me money, Allie. I spent part of it to get cleaned up, to get off the booze once and for all. I hate what I've done. Hate myself. Can't remember a time when I didn't hate myself. I think it started with my old man. You know the scars on my face? They're all from him and his fists. I turned into my old man with you and your mother, the last person I wanted to be. But now I'm sober and I got to try to make amends, even though it is far short of what you deserve.*

"*I bought the apple orchard for you. I remember how you always ate apples out of the orchard near our trailer. I remember thinking way back then that it was kind of cute how you always had apples with you. Now I know you were always looking for apples to eat because you were hungry, because your loser dad did not provide food for you. I spent my money at the bars. I failed you because I was too drunk to do anything different. Allie, I am sorry with everything I got. My gift to you is all the apples you could ever want or need. What I should have given you and what you had a right to expect.*

"*I love you, Allie, and I wish you the very best. I am truly sorry.*"

I choked up over that box, and when I got myself together, I walked through the apple orchard my dad left me. My apple orchard now.

I picked a Jonagold off a tree as Bob went running after those tantalizing squirrels, Margaret following her man with her tongue hanging out.

Mr. Jezebel Rooster cock-a-doodle-doo'd. He gets his times messed up.

The apple was delicious.

I found the ring in the middle of an apple pie we were sharing on Jace's deck as the sun went down over the blue mountains in the distance, pinks and yellows settling over my apple orchard down the hill.

At first, I couldn't even figure out what I was looking at. What was it and what was it doing in my pie? I pulled the ring out of the crust and licked it. It was quite the sparkler— absolutely stunning.

Jace reached for my hand and dropped down to one knee. Gotta love that. "Will you marry me, Allie Pelletier?"

"Oh yes. Yes, I will." He picked me up, swung me around, and kissed me the way he always kisses me, full and passionate, with love, bodies together tight.

"I love you, Allie. I've loved you since I met you, and I'll love you when we're old and making apple pies together for our great-grandchildren, using your mom's recipes."

"That's a really beautiful image." I held his face and kissed him, loving him wrapped around me, loving us, loving our future.

"Sure is," he drawled. "As long as you don't burn the pies."

I laughed and elbowed him and he grabbed me, flipped me over his shoulder, and shut the bedroom door with his cowboy boot.

I was a fool.

A hopeful fool.

I called a baby doctor.

She had a cancellation the next day, so I took it. She did the exam.

She said, "We can fix it."

I was stunned.

I told Jace the news as soon as I saw him.

He picked me up and swirled me around.

I told Pearl the news about our engagement.

She hugged me and asked for the pieces of my mother's purple-flowered china plates that my father had shattered.

I didn't know why she wanted them, but I handed them over.

For a wedding gift, she created a four-by-five-foot mosaic of Jace's house, which is where we are going to live. She used the pieces of the plates to form the flowers in the trees near his home.

"Welcome home, dearie," she said. "Now get in there and bang out some babies."

I received a call from the owner of Mackie's Designs.

"We want you back, Allie," Belinda Carls, the chic owner, said in her soft Texan drawl. "Annalise is gone. We checked out your claims and you were right as rain on a desert. Shane, Jeremy, and David said they were bee-bopping on the mattress with her, and they appreciated the promotions, but that's wrong as a skunk's scent and it's not how we work, not how Mother would have wanted it. Did you know Annalise threw her Manolo Blahniks at people who made her mad? I just found out that many of her employees have had nervous breakdowns and plumb lost their minds. She was fired quick as a wink. How would you like to be president of Mackie's Designs?"

I thought about it for a long . . . two seconds.

"No, thank you." I could not imagine wearing four-inch heels again, and I don't need to hide myself or my past behind couture or high-end fashions anymore.

"No?" Belinda was astonished, baffled. "What do you mean *no, sugar*? I've told you the salary, the benefits. This is a Texas-sized opportunity for you, Allie, and that's no bull . . ."

"Sorry, Belinda. I'm going to bake pies."

"Pies, dear?"

"Yep. Pies. Most especially, apple pies. My mother's favorite. I'll send you one."

Epilogue

I'm selling pies.

I started selling them at a local Saturday market. The first time, I sold twelve pies. The next Saturday I tripled that, and the next Saturday I doubled *that*. I was mentioned in an article about the best food to buy in local Saturday markets. I started getting orders from local stores in addition to the country café down the road.

I decided to turn my dad's house into a country store where I could bake and sell my pies. I bought new industrial appliances, took down a wall, hired a few local women, and we baked, sold, and shipped pies to other stores all day. I covered a table with my mom's tulip tablecloth and her apple orchard photograph is on a wall. I wear her apple apron.

I love my new life. I love watching the leaves of the apple orchard change. I love the smell of all the pies we make: raspberry, rhubarb, lemon meringue, chocolate, etc. and, most especially, apple pies, which I have named MaeLynn's Apple Pies.

I love remembering my mom and baking pies with her.

Sometimes I can hear her voice, her laughter. I look at the photos of us in Bigfork often.

I have brought the happiest memories of my mother right into this kitchen. Her memory is not blotted with grief and simmering resentment anymore, and I revel in the joy of who she was, the light she brought to my life. I love the time I had with her, however short. I have no room in my heart for anger, grief, or hatred toward my dad. I lived with it for too long; it wore me down to nothing and turned me into someone I am not.

At night, I hug my husband.

We cook dinner and sit by the fire. We locate the constellations, we put puzzles together. We hike through the gorge, by waterfalls, up to magical viewpoints. I go with him on photography forays because he likes taking pictures. We let the dogs run and we ride the horses. We bike. I read Jane Austen out loud. We read the same crime thriller together and talk about it. We have planned a trip to Yellowstone.

And we laugh. We always laugh.

My name is Allie Pelletier.

I had some trauma in my childhood.

I was often lonely and miserable.

I ate a lot of apples.

I made pies with my mother.

I fell in love in Yellowstone. I am still in love with that same man.

I have found peace with my past.

I am pregnant. We're having a little girl.

We will name her MaeLynn, after my mother.

We are going to give her brothers and sisters, too.

Jace and I are very excited.

A Kiss Before
Midnight

Mary Carter

Prologue

Many moons ugo

Like her mother and grandmother, and on up the maternal line, young Rose had the gift. But it wasn't until she fell in love herself that her powers truly progressed. In fact, ever since George first kissed her, women of all ages began flowing into the shop and begging for her love spell. It seemed everyone who used the secret tincture—purple clover, a drop of George's cologne, petals from the roses he'd given her—soon fell madly in love. Rose was happy she could help. When you were in love, you wanted everyone in the world to feel the same. And it was all because of George. Everything good in life was because of George.

Her first date, her first kiss, her first time. He laid a silver blanket down on the cemetery's soft grass. He gave her a thick red rose that was just beginning to open, and even brought two crystal flutes and a bottle of champagne. To this day all she had to do was close her eyes and she could hear the pop of the cork, see the fizz explode and drip down the long green neck of the bottle, listen to the clink of their glasses, and feel the golden liquid drip onto her fingers as she held the glass up for more. He was the center of her world.

And he looked at her as if she was the most beautiful girl he had ever seen, as if he couldn't get enough. Everyone else had trouble looking into her eyes—one blue and one green—but not him. Everyone else called the color of her hair "mousy." George called it chestnut. Others called her weird, or strange. George called her special and magical.

It was easy to say yes, and oh, how she wanted him to make love to her, because that would make them like husband and wife. And he was so slow, and so tender, and it didn't hurt as much as she thought it would, and it didn't last but a few stolen minutes, and their love was lit by a magnificent moon.

Someday it would be different. Someday she would be his legal wife. Then they could stroll hand in hand in the daylight and no one would look twice. For now they were destined to meet in the dark. Tonight marked an entire year that they had been seeing each other. She wondered what he would bring her. A rose, of course, as always, but maybe something else? Maybe a little necklace she could wear underneath her dress. A little heart, a promise she could wear when they were apart. Oh, how lucky she was. He was the handsomest man she had ever seen.

And that was the problem. He was a man. She was just shy of sixteen; he was thirty-six. Everyone else thought she was just a girl—a strange girl, a mousy girl—but George knew different. She was a woman, and she was in love. She couldn't wait to see him again. She wore her best dress, blue with a green silk ribbon, to bring out the best of each eye, and brushed her chestnut hair until it shone. When her mother wasn't looking, she had applied pink rouge to her cheeks and mascara to her lashes, and just a touch of shimmering gloss to her eager lips. It was just before midnight. The moon was ripe and drooping so low she felt as if she could reach out and touch it. George had yet to appear. It was a little odd. He was always the first one there, waiting for her, standing with one hand propped against a tombstone, the other holding her rose. Posing with a silly grin and waiting for the moment when he could say, *There's my Rose.*

She touched the note in the pocket of her dress, the one he slipped under the door to the shop. He was lucky that she found it first. She would have to warn him about her grandmother's prying eyes. *My Rose, meet me tonight by our favorite statue. I wish to steal a kiss before midnight.*

So here she stood by his favorite statue—a young maiden kneeling with her arms outstretched, palms out, as if pleading with her lover to take her into his arms. She couldn't stay long, for someone might notice she was gone. Something must have come up, because he would never leave her alone this long in the dark. She had just turned to go home, hurrying along the back row of headstones, when she tripped over something in her path. Startled, she lifted herself from the ground and whirled around.

His beautiful body lay faceup in the grass. His eyes and mouth were open, gaping blankly at the full moon. Just a body, a lifeless vessel incapable of saying *There's my Rose.* She knelt down beside him, took the rose out of his clutched fingers. How she wanted to kiss his lips, but the foam—it was too much. She couldn't bring herself to go near them. "I'm sorry, I'm sorry, I'm so sorry." She didn't wonder what had killed him; poison was the easiest spell to spot. It worked quickly and caused the lips to foam. Her mother and grandmother had seen the note. She brought the thorny stem of the rose up to her wrist and cut as deep as she could. It wasn't deep enough. She was still alive. She cursed her mother and grandmother, she cursed all lovers, she cursed anyone who was lucky enough to steal a kiss before midnight.

Only sweet sixteen but already condemned to the life of a lonely old maid. Her lover had died waiting for her. She, too, would spend the rest of her life waiting for him, waiting for death.

Chapter One

It began with a scavenger hunt. Imagine Rebecca Ryan, a junior, invited on the senior trip by Allison, Cathy, and Grace
(ACG!), the most popular girls in school. For the first time in
her life, Rebecca wished her long, dark hair looked more
like their light, fringed bobs. And what was she thinking,
bringing her fanciest clothes? The other girls were dressed
casually, yet somehow still looked runway ready. Rebecca
was a phony. She just wasn't like them. They were skinny;
she was curvy. They were loud and carefree; she was reserved and shy. They wore designer clothes and drove
to school in shiny new cars; she trolled thrift stores and
took the bus. They summered in Europe, pierced their ears,
and never missed a salon appointment. They were girls
who up until now hadn't said so much as hi to Rebecca in
the halls.

Normally she liked trolling thrift stores for clothes,
watching their town go by from the window of the bus, and
she truly enjoyed her yearly trips to Miami to see her grandparents, (anywhere warm was better than Buffalo in the winter time!), or trips to Gettysburg to see ancient cannons. Of
course she was dying to go to London, or Paris, or Rome.

But there was time. She would tour Europe when she graduated college. Or so she thought.

But here she was, in New Orleans, with ACG. She felt a rush of joy that buoyed her to a whole new level of happy. Why not take crazy risks for your new best friends? Perhaps she had always wanted to be popular, but since it never seemed remotely possible, she shoved the desire into a secret room in her heart and locked the door. Now the lock had been sprung and she was free. It was surprising how easy it had been to pull off.

She told her parents it was a school-sponsored band trip. Rebecca had grudgingly played the clarinet for years. She even forged a fake permission slip and watched guiltily as her mother lovingly applied tags to her suitcase and peppered her with questions about the trip. She vowed she would never lie to them again; she didn't have the stomach for it. It wouldn't be long before the Ryans found out that no one else in the band had gone to New Orleans, but by that time Rebecca would be back to face her punishment.

And now here they were, just hours off the plane from Buffalo, and Bourbon Street was already spinning under the influence of apple-green and berry-red drinks appropriately named Hurricanes and Hand Grenades. The four beauties linked arms and danced down the street, laughing loudly, exposing a breast here and there even though it wasn't Mardi Gras. And perhaps the rebelling would have ended with the three of them passing out in the Friends Motel, waking up with a wicked hangover and watery recollections of the phone numbers stuffed in their purses, had it not been for the scavenger hunt.

The first two items on Rebecca's list looked harmless enough:

1. <u>Drink three more Hurricanes</u>. Bartender *must* sign and swear you drank them, plus you must show us all three glasses.

2. <u>Get a psychic reading from the old witch at the Voodoo Shop</u>. Tell us what color the witch's eyes are so we know you've seen her. Tell us your fortune.

3. <u>Kiss a stranger in a cemetery</u>. Have someone take a picture of the two of you making out by a headstone.

The third item stopped Rebecca in her tracks. *Make out with a stranger in a cemetery*. Like she would. Like she could. Were the other girls really going to do that? Making out with a total stranger was worrisome enough. But a cemetery? At night? There was absolutely no way. As Rebecca made her way to a little jazz club she read about in a local paper, she obsessed about how she was going to fake that one. And maybe the creepy graveyard wasn't the worst bit. Rebecca was sweet sixteen and never been kissed. Juvenile games of spin the bottle didn't count. Neither did Jocy Garden sticking his tongue in her ear. But really, really kissed? She'd dreamt of it, of course, but guys didn't look twice at girls like her. She didn't want to do the scavenger hunt anymore. This wasn't why she came on the trip. She didn't want her first real kiss to be some kind of silly game. And why was she suddenly all alone? That hadn't been part of the plan. It struck her that it probably wasn't particularly safe for a sixteen-year-old to be roaming tipsy and alone through the streets of the French Quarter. If her mother knew, she would be out of her mind. Here she was, a trusted daughter, Reliable Rebecca, doing something incredibly stupid. She'd never even had so much as an overdue library book. She was suddenly ashamed. If anything happened to her, her parents' lives would be ruined forever. All because of her lies. All because she wanted to be liked and win a scavenger hunt. She didn't even ask what the prize was. How crazy was that? Should she turn around? Try to find them? Go back to the hotel? No. She was here, wasn't she? She had to at least listen to some local music. After all, that's what the band would have done if they really had come on a school trip.

Rebecca had wanted Allison, Cathy, and Grace to join her, but they insisted they each had to work on their own list. Rebecca got the feeling they couldn't care less about listening to a live jazz band. But this was New Orleans, the city of jazz—how could they not want to go hear the local talent? *Because they aren't like you*, her little voice said. So why had they invited her?

And why was she suddenly so ashamed of herself? When Allison asked her why on earth she wanted to go to a stinky old jazz club, Rebecca said she needed to have a story for her parents. That was true, but she would have gone anyway.

"Yeah," Grace had said. "Who are you going to find to make out with there? Some fat old trombone player?" Then the threesome laughed as if it were the funniest thing they'd ever heard. All Rebecca could manage was a pained smile.

Then Rebecca had insisted she wouldn't be there long, just long enough to tell her parents she saw some local jazz. The truth was, she couldn't wait to see where the locals played, where the true musicians hung out, tucked far enough away that they weren't burdened with entertaining tourists. For even though she wasn't very good on the clarinet (all right, she stunk—no matter how she pursed her lips, the darn thing always squealed when she least expected it), she absolutely loved listening to jazz. Something about the freewheeling brass instruments struck Rebecca as one of the sexiest things in the world. What she didn't tell the girls was that she probably *would* make out with a fat trombone player as long as he could play. Yes, good jazz made Rebecca feel alive.

And looks-wise, despite her desire to be more like her new friends, Rebecca Ryan certainly fit in with the sexy music. With a height of five feet eight inches, wavy jet-black hair, and blue eyes that turned aqua in certain lights, she almost personified jazz. Despite the lack of attention from high school boys, Rebecca Ryan was a beautiful woman.

* * *

It was a small bar, dim and dive-y, but lively and packed. A group of five men were playing on a little stage. As the brass and drums infused her with life, she made her way to an empty table just off center stage. She wished something farther back and more discreet were available, but since everyone seemed to be looking at her, she couldn't turn back now. Most of the patrons were older, and black, including the musicians. If they thought it was odd that a young white girl was in their midst, they didn't show it. She was greeted with huge grins—and not the kind that made her feel sick to her stomach—but the kind that made her smile back.

After establishing herself at the table, Rebecca went to the bar. She showed her ID to the bartender, then ordered a Coke.

"A Coke?" he said. "Sugar, why you bother with a fake ID if all you want is a Coke?"

He had a point there. Besides, the other drinks were wearing off a little. "Put some Jack in it," Rebecca said.

"You sure?" He leaned over. "How old are you, anyway?"

"Twenty-one," she said.

The bartender shook his head. "If you say so."

She felt guilty for lying again, but she knew she could pass for twenty-one and she had the fake ID to prove it.

"Can I get it in a Hurricane glass?" Why not try to fake part of the scavenger hunt, just in case?

"Not unless you're drinking a Hurricane. You think you can handle one?"

"I've already handled two."

"Well, be careful. They don't call it a Hurricane for nothing." He winked and held out his hand as if pointing to a distant storm on the horizon. "One minute it's all peaceful and quiet, real still. The next minute—there it is." He shrunk back theatrically as he talked. "Coming to suck up all the cows and houses in the hood!" When his little "storm" was over, he straightened up and laughed. "You get me?"

"I get you. I'll take one."

He whistled low and shook his head, then to show her he was teasing flashed her a smile. He had a gold tooth in the front. She smiled back. She dared to lean on the bar, even though she knew the neckline of the blue silk dress she was wearing was already low-cut enough without the counter tugging it down any farther, but if she was going to get anywhere in the scavenger hunt, she knew she was going to have to use a few feminine wiles.

"I'm on a scavenger hunt," she said as he slid the tall hourglass drink in front of her. "And I'm supposed to drink three of those."

"Oh boy. You shouldn't do that. This is your third already."

"I know, I know. I just need to show three empty glasses and have some nice bartender sign a napkin saying he saw me drink all three."

"Well, how about you drink that one and we'll cheat a little on the other two?"

"Perfect," Rebecca said with a smile and a wink. She swayed a little as she walked back to her seat. What was she doing? Who was she fooling? She had just finished her sophomore year of high school. She should not be here. What if the bartender got in trouble for serving someone underage? She was going to drink this one Hurricane, listen to some music, then call a cab home. And even if she did find someone she wouldn't mind kissing, there was no way she was going to a freaking cemetery at this time of night.

She was halfway through her stormy drink when he was called onstage. And although he looked completely out of place with his white skin, tousled chestnut hair, and blue eyes, he certainly didn't act it. He stood in the spotlight cradling a trumpet and grinning as the older musicians treated him to pats on the back.

"Miles Davis, move on over," a sax player yelled out. "We've got Grant Dodge right here. He may be young and white, but he plays like he's old and black." The crowd roared with laughter. "Folks, let's hear it for Grant Dodge."

He was the handsomest young man Rebecca had ever seen. And then he put that shiny trumpet up to his beautiful lips and blew.

Rebecca froze in midair, like a giant storm being put on pause. Grant Dodge played the trumpet like he'd been born with it glued to his lips. For a few seconds Rebecca couldn't move or even breathe. The feeling that washed over her as he played transcended everything she had ever known. This was madness, this was passion—this was love at first sound.

When he finished, she leapt to her feet with everyone else, screaming his name, and the sound of her voice must have made its way through the air thick with cigarette smoke, and the sounds of clinking glasses and blaring instruments, for every cell in her body recorded the moment when he heard her, when his head slowly turned, and his eyes met hers in the crowd. She felt a jolt as his eyes locked on hers, and stayed locked as the rest of the bar disappeared. Holding his trumpet across his chest like an easy, extra appendage, he first regarded her with open curiosity, and then, because she spontaneously smiled, he smiled back and there they stood for what felt like eternity, complete strangers grinning at each other across the room. Rebecca Ryan knew right then and there that he was going to profoundly change her life, but in that instant she just assumed it was because she knew two things without a single, solitary doubt. One: he was going to be the stranger she kissed before midnight. And, two: she was never going to play the freaking clarinet ever again.

Chapter Two

Rebecca Ryan leaned back in her seat and gazed out the window of the plane. *Prepare for landing*, she thought. *You're here. You're really here*. Twenty-one years, yet she remembered every single thing about that night. How could she not? How many people could say they lost their virginity in an ancient New Orleans graveyard beneath an engorged yellow moon? Although innocent probably wasn't quite the right word for her that evening. In fact, it was as if she was possessed. Oh, what a night.

It was humid and the sultry night air clung to their bare skin. Headstones, statues of virgins and angels—neither of which she would be after that night—rose protectively around them. Someone must have mowed that morning; the air still smelled of fresh-cut grass. Grant bought her a rose on Bourbon Street and it lay beside them on the soft grass. Every time she turned her head, its petals brushed like velvet against her nose, cheek, and lips. And then there was that moon. In her whole life, she had never seen such a huge, glowing moon. Complete with a statue of a kneeling maiden reaching out her arms, Rebecca never knew a cemetery could be so hauntingly beautiful.

Sometimes when she replayed that night, she added stars. You could do that with memories. Play with them, caress them, mold them. Microscopic little changes. Who remembers everything exactly the way it happened? So sometimes she remembered stars. Millions of them, glittering, spinning, and softly singing just to them. She imagined it was the last night on earth and they were the only two lovers left in the world. A handsome older boy. He was twenty-one, she was sixteen. How easily the lies tripped off her tongue that weekend. She told him she was nineteen.

The sounds, she didn't need to mold; they played like an orchestra when she closed her eyes. Zippers, and buttons, and soft kisses, and sighs, and all the little things they whispered to each other. Even when she cried out, it was only because it felt so good. She never imagined it could feel so good. Oh, the sounds they made that night. They should have woken the dead.

Twenty-one years since that fateful night. At times it was impossible to believe it had been that long. Other times it felt as if it were someone else's life entirely. It was a night filled with the promise of magic. She'd never felt anything like it before and she'd certainly never come close to it since. It was the night she lied to her parents, the night she was betrayed by the three most popular girls in school, the night she quit the clarinet, the night she was cursed, the night she not only kissed a boy for the first time, but made love to him as well, the night Rebecca Ryan's son, Miles, was conceived underneath that fat, glowing moon.

It was the night that swallowed her whole. And here she was, daring to go back. What was she so afraid of? Did she really think Grant Dodge would be waiting for her at the airport with an accusatory glare and a handheld sign that cried out: WHY DIDN'T YOU TELL ME I HAVE A SON?

She deserved that and more. And ironically, it was because of their son that she was here in the first place. His gift for her thirty-seventh birthday: a trip to New Orleans. Even her birthday card was an artist's rendition of the French Quarter featuring a trumpet player raising his instrument beneath an old-fashioned street lamp.

> *Mom,*
> 　*Happy birthday! I hope you find everything you're looking for.*
>
> 　　　　　　　　　　　　　*Love,*
> 　　　　　　　　　　　　　*Miles*

That was her Miles. And what a feat—convincing her parents to chip in for this trip, for there was no way her strapped college kid could have afforded this on his own.

"You're always talking about New Orleans, Mom," Miles had said with an excited grin when she opened the card and held up the itinerary tucked inside. "You've got to go back while you're still youngish."

Always talking about New Orleans. Little did he know why. He'd been told a much more discreet story of his conception: a long-term boyfriend who passed away in a car accident shortly after he was born. It was a hideous story, made up by her father. At the time, Rebecca hadn't been in any position to argue about it. She was an unwed teenage mother who needed the support of her parents.

But giving him that decent upbringing came at a price. She hated lying to Miles. Over the years he gently questioned her about his father. Where were his grandparents? Did he have aunts and uncles? Why didn't his father's family stick around to meet him?

It was a scandal, he was told, and that was true. Teenage pregnancies were shameful back then. *True, true, true.* Sometimes Rebecca did this with her lies, culled through them to sift out bits of the truth, as if that could mitigate some of her guilt. So Miles was told that his grandparents were so devastated by the loss of their son, Chris—this name was supplied by her mother, but he was never given a last name in case Miles wanted to go hunting—that they moved far away and never wanted anything to do with their grandson. It was too painful, Miles was told over and over again. Too painful. This, too, was partial truth.

But the minute Rebecca saw the card in Miles's sloppy handwriting encouraging her to go for it, she knew what she had to do. She was going to confront her past once and for all. If Grant Dodge was here, she would find him. If he wasn't, she was going to tell Miles the truth anyway, and if he wanted, he could try to find his father. It was high time she swept clean the lies that dirtied her life. She *was* still youngish, and for the first time in her life she was on her own. Miles was in college, and in order to pay for it, she'd sold her small house in Buffalo. Her parents, who had been saving for his college fund, lost a bulk of their retirement to a shady hedge-fund manager. Rebecca refused to let them drain the rest.

She missed her little home, but it was worth it. Not that she'd be able to pay for all four years with the money, but at least his first year was taken care of. He was an amazing trumpet player, so she had no doubt that he'd be able to get scholarships to see him through. If nothing else, he'd definitely inherited his father's musical ability. If she did find Grant Dodge, she couldn't wait to tell him this. Or would their conversations never get past *Why didn't you tell me I have a son?*

Tell you? How could I tell you? What a state his phone number was in when she had pulled it from her purse. Smeared and torn and illegible. It was really no surprise. Her purse had been lying on the damp grass beside them, or perhaps she was lying on top of it, sinking it farther into the ground each time he thrust into her, a memory which still turned her on so much she could only visit it in private. God, what a night. She couldn't remember ever surrendering to anyone or anything the way she did to Grant Dodge that night.

He'd even tried to talk her out of it. Was it too soon? Was she too tipsy? But a thousand stampeding horses couldn't have stopped her. It was silly to say, and so of course she'd never told this to a soul, but the way she felt that night, it was almost as if she were possessed. She had to have him, she was filled with this overpowering need. And it had been everything she wanted and more. It was quite simply one of the best nights of her life. But it came with a price, as everything did.

Her father, an attorney, went on a warpath to find and punish "the man who forced himself on my innocent daughter." Oh, the shame that went through her whenever she heard him say this to anyone. So she refused to say anything about Grant. She wouldn't give so much as a name or the color of a single hair on his head. Even after her father threatened to disown her and Miles, she remained resolute. And thankfully, since she complied with every other demand he ever gave, she and Miles continued to have her parents' support. She was grateful, yet resentful.

If her father had acted like a normal human being, maybe Grant could have been a part of their lives. They would never know. What's done was done. And in many ways, she'd paid her dues. She'd been ostracized by almost everyone in school, except Cathy. It turned out the scavenger hunt was a prank on Rebecca. The other three went dancing that night instead. The only reason she'd been invited on the trip was to get back at her. Allison thought Rebecca was the one who told her mother she saw Allison kissing her history teacher in the mall. It was actually Renee Rogers. But when the rumor mill started grinding, people began saying it was "RR" who told Allison's mom. Rebecca was simply a victim of her initials.

But Cathy, the only one of ACG who felt guilty about

what they did to Rebecca, stepped up and did the right thing. She ditched A & G and stood by Rebecca during the darkest time of her life. They were friends to this day, and Cathy would be arriving on Saturday to spend a portion of the weekend. She was the only one in the world who knew all about Grant. She was a busy wife and mom, so she couldn't take the entire weekend off, but Rebecca was grateful she was on the way. Otherwise, she was afraid she might crack.

Because, sixteen or not, drunk or not, rebellious or not, Rebecca was pretty sure she got one thing right. Grant Dodge, at least then, had been a remarkable person. Was he still? Was he even in New Orleans? If she told him about Miles, would either he or her son ever forgive her?

And what if he wasn't remarkable anymore? What if he was married with a dozen kids of his own? Maybe he was fat and bald. Not that he couldn't be a nice, fat, bald man, but it would still be hard to see him that way. In her mind, he epitomized sexy. Maybe he was dead. Rebecca crossed herself even though she wasn't a regular churchgoer. Or maybe he was a drunk on the street playing his trumpet for booze.

But what if he was still sexy and single? What if he traveled all over the world mesmerizing people with his trumpet? What if he had everything he'd ever wanted, except her? Maybe he felt a hole inside him and he didn't know why. Maybe every once in a while, he visited the cemetery where they made love, stood under a full moon, gazed at the soft, dark grass and wondered if he would ever see her again. But whoever and wherever he was, one thing was certain. He had never tried to contact her, either. It was the only thing that gave her any relief from her guilt. She had given him her phone number, but he never once called.

As the plane descended, Rebecca leaned her head back and tried to clear her mind of worry. She was here to celebrate her birthday: enjoy some good Creole cooking, tour the mansions in the Garden District, listen to some good jazz, stroll the shops in the French Quarter, and definitely check out a few jewelry shops. Maybe she'd even bring some of her own pieces to show them. She'd been making jewelry ever since her first trip to New Orleans.

Her very first creation was a locket that housed a tiny petal from the rose Grant gave her. She wore it all through her pregnancy and the delivery. It astounded her how comforting a piece of jewelry could be. It almost kept her sane. And she still had it, was even wearing it now. Making jewelry was her passion in life. And most of her pieces came from recycled material. For one, she thought the quality was much better. For two, she liked the idea of not wasting metals or gems. And she liked to think that some energy remained from the person who had worn it before, even if, by the time Rebecca put something together, it was a completely new creation.

Yes, all of those things would definitely make it a worthwhile trip. But there was one more thing she'd come to do, if she could summon the courage to do it. She was going to march back to that Voodoo Shop, and if that horrible old woman was still alive, she was going to do everything in her power to make her take back that ridiculous curse.

Chapter Three

New Orleans, 1992

All through the reading, Grant never let go of her hand. Could he feel how sweaty her palms were? Even so, she was grateful. The old woman was not easy to look at. It wasn't her hard, wrinkled face—in fact, Rebecca found the woman beautiful—nor was it her distracting eyes, one blue and one green; rather it was just a strong vibe the woman gave off. Rebecca couldn't quite put her finger on it. It was as if the woman were trapped, and she was silently begging them to free her. A quiet desperation clung to her, and it made Rebecca want to flee.

She never would have even found this little Voodoo Shop, let alone entered it on her own. Grant, who came over to her table the minute he finished his set, and turned her world upside down with his smile, chiseled face, and Southern drawl, was on a mission to help her win the scavenger hunt. And so here they were in this tiny, creepy little shop, sitting at a card table across from the saddest woman Rebecca had ever seen. A single candle flickered in the middle of the table as the woman shuffled a deck of tarot cards. Then her eyes flicked to the rose Rebecca had laid on the table in front of her. Grant bought it from a man who sold them out of a bucket.

No one had ever bought Rebecca a rose before. No matter what, she was going to keep it forever. The rose seemed to stop the woman in her tracks. She went back to staring at Grant and Rebecca, and suddenly flung the cards across the room. They rained down on shelves filled with little straw dolls, and worry beads, and incense, and books of potions. They dropped to the floor near their feet. One stuck to the dirty window beside them. Rebecca jumped and Grant squeezed her hand, although he, too, was clearly startled. The woman leaned forward.

"What time is it?" she said.

"Half past eleven," Grant said.

"It's not too late then," she said. Rebecca and Grant looked at each other. He raised his eyebrow and gave her a smile. It bolstered Rebecca's courage. This was probably a show. The old woman probably threw her cards at everyone.

"Too late for what?" Rebecca said.

"Stay away from the cemetery," the high priestess said.

Grant was delighted. "You're good," he said. "It's our next stop. How did you know?"

Rebecca wondered the same thing. Had she seen the list? Impossible; it was tucked inside her purse. The high priestess, as the woman had introduced herself, stood and leaned over them. And even though she couldn't have been much over five foot, Rebecca was terrified. She gripped Grant's knee, and he placed his hand on top of hers protectively.

"I'm warning you. Do not go anywhere near a cemetery." This time, she was only looking at Rebecca. "Are you listening?"

The high priestess wasn't shouting; in fact, her words came out in a strangled whisper, so why did Rebecca want to slap her hands over her ears? "It's just a scavenger hunt," Rebecca said.

"Then go. Get out of my shop."

Grant stood and put his arm around Rebecca. They had already paid; the woman had insisted on it up front. "I hope you have a very nice evening," Grant said as they headed for the door.

Rebecca was almost free when she felt bony hands on her shoulders. The old woman whirled Rebecca around, keeping a firm grip on her. Up close Rebecca could see a milky white film covering her mismatched eyes.

"Whatever you do," the high priestess said, "do not kiss before midnight. If you do, you will be cursed. I promise you. You will be cursed."

Rebecca glanced at Grant, who was struggling to open the door. That was odd—it had been wide open when they entered.

"Listen to me, little one. If you steal a kiss before midnight, you will be cursed. It will be the best and the worst thing that's ever happened to you, but you will still be cursed. It will follow you, and follow you, and follow you. It will torment you."

The relief of getting out of there was nothing like Rebecca had ever known. She was so angry at the reading, so mad at herself for allowing the woman to scare her to death, fall for her scam. No matter what, she was going to that cemetery and she was going to kiss Grant Dodge before midnight. This weekend was all about adventure, all about taking risks. Some little old lady wasn't going to stop her.

And when she did indeed steal that kiss, one minute before the clock struck twelve, she couldn't believe how good it felt. So good that she let his lips and hands trail all over her body, and once they started, it kicked up a storm of passion so overpowering that there was nothing they could do to stop it.

In some ways, the old woman had been right. Miles was conceived that night and he was hands down the best thing that had ever happened to her. But she also lost Grant. And she'd never come close to feeling with any other man what she felt with him that sultry, magic-filled night. She was married for a time, to a very nice man named Jim. But she didn't feel passion, she didn't feel need, she didn't feel magic, or longing. Jim was willing to do without it, but Rebecca just couldn't.

Whatever you do, do not kiss before midnight. As silly as it was, Rebecca couldn't help but wonder. Would things have turned out any different if she'd waited those sixty little seconds? Would Grant Dodge still be hers? And what about Miles? Would he know his father? Would Miles exist at all? It was too much to contemplate. She was here to find Grant and face whatever consequences came her way. Even if it meant losing the two men she loved most in this world. But if the other predictions of the high priestess had come true, then how could she ignore the last one? *The curse will follow you, and follow you, and follow you. It will torment you.* Well, not if Rebecca had anything to say about it. Twenty-one years was long enough. She would not have this threat hanging over her head for one more second of one more day.

Her hotel, situated right in the middle of the French Quarter, was a delightful mix of French and Spanish architecture. It was only four stories, with a gray stone facade and a series of balconies framed with ornate iron gates. Multiple baskets, swollen with colorful peonies, hung from the balconies. The interior lobby looked more like an old Southern mansion than a hotel. With its high ceilings, crystal chandelier, and red velvet treads on the winding staircase leading up to the first floor of rooms, it was both regal and welcoming. A wall of windows formed a horseshoe shape around a courtyard complete with private garden, fountain, and small swimming pool. Rebecca could see herself easily enjoying the weekend in just the hotel alone. Of course that wasn't going to happen. Now that she was here, she was itching to walk around, reminisce, hit the jewelry shops. She would have to carefully pick out which pieces to bring, and which to wear. Strangers often stopped her to remark on her jewelry, and several even purchased pieces from her when she told them she'd made them herself. Rebecca had so many favorite pieces, it was hard to pick. She loved gems, and brooches, and beads, and brass, and silver, and copper, and coins, and lockets. It was such delicate work, but she loved the feeling that came over her whenever she worked on a piece. The concentration it required left very little room for anything else, including worrying. Hours would pass quickly whenever Rebecca was bent over her black felt work space. She sold most things online, and when she had the house, friends came over and purchased custom-made pieces.

It was a nice little living, but her dream was to someday open a shop of her own. She knew she would love the face-to-face interaction with her customers. She wanted to watch them try on different pieces, and be able to recommend what she thought would work for them. Jewelry was more like clothing than most people realized. Everyone had certain things that looked better on them than others, but not everyone was able to recognize this. And she'd always imagined what her store would look like. She would have fresh-cut flowers, and approachable displays with little handheld mirrors on each table. She would have a chandelier, and hopefully a little fireplace, and gift boxes with her logo: a replica of the first locket she made, along with the name in fancy cursive:

Rebecca's Renditions.

And as she walked the streets of the French Quarter, she couldn't help but imagine owning a little shop here. She loved the warm air and the easygoing smiles of most everyone she passed. Artists were everywhere. Selling their paintings on the street, playing their music on the corner, giving fortune readings from fold-out chairs. Imagine owning a little shop in the French Quarter. Imagine living in one of those apartments with a sweeping balcony. Imagine the noise, and the music, and the food, and the visitors all the time. Most people probably wouldn't be able to fathom it. Her circle of friends thought of New Orleans as nothing more than a fun sideshow, a circus blowing through town. Fun to visit, but sooner or later the tents must come down. And of course there was poverty, and hurricanes, and drunken debauchery.

But Rebecca knew she would thrive on it. Buffalo, New York, had been a decent place to raise a kid, but she never really felt at home there. Not the way she did here. Imagine warm weather most of the year. Buffalo winters were brutal. Rebecca wasn't one for bundling up and shoveling sidewalks and scraping ice and snow off her car, which she didn't want to drive in bad weather anyway. If she lived here, right in the French Quarter, she wouldn't even need a car. The possibilities followed her all the way back to the hotel.

After a swim and a brief nap by the pool, Rebecca took a long shower, then brewed herself a cup of coffee and curled up in an armchair in her robe. She loved this most of all about going on vacation, a few stolen moments where doing nothing was the only goal. Not that her mind took a break; it hardly ever did. She mulled over the rest of her day. She would take her time getting ready for the evening, then dress, pick out a few of her best jewelry pieces, and head back to the shops. She would wander until she was absolutely weak with hunger, then find a cozy little spot for dinner. Then, and only then, would she go in search of the little Voodoo Shop. The chance it was even still there was slim. The high priestess, as she called herself, was an old woman back then. She'd probably passed years ago. At least it would be over and done with. Rebecca could cross it off her list, and she could stop obsessing on the so-called curse. If the high priestess was dead, Rebecca would firmly take the position that all curses had died with her. Maybe she'd even visit her grave, say her own little adieu.

She dressed in a light wrap-around skirt, black tank top, and slip-on sandals. The heat outside was cloying. She put on one of her best necklaces, a string of gray pearls with a black onyx stone front and center. Rebecca loved chunky jewelry, although she made daintier pieces for those who didn't. She put on a pair of large sunglasses and was out the door.

The minute she stepped outside, she received a text from Cathy.

Are you there? Have you seen him?

Rebecca laughed, as she could imagine Cathy going crazy with curiosity. Rebecca texted back immediately.

Yes and NO. Waiting for you. ☺!!!!!!!!

No use going into anything longer in the text. Like the fact that finding a boy she met twenty-one years ago was going to be a long shot at best. At least Cathy would be around to console her. Rebecca soon lost herself in a series of shops. In the cute little boutiques, she didn't even need to spend money to enjoy herself. Just feasting her eyes on all the offerings was thrill enough. Even the touristy shops with their Mardi Gras masks, bottles of hot sauce, and voodoo dolls were fun. Who didn't relish a red-feathered boa, glittery eye mask, or can of alligator meat?

Next she feasted on paintings and photographs done by local artists. From the Garden District, to the plantations, to the swamps, to Mardi Gras, to the colorful French Quarter, New Orleans held a plethora of subjects to photograph and paint. If Rebecca ended up with a shop here, she'd love to hang some of these on her walls.

Finally, Rebecca was ready to scout out the jewelry shops. A few of the touristy places sold jewelry along with their other wares, but she wouldn't consider them competition. In addition there were a few shops that were much fancier in origin, selling diamonds and other high-priced gems. Also, not her competition. She soon hit on a boutique that was exactly as she imagined hers would be. It was a modest space, but clean and inviting. The jewelry was on display on little tables all over the store. But when Rebecca went to touch a bracelet, the girl behind the counter flew out from behind her perch, her voice raised in alarm.

"No touching!"

Rebecca's fingers were poised to do just that. She let them dangle there for a minute before turning to the young girl. "Customers aren't encouraged to try things on?"

"Absolutely not. The artist would kill me. She says the oils from our fingers will smear the stones."

"Ah," Rebecca said. At her shop, things would be different. Customers would be encouraged to try things on, not scolded. Keeping her hands to herself, Rebecca surveyed the rest of the inventory. Like hers, the pieces in here were all handmade. There was a section of New Orleans jewelry with the fleur-de-lis theme, voodoo offerings, and even an alligator bracelet.

"It's not just one artist, is it?" Rebecca asked.

"Of course not," the girl said. "But there's one who yells the loudest."

Rebecca laughed. In every other shop she'd been in, the sales associates had been overly sweet, as this section of town depended on tourists. This shop would be direct competition, yet this young girl was more worried about getting yelled at than making a sale. Rebecca would have a leg up there. And she wouldn't offer alligators, or fleur-de-lis pieces; instead she would make pieces that echoed the jewelry worn by women in the South during different periods in history. She liked her pieces to come with a sense of history, a story, and characters. She could even have a few mannequins whose outfits she would change periodically to show how dramatically jewelry could change and enhance any look. The visit completely perked Rebecca up. She whipped out her credit card, and before the girl could speak, she picked up the bracelet and put it on. It was made of black, blue, and green shimmering beads.

"What's this called?" Rebecca asked. Not all artists named their works, but she was curious what the girl would say.

"The Curse. And we only take cash."

Rebecca knew her mouth was hanging open.

"There's an ATM around the corner," the girl said, misreading her shocked expression.

"The Curse?" Rebecca said. Was this some kind of sick joke? Or was the universe reminding her that she was doomed?

"I'm just the messenger," the girl said as Rebecca handed her the cash.

"Speaking of curses," Rebecca said, purposely keeping her voice light so the girl wouldn't think she was getting to her, "is there a little voodoo shop nearby?"

"Tons of them," the girl said.

"Do you know if the one with the high priestess is still around?"

"No idea," the girl said. Rebecca smiled again, although she really wanted to bring back the old kill-the-messenger philosophy. With this kind of attitude, she could only pray the girl would work here for a very long time.

"Well, thanks for your help." This time Rebecca didn't try to disguise her sarcasm. Seriously, the Curse? No artist would name their bracelet that, not even in this town. Would they? Rebecca couldn't help but think the girl had said it simply to be mean. She wanted to rip it off her wrist, but she certainly wasn't going to give the girl the satisfaction.

"Do you mean the old witch?" the girl said when Rebecca was nearly out the door.

"I might," Rebecca said. It certainly fit the description.

"She's like, ancient?"

"For sure. And she gives readings. There used to be two child-sized voodoo dolls hugging the entrance—"

The girl pointed left. "Just around the corner," she said. "It's pink."

"That's it," Rebecca said. "Is she still alive? Still giving readings?"

"I don't think she's ever going to die. She must be like a zombie or something."

"Zombies are already dead." Rebecca realized, too late,

that she probably shouldn't antagonize the girl. The scowl was back on her face. "Sorry," Rebecca added. "I know exactly what you mean." She headed back to the counter and lowered her voice as if she and the snarly sales girl were the best of friends. "She put a curse on me," Rebecca said. "Twenty-one years ago."

The girl's eyes widened. "Seriously?"

"Seriously. And here I am, twenty-one years later." Rebecca leaned in even farther. "I've come to make her take it back." Just saying it made a ripple of fear run through Rebecca. But there was relief, too, in letting the words live outside her head.

"Oh my God." The girl was almost smiling now and it transformed her entire face.

"Right?"

"Totally. Like. What did she do to you?" The girl scanned Rebecca as if looking for extra heads or limbs.

"I lost the love of my life," Rebecca said.

"Is that all?" The girl's response was accompanied by a sarcastic snort.

"Is that all?" Rebecca repeated.

"There's no such thing as the love of your life. There are like a gazillion people in the world. Do you really think there's only one right person? It's total bull."

"Maybe," Rebecca said. "But I've only ever met the one."

"I don't think you're the only one who has that curse, by the way," the girl said. Rebecca headed for the door again when the girl stopped her. "Your bracelet?"

"Yeah?"

"It's called Midnight."

"Thank you."

"You shouldn't believe everything everyone tells you, you know," the girl said with a wisdom much older than her age.

"And you shouldn't give up on your soul mate," Rebecca said with a hopefulness much younger than hers.

Chapter Four

It was right around the corner, just as the girl claimed. And it looked exactly the same. The front of the small shop was painted bright pink. Two child-sized voodoo dolls made of spiky straw and soft linen flanked the doorway. In large black letters, a sign above the doorway simply spelled out VOODOO. To the point, Rebecca thought. Although the pink paint made it all seem so harmless and fun, Rebecca knew it was anything but.

She entered through a film of hanging beads, liking how it felt to brush through them, the soft rattle announcing her entrance. It took a few minutes for Rebecca's eyes to adjust to the dark. The shop consisted of two small adjoining rooms and a hallway leading to a shut door. The shelves littering the small space were crammed with herbs, potions, books, worry dolls and beads, incense, and colorful little figurines. Rebecca stood still. She was once here with Grant Dodge. She could see the two of them bursting in, hand in hand, laughing.

"Can I help you?"

Rebecca jumped at the sound of the woman's voice. Just inside the entrance to the second small room stood an attractive woman somewhere in her fifties. She was dressed in a flowing pink gown, the same color as the shop. Her dark hair was swept up, her eyes heavily rimmed with black eyeliner and topped with fake eyelashes.

"I didn't see you there," Rebecca said.

"I blend in," the woman said. "What can I do for you? Love potion? Hate potion? A little sage to rid your space of negative energy, perhaps?" With that the woman reached for the nearest shelf and snatched up a bundle of herbs. Then she pulled a lighter from her pocket and set it afire. Smoke billowed out and began snaking toward Rebecca. Soon the place was overcome by a thick, sweet smell. Rebecca, who'd always been hypersensitive to certain smells, began to cough. She could feel her nose stopping up and her chest tightening.

"Oh dear," the woman said. "What have I done?"

Rebecca couldn't speak; instead she waved at the smoke and pulled up her tank top to cover her mouth. The woman quickly turned to a small sink behind her and doused the sage in water.

"Thank you," Rebecca choked out when she could speak again. "I'm allergic."

"Pity," the woman said. "You must have a lot of trapped negative energy in your space."

"Not really," Rebecca said. *Just in my head. There's a whole lot of negative energy trapped up there.*

"We have other incense—"

Rebecca threw up her hand before the woman could light up anything else. "Actually," she said, "I'm looking for the high priestess."

The woman barely moved a muscle. Only her eyes moved, to the hallway leading to the closed door.

"She's still here," Rebecca said.

"She's not well. I run the shop now."

"Oh, but I'd love to see her. Just say a quick hello."

The woman moved in closer and folded her arms across her ample chest. "What kind?"

"Excuse me?"

"Work, money, health, or love?"

"Love," Rebecca said. "It was a love curse."

The woman sighed, then gestured for Rebecca to follow her into the second room. There she perched herself on a stool near the one window. "They're the hardest kind to remove," she said. She stared out the window as she spoke. "And as I told you, my aunt is not well."

Rebecca took this in, wondering which way to play it. Did the woman want money? Is that what this was? From the way she'd spoken it was obvious Rebecca wasn't the first unhappy customer to storm in, demanding a cure. What a racket they had here. Frightening vulnerable people like her with this hocus-pocus.

"I suppose if I wanted to have this curse removed, it would be very expensive. Am I right?" Rebecca said. In a strange way, it made her feel better, knowing it was all just a big scam.

But instead of continuing the conversation, the woman jumped off her stool and pointed to the door. "Get out," she said. "Now."

"But . . . I'm sorry. I thought—"

"I was scamming you," the woman finished for her.

Rebecca felt little pinpricks up and down the back of her neck. It was hot in here. And she could still smell the cloying scent of sage. Little colored spots littered her vision. She wasn't sure she could keep standing. She reached out to steady herself on a shelf. She hadn't leaned on it too heavily, yet suddenly the shelf seesawed to the floor, and before Rebecca could react, items rapidly began sliding downhill.

"Oh God," Rebecca said. She tried to hold the end of the shelf up, but it was heavy and the bracket was wrenched from the wall. Bowls of crystals, little voodoo dolls, and glass bottles slid down. Rebecca was able to catch only a few things, and by the time she got a grip on the shelf, it was too late. Voodoo trinkets were scattered everywhere. Rebecca wasn't quite sure what the supernatural rules were, but this couldn't be good. And she didn't know how long she could hold this shelf up. It was heavy. And it was so hot in here. The little colored spots were back.

"Heavens," the woman said. "Don't faint on me." She stepped over to Rebecca and took hold of the shelf. In a few swift moves she had the bracket temporarily pinned back into the wall.

Rebecca had to get out. She started for the door and stumbled. She had destroyed the shop, and now she was crushing everything underfoot. She tried to take another step. Why was the floor so slanted? Why was the ceiling spinning? Suddenly, she felt arms around her waist. The woman guided Rebecca back into the entrance room, but instead of showing her the door, she helped her into an old armchair shoved in the corner of the room. Although bone-dry, it smelled like it had been left out in the rain, but Rebecca wasn't in any position to complain.

"Auntie," the woman shouted. "Can you come out here, please?"

Rebecca was startled by the tone of the woman's voice. She sounded worried. Rebecca wanted to tell her she was fine, that she didn't want to see the priestess after all, she just wanted to go, but she couldn't find the words. She closed her eyes, then heard a door squeak open and slow, plodding footsteps down the hall. Suddenly a blast of cold air hit Rebecca. Her eyes flew open. Standing just a few feet from her, supported by a cane, was the high priestess.

"She's one of yours," the woman said.

"I can see that," the priestess said. She waved her niece aside with the cane, then came a few steps closer. Rebecca knew it was impolite to stare, but she couldn't help herself. The old woman hadn't changed a bit. Of course she looked like an old prune back then, so it wasn't saying much. But still. Just seeing the old woman brought back a wave of sadness. It was as if someone were wringing her heart like a dishrag. Rebecca forced herself to stand.

"The love you seek is near," the old woman said.

Rebecca looked at the door. She should leave, just get out. Never look back. For that matter, she should go straight to her hotel room, pack, and head for the airport. She wasn't ready for this; she didn't want this. "I'm sorry," she said, taking a few steps toward the door. "I have to go."

"He's right here, darling. Right up the street."

Rebecca froze. The old woman was staring at her with a vacant smile. "I don't know anyone here," Rebecca said.

"As you say," the old woman said. "But if you do—"

"I don't."

"Then you won't try to rekindle the flame?"

Rebecca shook her head and made it to the hanging beads.

"Because once lit it will burn down everything in its path."

"Auntie!"

Rebecca squared her shoulders and faced the old woman. "I don't believe you," she said. "That's why I came. To tell you I don't believe you."

The high priestess took a few steps toward Rebecca. "You flew all this way to tell me that?" She cocked her head and put her index finger on her wrinkled chin. Her eyes were as disconcerting as ever; one blue, one green, both reproachful.

She knows I flew here. Well, lucky guess. Probably all of their guests are tourists. "I have to go," Rebecca said.

"So soon?" the priestess said. "In such nasty weather?"

"It's not—" And just as the words came out of her mouth, Rebecca heard the wind howling. Startled, she turned to see rain lashing at the windows, coming down thick and heavy.

"You came to undo the curse," the priestess stated.

"I am not cursed," Rebecca said with as much strength as she could muster. "I am not cursed."

"You're not?" the priestess said. She sounded almost joyful. "With all your lies? Have you not cursed yourself with all those lies?"

Your father and I were high school sweethearts. He died in a car accident shortly before you were born—

"Have you come to set things right?"

"Can I?" Rebecca asked. "Set things right?" Perhaps this was going to be simple. Perhaps the woman would give her some basic spell or chant, and Rebecca would pretend to believe it, but she would finally see through the act, and she would leave knowing she wasn't really cursed, had never been cursed.

"It won't be easy," the priestess said. "It never is."

"You don't even remember me," Rebecca said. She parted the beads.

"You kissed him before midnight, didn't you?"

Rebecca whirled around, dumbfounded. "Yes," she whispered. "I did."

The old woman gave a low laugh. It was startling to hear, even if it wasn't very merry. "Do you have a recording device?"

"My iPhone." She'd forgotten it could record. She'd never used it to record anything. "But really, it's not—"

"Turn it on, because I'm only going to say this once." Fumbling and shaking, Rebecca set her phone to record. The priestess held up a crooked finger and her words tumbled out like rocks sliding down a mountain. "The one with red feathers will betray you. You will be crushed. You will draw blood. Your heart will be ripped from your chest. Your wildest dreams will start to come true. You will encounter sudden wealth. You and your love will be caught in an endless cycle of passion and fear. Oh, but the love, the passion." The woman stopped, caught her breath, and looked away, her voice soft but heavy with emotion. "So few people get this. Such love."

Rebecca stood, openmouthed.

The priestess looked as if she'd had the wind taken out of her. Her niece stepped up and gently wrapped her arms around her. "Come, Auntie," she said. She looked at Rebecca. "I haven't seen her this upset in a long time. Please. Don't come back."

"I won't."

The priestess straightened up, as if all her energy had returned, and she whirled on Rebecca. "You blame me! The child you bore that night. Is that my fault as well?"

"Oh my God," Rebecca said. "Please. Will they ever forgive me?"

"Since that night you've lived your life in total fear. Since then, you've sacrificed everything for someone else."

My son—

"You've hidden your talents away."

Rebecca absentmindedly touched her necklace, made by her own two hands.

"Afraid, afraid, afraid! I warned you, didn't I? That kiss would change the rest of your life. Be warned again, my dear. I'm going to give you a second chance. From now on *any decision you make out of fear will take away bits of your life one piece at a time.*"

"Please," the niece said. "She needs her rest."

Rebecca stumbled forward. "I believe you," she said softly. "Just, please. Tell me how to lift the curse."

The old woman looked as if she almost felt sorry for Rebecca. She reached out but stopped short of touching her. "Ah, still such hope. I'm sorry to be the bearer of such bad news. Because the cycle will not end until you've caused the death of someone else."

"What?"

"Death. It's a cycle, my dear. Only death breaks the cycle."

"You can't be serious."

"Oh, I am," the high priestess said. "For you to be free, someone else must die."

This time Rebecca didn't wait to be asked to leave. She stumbled out and the minute the shop was no longer in sight, she began to run.

Chapter Five

Crazy old woman. Crazy, crazy old woman. And crazy of Rebecca to go looking for her in the first place. And still, all she could think about as she continued down the street in what was now a misty rain peppered with bursts of sunshine, was: *Right down the street? Grant Dodge is right down the street?* She wondered if it was literal. If she literally continued right down the street, would she run into him? She glanced down at her iPhone, still clutched in her hand. It was all recorded. She could play it for Cathy, get her unbiased opinion. She texted her: Wish you were here.

She didn't say anything more; no point in raising the alarm. Cathy would be here tomorrow and the two of them would discuss this calmly, and Cathy would assure her that bits of her life weren't going to be stolen from her, or whatever it was the woman had predicted. And she certainly wasn't going to break the cycle by killing anyone. My God, it was so melodramatic.

How sad. It was easy to see how lonely the old woman was. It was written all over her face. Some people just enjoyed seeing other people as miserable as they were, and that was that. She had planned on going back to the hotel for a rest, but now all she needed was a cool dark place to sit and a drink to calm her down. She was in a state, but it would soon pass and someday she would even laugh about this.

After finding the perfect little Cajun restaurant and having a shrimp cocktail and a glass of white wine, she felt even more reassured. Where was the old jazz club she wandered into twenty-one years ago? Would she be able to find it? Did it even exist?

"More wine?"

"One more glass," Rebecca said. "And then I'm cut off." The waiter laughed as if he'd heard it before, and presented her with a basket of warm fresh bread and a complimentary cup of Creole stew. It was pure bliss.

"I love your necklace," he said.

Rebecca lifted her hand to remember which piece she was wearing. The chunky black onyx with the gray pearls.

"My girlfriend wears jewelry like that."

Rebecca beamed. Maybe it was a sign. "Well then," she said, "she must have it." Rebecca took the necklace off and handed it to the astonished waiter.

"I couldn't," he said.

"I made it myself, and I insist," Rebecca said.

"Thank you," he said. "Then you're definitely having a third glass of wine."

After this meal and three glasses of wine, she would be comatose for the rest of the evening. She was about to protest when she realized she couldn't think of a more perfect way to end this crazy day. The encounter with the waiter made her feel good. She was a good person. If she was destined to kill someone, then it was going to be with kindness.

Saturday morning Rebecca woke up to the shrill ring of her hotel room phone. She pawed for it and answered without opening her eyes.

"Mom?"

"Miles!" She was immediately awake, and smiling.

"Ah, I woke you up, didn't I?"

"Never you mind," she said.

"Partying all night?" Miles laughed. He knew she was the type who was always in bed with a book by nine. And true to form, she had been.

"I'm saving that for tonight," she said. "Cathy will insist on it."

"How is it, being back?"

Her son was so sweet. He was genuinely invested in her happiness. For a split second she felt the wringing guilt that always accompanied her lies.

"It's the same as I remember," she said. *Except I haven't seen your father. And I'm destined to be a killer.*

"Oh God, Mom," Miles said. "You sound teary."

"Just groggy," Rebecca lied. Maybe she should tell him now. Get it over with. But something stopped her. It was Grant she should tell first. Until she squared things with him, she couldn't completely explain it to Miles. "How do you feel about tonight?" she asked her beautiful son. He had a jazz competition. Miles laughed. He never got nervous about competitions. She wished Grant could be there to hear him. She wished she could see them play side by side on-stage. A familiar pain sliced through her—regret, guilt, longing.

"It'll be a blast, Mom. Look, I gotta split. You have fun. And remember—what happens in New Orleans—"

"I think that's Vegas."

"It's N'Orleans for you, Ma. Just have fun. Listen to some jazz if you get a chance. And next time, I'm coming with you." They said their good-byes and their I-love-you's, and when Rebecca hung up she sent up a little prayer, asking for forgiveness for the things she'd done and the things she'd failed to do. *What happens in New Orleans, stays in New Orleans.* Vegas or not, she could only hope Miles would still be on board when he found out how good she was at sticking to that particular motto.

Cathy, who loved surprising people even when they knew what was coming, didn't text until she was already in the French Quarter, sitting at the popular beignets café, famous for their powdery little doughnuts that were so addictive they should be illegal. Rebecca, who pretty much had to watch everything she ate for fear of crossing from voluptuous to overweight, couldn't believe the amount her tiny best friend could put away. She was easy to envy, but Rebecca wanted nothing but happiness for Cathy. She had given up her throne as a popular girl in high school to stick by Rebecca, who wouldn't have made it through that horrendous year without her. Cathy had a privileged life, but she deserved every second of it. Cathy had three beautiful daughters and a doctor husband who was busy, but from everything Rebecca could tell, they were happily married. She was also thrilled to be with Rebecca in New Orleans for the weekend, so much so that she didn't even bat an eye when all the powder from her beignets caked her Chanel bag and tailored suit. She simply brushed it all away with her pretty new nails, laughed, and reached for more. Rebecca ate only two of the evil little morsels and then forced herself to drink her coffee and pretend eating another one was the furthest thing from her mind. So far they were having a lovely reunion, catching up on everything, and for the moment ignoring the elephant in the room.

Cathy was the only person in the world who knew all there was to know about Grant Dodge. And instead of judging her, telling her it was ridiculous to love a man she'd spent only one night with, Cathy listened to the love story over and over again without once losing patience. And here she was again, just when Rebecca needed her. Tears suddenly filled

Rebecca's eyes. Cathy immediately stopped talking and tried to hand Rebecca another beignet. Rebecca laughed, refused the treat, and tried to think of something, anything that would stop the waterworks. She hated this, how Cathy always took care of her, how just the sight of her best friend made her want to break down, how she didn't know how she was going to make it if she didn't find Grant Dodge and get this huge poisonous secret out of her for once and for all.

"Let's walk along the river," Cathy said. "Check out the steamboats, work off the four thousand calories from these evil little doughnut balls."

It worked—Rebecca laughed, and soon the two were off, arm in arm, strolling along the Mississippi River, just two good friends enjoying the early morning sun, with nothing but shopping, eating, drinking, and dancing ahead of them. Rebecca was able to get Cathy an adjoining room, and she looked forward to being like young girls again, sharing gossip and makeup, running back and forth to each other's rooms.

After a nice walk, they headed back toward the hotel, and without even having to discuss it, knew they would end up wandering into little boutiques along the way. Cathy, who loved to cook, bought several spices and an apron decorated with an openmouthed alligator that said KISS MY ALLIGATOR. When they passed the jewelry store where Rebecca had purchased the bracelet, Cathy immediately stopped.

"This could be you," she said, peeking in the windows. "In fact, your stuff is so much better than this." Cathy, along with being a good friend, had always been one of Rebecca's best customers.

"I thought the same thing," Rebecca said. "I could open one of my own."

Cathy squealed and grabbed Rebecca's hands. "You totally should. Our little town needs you. You could open it right near—"

"Here," Rebecca said. "I was thinking about opening a little shop here."

Cathy stopped talking and even walking. "I knew it," she said. "Rebecca, I think I'm psychic." Cathy sounded so serious, and her face was radiating a childlike wonder.

"Do tell," Rebecca said. Again, without the need for words, they left the little jewelry shop without even going in, and headed for the hotel.

"I was on the plane, right? Just thinking about you, and wondering if the weekend was going to turn out how you wanted—and I was thinking, God, Rebecca could move to New Orleans. And suddenly it was like—oh my God! Of course. That's exactly what she'll do. And I saw you. I saw you in this little jewelry shop and living . . ."

They both stopped and looked up at an apartment above them with one of the infamous sweeping balconies. They both pointed.

"In a place just like that!" Rebecca said.

"Exactly!" Cathy said.

"So you don't think I'm crazy?"

"I think it's fate, Rebecca. And with Miles in college, you're as free as a bird. You'd fit right in here. I've always thought of you as this sexy Southern woman, even though you're from Buffalo."

"I don't want to leave," Rebecca said. "I don't even want to go home to pack."

"I'll ship you whatever you need and put everything else in storage. Didn't you get rid of a lot anyway, when you sold the house?"

"Almost everything. But I still couldn't ask you to do all that."

"Are you kidding me? It would be nothing. And I'd have this great place to come and stay for Mardi Gras!"

Rebecca and Cathy daydreamed a little more on the way to the hotel, and continued talking about it in excited bursts as they lay by the pool with a cocktail. In that moment, in the fantasy of all that was possible, Rebecca was giddy and excited, and so, so grateful that she had a friend like Cathy. She told her so.

"I'm so glad you feel that way," Cathy said.

There was something in the way Cathy said it that raised a slight alarm in Rebecca. It reminded her of the way her voice changed whenever she lied to Miles about his father.

"I want you to be happy, Rebecca. Really, really happy."

"I know that."

"You deserve it. If anyone freaking deserves it, it's you."

Rebecca pushed up her sunglasses and sat up. "Cathy. You're scaring me."

"I hired a private detective."

A chill went through Rebecca. *The love you seek is closer than you think.* "And?" Rebecca's voice was barely a whisper.

Cathy reached over and took her hand. "He's still here," she said. "And tonight we have reservations for opening night at his new jazz club."

A feeling that could equally be described as excitement or fear bubbled through Rebecca. She could feel her heart beat all the way down to her fingertips.

"Rebecca's," Cathy said.

"Yes?" Rebecca said, her voice still a mere gasp.

"That's the name of his new jazz club," Cathy said. "It's called Rebecca's."

Chapter Six

Opening night, and so far everything was coming together nicely. Grant Dodge had his general contractor go over the place and he proclaimed everything ready to go except for a two-foot section of the balcony overlooking the main stage. It was still loose despite their attempts to fix it. Grant decided he would put his private table against it and stick a reserved sign on it. After more worrying, he also decided he would make up a sign warning people not to lean against the balcony. That didn't sit well with him, either, because people rarely paid attention to signs, especially when it was dim and they were drinking. So he tried to fix the loose section himself, but the contractor was right, you couldn't do it without taking down the entire railing. In the end he decided not to put any tables upstairs at all. It would be off-limits to patrons, which would of course reduce the number of people allowed in, but at least he wouldn't have an accident or a lawsuit on his hands. He just couldn't afford to delay the opening.

He looked over the balcony, surveying the main floor, and tried to soak it all in. Twenty-plus years of dreaming of this very day, and here it was. A club evoking the Roaring Twenties. Oh, the plans he had for this joint. He would hire big-name bands, and little-known guys, and hold small jam sessions along with huge swing-dance parties. The décor was classy yet simple. Mostly dark wood and a little trim of gold here and there, with one extravagant exception: the chandelier that hung from the center of the ceiling. It was so ornate you could drop it from Times Square on New Year's Eve.

Rebecca's. Just outside the French Quarter, nestled in between the tourist sections and Louisiana mansions. Opening at last. Everyone he hired was in the spirit, working nonstop to get things ready. A local florist was dropping off elaborate displays of flowers: roses, calla lilies, peonies—all white with one pop of red in each bouquet like a burst of sound after a quiet intro. It was amazing how everything in life was like music, with its own beat, rhythms, and innuendos. His bartender was stocking the shelves with their finest liquors and putting champagne on ice for the formal opening toast, and several barbacks were polishing the small round tables. No reservations—Grant preferred an open concept, where anyone and everyone was welcome to walk in at a moment's notice—but he knew from the word on the street that they'd be jammed.

He was most proud of the sign. Flowing black letters spelling out the name against a blue background, starting with one swirl of jet-black hair before the R, and ending with a painting of a vibrant red rose. Everyone wondered why he named it Rebecca's. He told them a tale about a great-great-grandmother with a beautiful voice. In reality his great-great-grandmother was a seamstress named Myrtle. The truth wasn't something he wished to share. You never forget your first love. Or, should he say, your first time—because it just didn't seem possible to fall in love after one night. But she was his first, and that night set a precedent of passion and on-the-edge excitement that he'd never experienced before or since. Just saying her name turned him on. Sick, maybe, but there it was. He'd whispered her name so many times to himself that it was almost a relief to see it in print.

Rebecca. You never forget your first. It was fitting, the sign. Besides this club, she was the only thing he'd ever really dreamt about these past twenty years. Now, at least, he was about to have one of his dreams come true. His ex-wife would have a royal fit if she knew who he'd named the club after. But wasn't she the one who left him? Went back to Megan's biological father, even though Grant had been the one to practically raise her. But even that he couldn't blame her for; he'd tried to be a good husband, but his mind was always elsewhere. On playing the trumpet, on opening a club of his own some day, and on that curvaceous raven-haired beauty who almost seemed to possess him. Some days he wasn't even sure if she was real. Just a figment of hormones and alcoholic concoctions that should be illegal.

He'd even gone back to the old witch's shop a few times and stood outside the door. That's as far as he ever got. Because he didn't trust what he'd say to her if she was even still alive. After all, she was the one who'd cursed them. The one who said they'd lose everything if they kissed before midnight. What a fool he'd been. He hadn't believed a word of it, so he'd egged Rebecca on, practically dared her to kiss him before midnight. He wasn't thinking beyond the overwhelming need to press his lips against hers. And oh, what a kiss, and what followed it. He hadn't planned it, certainly didn't go into that cemetery to take advantage of her, but once they started they just couldn't stop.

Sometimes now, secretly, he tried to replay the evening, delaying their kiss another minute, and wondered what could have been. Would they be married with a ton of kids right now? Could he have had a lifetime of her flashing blue eyes, silky hair, and laugh that made him want to scale skyscrapers? Could he have had it all?

Not that he'd had a horrible life. Parts of it he wouldn't trade for anything. And there was his stepdaughter, Megan. He'd raised her since she was four. So at least the father bit he got right—if the close relationship he had with Megan was any indication. And last year had been the most trying of their lives, what with Megan and that older boy. He was such trouble, you could see that a mile away. Megan almost stopped speaking to Grant when he sided with her mother that she was way too young and the boy, who was twenty-one, was way too old.

Thank God, they'd survived it. It still made him furious, how a twenty-one-year-old would even consider getting involved with a teenager. Made his blood boil. At least they'd stopped it before it had gone too far. Grant rarely let himself imagine what would have happened if his little girl had actually engaged in sex so young. He would have absolutely lost his mind. He didn't think he would've been able to stop himself from getting violent. Megan's biological father—if Grant did say so himself—was a wuss. Grant was the one who went to the boy's work—he was a bartender, no less—and threatened the life out of him if he ever contacted Megan again.

Speaking of Megan, she was going to be here tonight; another thing that had started a giant argument between him and his ex, Amy. Only after he invited Ken, Megan's biological father, who Amy had recently remarried, did Amy finally relent. Grant didn't mind. He wasn't jealous of either of them. Even though he thought of Megan as his daughter, he wasn't going to deny her a relationship with her biological father. Even if he was a complete wuss. Even if he had disappeared on her when she was four. Blood was thick; kids longed to know who their real parents were. It wouldn't change a single memory he had, nor would it affect the ones they would make in the future. He wanted both women in his life to be happy. For a split second, as he did on numerous occasions, he once again thought of Rebecca. God, what beautiful children she would have made. Probably did make. On one hand, he'd love to know what she was up to now, and on the other, it would probably ruin his romantic notions. Reality could never compare to the imagination. She might no longer even be beautiful, although that was hard to imagine. He would toast her tonight, silently, the sexy girl who started it all, and made all others pale in comparison.

It was all shaping up. It was time for him to go home and freshen up. Maybe catch a little nap. If he was lucky, ex-wife notwithstanding, it was going to be one hell of a night.

From a balcony across the street, Rebecca and Cathy spied on Grant's club. Rather, Rebecca spied and Cathy sat on the railing eating beignets. Through her binoculars, Rebecca stared at the sign.

The minute she saw the wavy strand of black hair and the rose painted on it, there was no doubt. He named his club after her. The color blue against which black letters splashed out her name was the exact shade of the dress she'd worn the evening they met. It hadn't been all in her head; it hadn't just been youth, or alcohol, or sex. That night meant something. She meant something. But Rebecca was still making excuses, still pretending the sign had nothing to do with her. "Maybe he has a wife, or girlfriend, or aunt, or grandmother, or dog named Rebecca."

Cathy was quick to counter. "According to Bernie, his ex-wife's name is Amy. Their daughter is Megan. I got nothing on an aunt, a grandmother, or a dog."

"Bernie?"

"My private investigator."

"You're on a first-name basis with your PI? That's just weird."

"Oh, I'm weird? You're the one who just paid a little old lady eighty bucks to stand on her balcony with dollar-store binoculars, and sunglasses that make you look like the Unabomber, so you can stake out the man who took your virginity."

"Touché."

"Can you see anyone?"

"There are a lot of men coming and going. So far, no Grant." Rebecca sighed and allowed Cathy to take over the binoculars. "I can't do this. Let's go to the airport. Get me on the first flight home."

"Or, we have a nice little drink at the hotel, gussy up, and come back to the club."

"Why didn't he ever contact me?"

"Who knows? You ruined his phone number while you were mucking around—maybe he did, too."

"I gave him enough information to locate me."

"Well, he obviously remembers you. Nobody ever named a club after me."

"Maybe I should go in right now, so I don't mess up his show tonight."

"Now who's being dramatic?"

"He named his jazz club after me, Cathy. I've been trying to be humble, but that's huge. Isn't it?"

"It's pretty damn huge."

"God, this is terrifying."

"I know. I can feel you vibrating."

"Let's go get that drink."

"Good," Cathy said, linking her arm through Rebecca's. "Because you suck at surveillance."

"Hey." Rebecca pouted. "Why do you say that?"

Cathy sighed, took the binoculars and turned them the other way around. Silently she handed them back to Rebecca, who, doubtful, looked through them again.

"Right," Rebecca said, handing them back. "If you're the type who prefers everything magnified and in focus."

Cathy laughed and Rebecca joined in, and before long they were back at the hotel bar having a glass of wine and playing out every scenario that could possibly unfold that evening. Cathy's were romantic and usually ended with Grant on his knees proposing; Rebecca's usually ended with the club on fire and patrons stampeded to death in the race to get out.

Cathy soon had enough of Rebecca's doom-and-gloom scenarios. She shook her finger at Rebecca. "You can't be so negative," she said. "Close your eyes. Remember that night? It was the most romantic story I'd ever heard. And I should know, because you told it a hundred thousand times. You were young, and felt confident and on top of the world."

"That's because I was young and confident, and on top of the world," Rebecca said.

"No, you weren't. You were a geeky clarinet player getting punked by a trio of bitches." Cathy said it like it was. It was one of the things Rebecca loved most about her. "And yet," Cathy continued with a gentle hand on her arm, "you somehow transformed from a geeky clarinet player to this magical, voluptuous woman who reached out and grabbed a stranger's heart."

There it was again, that word. Magical. Rebecca closed her eyes and for a few seconds she really felt like that young girl again.

"That's it," Cathy said. "You've still got it. And you're going to blow his mind."

"Absolutely," Rebecca said. "Especially when he hears I've denied him twenty-one years of his son's life. Now that's going to be a showstopper." Unfortunately, once in a while, Rebecca, too, could call it like it was.

Chapter Seven

Rebecca bought a dress, just for the occasion. It was a similar color to the blue dress she wore on that night twenty-one years ago. It had a low-cut V-neck and was made of a satiny material that hugged her curves and twirled around her shapely calves every time she moved. She tucked three pictures of Miles into her purse—a baby picture, one from his tenth birthday, and one she took on his first day of college. Just looking at the brief recap of everything Grant had missed out on, almost brought Rebecca to her knees.

Miles had Grant's tousled brown hair and her blue eyes. There was no doubt he was his father's son. Rebecca decided that if she did indeed see Grant tonight, she wouldn't approach him until way after the show. It wouldn't be fair to ruin his opening. She'd waited this long; she could wait several more hours.

Cathy looked lovely in a little black dress. The pair of them turned many a head on the walk to the club. Several times Rebecca almost turned back. Cathy, who sensed this, kept her occupied with constant upbeat chatter. It was less than a fifteen-minute walk, but it felt like forever. When they finally neared the street, there was already a long line forming around the corner.

Rebecca turned to Cathy and clutched her arm. "Listen," she said. "If we don't get in—that's fate telling me it's a mistake, and I'm never coming back here again. If that happens, I want you to promise never to mention him again."

Cathy glanced at the line snaking its way down the block. "You're scared," she said. "I get that. But this isn't about you, remember?" Before Rebecca could react, Cathy snapped open Rebecca's purse and whipped out a baby picture of Miles. Rebecca wanted to reach out and touch his chubby cheeks. What if he hated her for this? What if he never spoke to her again? She spoke her fears out loud.

"That kid would defend you to the ends of the earth, and you know it," Cathy said. "He'll understand, Rebecca. Maybe not right away. But eventually he'll understand."

"What if Grant is a horrible person?"

"Then you walk away."

"What if we don't get in?"

"Then we come back until we do."

A man carrying a bucket of red roses passed by the line. He walked by Rebecca, stopped, and continued to the front. In the distance, Rebecca could see him looking up. Within seconds, he came back with a rose in his outstretched hand. "You match the sign," he said. "But you need this to complete the circle."

Rebecca held her breath and didn't move. Cathy bought the rose, snapped off the stem, and gently placed it behind Rebecca's ear. Just like Grant did with the rose he gave her way back when. The rose she'd preserved in a heart-shaped locket she usually wore around her neck. She had it on tonight—how could she not?

"It's a sign," Cathy whispered. "We are so getting in." Cathy had barely finished the sentence when a collective groan rose, and throngs of people began walking away from the club, blaming each other for not arriving sooner and bickering about where they would go instead. Rebecca craned her neck to have a look. Ahead, a velvet barrier was blocking the entrance.

"We're to capacity," a large man at the front of the line called down. "Sorry, folks. That's all for this evening."

Rebecca turned back. Cathy grabbed her arm, whirled her back around and began marching to the entrance. Uh-oh. Cathy was on a mission. Whoever the eleven-foot bouncer was, Rebecca felt sorry for him.

She stayed out of the way and surveyed the ornate wooden doors in front of which the bouncer stood, legs shoulder-width apart, hands folded over his chest, wearing sunglasses despite the lack of sun. A pretty young blonde leaned against the front brick wall, smoking a cigarette. She was wearing what appeared to be an old-fashioned wait staff dress: black with ruffles and a white apron. The only color she wore was on her shoes, sparkling red stilettos. Grant was obviously trying to recreate the twenties. The lights from the club were cozy, the air was sticky sweet and smelled like baking bread. Even the smoke curling from the cigarette before vanishing into thin air added a very Big Easy feel. Although there wasn't a band playing yet, Rebecca could hear music being piped in over loudspeakers, and animated voices could be heard from within.

"Look," Cathy said suddenly, head craned to the sky. "The moon." It glowed low and fat. It was the moon from that night.

Cathy tugged on her sleeve and Rebecca forced herself to look away. She was being silly. She wasn't some love-struck teenager reading signs into everything she saw. It was a normal night, and a gorgeous moon, and there was nothing more to it. They had simply gone out to listen to a little jazz, see an old acquaintance, and too bad, they weren't getting in anyway. Tomorrow all of the mystery would vanish with the morning light.

She hoped Grant had a fabulous night. He certainly had a

spectacular turnout. She was thrilled he'd stayed with music, and from the looks of the place, he had many admirers in town. She was happy for him. She hadn't ruined his life at all. Maybe this was what she was meant to see. Maybe now she could let go of some of her guilt.

"Let's go," Rebecca said.

"Not on your life," Cathy said.

"Unless you want to take on the beef kebab guarding the door, I don't think we have much of a choice."

"But I've come all this way," Cathy said, raising her voice to a near shout. "I can't miss this."

"Sorry for your loss," Rebecca said.

Cathy nodded to the bouncer. "Why don't you just tell him you're the mother of Grant's child?"

Rebecca was about to tell Cathy to keep her voice down when suddenly the waitress from the wall was advancing on them, throwing out her cigarette and crushing it with her heel as she did. God bless her, Rebecca thought. She wouldn't have been able to walk from a motel bathroom to bed in those things, let alone wait tables in them.

"Oh my God," the waitress said, taking Rebecca's hands. "You're Megan's mom? Amy?"

"No—"

"Hey," the bouncer said to the blonde. "You're late. You missed the opening meeting—all the dos and don'ts—"

"Relax. I'll ask one of the girls," the waitress said before returning back to Rebecca. "I'm so sorry. I just saw Megan go in with a man and a woman, and I just assumed the woman was her mother, Amy—"

"Honest mistake," Cathy said. "You know how messy divorce is."

"I thought you remarried your first husband. That's on the skids, too?"

Cathy gently pushed Rebecca out of the way. "She doesn't want to talk about it."

"You poor thing." The waitress smiled, revealing a little

gap between her teeth. It produced a slight whistling noise when she spoke. "And he brought his new girlfriend?" she said, leaning in. "Scum."

"Total scum," Cathy said.

"It's fine," Rebecca said. "I'll come back another night."

"No no, please," the waitress said, still hanging on to Rebecca's hands. "You're so beautiful. I know—I'll sit you at Grant's private table."

"Perfect!" Cathy said.

"No!" Rebecca said.

"Now that you're single again, and looking so gorgeous— who knows, right?" The waitress winked. Cathy winked back.

Still holding on to Rebecca, the waitress nodded to the beef kebab, who opened the door and gestured them in. From there, the waitress almost broke into a sprint as she led them through the crowd to a set of stairs leading to a balcony overlooking the stage. With one smooth move she reached out and unclipped the rope blocking the stairs.

"I can't do this," Rebecca said. "I can't just plop myself down at his private table."

"I don't think you have much of a choice," Cathy said. "I think the spirits are controlling this one." It was hard to hear Cathy over the noise of the crowd and the music playing over the loudspeaker. "I just love this song, don't you?" Cathy said.

Rebecca was glad she was walking ahead of Cathy so that she didn't have to look at her. It was shaping up to be a strange evening: the man with the rose; being led to Grant's private table; and of course the song blaring over the loudspeakers. "Black Magic Woman." Maybe Cathy was right. Maybe the spirits were in charge this evening. She just hoped they were on her side.

At least Grant wasn't up here. She certainly didn't want to ambush him. The table was a two-seater right at the edge of the balcony, with a perfect view of the stage. What in the world was Grant going to do when he found out a couple of strange women, one of them claiming to be Megan's mom, had taken over his table? In fact, nobody else was allowed upstairs, which was strange because it was a pretty large space. He could have definitely fit more tables up here. Maybe he was just trying to be exclusive and generate excitement.

Rebecca scanned the crowd below, wondering which ones were his daughter and ex-wife. She wondered if Megan looked like Grant. Miles had a sister. Yet another facet of his life she'd denied him.

"Stop hovering over the balcony," Cathy said. "You're making me nervous."

"I know. I could fall to my death." Suddenly the waitress appeared with a bottle of champagne, two flutes, and a bucket of ice.

"On the house," she said with her slight whistle.

"Perfect," Cathy said.

"We'll pay," Rebecca said. "I insist."

"Can't have the boss thinking I'm treating the mother of his child poorly, now can we?" The waitress grinned, popped the champagne, and poured them each an overflowing glass. Then she set the bottle in the bucket and trounced off.

"We're going to end up in jail," Rebecca said.

"There's no one else I'd rather be locked up with," Cathy said, holding up her glass. "Except maybe George Clooney."

Rebecca laughed and toasted. Maybe she should just relax and enjoy herself. It wasn't exactly her fault the evening was turning out like this. It's not like she was deliberately trying to sneak in and crash the party. Besides, it was so crowded and the wait staff was so busy that the chances of their waitress running into Grant and explaining what happened were slim. He would probably just think they had been accidentally seated at his private table with a reserved sign on it and served the finest champagne on the house. It wasn't too late; they could leave now, and no one would be the wiser. Just as the thought hit and Rebecca geared herself to stand and flee, the lights dimmed onstage and musicians began to take their places. The anticipation of seeing Grant again and hearing him play overrode everything else. Rebecca leaned forward as her stomach twisted into a series of tight braids.

And it hit her, harder than anything else had so far. She hadn't come here just to confess her sins. She came because she had to see him. Just one more time. Twenty-one years of pent-up longing. It was no wonder she had almost single-handedly finished the champagne.

Soon the seven musicians onstage began playing an up-beat Dizzy Gillespie tune. Rebecca was immediately en-tranced.

"You should see your face," Cathy said. "It's glowing."

Rebecca just smiled. She didn't want to talk or even breathe too loud over the music. For a few minutes she allowed herself to be transported to another world. Great jazz was like being hoisted atop a crowd of people and gently thrown from one stranger's arms to the next. Some people didn't get as lost as others in jazz. Cathy was one of them. Rebecca didn't know how she could be checking her cell phone at a time like this.

"It's a long song, isn't it?" Cathy whispered.

Before Rebecca could answer, the downstairs room erupted in applause. At first she thought they were just applauding the song, and she heartily joined in. Then, as she leaned over the balcony, she noticed heads turning toward the back of the room, following someone's path toward the stage. Tall. Tousled brown hair. Easy smile. Trumpet held as if it were a part of his body. It was him. It was Grant, coming onstage. Every nerve ending in her body started firing.

And just like that, twenty-one years faded away. He was older, of course, but sporting the same boyish grin and confident stride as he took the stage. Rebecca held her breath, and although she didn't slink back into the safety of darkness, she half prayed he wouldn't look up. Not yet. Instead he looked straight ahead as he raised his trumpet. Just when he reached center stage and it seemed as if he was about to play, he lowered his trumpet and leaned into the microphone.

"Good evening, ladies and gentlemen," he said. "Welcome to Rebecca's. This dream was a long time coming, and I'm honored you're here to share it with me." The crowd showed their support and Grant smiled and waited for the applause to die down.

My God, he was still the sexiest man Rebecca had ever seen. *I'm here. I'm right here.*

"I'm going to slow it down with a little Miles Davis."

Rebecca gasped, and the sound was like a thunderbolt in her head. Cathy reached out and touched her hand as Grant began to play "I Thought About You." It was instrumental only, but Rebecca could hear the words in her head as the poignant voice of his trumpet conjured up a dozen images in rapid succession: rain coating the side of a kitchen window late at night, lights glittering off train tracks, lonely alleys, soft kisses, and his body on top of hers on the damp cemetery grass. All this went on in her head as down below his trumpet carried on, as if calling out just for her. It was official. She was under a spell, and it hadn't lost an ounce of its power.

I took a trip on a train, and I thought about you.

"Sweetie, are you okay?" Cathy handed her a cocktail napkin. Rebecca hadn't noticed the tears running down her cheeks until then.

And I thought about you.

"I used to sing this to Miles when he was a baby," Rebecca whispered. She did, too. Every night. And every night she thought about Grant. And this was the song he opened with. It was some kind of sign. It had to be. The magic between them wasn't all in her head. It was happening all over again, right now. Rebecca folded her arms over the balcony and leaned in.

"You're making me kind of nervous," Cathy said. "Is that safe to lean on?"

The moon shining down, on some little town . . .

Suddenly, a creaking sound rose above the blare of the trumpet and it felt as if the railing was moving. What was happening? Were the vibrations of the music giving her the illusion of movement? Something bad was happening, she could feel it, but she still didn't know what. This time when she gasped, everyone heard. Heads from below snapped up, and other gasps joined hers. It wasn't until she heard someone shout, "She's going to fall!" that she realized they were talking about her. A small section of the balcony was tearing off, teetering over the edge, and she was going to plunge to her death.

I've ruined his night, was her first thought as she began to fall. *I hope I don't kill anyone*, was the second.

Grant Dodge sprung into action. He couldn't believe what was happening, but he didn't have time to analyze it. It wasn't a long fall, and he knew there was a space between two tables where the woman would land. As he sprinted to the spot, he yelled at others to get out of the way, which most of them were already doing. It happened so fast, and yet in some ways seemed in slow motion. Right behind him were his bouncer and a couple of his bigger jazz players. Thank God the balcony almost directly overlooked the stage. They all held their arms out, like a human net, and braced themselves. Still, the impact took most of them down. Grant ended up with his hands on the floor, the woman's bottom pinning them down. Even before he knew if everyone was all right, his testosterone kicked in and he found himself thinking it felt like a nice ass, even if it was crushing his wrists.

"You okay?" he said to the stunned woman. "Everyone okay?"

One by one, his musicians and bouncer helped everyone up. The woman who fell was shaking, but appeared to be unharmed. With help, she was able to stand. She had a gorgeous hourglass figure, something else he shouldn't have been thinking about given the circumstances.

Grant held his hand up to the crowd. "We're okay," he shouted. "Everyone is okay."

There was a second of silence, then from the stage came a drum roll topped off with a couple of hits to the cymbals, and the crowd went wild with shouts and applause.

To Grant's bewilderment, his bouncer leaned in to the lady and said something strange. "See how handy a beef kebab can be?"

"Just like we rehearsed it," one of the large musicians called out. "Just in time for us to play a little tune we like to call 'I Fell For You.' " Laughter again from the crowd.

Grant put his arm around the woman's waist—she was still shaking—and he gently walked her over to the stairs, where her friend was waiting, frozen in place. The band began to play as if nothing had happened, and soon the crowd settled back in, seemingly enjoying themselves more than ever.

They bought it, Grant thought. *They thought it was planned.* He'd have to give Reggie a bonus for coming up with that one. Now he was going to have to figure out how to avoid a lawsuit from the woman who almost died in his club. How in the hell did she get up to the balcony? What happened to his strict orders not to let anyone up there? He even had it roped off, just in case. He should have known some idiot would try to get around it. He was going to have to be careful not to let the woman have a piece of his mind. The more he thought about it, the more furious he became. In fact, he wanted to shake the living daylights out of her. Instead he gently sat her on the step.

"Do we need to call an ambulance?" he asked her. The woman quickly shook her head no. He couldn't see her face; she was keeping it down, her long black hair covering it. It was hard to stay mad at someone who was so shook up. He sat next to her on the stairs and put his arm around her. In seconds, he'd gone from wanting to kill her to wanting to take care of her, comfort her.

"I tried to rope off the balcony," he said to her friend, who was still hovering above them. "I told them not to seat any-one up there."

The friend leaned down next to the woman. "Are you okay?" she said. "Rebecca, look at me."

Rebecca? Grant started at the name. Well, what about them apples? Imagine the headlines. Stranger named Re-becca killed at the opening of Rebecca's. He almost laughed.

"Your name is Rebecca?" he asked. And then she looked up, and into his eyes. And then he couldn't tell if he was shaking because she was shaking, or if his body was doing it all on its own. He literally felt a series of jolts, as if a firing line had just unloaded on him and not one of them had missed. It was her. It was her, it was her, it was her.

Rebecca. Had he said it out loud? Did he even have a voice?

"Hello, Grant," she said. "Sorry to just drop in on you like this."

Chapter Eight

Rebecca didn't get another chance to apologize. Grant was beside himself. "This is unbelievable," he kept saying. "It's you. It's really you." He quickly set Cathy and Rebecca up at his reserved table downstairs, and saw to it that they were treated like queens. He squeezed Rebecca's hand and whispered that he'd talk to her after his set. He played with his eyes fastened on her and as soon as he finished, a huge grin lit up his face. It didn't take long before his ex-wife, Amy, was glaring at Rebecca's table. Megan, on the other hand, was a delight. During his next quick break, Grant introduced them.

"This is my daughter, Megan," he said.

"Stepdaughter," Megan corrected. "But he's like a real dad." She glanced at the table where her mother was sitting.

"Sorry," Grant leaned in and whispered. "That's the biological dad there. No disrespect meant, Megan."

"None taken, Dad," she said good-naturedly. "He's the real deal," she said with another flash of a smile.

Stepdaughter, Rebecca thought. And although it was obvious they had a true father-daughter relationship, it conjured up strange feelings in Rebecca. Grant had a biological child as well. She felt ashamed of herself for thinking it would be a stronger bond. After all, he'd actually known Megan most of her life, raised her, sang to her, tucked her into bed, laughed with her, played games with her, and on and on and on. He'd never even set eyes on his son.

Grant carefully dodged the question when Megan wanted details of how he and Rebecca knew each other. It wasn't hard to do with all the commotion. During the second half of the evening, patrons took to the dance floor, and there was so much merriment, there wasn't much time for chatter.

"So, will I be going back to the hotel alone?" Cathy asked with a smile.

"Absolutely not," Rebecca said. "Whatever you do, do not go home without me."

"Miles looks just like him," Cathy said.

Rebecca looked up. Grant was smiling at her from on-stage. It was true. They even had the same dimple in their chin when they smiled.

"Next break, we've got to go," Rebecca said.

"Are you okay?"

"No. I can't keep this secret bottled up, not after drinking all this champagne. And I can't tell him tonight. This is his night. So next set, we say our good-byes and we're out of here, okay?"

"Whatever you think."

At the next break, Grant appeared. Just as he started to sit down, Cathy and Rebecca stood.

"I'm afraid we have to go," Rebecca said.

"You're kidding," Grant said. He seemed truly surprised, but to his credit, he quickly recovered. "By all means. I just—it's just—it's so incredible seeing you."

"She has all day tomorrow," Cathy said. Rebecca wanted to kill her, but Grant didn't give her a chance.

"Fabulous. Will you see me tomorrow?" he said. "I might need a bit of a lie-in after tonight, but what about getting together in the afternoon?"

"I'd love that," Rebecca said. She told him the name of her hotel, and he agreed to meet her in the lobby at one. She and Grant did an awkward dance, not knowing whether to hug, or kiss, or shake hands. He ended up extending his hand, but when she went to shake it, he held it instead. Then he brought her hand up to his lips, and without breaking eye contact, he slowly turned her hand over and kissed her palm. It was so erotic, she wanted to kill him for turning her on in public.

It was still there, as strong as ever, that current of electricity between them, Rebecca thought. It was good to know that some things never change. That is, until she spilled her secrets.

As she and Cathy walked back to the hotel, doubt began to creep in. Was she making the biggest mistake of her life? Should she stay and dance, and end the night in his arms? Have one more night to cherish before she ruined it once and for all? She couldn't imagine someone telling her she had a grown child, a whole life that she could have been part of. She only prayed that no matter how angry they were at her, Miles and Grant would have a chance to get to know one another. Better late than never? She could only pray that would be the case.

Once they were back in their hotel room, Cathy hung out in Rebecca's room. She kicked back on an easy chair, but Rebecca couldn't sit still. "I don't know who to tell first," she said, pacing. "Grant or Miles. Who should I tell first?"

"Oh, sweetie. I don't know."

"I think I should tell Miles first. Miles at least knows he has a father, so it might be less of a shock."

"True, but he thinks his father was killed in a car crash before he was born."

Rebecca sat on the edge of the bed and put her head on her knees.

"Sorry," Cathy whispered.

"Don't be," Rebecca said. "I need a cold, hard dose of the truth."

"It's been twenty-one years," Cathy said. "I know you're feeling all guilty, but I don't think there's any reason to rush your decision now, is there?"

"Other than a ton of bricks weighing me down every day?"

"I just think you need to calm down, get to know Grant again, and take it a step at a time. Maybe you can invite Miles here and tell them at the same time."

"Miles is my son. He's the one I have the real relationship with. I should tell Miles first."

"Okay."

"But I robbed Grant of the joy of finding out he was having a child. In an ideal world, he should have been the first person I would have told. But what if it's too late? What if he doesn't even want to get to know Miles? In which case, if I tell Miles first, then I've set him up for a huge rejection. Then again, after all these years, maybe Grant has a right to choose whether or not to step in now."

"That makes sense."

"So I'll tell Grant first."

"I agree."

Rebecca leapt out of bed, pulled a pair of jeans out of her suitcase, and began to dress.

"What are you doing?"

"I'm going back to the club. I'll bet he's still there."

"It's two thirty in the morning."

"You think I should wait?"

"Yes, my dear friend, I think you should wait."

"You're right." Rebecca left her jeans on but got back into bed. Cathy started for her room.

"I know it's silly but—"

"Do you want me to stay in here for a bit?" Cathy guessed.

"Please," Rebecca croaked. "I don't want to be alone with

my thoughts. Oh God, I'm like a crazy person. I think she really did curse me."

"Relax," Cathy said. "I'll just lay here for awhile." Cathy clicked off the light. "It's going to be okay," she said.

"Promise?" Rebecca said.

"You were only sixteen," Cathy said. "A child."

"Okay," Rebecca said. She closed her eyes, hugged her pillow, and began counting the seconds until one p.m.

Grant was already standing in the lobby, hands in pockets, looking out at the back pool, when she came down. He turned as she descended the staircase, and she saw him take her in. She felt like the star of a romantic movie, making her grand entrance. He was so handsome, and tall, and clean shaven—she wanted to reach out and rub her hand along his smooth jawline—and he wore cologne that should be illegal in public. Instead, she smoothed her hair and laughed nervously, and this time they decided on an awkward hug. It lasted longer than your average friendly hug.

"Are you hungry?" he asked.

"Starving," she lied. How could you eat when your stomach was in total knots? How could you choke down a single bite when you knew you should be using your mouth to say *I gave birth to your son*?

"Great. I know a little place near the Garden District. Then I thought we could have a stroll around the mansions. I can point out where all the celebrities have lived."

"Just what I came for," Rebecca said. She laughed again.

"I never thought I'd hear that laugh again," Grant said.

"Before we go," Rebecca said, "I hate to do this." Grant looked as if he were bracing himself for really bad news. Rebecca made note of it: he wasn't very good at hiding his emotions, anxiety clearly splashed across his face. "My friend Cathy is only here for one more day, and—"

"Is that all?" Grant said. "The more the merrier."

"Are you sure?"

"We couldn't just leave her here by herself on her last day."

"Thank you, thank you, thank you." Rebecca started toward the stairs to go and tell Cathy.

"How many days are you staying?" Grant asked. It was almost a whisper.

Rebecca turned. "I'm—here for a while," she said. "On business."

He immediately relaxed, and broke into a huge grin. "Good. That's very, very good."

And she knew, as she walked back up the stairs, that his eyes were glued to her every step of the way.

They ate in an adorable little bistro with a back garden patio. It was somewhat obvious that Grant had picked a romantic place, but the three of them chatted away and enjoyed themselves nonetheless. When he casually asked Rebecca what brought her to New Orleans, Rebecca couldn't speak. Cathy jumped in.

"She's checking out possible locations to open a jewelry boutique."

Rebecca just looked at her.

"You mean you might stay?" Grant said. He sounded excited.

"Everything's up in the air right now," Rebecca said.

Grant grabbed a napkin and wrote down a name and number. He slid it to Rebecca.

She looked at it and said the name out loud. "Mae Lin."

"She's looking for someone to sublet her apartment. She's already in San Francisco, but a friend of hers has the key and can show it to you anytime."

Cathy grinned. "It's fate," she said.

Rebecca smiled but went back to being mute. Cathy picked up the slack, talking about her husband and kids and job. So far, Rebecca had talked of her jewelry business and where she lived, but little else.

Every once in a while, Grant would say "Buffalo," as if he were fascinated by the word. Finally, after about the third time, he caught Rebecca looking at him. "I just . . . always wondered," he said. "Where you lived."

A wounded feeling came over her as if she were that rejected teenager once again. Sitting by the phone, touching her belly, praying for him to call. "I told you where I lived, and I gave you my phone number."

He looked stunned for a second, and then sheepish. "I wasn't always listening to you."

"You. What?" All these years of replaying every word he'd ever said to her like a favorite song, and he couldn't even remember where she lived? Maybe this wasn't the fairy tale she thought it was.

"You were so bewitching," Grant said. He turned to Cathy. "She was so gorgeous."

"I know," Cathy said. "I was here that weekend, too."

Once again, Grant didn't try to hide his genuine surprise. "You were?" He snapped his fingers. "The scavenger hunt!"

Cathy grimaced, gulped her wine, and poured them all more. "Guilty," she said, sneaking a look at Rebecca.

"Who won that, anyway?" Grant said.

"I did—" Rebecca said.

"It was a trick," Cathy said.

Rebecca wished her friend would have stuck to the lie, but Grant's ears were already perked up.

"We were horrible to Rebecca that weekend," Cathy said. "Three nasty girls out to set her up."

"No," Grant said.

"Unfortunately, yes," Cathy said. "We dared her to get drunk and seduce a handsome stranger while we went dancing." Cathy immediately flushed, and for that matter, so did Rebecca.

"Well," Grant said, "I can't say I'm completely sorry." He stared at Rebecca across the table. She was the first to look away. "The two of you obviously patched things up—friends to this day."

"Oh yes," Rebecca said. "She made up for it. Stood by me when everyone else—" *Shunned me for getting knocked up.* Rebecca let the sentence drop.

Grant must have sensed the subject put Rebecca on edge, for despite looking as if he had a sea of follow up questions, he didn't pursue the matter any further. "Anyway," he said, "you wrote your number down—but it was smeared—"

"Yours too!" Rebecca said.

"If only I had remembered you said Buffalo," Grant said. "I'm sure I would have called information. I was so mad at myself. For being so entranced with your beauty that I wasn't a very good listener."

Okay, maybe she could forgive that. "We were so young," she said.

"Nineteen and twenty-two," he said.

Cathy started to cough.

This was it, Rebecca thought. Time to drop a little bit of the truth and see what kind of detonating power it had. "Sixteen," she said. "I was really sixteen."

Cathy froze with her wineglass poised midair, as if she couldn't believe Rebecca had just spit that out. Rebecca stared at her plate.

"Oh," Grant said. Then, after a minute, "Oh."

"I'm sorry."

"Oh," he said. "So I—oh my God. I would have never—" He glanced at Cathy.

"It's okay," Rebecca said. "She knows."

"I. It's just. Wow. Sixteen. I feel like such a jerk."

Rebecca immediately put her hand on top of his. "I was the jerk," she said. "I was the jerk."

"You were completely blitzed on Hurricanes," Grant said. He stopped eating, pushed away his plate. "I was an adult. And you were a drunk sixteen-year-old girl. Sixteen."

"Grant. It wasn't like that. I—" *Was madly in love with you.* No, that wouldn't sound right. *Was under a spell—*

"Megan is fourteen," Grant said. "You were only two years older than my stepdaughter, Megan."

Oh no. Rebecca had forgotten all about his teenage daughter.

"She had an older boy hanging around her last year and it scared me to death. I wanted to kill him. I absolutely wanted to kill him." He pushed his chair back from the table. "I was him," he said. "I was no better than him."

Rebecca felt as if the patio floor were tilting forward, but she didn't know how to straighten it out again.

Cathy cleared her throat. "Weren't you almost seventeen?" Cathy croaked.

Grant looked at Rebecca. Rebecca opened her mouth, but she couldn't lie to Grant again. No matter what else, she wasn't going to lie to him again. Silently, she shook her head.

Grant put his hand up to his head as if it were throbbing. "I should have known better," he said. "I should have asked for your ID."

"I had a fake ID," Rebecca said. "And you wouldn't have been able to stop me." She surprised them both by the passion in her voice. "Sorry," she said. "Despite—my age—it was a magical night for me."

Grant nodded, but he still didn't touch his food. He looked at his watch. He checked his phone.

Rebecca could feel Cathy staring at her from across the table, offering her support. Grant's reaction to this little hiccup didn't bode so well for her other zinger.

"Grant," she said. "I'm sorry I lied—"

Grant screeched his chair back and abruptly stood up. "Ladies," he said, "I'm terribly sorry. This meal is on me.

Enjoy." He threw a wad of cash down on the table. Stunned, Rebecca just stared at it. "It's been great catching up with you, Rebecca. I, uh, have this thing back at the club." He gestured wildly and knocked his silverware off the table. The clatter caused a number of heads to jerk their way.

Rebecca hated seeing him like this. "Grant," she said. "It was a long time ago."

"I'm going to the restroom," Cathy said.

Grant held up his hand. "No need," he said. "I'm not staying."

"I didn't realize you'd be so upset," Rebecca said.

"I'm not having this conversation here," Grant said.

"I wasn't trying to trick you. I was young—"

"Oh yes," Grant said with a wry laugh. "I think we've covered that part. You weren't just young, you were jailbait."

Jailbait. He'd taken their beautiful night and twisted it into something ugly. Or had she taken an ugly night and twisted it into something beautiful? Looking at him now, so angry with her, she couldn't decide.

"I . . . can't change it now," Rebecca said quietly.

"Of course," he said. "What's done is done, right? I'm sorry I have to run, but, well—running a club is a full-time job. Married to my job, you might say. Can't be helped." He was talking nonstop; he wanted nothing more than to flee.

Rebecca had never felt so mortified in her life. "Of course," she said. She felt as if she'd been hit on the side of the head with a two-by-four. *Come on, Grant!* she wanted to say. *You didn't force yourself on me. I was the seducer!* But it wasn't fair to discuss this in front of Cathy, and he was so obviously disturbed. She'd forgotten how passionate and temperamental artists could be.

What a fool she was for bringing it up in front of Cathy. Now he knew that Cathy knew what he'd done. Oh, what a mess she'd made of things less than an hour into it. Even so, Rebecca was still stunned when he actually turned and walked out. So, for that matter, was Cathy. She pushed both their plates away and poured the rest of the wine.

"Rebecca," Cathy said after a few minutes of silence.

Slowly Rebecca fell back into her chair. "Yes?"

"I don't think you should tell him," Cathy said.

"What?"

"Can I be brutally honest?"

"Please."

"Forget your guilt."

"Are you kidding? You know I can't do that."

"Rebecca, I'm telling you. He looked as if he were about to explode."

"He was just taken aback."

"Taken aback? I've seen 'taken aback.' I've been 'taken aback.' That, my friend, was—at the very least—seriously pissed off."

"It was kind of weird, right?"

"It was definitely kind of weird, Rebecca. It was twenty-one years ago, for God's sakes. And he couldn't even stay and finish dinner? He had to throw a little fit and make us all totally uncomfortable? My God, he acted like you came here to accuse him of something."

"I think because of his daughter—"

"His stepdaughter, remember?"

"He raised her since she was four."

Cathy held her hands up. "Okay, okay, so he has a teenage daughter. He still overreacted. I'm sorry. I don't know what that was. But I don't like it. I think you should come home with me, put the past to bed, and whatever you do—I don't think you should ever tell that man that he has a son."

Chapter Nine

Nothing like a stroll past historic Southern mansions to get your mind off a man. New Orleans's Garden District was an area the girls had ignored when they were teenagers, but it was quickly becoming one of Rebecca's favorite places. They followed the route of the St. Charles Streetcar line on foot, marveling. Each mansion, stately and beautiful, advertised its unique identity through color, ornamentation, and landscaping.

But it still wasn't enough to get Rebecca's mind off of what had just happened. Grant threw a fit and took off. All because she lied by three little years.

Maybe Cathy was right. She'd come here fully prepared to do the right thing, and the man couldn't even handle the first part of the conversation.

Wasn't it time she let go of the guilt? The past was the past. Who was judging her anyway? The big guy in the sky? She didn't even know if she believed in him. She suspected some kind of energy was formed after a human being died, but she wasn't quite sure what. And she didn't believe she was going to be punished. How could anyone on this planet be punished for anything? Sometimes life was just a total zoo, still nothing more than a fight for survival despite the invention of the iPad.

Miles was a grown man. The "damage" of growing up without a father had already been done. No matter what she did now, she'd never be able to make that up to either of them.

Without speaking, Cathy and Rebecca turned left into the neighborhood. This street, too, was filled with glorious mansions, and iron gates, and towering trees, and blooming flowers, and secrets dotting each house, each yard, hanging from every window. *We're all just masquerading to some degree*, Rebecca thought. *New Orleans just chooses to celebrate it.*

"City of wealth, and masks, and ghosts," Rebecca said as they finished their tour.

"And hurricanes," Cathy said. "The drink and the storms."

"And psychics and secrets," Rebecca said.

"And cemeteries. Where things should stay buried. Things like secrets," Cathy said, taking Rebecca's arm. "Come on, I'm taking you back to Buffalo."

Once back in the Quarter, Rebecca wanted to drag Cathy to the Voodoo Shop, but Cathy refused to go anywhere near it.

"I don't like anything hokeypokey," Cathy said.

"I think you mean hocus-pocus," Rebecca said.

"Whatever. Not on your life. And you shouldn't be listening to crazy, swindling old ladies, either."

"Don't you believe in signs?"

"Yes. Stop signs. Now let's get into our bathing suits and try to break into the pool."

"Are you serious?"

"Yes! I didn't come to New Orleans to be good. I want to do one bad thing before I go back to being a boring old mom."

"Going swimming in the hotel pool? That's your bad thing?"

"Going swimming in the hotel pool *after hours*."

"Skinny-dipping?"

"Are you kidding me? No way."

It was always the skinny girls who were most self-conscious. Rebecca laughed. "I admire your enthusiasm, but it's an intimate courtyard. I don't think we're going to be able to get away with it."

"That's the beauty of it."

Rebecca so didn't want to go along with it. She wanted to go see the psychic. She wanted to see if there would be any change in her reading now that she'd seen Grant again. She wanted an excuse not to go back to Buffalo.

From now on, anything you do out of fear will steal little bits of your life away, one piece at a time . . .

Was she afraid to stay, or afraid to go? How could the old witch give her such cryptic readings?

Back at the hotel room, she changed listlessly into her swimsuit despite Cathy's giddy mood. This was simply a getaway for Cathy, a reprieve from her routine at home. Rebecca didn't have a routine at home. She didn't even have a home anymore. She wanted to be here, in New Orleans. All night she'd been thinking of the napkin Grant wrote on. A friend with an apartment to sublet. And just yesterday Cathy was encouraging Rebecca to stay. Was she really going to let Grant Dodge shame her out of town?

The pair crept down the stairs in their swimsuits, towels wrapped around them. Cathy started to giggle. Rebecca rolled her eyes in the dark, but smiled nonetheless. Cathy was fun to be around—a great mom, too. Had Rebecca been a great mom? She'd tried, but being both mother and father wasn't an easy job. Cathy's husband was the disciplinarian, so Cathy had always been free to be the fun parent. If Cathy's girls were here with them now, they would all be sneaking down the stairs in their suits and giggling.

They reached the lobby, and even though the hotel was dead silent (guests were not allowed to check in after midnight, and therefore no one was staffing the desk), Cathy crept anyway, stepping on her tiptoes up to the door leading to the courtyard.

"It's locked," she whispered.

"Told you," Rebecca said.

"Shit."

"We could put on heels and walk the streets," Rebecca said. "Wouldn't that be fun?"

"Do you think we could pick it?" Cathy said, pawing her head for a bobby pin.

"No," Rebecca said. "There's a nice big vase over there, though. We could hurl it through the French doors."

"Funny." Cathy sighed, folded her arms across her chest, and stared out at the dark courtyard.

"We were *going* to do it," Cathy said, heading for the stairs. "That counts for something, doesn't it?"

"That counts for a lot," Rebecca said, thinking of Grant. "That counts for a hell of a lot."

The next morning, Rebecca awoke before the Louisiana sun. She and Cathy were supposed to pack, go to breakfast at the doughnut place, and head for the airport. Rebecca wanted some time alone to roam the streets, take one last stroll around. As the sun came up, she wondered once again what she should do. Cathy insisted again last night that she should go home with her. Give this some distance. But Rebecca couldn't imagine leaving without doing what she came here to do. She knew it wasn't going to be easy, and maybe it shouldn't be.

She took little side streets she'd never been down before and relished the fact that most of the city was still sleeping off last night's party. After thirty minutes or so, she was just about to head back to the hotel when she noticed something shining on the ground. She bent over to examine it, and came back up with a gleaming silver heart. *I could make my second New Orleans–inspired necklace out of this*, she thought. *Maybe it's a sign*. She pocketed the heart, laughed at herself, and was just about to turn back when she looked up. Across the way, wedged in between a T-shirt shop and a cooking shop, was an empty storefront. Hanging from the window was another sign, the clearest one she'd seen to date: FOR RENT.

"You're not eating your share of doughnuts," Cathy said.

Rebecca was already seated at one of the little tables when Cathy joined her. The place was hopping. "I ate twelve of them before you arrived."

Cathy's eyes swept over her like a laser beam. "Then where's all the powder?"

Rebecca laughed. "You don't miss a trick."

"Speaking of which, I brought your things."

"What?"

"You left all your luggage at the hotel, so I packed your things and checked out for you."

"You didn't."

"I didn't."

"You shouldn't have—you what?"

"I left your things in the room. And I didn't check you out."

"So why—"

"I'm just confirming what I already suspected. You're staying, aren't you?"

Rebecca reached over and grabbed Cathy's hand. "I went for a walk this morning."

"Uh-huh."

Rebecca pulled the silver heart out of her pocket. "I found this."

"Okay." Cathy didn't even touch it.

"It was lying on the street right in front of a shop for rent!"

"And you took it as a sign."

"Well, it was a sign. Like 'Stop.' Only this one said 'For Rent.' "

"Is this about Grant?"

"Absolutely not. This is about me. It's about starting a new chapter in my life. What do I have back in Buffalo?"

"Your parents, your son, and incredibly good friends."

"My parents drive me crazy, my son is off to college, and my incredibly good friend loves weekend getaways and can visit me."

"I don't want to see you get hurt."

"I have to do this. Correction. I want to do this. I've been dead inside, Cathy. I don't always tell you, because I've dumped on you enough over the years. But I haven't felt really happy in a long time. This place makes me happy."

"Powdered doughnuts and sunshine make everybody happy," Cathy said. "But this city isn't all powdered doughnuts and sunshine, and you know it."

"I'm not expecting perfection. I just—I want to take a chance on it, see what happens. Buffalo will always be there if I fail."

"Let's get out of here so I can see this shop before I go," Cathy said. They paid the bill and started to leave the table. Cathy ran back and grabbed the last two beignets. "They don't feed you on the plane," she said, and stuffed both of them in her mouth at the same time.

Chapter Ten

Rebecca stood behind the counter of her small shop, surveying the territory. She loved the moments just before and after closing when she could pause for a few minutes of silent reflection. She glanced at the calendar on her wall. She couldn't believe she'd been here three months already. The shop was small but perfect. A good deal of her business was still from the Internet, although foot traffic was starting to pick up. She loved the little bell above her door; it brought a rush of pleasant feelings every time someone jingled in. She also lucked out on the apartment. Mae Lin was going to be in San Francisco for the whole year, and she had left her place completely furnished.

The apartment was in the French Quarter, only a few blocks from the store, and as Rebecca dreamed, it was one of the old French Creole apartments with a long balcony overlooking the street. Rebecca couldn't wait for Mardi Gras. Mae Lin had an eclectic and colorful flair, and Rebecca was completely at ease in her space, but spent most of her time on the balcony curled up in a chair, watching the world go by.

It was on such a Saturday morning, sitting on the balcony with the newspaper and a giant cup of coffee, that she had seen Grant Dodge pass by. Rebecca's heart began pounding immediately, and she spilled hot coffee all up and down her arm. She'd had a foolish urge to hit the deck, but Grant hadn't even glanced up. As far as he knew, she was gone. Would he be furious that she rented Mae Lin's apartment after all? He'd been carrying his trumpet case and walking with his eyes straight ahead. He had such a confident way about him. She wondered if he'd even thought about her since that night. Maybe she'd just imagined the connection between them.

Jerk. For days after the sighting, she'd sat in the same spot at the same time, but he didn't pass again. Yes, it had been three months and she still hadn't approached him. She just wanted to get settled in first. If he reacted as badly as she suspected, it would be tempting to skip town the minute he let her have it. And she couldn't let him ruin her dream. She loved her little shop. She loved New Orleans, with its plethora of things to do and places to eat and streets to explore. And lately she'd been pouring all of her passion into making new jewelry pieces. She'd been working with red stones, placing them in circles and triangles. Red was the color of passion and a symbol of strength. The younger girls who came into the shop always gravitated toward red. Were women just destined to be drawn to danger, to fire, to signs that shouted *stop*?

It made Rebecca smile to see girls come into the shop and try on her work. She never yelled when her pieces were touched; in fact, she prodded those who seemed shy to try things on. Earrings were an exception; she couldn't have people trying them on, but she would encourage them to hold them up to their ears and look in one of the many handheld mirrors lying about the shop. She usually sold at least five pieces a day. With that, her savings, and her Internet business, she was just getting by.

Today Rebecca was looking forward to getting back to the apartment and taking a bubble bath. She bought some candles from the shop next door along with a bottle of wine. The apartment itself was so gothic, and so romantic, that she didn't need a man to evoke a lovely evening. She even had a new nightgown to put on. After her bath she would sit on the balcony in her new nightgown, sipping wine. Because one thing she'd learned, one adage that turned out to be true—nobody ever looked up.

Mae Lin's bathroom looked like something out of a five-star hotel. It was as big as a bedroom, with pristine cream-tiled floors and soothing ocean-blue walls. A standing glass shower came with dual rotating showerheads with settings that varied from "light mist" to "Amazon rainforest." A CD player was on its own shelf with a stack of CDs next to it. Mirrors and candles were positioned everywhere. Built-in shelves were stacked with designer towels. A silk robe hung on the back of the door, and a tall cabinet housed an impressive collection of bath salts, bubbles, and lotions. This was one clean chick. So far Rebecca had tried every setting on the showerhead. "Rain massage" was her favorite, but tonight she definitely wanted to take a long bubble bath in the deep, old-fashioned tub that took up the center of the room. She brought a bottle of wine, a glass, and a corkscrew into the bathroom with her.

She put on a compilation jazz CD, then turned to the cabinet. So far she hadn't used any of Mae Lin's products, but she clearly remembered Mae Lin saying she could help herself to anything. *Make yourself at home; use anything you'd like; what's mine is yours.* Still, she wouldn't use too much of anything. She chose a large glass bottle on the top shelf. It hadn't been opened, but there were so many bottles, that wasn't a surprise. This one had a pewter lid shaped like a dragonfly. Rebecca would only pour a drop of it into the tub. She placed the plug in the tub and turned on the water. The handles were hard to turn and when Rebecca finally did force them into submission, they let out a scream worthy of any torture victim. Rebecca jumped at the sound, then scalded herself as she reached in to touch the water. She tried the cold tap, and although she had to put her entire body into it, the knob finally produced enough cold water to bring the bath to a temperature that wouldn't scald her. Then she carefully measured out a small amount of the bubble bath and set the bottle on one of the many little metal holders hanging off the side of the tub, just in case she wanted to add a drop or two later.

She glanced at the standing candelabra next to the tub. It was shaped like a tree, its metal branches each holding little candles. There were at least twenty; it would look incredible lit. She wasn't surprised to find a long, elegant lighter next to the tree, and feeling like royalty (who had to prepare her own bath), Rebecca set about lighting each little candle. Then she dimmed the chandelier and stood back to marvel at the effect. How gorgeous. Little sparkling flames casting dancing shadows on the walls and ceiling, creating a romantic glow. If only Grant were here to join her . . . but she would have plenty of time to fantasize about that later.

Rebecca hummed to herself as she walked around the apartment wrapped only in an enormous lavender towel, sipping wine, listening to jazz, and waiting for her warm bubble bath to fill to the top. This was the life. But when she entered the bathroom again, the water in the tub was dangerously close to overflowing. Setting her wineglass down next to the bottle, she hurried to shut off the knobs. She leaned in and put her entire body into it once again, but this time they didn't budge. The water was about to spill over. What had she done? She didn't remember Mae Lin saying not to use the tub, so the knobs had to be working. She was just too weak. Maybe her hands were too wet. She wiped them vigorously on the towel, then used the towel for a grip and tried once again. Still no movement. No-no-no, this could not be happening. She was just trying to take a bath!

What was she going to do? Mae Lin had casually mentioned to call her if she needed the super. Why hadn't she just left her the super's direct number? Tools. She needed tools. There was no time for calling anyone. Mae Lin had to have tools, right?

Rebecca ran to the kitchen, slipping several times, but managed to right herself, and she looked in the first place she would have left tools: under the kitchen sink. To her immense relief, she found a wrench. She didn't know if it would work, but she had to try. But when she reached in and grabbed the wrench, something skittered across her hand, then flew out of the cabinet.

It was a mouse. Rebecca, who was normally the type who would carefully scoop critters up and shoo them outside, was overtaken by a primal fear. Already highly adrenalized, Rebecca reacted instinctively. She brought the wrench down on the mouse, killing it instantly. As she stood staring at its lifeless body in disbelief, she wondered if this was it. *You will cause the death of someone else.* Could it be a mouse?

No time to even get rid of the body. Rebecca had a serious situation going on. She ran into the bathroom with the wrench and hurried over to the tub. The water was already leaking over the edge. Rebecca swiped every sweet-smelling designer towel from the shelves and spread them on the floor to absorb the oncoming flood. She grasped the wrench and attacked the knobs with everything she had. From the living room, her cell phone began to ring. Her hand kept slipping, forcing her to constantly readjust, but finally she was able to get a tiny bit of movement out of one knob. The water decreased, although it did not stop, and not only was her entire front wet, but so were most of the towels protecting the floor. She could feel the water swishing around her ankles. Even if it stopped now, it was already a disaster. Bubbles lay atop the surface of the towels like alien creatures dropping in to check out the landscape. Rebecca let out a loud yell as she took the wrench and whacked the knobs as hard as she could. She drew her hand back for another blow and knocked over the bubble bath. It flew out of the rack, landed on the one spot of tile not protected by the towels, and smashed apart, splattering shards of glass and amber liquid far and wide. She really wanted to hit something now, but she still had the damn knobs to deal with. *Please God, please God, please God, I'll do anything*.

Her phone was ringing again. With the panic of a woman lifting a car off her trapped children, Rebecca went after the knobs for the zillionth time. The left one began to scream, then finally she felt it move, and then it was shut off. By the time she got the other knob to turn as well, Rebecca felt as though she'd been battered in a storm at sea.

There was an inch of water on the floor and all the towels were soaked. The doorbell rang. Obviously someone had heard the pounding, and the smashing, and her screams. Her nightgown was still in her bedroom, and she couldn't wrap a towel around herself because they were all soaked. Rebecca swiped the robe off the back of the door and put it on. It was way too small for her. She tried adjusting the tie, but instead it flicked out like a whip and caught the tip of the wine bottle. Rebecca lunged for the bottle, but as she grabbed it, it slipped out, splashing wine on Mae Lin's beautiful white robe. Then the flaming tree of candles tipped over. Orange flames licked at the creamy white tiles. "You've got to be kidding me!" Rebecca said aloud. She lunged for the wet towels and soon smothered the fire, but long black scorch marks streaked the tiles and the towels, candle wax lay in wet clumps all over the floor, and a burning smell lingered. *To hell with it*.

Rebecca drank straight out of the bottle as she headed for the door. She was about to call out *Who is it?* when she heard the sound of a key in the lock and the door began to open. Rebecca was too shocked to move. Even more so when a gorgeous petite Asian woman with long wavy hair and eyelashes that could wink at you from a football field away burst in. She wasn't alone. Behind her was Grant Dodge.

Rebecca knew she should say something, but she was too stunned to move. Mae Lin took it all in with a series of quick glances.

"Oh my God," she said. "What's burning? Why is there water on my floor?"

Rebecca glanced down. Water from the bathroom was winding its way out into the living room, spreading like a river.

"Mae Lin? I'm Rebecca." She offered her hand for a shake. The woman ignored her and stormed into the bathroom.

"My towels! The floor!" She noticed everything in rapid succession. The wine, the candles, the standing water, the full tub. But the worst was the broken bottle of bubble bath. Mae Lin swiped up the dragonfly lid and screamed, "This was the last gift my mother ever gave me!"

"Oh my God," Rebecca said. "I'm sorry! I'm sorry!"

"Before she *died*," Mae Lin said, in case Rebecca hadn't quite grasped this.

Rebecca launched into a rambling explanation. She'd never taken a bath in here before, the knobs were stuck, she had to get a wrench, she had to kill a mouse. Rebecca didn't think Mae Lin was listening until she mentioned the little rodent.

"A mouse?" Her eyes were huge saucers, her mouth open. Then she ran for the kitchen. Rebecca, who hadn't dared look at Grant up until now, slowly lifted her eyes. He was standing in the doorway to the bathroom, watching her. She thought she was going to cry.

"Yikes," he said. Then he gave her a little wink. "She'll calm down."

"Everything happened just the way I said."

"I had no idea that you were still here, that you took the apartment—" They were interrupted by a piercing scream. Rebecca and Grant ran into the kitchen. Mae Lin was sitting cross-legged on the kitchen floor, rocking the dead mouse in the palm of her delicate hands.

"You probably shouldn't be touching that," Rebecca said.

"That?" Mae Lin shrieked. "*That* has a name!"

Please tell me it isn't Mickey.

"Louis," Mae Lin cried. "You killed Louis!"

"It—*he*—startled me. I just reacted."

"You murdered him. You murdered Louis Armstrong."

"Mae Lin, enough," Grant said.

Mae Lin gracefully uncurled her pretty legs and stood. She shoved the mouse at Grant. "I painted his nails," she said. "Do you see?"

Rebecca leaned in. Sure enough, there was a spot of red on his little toenails.

"Mae Lin, please. Why don't you put Louis on the balcony for now, and I'll pour you a drink." To Rebecca's astonishment, Mae Lin followed Grant's suggestion, although she did so while raving out loud about the dangers of renting your apartment to a total psycho off the street.

"She's not a psycho off the street . . ." Grant said. "Exactly. Rebecca and I go way back."

"Say what?" Mae Lin said.

"Grant is the one who gave me your phone number."

Mae Lin gave Grant what could only be described as a death stare before turning back to Rebecca. "I don't care if you were raised by Mother-freaking-Teresa and Elvis is your best friend. I want you out."

"What are you even doing here? Why didn't you tell me you were coming home early?" Rebecca was hardly in a position to be defensive, but she couldn't help it.

"I've been calling the house for days and days and days," Mae Lin said. She hung her head to the side as if she couldn't make the effort to keep it up.

"My cell?" Rebecca said.

"No, the home phone," Mae Lin said.

"I wouldn't answer your phone," Rebecca said.

"Oh, but you'll destroy the rest of my home and murder my beloved pets?"

Rebecca glanced around before answering, wondering what other pets were in store. Grant handed Mae Lin a glass of Scotch.

"More wine?" he asked Rebecca with a glance at her robe.

"Is that my robe?" Mae Lin screeched. "With wine stains?"

Mae Lin stepped uncomfortably close to Rebecca and stuck out her neck. "Here," she said, pointing to it. "Why don't you just slit it and get it over with?"

"I'll change instead," Rebecca said. She ran into the bedroom and slammed the door.

"I'd say change in the bathroom," Mae Lin yelled through the door, "but there's no room in there what with Noah and his ark."

Funny.

"Except he's short a mouse!"

Chapter Eleven

Rebecca came out of the room wearing her own nightgown and robe, fully prepared to offer Mae Lin compensation for all the damages. She wasn't quite sure how to make up for Louis or the dead mother's bubble bath, but at least it would be a start. But when she came back out, Mae Lin and Grant seemed to be in an intense conversation on the balcony. That's when Rebecca noticed the luggage by the door. There sat two matching leopard-print suitcases on wheels and a beat-up gym bag. The gym bag must belong to Grant . . . Had he come to spend the night? Were he and Mae Lin lovers? She was certainly beautiful, if you liked your women with a stinging bite. But would Grant have actually done that? Would he have sent her to live with his *girlfriend*?

Well, why not? What did she think? She would come to town and he would fall magically in love with her and there would be no other women in his life? *You had better get a grip*, Rebecca told herself. *You're here for Miles, nothing else.* Besides, she didn't know anything about the man. She didn't back then, and she certainly didn't now. Rebecca quietly stood at the entrance to the balcony until Mae Lin and Grant looked up.

"I can write you a check for damages," Rebecca said. "And leave as soon as I find a new place."

"Make it out to cash," Mae Lin said. "And write 'I'm pathetic and sorry' in the subject line."

"Mae Lin," Grant said.

Mae Lin rolled her eyes, then threw her head back and cackled. "Grant has fought for your honor," she said dramatically. "I've decided to spare your head."

"Thank you?" Rebecca said. She didn't try to hide her sarcasm; she had a little bite in her as well. Besides, Rebecca was the one without a place to live. Mae Lin was supposed to be gone for an entire year.

"Funny," Mae Lin said, sliding her eyes from Grant to Rebecca as if she were the queen and they had both just betrayed her. "I work at Rebecca's and I live with a Rebecca."

"Well, not for long," Rebecca said. "Live, that is. I'll start looking for a place tomorrow."

Mae Lin fluttered her eyelashes dramatically and threw out her arms. "I told you I'd spare your head. What more do you want?"

"You'll have to excuse Mae Lin," Grant said. "It seems she left her heart in San Francisco."

With those words, Mae Lin was off again, ranting about some scumbag music club producer who, Rebecca gathered, was behind Mae Lin's early departure.

"He didn't even want us to *drink* on the *job*. I'm like, *hello*! I'm a *singer*. In a *nightclub*!"

Rebecca suppressed a little smile. Mae Lin was stressing about every third word in her sentences and bouncing her pretty head when she spoke. She sounded part drill sergeant, part cheerleader, and of course a lot diva nightclub singer. Rebecca was actually starting to like her. From a distance. As if she were a tiger in a zoo. Suddenly, Rebecca felt someone's gaze on her. When she looked over, Grant was openly staring at her. She quickly averted her eyes, then regretted it.

She didn't want him to think she was nervous around him. She didn't want him to see her cheeks heat up.

"Any-har-har," Mae Lin said, propelling herself into an upright position, and leaning dramatically over the balcony rail. "You can't leave. I just got *fired*. I'm broke and you signed a sublease agreement."

Actually, Rebecca hadn't signed a thing. They talked about it, but Mae Lin never did get around to sending it. Rebecca didn't see the point of mentioning it, at least until she had another place to stay.

"We'll split the rent in three," Mae Lin continued, marching back into the living room. Rebecca reluctantly followed, and Grant quickly joined them.

"Split the rent in three?" Rebecca said.

"Never mind," Grant said.

"Grant is staying here, too!" Mae Lin said. "His girlfriend kicked him out."

This time Rebecca had no qualms about looking at Grant. Jealousy flared in Rebecca. He never mentioned a girlfriend. Then again, she never mentioned a son.

"Mae Lin, I'm not going to stay here," Grant said.

"We already agreed," Mae Lin countered.

"That's before I knew about your roommate," Grant said. Was it Rebecca's imagination, or did he stress the word *roommate*?

Mae Lin turned to Rebecca with a grin that almost devoured her petite face. "Grant had a big scandal with his girlfriend after the grand opening of his club. And I missed it!"

Rebecca didn't remember seeing another woman with Grant at the club. Then again, she was kind of busy falling over the balcony and into his arms.

"She doesn't want to hear this," Grant said.

"Oh, but I do," Rebecca said. She flopped down on the couch, crossed her legs, and smiled at Grant before turning her attention back to Mae Lin.

"A woman crashed through the balcony and into his

arms," Mae Lin said, throwing both her hands over her heart and cocking her head like an old-fashioned damsel in distress.

"Wow," Rebecca said. "It was a good thing he was there."

"That's not the wow part," Mae Lin said. "It wasn't just any woman. It was the love of his life."

"Mae Lin!" Grant said.

"Like a ghost from the past, *whoosh*, into his arms. Later his girlfriend, who couldn't attend opening night because she was too busy—"

"She was dancing," Grant said. "She's a ballet dancer."

Terrific, Rebecca thought. *A ballet dancer. Must be very flexible.*

"Later his girlfriend heard Grant talking to his best friend. Telling him how he knew the woman who fell on him. She was the one that got away. The woman of his dreams! The one who took his virginity. The best sex he ever had!" Mae Lin hit Grant playfully on the shoulder. "Some people just don't know when to shut up, right, Rebecca?"

"You've got that right," Rebecca said.

"I'm exhausted," Mae Lin said. She got up and grabbed a liquor bottle from her cabinet. "I'm going to bed."

Rebecca was just about to do the same: shut herself in the bedroom and away from Grant. The love of his life? Did he really say it? Did he really mean it? He certainly didn't look comfortable now, standing by the door with his hands shoved in his pockets, softly kicking his duffel bag. But before Rebecca could escape, Mae Lin sprinted into her bedroom, yelling, "My bed, my bed, my bed, my bed. How I've missed you so." She jumped on it and spread out like she was making snow angels.

Rebecca got up from the couch and stood in the doorway of Mae Lin's bedroom, not sure what to do. Was Mae Lin really going to sleep in the bed that Rebecca had been sleeping in? Mae Lin lifted her head. "There are pillows and blankets in the closet out there. Shut the door! And be quiet out there!"

Rebecca shut the door and turned to Grant. He was still kicking his duffel bag. "Quiet as a mouse," he said, looking at Rebecca.

The comment took her by surprise and she burst out laughing. Grant stopped kicking his bag and grinned. A few moments of silence fell as they considered each other.

"Should I go?" Grant said. "I can sleep at the club."

The living room had two sofas facing each other.

"It's late," she said. "I don't mind."

She went to the closet, grabbed sheets and blankets, and pretended the father of her son wasn't standing just a few feet away. He hurried over to help her carry them to the couches, and Rebecca was surprised when he began making them up. A man who makes his own bed. He could have taught their son a thing or two. As much as she loved Miles, even she had to admit he was one of the messiest kids she'd ever seen. He was perfectly happy to coexist with clutter. As she watched Grant tuck the sheets into the edges of the sofa, she realized he didn't get that from his father. What traits were just Miles's? Or did Grant come from a long line of messy men and it just skipped a generation? It wasn't just time with his paternal family that she'd robbed Miles of, it was vital information. What about health? Didn't he have a right to know all the risks and benefits of being a Dodge? Of course he did.

"Grant," Rebecca started to say.

"I owe you an apology," Grant interrupted. "I overreacted that day."

"You think?" Rebecca said. She hadn't meant to sound so harsh, but it just flew out of her mouth.

Instead of taking offense, Grant just laughed. It was a nice, deep laugh. "We had an incident—actually an ordeal— with Megan last year. She got involved with an older boy."

"You mentioned it," Rebecca said.

"I don't want to go into all the details right now, but it was quite honestly the worst year of my life."

"I'm so sorry."

"When I found out you weren't much older at the time we . . . than Megan . . . the things I said about that boy . . . the hatred . . . the minute you said you were sixteen, I just— locked up. I was just like that asshole kid that wouldn't leave Megan alone."

Rebecca crossed over to Grant but stopped short of touching him. "No, you weren't," she said. "I was the seducer."

Grant chuckled again. "You weren't exactly shy," he agreed.

"A hundred horses couldn't have stopped me," Rebecca said. Silence fell as they stared at each other. The only light coming into the room was provided by outside streetlights. She was suddenly very aware of her nightgown, and his eyes on her body.

"You are so beautiful," he said. "It's astonishing."

This time it was Rebecca's turn to laugh.

"I sound melodramatic, do I?" Grant said.

"A bit."

"It's just that I've imagined this— -seeing you again—but I always figured—I mean, it was likely that—"

"I was old, fat, and bald?"

"Bald? Uh—maybe the first two, but not bald."

"Right. That was how I imagined you." This time they both laughed. "Sometimes I pictured you homeless, too. Playing your trumpet for booze."

"That's not far from the truth."

"Don't be modest. You're the owner of a hot new club."

"That experienced a near tragedy on opening night. And something of a miracle, too," he added shyly.

"That was entirely my fault. And your waitress's. She ignored the rope."

"For some reason she thought you were Megan's mom," Grant said. "She kept saying she couldn't turn away the mother of my child."

This was it. This was her opening. "I am—" Rebecca started to say. But she never got the chance to finish. Grant was in front of her, reaching for her, and he planted his lips on hers before she could say another word. Slowly, she yielded to him. Desire crashing over her like a powerful wave, she clung to him as their kiss deepened. Just as suddenly, Grant pulled away.

"Oh God," he said. "I shouldn't have."

"It's okay," Rebecca said. "I feel the same—"

"I have a girlfriend," he said.

"I have a son," Rebecca said. She lay on the couch and pulled the covers around her. She was suddenly furious, but she didn't want to show it. Right. A ballerina girlfriend— how quickly she forgot. What was he doing kissing her then? Getting her all hot and bothered and then making her sleep a few feet from him? It was downright cruel. In the morning, either Grant would be gone or she would.

Grant still hovered over her. "Married? Boyfriend?"

"Not for a long time," Rebecca finally said.

"How is that possible?" Grant asked.

Rebecca laughed. "I guess I've been cursed." She had been joking, but as soon as the words were out of her mouth, she thought of the high priestess. *If you kiss before midnight . . .*

"Do you believe in such things?" He sounded kind but cynical.

"Don't you?" she asked. Rebecca sat up. Grant slowly sat down on his sofa but leaned forward as if to bridge the gap between them. How could he forget that night? How could he forget everything that followed because they dared to flaunt—

Oh. Because he didn't realize everything that resulted from that night. Except that he lost her. Or did he just assume they would part ways?

The love of your life, Mae Lin had teased. She had meant something to him—even if he tried to deny it, she knew it was the truth.

"You named your club Rebecca," she said softly.

"Hold off on that for a second," Grant said. "Do you mind explaining all this to me?"

Rebecca fiddled with a loose thread on her blanket and cut off all eye contact. "Explain all what?"

"Why are you here? Is it just some kind of crazy coincidence?"

"You gave me Mae Lin's number—"

"I mean here in New Orleans. In my club opening night. Was it just coincidence?"

Rebecca dropped the blanket and sat up straight. "Not exactly."

Grant came over to her couch and knelt beside it. "Go on."

"I've always wondered about you."

"Have you?" They were having it. They were having the conversation. But Rebecca wasn't ready for the conversation. She hadn't practiced it. She was exhausted. She was off guard. Mae Lin wasn't supposed to be here, let alone Grant. She didn't have to let him control this conversation. They could have it at her leisure when she looked refreshed and she knew what the hell was going to come out of her mouth.

And she wasn't going to flatter him, either. She wasn't going to tell him that she thought of him practically every second of every day, especially when she looked at Miles.

"I originally just came here for a weekend getaway—"

"That almost got you killed."

"Until you and your bodyguards saved me."

"We aim to please."

"And then you gave me Mae Lin's number, and next thing I knew I saw a 'For Rent' sign on a little shop—and even my son said—"

"Your son said?"

Hearing the word *son* out of his mouth was too much. *Your son. Our son. Say it. Say it!* Why couldn't she just say it?

"Are you okay?" Grant brought his hand up and wiped away a tear rolling down her cheek. Then he slowly began to caress her cheek. It felt as if it were on fire, and maybe he felt it, too, because he suddenly dropped his hand and shifted away from her. "Is something wrong? Is your son okay?"

"Yes, yes, he's fine. It's just . . . I love him so much, you know?"

"Of course, of course."

Rebecca could hear the kitchen clock ticking, only it seemed as if it were an extension of her heartbeat, synched up with the hollow tick of the second hand.

"How old is he? What's his name?"

"Miles. I never married his father—"

"Miles," Grant said. "Nice name." They looked at each other for several seconds. "How old is—"

An obnoxious cell phone song interrupted them. They both looked at Grant's gym bag.

"That's my . . ." Grant said.

"Ballerina?" Rebecca said.

"Yeah," Grant said.

"You should get that."

"I probably should. If I don't—she might *escalate*."

Rebecca laughed; she couldn't help it. Was he doomed to be with feisty women? Grant gave her a sheepish look and took his phone call out on the balcony. Rebecca exhaled, lay down, and shut her eyes. So close. Maybe it was for the best. At least Grant knew that Miles existed. He caught on to the "jazz" name. He knew she never married the father of her son. And she had been just about to tell Grant how old her son was. *Their son*. It should have been the last piece he needed to complete the puzzle. All these years and nothing had changed. She was still a coward, still so afraid to face up to what she'd done. *Next time*, she told herself as she drifted off to sleep. *There's always next time*.

Chapter Twelve

Rebecca stood in her shop and tried to concentrate on her inventory list. It was a little difficult with Mae Lin bouncing around. She couldn't believe three weeks had passed since Mae Lin burst onto the scene. But currently it wasn't so much Mae Lin's frenetic energy that was distracting her; instead it was that thing in her hand. Mae Lin had had Louis Armstrong stuffed.

"I'm glad you killed him," she had announced one day, whipping him out of her pocket and holding him up. "Now we'll be together forever." And every day Mae Lin made a point of displaying him in Rebecca's presence.

At first Rebecca wondered if Mae Lin was mentally disturbed; now she just concluded that Mae Lin lived to be outrageous and wore her eccentricity like a coat that was too big in the sleeves. Besides the mouse, Mae Lin was wound up about Mardi Gras. It was weeks before the big day, but the streets were already starting to crackle with anticipation. Every once in a while a partial float would go by, and on the sidewalks one would increasingly see bits of feathers, beads, and pieces of silk flapping in the warm breeze. Business picked up as tourists began arriving, filling the streets, the restaurants, and the shops, as one by one hotels and inns turned their signs to NO VACANCY.

Some of those tourists found their way to Rebecca's Renditions. Mae Lin, it turned out, in addition to rodents, was obsessed with jewelry, and she began recommending the shop to her friends. Grant wasn't one of them. He left the apartment the day after his return with Mae Lin and he hadn't been back since. Nor had he called.

Rebecca couldn't believe how much it stung. It brought back bad memories of waiting for his call. And this time there was no excuse: he knew exactly where to find her. After that kiss—how could he just cut her off like that? And although she didn't know for sure, she assumed Grant simply went back to his girlfriend. And she wasn't the only one who missed Grant. Mae Lin, too, began to pout about his absence. So one day, while painting her toenails with a Q-tip, Mae Lin announced that they were going to throw the Mardi Gras party of the century.

It was only a few days after the announcement of the party when it happened. Rebecca and Mae Lin were eating takeout in the living room—breaded Creole crab cakes on a stick, which Mae Lin had taken to calling "crab dogs"—when Mae Lin glanced up at the fireplace mantel and screeched. Before Rebecca could even react, Mae Lin flew across the room and swiped up Miles's portrait. Rebecca had placed it on the mantel within hours of moving in, and had completely forgotten to remove it after Mae Lin's return to the nest. Hopefully, Mae Lin wouldn't ask too many questions. Rebecca just had to play it cool. Rebecca waited for Mae Lin to say how handsome Miles was. Everyone did.

"He looks so young here," Mae Lin said. "Where did you get this?" Rebecca's thoughts jammed. Had she even mentioned Miles to Mae Lin? No, she hadn't. Mae Lin thrived on gossip and so Rebecca put off mentioning him.

"He sent it to me," Rebecca said.

"What is this—high school?"

"First year of college."

"I didn't know Grant went to college."

"He didn't—"

"You just said he did."

"That's not Grant." Rebecca didn't like Mae Lin's fingers all over Miles's face. She approached and held her hand out for the picture. Instead Mae Lin brought it so close to her face, Rebecca thought she was going to kiss it.

"You are kidding me."

"I have a lot more pictures, from birth on, if you don't believe me," Rebecca said. She'd brought the best photos she had of Miles, partly because she knew how much she would miss him, but mostly because she wanted to share them with Grant. Mae Lin stopped studying the picture and started studying Rebecca instead. Rebecca swiped the picture out of her hands.

"What's his name?"

"Miles."

"As in . . . Miles Davis?"

Rebecca gave a small smile. Only musicians picked up on it. "As in."

"How old were you when he was born?"

Rebecca sat in the easy chair next to the couch and curled up, still clutching the picture.

Mac Lin sat across from her on the couch and began to nibble on another crab dog, all the while staring at Rebecca. "Very handsome boy," she said when Rebecca didn't answer her question.

"Thank you," Rebecca said. "He's a good kid, too."

"Musical?"

"Plays the trumpet."

"Hmmm. And you literally crashed Grant's opening."

"Didn't quite plan it that way."

"His club is named Rebecca."

A tiny thrill ran through Rebecca. Just picturing her name on the sign, with a strand of her hair and a swipe of the color blue she'd worn that night, made her swell with passion. Shoot. The crab dogs were gone. Now Mae Lin would have nothing to keep her mouth occupied.

"I can't believe he didn't tell me he has a son!"

"Mae Lin—"

"I tell him everything. How dare you both play me! Mae Lin is nobody's fool! I'm going to let him have it. I could've been Auntie Mae. I would've sent the kid Christmas cards—" Mae Lin swiped up her cell phone.

"Please," Rebecca said. "Put it down."

"Grant and I are like this!" Mae Lin crossed her index and middle fingers together and thrust them out. "He can't get away with this doozy of a secret. I even told him about giving that scumbag producer a blow job in the back of the Korean deli." Mae Lin furiously began to dial.

"End it," Rebecca said. "Now."

"Grant," Mae Lin said. It didn't sound like she had reached a recording. "My old buddy. You are my buddy, aren't you?"

"He doesn't know." Rebecca had to shout it, but there was no other choice. It worked. Mae Lin's eyes tripled in size and her jaw dropped open in her typical dramatic fashion.

"I'm just calling to see if you're coming to my Mardi Gras party, darling. If you don't, I'm going to hunt you down and strangle you, then have my way with your dead body." She winked at Rebecca. Rebecca couldn't believe she was actually going to give that comment a thumbs-up, but she did anyway. "Great," Mae Lin finished. "Bring the ballerina if you want." At this Mae Lin looked at Rebecca and shrugged. "See you then." She clicked off and then tossed the phone on the couch like it was infected. "Oh my God," she said, putting her hands on her heart. "I just lied to Grant Dodge. Oh my God, oh my God, oh my God."

"I'm going to tell him. That's why I came. It's just . . . every time I try, something gets in the way."

"He's my friend. I can't keep something like this from him. And I won't."

"It's not your secret to tell."

"It's not yours to keep! That man would've been there for him. In every way."

Rebecca couldn't take it. She couldn't take Mae Lin of all people hitting her over the head with what she already knew, what she'd been torturing herself about for the past two decades.

"Don't you think I know that? You have no idea what it's been like. What a secret like this does to a person. I came here to tell him. So just back off and give me a chance. All right?"

Mae Lin took a few steps back. "Whoa," she said, holding up her hands.

"I was sixteen," Rebecca said, still explaining. "My father was on a rampage. If he had tracked Grant down, it wouldn't have been pretty."

"You've been out of your father's house for a long time," Mae Lin pointed out.

Rebecca didn't like how hard Mae Lin stressed *long*. She drew it out like it was one of her songs. "His phone number was smudged. I couldn't read it. I didn't have Facebook."

"Hmmm."

"He didn't call me, either. Not once. I gave him my name, my number—maybe he lost it, too, I don't know. Maybe the high priestess really did curse us."

"The high priestess?"

"Yes. She's a psychic. She lives and works out of—"

"The Voodoo House."

"You've heard of her." Rebecca wasn't surprised. There didn't seem to be a soul in town who didn't know the old witch.

"She's a total nutter," Mae Lin said, whipping the mouse out of her pocket. "Isn't she, Louis?" She brought the mouse up to her nose and went cross-eyed staring at him.

"I saw her again when I came to town. Tried to make things right. But she just cursed me all over again. I'm afraid if I tell Grant about Miles, it's going to set something awful in motion—"

"God, take a chill pill. You're hyperventilating all over my easy chair."

"She said I'd find the love I've been seeking, but I would cause the death of someone else!"

Mae Lin gasped and looked at Louis. Then she fixed her eyes on Rebecca. "Mardi Gras party. You'll tell him then."

"No, it has to be somewhere private—"

"You'll tell him then, or *we* will," Mae Lin said, moving Louis up and down so that it appeared he was nodding emphatically. She kept it up until Rebecca slowly nodded in agreement. Then, like a drug addict in need of a fix, Mae Lin began scouring the coffee table. "Shit," she said. "We're out of crab dogs."

Chapter Thirteen

It was indeed a party. The place pulsed with musicians who were so lively and animated—even before the impromptu jam sessions began—that for a few blissful seconds Rebecca simply leaned against the wall in the living room and took it all in. *Miles would have loved this*. His picture was gone from the mantel, tucked safely under Rebecca's pillow, but Mae Lin's ultimatum stalked Rebecca like a deranged shadow.

As Mae Lin had instructed—i.e., ordered—everyone was dressed as outlandishly as possible. Guests were highly feathered and sequined, and in some cases glowing neon. Women—and a few men—bared cleavage and displayed pierced belly buttons above shiny belt buckles. They wrapped themselves in leather and wore lots of war paint. One man was dressed as a walking float. The noise from the thrilling mob and colorful parade outside filtered in, as if it were one and the same. Outside, as in, people were drinking and flashing their breasts in exchange for beads—again, the men as well as the women. They were having an all-around juvenile good time.

Grant had yet to arrive. But just as Rebecca was thinking what a bullet she had dodged, the front door opened and in he walked. He was dressed like a normal human being in jeans and a dark blue shirt that set off his eyes, topped with a leather jacket that instantly made Rebecca want to make love to him on a motorcycle. God, he was a beautiful man. Rebecca immediately regretted dressing like a peacock. Her dark hair, piled loosely on top of her head, sprouted feathers. Her eyes were rimmed with black and topped off with shimmering purple and green eye shadow. She wore a skintight blue-and-green dress that showed so much cleavage she was getting beads by the bucketful. And, last but not least, she wore the peacock's proud tail. A bit of a lie, she supposed, when in reality it was the male peacock who flashed prettily. Mating rituals. In animal, as in human, nothing said *mount me* like flashing a little tail.

Not to be outdone, Mae Lin was dressed in a ruffled red dress with thigh-high white boots and silver sparkly eyelashes. Within seconds of his coming through the door, Mae Lin jumped on Grant, wrapping her hands around his neck and her pretty legs around his waist, forcing him to hold her. Yet, even as he did, it was Rebecca he stared at. She felt the familiar jolt of electricity thrum through her. It took forever for her to even notice the woman next to him. Tall and pretty and blond, she was dressed simply: high heels, blue jeans, and a red T-shirt that read SAXOPHONE PLAYERS BLOW. She beat Rebecca's peacock by a million Miles. Rebecca wanted to run from the room, perhaps toss herself off the balcony, but with the streets so jammed, escape was nearly impossible. Although being crushed by a drunken mob was starting to sound pretty darn good to Rebecca.

The second Mae Lin jumped off of Grant, she grabbed the blond goddess by the hand and began pulling her away. When she passed by Rebecca, she leaned in and said in a loud whisper, "Tell him." And then they were gone. Rebecca looked up to find that Grant, too, was being taken away, onto the balcony by a group of guys. Rebecca took a deep breath and followed.

Grant was with a group of four other men. They made room for her, and immediately teased her about her peacock feathers. Rebecca flirted with all of them, all the while aware of Grant's eyes on her.

"What do you think?" one of the men said with a nod to the street festivities below.

"It's amazing," Rebecca said. It truly was. Below, revelers sported greenish-yellow glow-sticks. Some had wrapped them around their necks or wrists; others held them aloft like batons. As the night sky began to make its entrance, people's features disappeared and the glow-sticks took on a life of their own, bobbing up and down the street like ghostly conductors at a night symphony. Laughter and cheers and music filled the smoky, dusky air.

"Want more beads?" one of the men said with a wolfish grin. "All it would take is a bit of flash to the boys below and you'll be covered in 'em."

Rebecca laughed. "I'm weighed down as it is, and I didn't flash a soul." *Except for Grant, a long time ago in a cemetery not so far, far away.* She'd better stop thinking about it. Grant hadn't taken his eyes off her. What if he could tell what she was thinking?

"Give her time," a third said. "She'll come around."

"Time? Hell. Give her another drink." Now all but one in the circle of five men had spoken to her. All except Grant. He had yet to say a word, but she felt as if they'd spoken volumes. Was this love? A connection that needed no words? Or was she just slightly feverish from her first Mardi Gras?

Grant was subtle about it, but he made his way over until he was standing directly beside her. When he leaned in to talk to her, he placed his hand on the small of her back. She wanted to freeze the moment in time, stand there like that for a thousand nights.

"We'll have to clear off the balcony in an hour or so," he whispered in her ear. "Those who are left tend to get sick or start fighting. It's not pretty."

It was settled: she was unhinged. You had to be when even that comment turned you on.

"It's her first Mardi Gras," another of the men said. "Let her have the full experience."

"Speaking of experiences," the oldest one, a short black man with white hair and an ample belly where he liked to rest his hands, said, "Joe isn't going to get the likes of this in his fancy college." The men all laughed.

"We were just talking about a buddy of ours," Grant said. "His kid just got into Juilliard."

College. Kid. Rebecca felt ill. Soon she was going to be the one getting sick, and it wouldn't be from drink. "That's fabulous," she said. The men exchanged strained smiles around the semicircle. "Isn't it?"

"Not if he wants to be a real musician," said a middle-aged man with a faded red beard.

"Hear, hear," the older black man said.

"What?" Rebecca said. "You can't be a real musician if you go to college?"

"Those who do, do," the black man said. "Those who can't, teach."

"We're not talking about teachers, we're talking about students," Rebecca said. She sounded defensive, but she couldn't help it. The sacrifices she'd made to get Miles into college. Selling her house, no less. Not that she would ever make it seem like a big deal to her son. She was so proud of him. And he loved it. Didn't he? "College is a wonderful experience." She hoped she sounded convincing. She hadn't gone to college, so she was striking out in the dark. "It's a supportive environment where you have a network of people with the same interests, talented teachers, music competitions—"

"Real musicians play," Red Beard said. "That's all."

"We're not saying kids shouldn't go to college," Grant said in a soothing voice.

His curiosity was piqued. She'd better be careful.

"Not one of us has a college degree," the older man said. "And we can outplay any Harvard—"

"Juilliard," Grant interrupted good-naturedly.

"Juilliard," the man said, over-pronouncing it in a jazz-like singing voice. All the men laughed. "We can outplay any Juilliard graduate any day."

"Maybe it's just jazz," Grant tried to explain to Rebecca. "It lends itself to more of a freewheeling lifestyle."

"I see," Rebecca said. She was suddenly relieved Miles wasn't here, and not for the most obvious reason. She wouldn't have wanted these men influencing him. Because at first Miles hadn't wanted to go to college. He wanted to take his trumpet and travel. Europe, New York, New Orleans. It absolutely terrified Rebecca. She couldn't imagine never knowing where he was, if he was okay, if he was making enough for a decent meal, if he had a place to sleep. She had never been a bully like her parent; thanks to her father, she didn't want to be *that guy*. She didn't want to parent out of fear; she didn't want to squash her only child's dreams. But she had lost it when Miles floated the idea. She just lost it.

She couldn't eat or sleep and she began crying frequently. Finally, she begged him—she out-and-out begged Miles—to go to college for at least one year. She said if he put in a year and still wanted to run off and see the world, he would have her blessing. She ordered every college catalogue from schools with good music programs and began placing them in his path: his bed, the dining room table, even the bathroom sink once, when he was in the shower. The day he picked one and applied was the happiest day of her life. The day he was accepted was the second.

Miles wasn't a pushover by any means, but he had a soft spot for his mother. He knew what she'd given up to have him, and he hated seeing her upset. It shamed her now, her manipulations, but she'd done the right thing, hadn't she? Or had she crushed his dream?

College, a waste! They couldn't really believe that, could

they? She was tired of feeling as if she'd always made the wrong decisions. This couldn't be one of them, it just couldn't. The Big Easy. Why didn't they just call it the Big Lazy?

"Surely there are plenty of famous musicians who went to college," Rebecca said.

"Of course," Grant said quickly. He looked at her with concern—he and Miles were so alike. "We're just a bunch of old dogs," he added with a wink. "Don't mind us."

"Soul comes from here," the older man said, stepping closer to Rebecca. He touched his gut. "And here," he said. He touched his heart. "Nothing good ever came from just using this." Last touch was to his head.

"Or this," another said, grabbing his crotch. Laughter broke the tension, and the mood lifted.

"Who needs anything?" Grant said. "Another drink? Something to eat? I think I saw pigs in a blanket—"

"They're crab dogs," Rebecca said.

Grant raised his eyebrows. Rebecca laughed. They were having a good time now. She should let it go.

"I just think you can't overestimate a college education—" she started to say.

Red Beard didn't even let her finish. He even gave her the hand. "If rich folks need something to waste their money on, who are we—"

"Rich? You really think most parents who send their children to college are rich?" *Stop, Rebecca, just stop*.

"Of course not," Grant said.

"Some people sacrifice everything they have."

"Not too smart, are they?" Red Beard continued.

"Joe," Grant said. His tone carried a warning.

"I can't believe you people," Rebecca said.

"What people?" said Joe—or Red Beard, as Rebecca was always going to call him.

"Musicians, New Orleaners—take your pick. I'm—"

"Lady. You want to send your kid to college, send your kid to college. We're talking about musicians. We learn by jamming, man. Jesus. Someone's got her feathers all in a ruffle."

Grant gently touched her on the arm. "Rebecca," he said softly, "don't be upset. We're harmless, I swear."

Before she could answer, Mae Lin popped into the group. She hip-bumped Rebecca. "What's up, lady? We can hear you inside even with a drummer and two guitarists jamming." Mae Lin laughed and Rebecca tried to smile, but she couldn't believe it. Mae Lin telling her she was loud? The world was upside down.

"Maybe this will calm you down," Mae Lin continued. She passed Rebecca a joint. Rebecca hesitated, then, what the heck. It was Mardi Gras. It was dressing up, and letting your hair down, and flashing them if you had them. Not lecturing aging musicians. She inhaled, held it in, then slowly let it out. Before she could take another drag, Grant took it out of her hand and gave it back to Mae Lin along with a dirty look. What was the big deal? Didn't all musicians smoke a little weed?

As if reading her mind, Grant leaned in and once again whispered into her ear. "Mae Lin's been known to lace it," he said.

Startled, Rebecca just nodded as if she totally understood. But given that was only her second drag of pot ever, and she had never remotely done any other drugs, she was clueless. Laced? With what? Was one drag going to do her damage? Should she be concerned here, or was the pot just making her paranoid?

"So," Mae Lin said. "Have you told him?"

Rebecca was floored. How could she say that right in front of Grant? "Mae Lin," she said. She had already come across as a shrew, and she didn't want to start a fight with Mae Lin on top of it. Besides, Mae Lin had been smoking a few of her own joints and she was looking at Rebecca as if Rebecca were a piñata and it was Mae Lin's turn at bat.

"It's a yes or no question," Mae Lin said.

"No," Rebecca said as quickly as possible. "Not yet."

Mae Lin shook her finger at Rebecca and made a tsk-tsk sound.

Grant took Rebecca's arm and gave her a reassuring squeeze. "Come on," he said. Arm in arm they started for the living room. There they ran smack into the blond goddess. She didn't look happy. She stood directly in their path, scowling.

"Careful," Mae Lin said, coming up behind them. "You already took a drag. That stuff is a truth-teller. And it's Mardi Gras. Fat Tuesday, baby. Also known as Shrove Tuesday from the word *shrive*, which means to *confess*."

Rebecca felt the room closing in on her. Everywhere she looked there were bodies. Standing, sitting, kneeling, lying down, doing headstands against the wall. The vibe was still lively, but slightly mellower as a group gathered around several musicians playing a set that would last well into the next morning.

"I want to go," the blonde said. "Now."

"So go," Mae Lin said. "There's the door." For a split second Rebecca liked Mae Lin again. Loved her even. The blonde turned with a huff and headed for the door.

"Grant," Rebecca said. "Before you go—"

"Go? Are you trying to get rid of me?"

"Your girlfriend," Rebecca said, pointing at the retreating blonde.

Grant laughed. "Never met her," he said. "That's not my ex."

"Oh," Rebecca said. Then, insert lightbulb, screw in. "Ex?"

"Yes," Grant said. "It's over. I moved into the club. Not glamorous, I know. And I don't have a college degree. Probably not what you're looking for in a guy."

"Grant—"

He pulled her away from Mae Lin, away from everyone, to a tiny unoccupied space against the wall and drew her to him. "Rebecca," he whispered. "Rebecca, Rebecca, Rebecca,

Rebecca. You're here. You're really here." He traced her lips with his finger. "I want you. I've always wanted you." And then he was leaning in. And then he was kissing her. Their bodies pressed together so tight, a feather couldn't have slipped between them. And then it all started to disappear, all of it, and they were moving in unison, still kissing, heading for Mae Lin's bedroom. And although Rebecca wished there was any other place to go, she had originally been told she could use the bedroom. And she couldn't think of any better use for it. Images flashed through Rebecca's mind—the cemetery, the fat yellow moon, Mae Lin's red feathers. Red feathers. Rebecca pulled away from Grant.

"I'm sorry, I'm sorry," he said. "You're right, not here, not now—"

Mac Lin stood on top of the coffee table with a microphone in her hand. It screeched when she turned it on, and silence descended upon the room. *The one with the red feathers will betray you.* Oh God, why hadn't she seen it?

"Has everyone met my new roomie?" Mae Lin shouted into the microphone. "Rebecca. Rebecca like the club. Rebecca like the mom."

Rebecca turned to Grant. "I have to tell you something."

"Who likes secrets?" Mae Lin belted out.

The guests—they did. They loved secrets. They laughed and clapped and encouraged her. Who didn't love delicious secrets? Tell us!

"Rebecca has a secret. Don't you, Rebecca?" And then Rebecca spotted what was in Mae Lin's hand. She was holding the picture of Miles. And Grant was trying to have a look at it, like everyone else.

Rebecca took her hands and put them on Grant's beautiful face, gently pressing until he looked at her. "Miles," she whispered. "His name is Miles."

Grant was still smiling at her; he was still a man who wanted to love her. "I remember," he said. "Your son."

"Yes," Rebecca said. "My son. And yours. He's your son, too." There was a split second of confusion. The smile faded slowly.

"Miles!" Mae Lin bellowed. "Rebecca and Grant have a son named Miles. Isn't he handsome? Like his father?"

Grant stumbled back. His expression gutted Rebecca. It wasn't anger. It was worse. He looked absolutely terrified. And then he recovered. He moved in on Mae Lin and swiped the picture out of her hands. Tears ran down Rebecca's cheeks as she watched Grant take in the face of his son for the first time. She stepped up to face Grant as her life with Miles flashed before her. Bringing him home from the hospital in a lavender blanket that belonged to her as a baby, feeling the soft, heavy weight of him in her arms. Looking into his big, curious eyes, his little smiling lips. His smell. His coo. His first step, his first word—*mama*. How big that trumpet was in his five-year-old hands, how it all but obscured his face when he played it. Elementary school, high school, he grew up so fast. She wanted it all back. Not for her; for Grant. She wanted to give it all to him. She was a liar. She'd kept father from son.

She couldn't breathe. Tears were running too fast, her throat was starting to close, and she could feel her body shaking. When Grant finally lifted his eyes and looked at her, all she could manage was the barest of whispers.

"I was sixteen," she said. "My father was furious. He threatened to make your life hell. But still. I tried. Your phone number—it was smeared—I couldn't read it. So I waited. But. You never called."

Grant nodded solemnly. Slowly he pulled something out of his pocket. It was a torn and dirty napkin. Rebecca knew what it was immediately. Through the blur, she recognized her scrawl.

"I don't always carry this around," he said. "But I brought it tonight. To show you. Why I never called." Gently he reached up to wipe away the tears still rolling down her cheeks. She grabbed his wrists and held them.

"Every day," she said. "I thought of you every single day. I wanted you to know. I wanted you to be there. Please, don't hate me. I think it would kill me. I really think it would kill me."

Grant lifted her chin with his finger and stared into her eyes. "I could never hate the mother of my child," he said. "Never." Then, still holding the picture, he took her hand. "Let's get out of here," he said.

Rebecca, heart swelling in her chest, held on to Grant's hand. He knew. He was still here. He was still talking to her. He was still touching her. She would follow him anywhere.

Chapter Fourteen

Even though the parade was long over, they found themselves in the middle of a giant mass of still-partying, squirming people. Grant kept a firm grip on her hand, which helped to somewhat lessen Rebecca's fear that they would be crushed to death and buried in a grave of glitter, feathers, and beads. Grant had the framed picture of Miles inside his jacket, and as they maneuvered through the crowd he kept his free hand on it the entire time. When they came to a spot where they literally could not move, Grant pulled Rebecca into him and wrapped his arms around her. Now the picture was sandwiched between them, and Rebecca could feel it against her chest. Music, voices, stomping, and cheers filled their ears. The air smelled smoky and sweet, the heat clung to their skin. There was something else in the air—the unmistakable feel of magic. They were magic together. He gazed into her eyes, and then slowly he came in for another kiss. It reverberated through her entire body. Then suddenly, from behind, they were shoved. Rebecca felt a thump, and then something sharp pierced her chest.

"Let's get out of here," Grant said. He pulled the picture away, then stared at the little drops of blood on the cracked glass. Rebecca looked at her chest, and to her relief, she'd been barely grazed. Grant, too, had been pricked.

You will be crushed. You will draw blood . . .

"Are you okay?" Grant said.

"We have to get out of here," Rebecca replied. "Now." Without further discussion, they began to push their way through the throbbing mass of bodies. From out of nowhere, a hand came toward Rebecca's neck, wrapped around her beads, and yanked them off. She didn't mind the beads, but her locket—she'd been wearing her heart-shaped locket, the first necklace she ever made, the one with petals from the rose Grant gave her —

Your heart will be ripped from your chest—

Grant navigated them through several side streets, and slowly but surely the crowds were less and less. "This way," he said, pulling her down a narrow alleyway. It led to a tiny park surrounded by a black iron fence. In the center was a fountain where two stone cherubs playfully squirted water out of their mouths. Three street lamps illuminated their shenanigans in a soft glow. Rebecca and Grant sank onto a bench and watched shadows play at the base of the fountain. The air was starting to cool, but the last traces of humidity still clung to their skin. Grant set Miles's picture down and touched the spot above Rebecca's breast where the glass had nicked her. His touch sent an electric thrill through her and she could almost hear the cherubs tittering.

"Back there," Grant said with a tilt of his head, "you were clearly frightened."

"The high priestess," Rebecca said. "I saw her a few days ago." Grant's brow furrowed, but he didn't interrupt. "She remembered me, Grant. She remembered *us*."

"I hope you don't believe all that stuff about curses—"

"We've lived it for twenty-one years, haven't we?"

"No," Grant said. "It's just life, Rebecca. You were only sixteen. How else was it going to end?" Grant took both of her hands in his, then kissed each of them.

"But she said things. Things that have come true. You will draw blood. You will be crushed—"

Grant touched the spot on her chest again. "Well, if this is the blood—it's not too scary, is it? Nothing to worry about. And if you need a transfusion, lovely lady, I'm right here." Grant rolled up his sleeve and winked.

"There was more. She said—my heart would be ripped out of my chest. And my locket—my heart-shaped locket, the first necklace I ever made, with petals from the rose you gave me—was just ripped off back there!"

"It's okay, it's okay, it's okay."

"It's not. She said—if we get back together—I'll cause the death of someone."

"Oh, Rebecca. She really got to you, didn't she?" He squeezed her hands tighter. "Listen to me. That woman doesn't have power over life and death and neither do we. You are not cursed. And no offense, but I just found out I have a son. I want to know everything about him. Okay?"

"Okay," Rebecca said. "But be warned. There's nothing I love talking about more than Miles."

"And there's nothing I'd rather hear about."

So, beginning with his birth, Rebecca began to talk. As the stories poured out of her, the moon revealed more and more of itself, until it was a fat, shiny globe against the black sky. And then, somehow, as she talked, the sky began to lighten, and the moon faded to a pale yellow, then just a whisper of white as the sky around it brightened. Neither of them knew how it was possible, but they had been talking about Miles the entire night. By the time the sun peeked over the horizon, Rebecca's voice was hoarse, and they were both exhausted. Grant put his arm around her, then dropped his head.

"You've had to do it all alone," he said. "You had to sell your house. I'm the father. I should have been providing all these years."

Guilt thumped through Rebecca. "It's my fault," she said. "It's all my fault."

Grant put his hands on her shoulders. "Listen to me very carefully," he said. "The past is the past. I don't blame you. I will grieve the years I've lost, but I will never blame you. And more than that, I will rejoice in what I've been given. A second chance with you. A son. Nothing else in this world matters. We're blessed, Rebecca. We're thrice blessed."

Rebecca moved out of Mae Lin's apartment the following morning. It was easy to do when you were living out of a suitcase. She wasn't so much moving out as "fleeing the scene." Rebecca correctly suspected that Mae Lin would be nursing the mother of all Mardi Gras hangovers, and no good-byes would be necessary. They had never become true friends, so Rebecca didn't see the point in talking through her feelings of betrayal. And in a way, she was grateful. Grant knew the truth, and he'd not only taken it remarkably well, he was excited about having a son. Now all she had to do was tell Miles. And the only way to do that was face-to-face.

So Rebecca did the only thing she could at the last minute: she moved into her jewelry shop. Grant wanted her to stay with him at the club, but understood when Rebecca said she wanted to take things slow, do it right this time. There was just enough room behind the counter to roll out a sleeping bag or some such. She would close the shop early today and buy one. Then she'd start the process of looking for a place to stay all over again. If she didn't find a place in a few days, she'd stay at a hotel. She kind of liked the idea of nesting for a few nights in her little shop, and she just wanted some peace and quiet where she could relish every moment of that night with Grant.

Rebecca laughed to herself as she unrolled her new sleeping bag and took the plastic off her new giant pillow. This was living; this was an adventure. She even had a small reading lamp and a paperback thriller. The best part of the evening was when Miles called and told her he booked a ticket; he would be here in three weeks.

Three weeks. She couldn't wait to tell Grant. She was so excited she couldn't fall asleep, and the paperback couldn't hold a candle to her real life. What a change. And for some reason, she couldn't get the high priestess out of her mind. She saw her face every time she closed her eyes. And then, something else took shape. A necklace. Rebecca often created pieces from dreams. But this wasn't a dream—she was awake. And she saw a necklace that she knew was meant for the priestess. It was a fragile gold chain made with a live rose. It would have to be encased in something, preserved forever. Like her locket? No, the rose had to be visible. Somehow she knew this was what she had to do. A peace offering. Would this be enough to cure the curse? It didn't matter; she would do it regardless. Once the decision was made, she fell into a deep and dreamless sleep.

The necklace came together perfectly. It was as if she was guided, as if it was meant to be. She found a beautiful crystal and cut a small hole in the top. Then she crushed several rose petals into tiny specks of blushing dust and poured them into the crystal. Finally she sealed the hole so the petals couldn't escape. It looked like a miniature snow globe raining tiny shards of rose petals. She added some liquid that kept the tiny petals floating in the crystal. It was one of the most beautiful and unique pieces Rebecca had ever made, and even though she suspected she could make a fortune by making more and selling them en masse, she wasn't going to do it. This one was meant only for the priestess. Rebecca was actually looking forward to giving it to her. Was it Grant making her feel this open and loving?

She was in love; that was the secret to everything. Mankind had certainly advanced on every front since crawling out of the sea, but love was still the same primitive force it had always been.

Grant was at her shop the first thing in the morning with powdery doughnuts and coffee. They couldn't stop looking into each other's eyes, and laughing, and gently touching each other wherever and whenever they could. Rebecca loved the expression on Grant's face when she told him that Miles was coming to visit. He picked her up and swung her around the shop. Then, because she was still so full of Miles, she showed him the beautiful card he'd given her for her birthday, the little street scene of the French Quarter. Grant read it, then looked quizzical.

"Are you sure he doesn't know about me?"

"Why would you say that?"

"I assume you read this," he said.

" 'I hope you find everything you're looking for,' " Rebecca said from memory.

Grant handed her the card. "Look closer."

Rebecca read it, then gasped. " 'I hope you find every*one* you're looking for.' " She looked at Grant. "I swear—I thought it said *everything*."

"What do you think now?"

"My mother," Rebecca said softly. "It has to be. She's always felt bad. She must have said something to him. She must have. And still—he never pressured me. He's gentle and protective. Like you."

Grant smiled. "I can't tell you how glad I am to hear that. Is it strange that I'm already proud? I mean, I know I have no right—"

"You have every right," Rebecca said. She kissed him. "You have every right."

"Three weeks," Grant said. "I guess we'll find out then."

Soon they were in each other's arms. She loved smelling his cologne, feeling his heartbeat against her, having his strong arms around her. She felt safe. She felt like she was home. It wasn't long before their soft caresses turned into passion. Then they were all over each other. Lips, hands, bodies, and voices united in soft little moans, as together they fell to the sleeping bag.

Rebecca wondered, very briefly, if they would ever make love in normal places. She couldn't care less. He was undressing her too slowly. She urged him to hurry. He laughed, and then gently pinned her hands above her head to show her he was in control, and he was going to take his time. By the time they were in the space where it was just his skin against hers, he entered her and they found their own rhythm as the city began waking up around them. Magic. It was magic. Afterward, they lay for a long time, just wrapped in each other, just being.

Every step of the way, Rebecca expected something bad to happen. A potted plant to fall on her head. The sky to open up and thunder down. The little box with the red bow to be swiped out of her hands.

When none of the above happened, and she was standing outside the Voodoo Shop, Rebecca then feared that the shop would be closed, or the old woman would be gone, or she would refuse to see her. But the doors were wide-open, just like every other time she'd been there. Rebecca stepped inside.

And there, sitting in a rocking chair in the main room, was the high priestess. She was staring at the door as if waiting for someone, perhaps Rebecca, to walk in.

"You," the high priestess said in a tone that made Rebecca want to turn and flee.

Rebecca took a breath and forced a smile. Then she stepped forward and held out the box.

The priestess stopped rocking. "What is it?" She sounded alarmed.

"A gift," Rebecca said. "For you." Without taking her eyes off the box, the old woman reached out with a trembling hand and petted the top of the box with her fingertips. When she looked up at Rebecca, she had tears in her eyes. Rebecca was so startled she almost dropped the box. And then a wave of shame crashed over her. The high priestess wasn't some kind of witch. She was a lonely old woman. Rebecca bridged the distance between them and knelt down by the rocking chair.

"It's one of a kind," Rebecca said. "Just like you."

With the smile of a child, the priestess took the box in both her hands and held it like a precious baby bird while she stared at it. Then she tore into it with surprising speed, held up the necklace, and gasped upon seeing the crystal with the rose petals. She watched the petals dancing inside. Slowly, she looked at Rebecca.

"It's my anniversary," she said. "How did you know?"

"Your anniversary?"

"My lover. We met this very day. Sixty years ago. He called me his Rose." She clutched the necklace to her chest. "My darling," she said. "My darling, you remembered."

Rebecca gently took the necklace and placed it around the old woman's neck. The high priestess reached out and took her hand. She squeezed it so hard Rebecca knew she'd have marks, but she didn't cry out or pull away. It was as if the woman were holding on for dear life.

"True love lives beyond the grave," the priestess said. "It really and truly does. I'm not alone. I've never been alone." Then she began to chant in a language Rebecca couldn't understand, all the while touching the crystal and rocking faster and faster. Rebecca pulled her hand away and stepped back. Was she having some sort of breakdown? Then just as quickly, the rocking eased up, the chanting stopped, and the high priestess began to quietly hum.

"Go, my child," she said to Rebecca. "You are free."

You are free. It was good news. It was the best news. So then what was this feeling of dread following Rebecca out of the shop? Why did she feel a hundred pounds heavier? The high priestess loved the necklace. She set Rebecca free. The curse had been lifted. Hadn't it? She was with Grant, Miles was on his way, and she certainly hadn't caused the death of anyone. Maybe it wasn't the old woman who'd been keeping Rebecca under a curse. Maybe Rebecca was the one who was cursing herself. She'd been keeping herself a prisoner all these years. A prisoner of her fears, a prisoner of her never-ending guilt. It was over. It was time to shed it all, and live a life without secrets. And that's exactly what she was going to do, starting now. She took out her phone and dialed the number she knew by heart. And although she'd planned on doing this face-to-face, the minute she heard her son's voice, she knew she had to tell him. It was now, or never.

"Miles," she said. "I have something to tell you."

Chapter Fifteen

It was one of the best moments of her life. Watching Miles and Grant on stage together, dual trumpets blaring, playing to each other, bouncing off each other. The father-and-son team had been packing the club every week for the past three months. Soon Miles would be returning to college, and they would have to wait until winter break to play together again. Rebecca watched them, front and center, gripping a tissue in her hands, blubbering through the entire performance like always.

Miles and Grant were alike in so many ways. They even held the trumpet with the exact same stance, fingers moving in unison, elbows relaxed, feet splayed the same distance apart. Like father like son. It was still astonishing to Rebecca that they'd only known each other for six months. All these years Miles knew his father was alive, but he hadn't pressed her for details. His grandmother, knowing that the lies were torturing her daughter, had explained all she knew to Miles when he was old enough to hear it. And he never even let on. Keeping secrets must be a family trait. He secretly hoped she would find his father in New Orleans, and here they were. It was unbelievable how much life could change. Besides her son and Grant being reunited, and the fact that she and Grant were so in love—as if that weren't enough—ever since Rebecca gave that necklace to the high priestess, business had been booming.

Girls were coming out of the woodwork to buy her pieces, and then they brought their friends. One girl said she met the love of her life shortly after buying a necklace. Whether or not the two events were related, rumors began to spread. Everything in New Orleans was coated with a bit of voodoo, so Rebecca didn't give it a second thought. If anyone asked her if it was true that her pieces could draw in true love, Rebecca would just smile and say, *It's been said.*

Money will flow in faster than you can catch it . . . She tried not to let it get to her—that this, too, had been one of the priestess's predictions. She was doing so well at the shop, and Grant was doing so well at the club, that they had started looking at buying a house together. It was perfect timing; the small hotel where Rebecca had been staying was quaint, but she was ready for something more. She was ready to give her heart.

You will cause the death of someone else. Despite how well her life was going, this prediction began to haunt her. Things absolutely could not be any better than they were right now, and she still couldn't be happy. *You will cause the death of someone else.* Absolutely everything else had come true, so how could she ignore it?

Had the curse been lifted? Was she safe? Was Miles? Grant? She had to know. She had to pay the high priestess one last visit and ask her straight out. Rebecca waited until the last customer was out of the shop, then she hurried down the street. A light rain started to fall as she ran, and by the time she reached the Voodoo Shop she was drenched; her hair was plastered to her face, her thin dress clung to her body. This time, the door was closed. Rebecca stood in front of it for a few seconds, and then pushed on it. It opened.

The shop was empty. As if it never existed.

"Hello?" She took a few steps inside. The second room was empty, too, except for a young woman who appeared to be cleaning the shelves.

"What happened?" Rebecca said. The woman turned with a start. "I'm sorry, I didn't mean to startle you. I came to see the high priestess."

"She passed away a few weeks ago," the woman said.

"I'm so, so sorry," Rebecca said. "And the daughter didn't want to keep the shop open?" Rebecca hated thinking it, but now that she looked at it, this space would be the perfect place to move her jewelry store. The little shop she had now wasn't big enough with all the traffic she was getting.

"She said it was never her dream," the woman said. "She went West."

"Good for her."

"Were you a friend of the priestess?" the girl asked.

"I have a jewelry shop in town," Rebecca said. "I made her a necklace."

The girl gasped, then reached into her pocket. "This necklace?" she asked.

Rebecca was surprised to see it. For some reason, she thought the priestess would have wanted to be buried with it. "Yes," she said.

"She died the day she got this," the girl said.

At first Rebecca was convinced she hadn't heard her correctly. "No," she said. "Are you sure?"

"Doctor ruled it old age, of course, but her daughter blamed you." She held up the necklace, and they watched the rose petals dance.

"Me?" Rebecca said. "Why me?"

"It reminded her of her true love," the woman said. "He used to call her Rose. Then you gave this to her on their anniversary. She said he was coming for her, that true love lasted beyond the grave. And then, just like that, she was gone." The girl snapped her fingers. "Her daughter said she died of a broken heart, but I think it's the opposite. I think she died be-

cause after all these years of being miserable, her heart was
finally full. She just couldn't take being so happy." The girl
gave a shy smile. "Or maybe he was sending her a message.
Maybe he was calling to her. And off she went." Silence descended on the little shop. "Here," the girl said, holding out
the necklace. "You should have it back." And then, before
Rebecca could protest, the girl placed the necklace in Rebecca's palm and closed her fingers over it. "She would want
you to have it," she said. "I'm sure of it."

The three of them stood, arms linked, and gazed down at
the grave of the high priestess. Miles had already joked
about being conceived here, and although Grant and Rebecca were too mature to point out exactly where the conception had taken place, they did share a little grin and hand
squeeze when they walked past the statue of the maiden with
the outstretched hands. She was faded, and overgrown with
moss, but she was still there, still reaching out for her unseen
lover. Rebecca laid the necklace on top of the priestess's headstone. Miles lifted his trumpet and softly played "Amazing
Grace."

True love. The road certainly hadn't been smooth, or
straight, and somehow it had brought them full circle, to
this cemetery, these sacred grounds where it all began. And
then, as they turned from the grave, Grant put his arm
around Miles and Rebecca and announced that he was taking his two favorite people to the "best restaurant in town."

When Rebecca went to kiss him, Grant pulled back. At
first she was stung. Then he laughed and made a show of
looking at his watch.

"A kiss before midnight?" he said. "Are you sure it's
safe?"

Rebecca grabbed the back of his head, stood on her tiptoes, and laid one on him.

"That's my girl," he said. "Not afraid of anything."

"Not anymore," Rebecca said. "Not with *my* two favorite people by my side."

Miles and Grant exchanged a grin, and Grant patted down his breast pocket as if checking to see if something was still there. Then, as they walked, and talked, and laughed, Rebecca could feel her future shimmering around them. She could see love, and happiness, and a long, magic-filled life ahead of them. And if she was right about what was in that pocket—what was waiting for her after the best meal in town—at least one thing was for sure. She knew the exact two-man band she was going to get to play at their wedding.

Romeo & Juliet . . . and Jane

Elizabeth Bass

"The best moment of playing Juliet is the nanosecond when they offer you the part."—Dame Judi Dench

Chapter One

Marcy poked her head into the exam room. "Could you come out here for a sec, Jane?"

Jane hesitated, but when she saw the urgent light in the vet tech's eyes, she smiled apologetically at Sandra, Fuzzy Weaver's mom. Sandra looked annoyed by the interruption. Not Fuzzy. The minute the dog saw the vet heading for the door, his tail began to twitch at the possibility of a hoped-for reprieve. "I'll get the vaccines ready and grab a few free food samples for you to try," Jane told Sandra.

Free was always a good way to unruffle ruffled feathers.

After the exam room door was closed, Marcy scooted ahead of Jane. "You've got to see this." She led her past the kennel cages and out the clinic's back exit, where the big deliveries were made. "Shane wants me to sign for this thing, but I think there's been a mistake."

Jane had been prepared to say that she didn't have time to sort out a delivery problem right now, but what she saw made her swallow the words. Next to Kaylie the receptionist's Honda Fit sat an enormous canary-yellow sectional sofa.

"What is *that*?"

"That's what I wanted to know," muttered Marcy. "There's obviously been a screwup."

Shane, the delivery guy, read off the invoice on his clipboard. "Dr. Carl Fenton, Mesquite Creek Animal Hospital. Says so right here, clear as day."

Jane aimed a wary glance at his clipboard. "To this address? Not Carl's home?"

"This thing wouldn't fit in Carl's little house," Marcy said. "Besides, this just isn't something he'd want. *Yellow?*"

"There's a set of matching chairs still on the truck," Shane informed them.

Had Carl really ordered this? Was he insane? That yellow fabric, so easy to stain, snag, and shred, would be a disaster in the vet clinic. In less than a week it would die the death of a thousand paws.

But the clinic was still Carl's business—he could put yellow couches in the waiting room if he wanted to. Heck, he could furnish the place in Louis XV antiques if he preferred. Or beanbag chairs.

Reluctantly, she signed.

Marcy shook her head. "This isn't right. Do you think Carl's finally gone crazy?"

Jane didn't want to have a discussion about Carl's mental health in front of Shane. The truth was, she'd thought Carl was showing improvement lately from his usual withdrawn, gloomy self. The happiest she'd seen him since Maggie had died six years ago. "Could you go tell Sandra I'll be right in?" she asked Marcy. "And Fuzzy'll need his rabies and *Bordetella*."

"What about this?" Marcy said, gesturing toward the massive couch. "You can't haul it in yourself."

"The couch stays out here until Carl gets back," Jane said. "The plastic sheeting over it should protect it in the open air for one morning."

Marcy appeared ready as always to put up an argument,

but she finally turned on her heel and marched back into the clinic.

Shane's gaze followed her, riveted, as if Marcy were a showgirl strutting across a Las Vegas stage instead of a petite twenty-something in surgical scrubs and sneakers, her lank hair pulled back in a ponytail with a rubber band snagged from the reception area.

Jane had to give the man a verbal nudge. "Chairs?"

He startled a little, then jogged back to the truck. "Hasn't changed since third grade."

"What hasn't?" Jane shook her head as she eyed the first chair off the truck. It was armless, with yellow fabric going up the high back.

"Marcy," Shane said, tossing a glance toward the clinic's back door. "I gave her a little heart-shaped box of candy when we were kids, and then during the next recess she knocked me off the monkey bars. Broke my arm."

Jane only half listened as she pulled her cell out and dialed Carl's number. Right now he was out dealing with some sick cattle in another county. She waited through a half dozen rings and then left a quick message for him to call her. No telling when he'd check his messages.

She'd been heartened when Carl had announced that he wanted to modernize the clinic a little after all these years, to brighten things up a little. She'd encouraged him. But this stuff was wildly inappropriate. How did you tell a man who was finally emerging from his shell that he was coming out the wrong way?

"Do you know if it's really serious between her and Keith Atkins?" Shane asked.

"What do you call serious?" Jane laughed. "Going out for three years? Won't look at anyone else? Seems depressed if he spends so much as a Saturday away from her on a hunting trip?"

"Oh." His face fell. "Guess that answers my question."

"I'd think one broken arm would have cured you," Jane told him, moving a couple of chairs farther out of the path of cars.

Shane looked at her blankly, and then lumbered back into his truck and roared away. She bit her lip. Maybe her words had come out more tart than she'd intended. The truth was, she sympathized with Shane completely. Some people got under your skin that way, making it seem no one else in the world compared.

She went back in, apologized to Sandra and Fuzzy for the interruption, and administered the vaccines. She left the room for a moment to retrieve the forgotten food samples and nearly slammed into Kaylie, who was standing next to the door and practically hopping from foot to foot with impatience.

"You'll never guess who's out front!" Before Jane could even attempt to answer, Kaylie blurted out, "Roy McGillam! Roy McGillam's out in our waiting room. Your Romeo."

The words broke Jane's stride only momentarily as she crossed to the shelves where the samples were kept. She forced her mind to stay on task. *Fuzzy. Food samples.*

Kaylie followed her. "Don't pretend you don't know what I'm talking about. I spent my four years at Mesquite Creek High School participating in Skeeter Theater, and the picture of you and Roy in *Romeo and Juliet* was right there in the hall going into the auditorium. My sister said y'all were the big couple in school that year. Everybody thought you two would run off and get married or something."

Jane snatched several samples out of plastic baskets. "It ended up being 'or something.' "

Kaylie lowered her voice. "I can show him into Carl's office, if you want some privacy."

Jane flicked her an exasperated glance. "We don't. The exam room will be fine."

"I saw that production when I was in fifth grade. I cried."

Jane took a deep breath and turned. "Why's he here?" Roy didn't even live in Mesquite Creek. Or in the state.

As if in answer to her question, Marcy appeared, her expression grave. "Roy McGillam's got his mom's dog with him. Buddy. Says he wants to put him to sleep."

The words knifed through Jane's heart. What had happened to Buddy? Euthanizing beloved pets was never her favorite part of the job, but there were some animals that made it even harder than usual.

She wrapped up the appointment with Sandra and Fuzzy and took a moment to collect herself. To steel herself both for seeing Roy and doing what had to be done with Buddy.

Buddy had been fine four months ago, when Wanda McGillam had still been alive and brought him in for his normal checkup. Apart from a little arthritis in the back legs, Jane had found nothing wrong with him. But Buddy was a big Great Pyrenees, and old, and he'd lost his owner a month after that last exam. The past three months had probably been stressful for him. No matter how gutted she felt, she had to think of Buddy, not her own emotions, and face what had to be done.

Facing Roy was a little more complicated. Her stomach fluttered uncomfortably as she quickly sprayed and wiped down the exam table and then, foolishly, checked her reflection in the stainless steel surface. She immediately regretted it. No makeup. Wiry hair needing a trim. *Knock 'em dead, Jane.*

She turned to the door, bracing herself for those blue eyes of his.

But when Roy came in, it was his back she saw first. Buddy weighed well over a hundred pounds, and he wasn't one of those dogs who dealt with vet stress by becoming super hyper. He handled terror in a way Jane understood completely—he froze up. Legs locked, head ducked, eyes half-clouded in cringing fear, poor Buddy had to be dragged into the room with Roy tugging at his collar and Marcy at the other end, grunting as she shoved against his ample rump.

He can't be feeling too bad.

Once they got him in and settled on the table, Roy straightened, then spent a long moment drinking Jane in. "Hello, Jane."

Her throat felt as if she'd swallowed sand. The eyes hadn't changed—they were as blue as she'd always imagined the Mediterranean to be. His hair was cut short, so he didn't have that youthful floppy appearance anymore. Overall, he seemed more substantial. Bulkier. He'd gained muscle, and a polish he certainly hadn't had back in school, when Levi's and a Weezer T-shirt were basically his uniform.

She allowed a smile of greeting to flicker across her lips and then she focused her attention on Buddy. The dog was shivering as if he expected to be hacked in two with a meat cleaver. Matted fur rippled. He'd gained weight, obviously, which didn't indicate a dog at death's door.

"It's been so long," Roy said. "But you look . . ."

"Older." She spoke to the dog, because it was easier. "We're all a little older, aren't we, Buddy?"

Buddy answered with another tremble and a whimper.

Roy cleared his throat. "I was actually hoping Dr. Fenton would be here today, not you."

Jane frowned.

"I mean"—he skimmed a hand through his hair the way he used to when there had been more of it—"I'm sure you're as good as Dr. Fenton, but . . ." He blew out a breath. "This is so hard. I mean, about Buddy. And then seeing you . . ."

She raised a brow. "What's wrong with Buddy?"

In a gesture she remembered well, Roy lifted his shoulders and dropped them. "He's old."

Buddy was ten, which was old for a big dog. But a quick listen to his heart and lungs indicated that he was still going strong. Just quivering in fear.

She stepped back and patted his head, even though it

made him flinch. Outside the vet, he had a heart like a lion. Inside, he was the Cowardly Lion.

"Buddy seems the same as the last time I saw him, about four months ago, which was when Wanda brought him in." She froze as soon as she spoke the name, then looked Roy in the eye. "I was so sorry about your mom, Roy."

He nodded, but his jaw popped with tension. "I expected to see you at the funeral."

"I wanted to be there. You know how much I loved her. But we had an emergency here—I had to do a surgery on a dog that had been run over. And then you left so quickly . . ."

"I had to."

Jane nodded, although she wondered if that meant he had business he needed to get back to in Seattle, or if he'd been so broken up he just couldn't stand to be in Mesquite Creek. Maybe it had been a little of both.

"I asked Aunt Ona to look after everything until I could come back and get Mom's stuff settled," he explained. "But Aunt Ona can't stand Buddy. She says he sheds and drools and"—he lowered his voice, as if to spare Buddy's feelings—"he has a problem with flatulence."

Jane would have laughed at that, but she felt her irritation rising. She kept her eyes trained on Buddy—a sweet, gentle giant of a dog who she remembered as a fuzzy white puppy. Wanda had gotten him to keep her company, since Roy was making noises about not coming back to Mesquite Creek after college. Buddy had been like a second son to her. Wanda had had three things she was proud of in her life: Roy, the fact that she hadn't touched a drink for twenty years, and her dog.

"Let me get this straight," Jane said, straining to keep her voice steady. "You're going to euthanize your mom's beloved pet because Ona thinks he farts too much?"

Roy's eyes widened. "He's an old dog. Great Pyrenees don't live past twelve. I looked it up on the Internet."

"The Internet?" Jane usually aimed for a professional distance when it came to how people dealt with their pets in crises, but Roy's words sent her professional demeanor out the window. She'd hoped his coming here had been on impulse, that he was looking for guidance. But this was just too cold. "You searched the Web to rationalize putting Buddy to sleep?"

"Only because I was sure—"

"All you needed to do was look into his eyes." She gestured toward Buddy. Unfortunately, he wasn't at his best at that moment. The raised tension in the room caused his entire body to shake, sending a cloud of dander up around him. At the same time, a thick strand of drool cascaded out one side of his quivering jowls. Also, a pungent odor now suffused the room.

But that doggy gaze, soulful and dark, so full of plaintive, heartbreaking uncertainty provided more fuel for Jane's anger. Three months ago he'd lost his owner, his beloved person. He'd been shunted off into exile with Aunt Ona, who obviously hadn't taken care of him. And now here came Roy, Mr. Don't-Look-Back, to snuff his life out completely.

"I will not euthanize Buddy," she declared.

Roy looked trapped, defensive. "What am I going to do with him?"

"You could take him home with you."

He thought for a moment, and then shook his head. "That wouldn't work. My place in Seattle is full of stairs, and I'm at work all day, and I travel a couple of times a month."

She'd heard about his life from his mom, of course. Wanda had always lavished Jane with details of Roy's successful life, wanting her to know what a prize she'd let slip through her fingers. Roy was the catch of Seattle, the playboy of the West Coast. Wanda had always considered the breakup to be Jane's fault, which was true . . . up to a point. Much as she'd loved Roy, Jane had already been accepted to vet school at Texas A & M for doctorate studies when he wanted to take off for Seattle. It would have been wrong to give up everything she'd ever worked hard for and dreamed of, not to mention everything her parents had dreamed of for her, to run off with him.

Of course, she couldn't have guessed that Roy would view her very rational decision as an excuse to turn his back on her forever.

"It might be inconvenient for you," she admitted. "Sometimes pets are demanding, especially in their later years."

Roy jumped in. "But that's just it. This has to be his last year or so. Wouldn't this be saving him from a lot of pain just to do it now?"

"*Kill* him now, you mean?"

Roy flinched. She did, too, a little, half expecting a bolt of lightning to strike her, courtesy of the American Veterinary Medical Association. *Kill* was not a word professionals preferred.

"I am not going to put Buddy to sleep," she repeated.

"But—"

"Don't worry, Roy. I won't try to shame you into doing the right thing. I'll find a good home for him."

For a moment, the only parts of Roy that moved were his eyes as he looked from her face to Buddy's. At the same time, Buddy glanced from Roy to Jane.

"Okay," Roy said. "That would probably be for the best."

His words hit her like a slap. No matter what she'd said, she had hoped that her offer would convince Roy to think twice. "You'd be okay with a stranger taking your mom's dog?"

Roy shrugged. "If they want him, why not? You'll see he winds up with good people, right?"

She gaped at him. Could this really be *Roy*? The same soulful boy who loved to draw, who had bowled her over when she was a geeky teen? The boy who had brought an entire auditorium to tears after he'd died on stage? The young man who had broken her heart when he'd left and never looked back? The man she had missed and wondered about for nearly ten years?

Couldn't be. That Roy had been body-snatched, leaving this cold, soulless husk.

She lifted her chin. "Sure. I'll find Buddy a good home." She fought to keep her rising indignation from coming out as a quaver in her voice. "You won't have to trouble yourself about him anymore."

He stared into Buddy's eyes, then looked at her. He was so obviously relieved, she wanted to smack him. Maybe this was the outcome he'd been hoping for from the start. "Great. God knows, I've got enough on my plate, getting rid of all Mom's other stuff. And especially dealing with Aunt Ona. And then, of course, there's the opening of McGillam Auditorium at the school next week. They're making a big fuss over that, you know."

Jane gulped back a knot of rage.

When she said nothing, he smiled a little awkwardly. "I'm going to be around town awhile. We should get together—maybe head over to the Blackberry Jam this weekend. It would be fun to catch up a little."

Uh-huh. Actually, she felt she'd just been brought up to speed on the new Roy McGillam. Mesquite Creek's big success story. Heel.

"You know where to find me," she said.

He tilted his head, as if trying to gauge how to take that. Maybe his interpersonal radar hadn't gone completely dead after all.

"Okay . . ." He leaned down and gave Buddy a quick pat. "Bye, Buddy. Be good."

When he straightened, smiled, and strolled quickly toward reception, it took all Jane's strength to hold Buddy back. The dog whined and tried to lurch toward the door, to follow Roy's disappearing form. She could remember the feeling well.

"You'll get over him," she murmured to Buddy, planting her feet so she wouldn't be dragged out of the exam room.

Marcy hurried in, then stopped short. "You didn't euthanize him." The relief in the statement was palpable. Euthanizing an animal, especially one they'd known as long as Buddy, always cast a pall over the clinic.

"Of course I didn't. He's perfectly healthy."

The vet tech petted him. "Why did Romeo leave him, then?"

"Because I offered to find him a good home."

Just then, Kaylie scooted up to the door, her expression nearly rapturous. "You saved him! That was such a sweet thing to do for Roy!"

"It was not a romantic gesture on my part, Kaylie. The jerk wanted to put Buddy to sleep for no good reason. Because he couldn't be bothered."

"And you saved him from doing something he would regret for the rest of his life." Kaylie sighed. "Remember how I'm writing a feature for *The Buzz*, all about Skeeter High's productions of *Romeo and Juliet* over the years?" Kaylie's other job was aspiring journalist for *The Mesquite Creek Buzz*. "I was going to call it 'Three Juliets,' and focus on the women who've played that part—that's why I've still got to interview you, Jane. But I'm thinking now maybe I should include you and Roy together. Romeo and Juliet, reunited. Wouldn't that be fun?"

Jane was shaking her head. She already regretted agreeing to be interviewed for the story as originally conceived. Thankfully, Marcy cut short any need to respond to Kaylie's newest bad idea.

"Speaking of regretting something for the rest of your life . . ." Marcy stepped back, crossed her arms, and darted a doubting look at Buddy. "Who's going to adopt a ten-year-old shedding slobber-factory like this?"

"Guess," Jane said.

Chapter Two

That hadn't gone well.

Roy kicked himself all the way back to his mom's place, without knowing quite what had bothered him most about the encounter. They'd greeted each other like adults, transacted their business. But still he felt a stabbing discomfort, as if he was guilty of something.

Guilty of abandoning Buddy?

Guilty of leaving Jane all those years ago?

But the problem had never been his leaving. Ever since they were high school seniors, he'd told Jane that he was going to flee Mesquite Creek as soon as possible, go far away and never look back. He had always expected that when the time came to go, she would be with him. That they'd ride off into the sunset together.

Instead, when the time came, Jane had applied to vet school, been accepted, and refused to consider other options. She'd dug in her heels, and a part of him was convinced that it was her parents talking to her behind the scenes that caused her to be so stubborn. They'd never liked him. Why would they? He was the son of the town drunk, a misfit of a kid who loved to draw and play silly pranks, although he never got caught doing anything really bad. The whole town had been waiting for him to take the same moral nosedive as his dad, but he'd tripped up their expectations by making good grades, winning a scholarship to UT, and capturing the heart of the town's good girl—Jane: lifelong honor student, class secretary four years running, daughter of the superintendant of schools.

It was the play that had done it. He and Jane had never paid that much attention to each other. Then, for *Romeo and Juliet*, she'd been the stage manager. During the first read-through of the play, sitting around a table in the cafeteria, he'd caught her looking at him a few times, as if she'd never noticed him before. Never mind that they had been going to the same schools for twelve years.

After that rehearsal, Jane had approached him, her usual shy reserve vanishing in her enthusiasm. "Good job, Roy! You made me understand things I didn't get even after reading the footnotes and seeing the movie."

Of course she would have studied the text and gone to the trouble to watch the movie, even though she wasn't actually in the play. And there wasn't even a grade at stake. It fit what he'd always thought of Jane Canfield—nose-to-the-grindstone goody-goody. But as he watched her during those weeks of rehearsals, she actually just seemed to throw herself into what she was doing for the sheer joy of it, the way he could spend hours over a sketchbook or messing around with computer animation programs. Everyone was a nerd when it came to the activities they loved.

He asked her to run lines with him during lunch, then after school. After several weeks, two things were clear. One, he was in love with Jane, and two, she already had the whole damn play memorized. When Lacey Butler came down with mono and had to pull out of the production at the last minute, Roy suggested Jane for Juliet. What choice did they have? Not many girls could memorize so many lines in two days. People were astonished at how good she was, how moving. But to Roy, she had been Juliet since that first read-through.

Red and blue lights flashed in the rearview mirror.

Roy's heart sank. A police cruiser was practically on his bumper.

When he pulled over and caught sight of the cop who got out of the car, he muttered under his breath and rolled down the window.

Speaking of the high school play . . . Jared Evans had been an unexpectedly enthusiastic Mercutio. Jared might be heavier now, with decidedly less hair, but he moved with the same shambling gait he'd had back then.

When Jared stopped and leaned in toward the driver window, he drew back in surprise at the sight of Roy. "Hey!" He laughed. "Romeo, Romeo, wherefore art thou going fifty in a thirty-mile-per-hour zone?"

Roy looked around at the empty street. Thirty? No signs were posted anywhere that he could see. "Is that how Mesquite Creek pays your lavish salary—as a speed trap?"

"Yeah, but don't worry about it," Jared said, laughing.

"No—"

Jared cut him off. "Heck, I couldn't give a ticket to the town's favorite son."

Roy rolled his eyes uncomfortably. He hadn't meant to wriggle out of trouble. "If I was speeding, go ahead and give me the ticket."

"No can do. Chief wouldn't hear of it after that new cruiser you donated—on top of everything else you've done. Heck, without you, the kids would be having graduation on Skeeter Field again. Everybody hated that. Turn those lights on this time of year and the poor kids were having to use their diplomas to bat away june bugs."

Roy smiled. "Look, I'm happy about the auditorium and the police car—I've been lucky—but I still think you should give me the ticket. You don't want to be accused of favoritism."

"Lucky?" Jared was grinning. "And when I think of how teachers used to ride you for doodling in class." A laugh burst out of him. "Doodling! I bet that one commercial—the dancing pretzels?—made about a gazillion dollars. Am I right?"

Roy smiled. "Well, thanks."

"Don't mention it. We should get together for a beer while you're in town."

"Let's do that."

Before Roy could get the window up, Jared leaned in. "You seen Jane yet?"

"I was just at the animal clinic."

"Yeah? My little sister, Marcy, works there now." Jared straightened, shaking his head. "I've been telling everybody for years that you and Jane wouldn't be able to stay away from each other forever."

"It wasn't . . ."

But Jared was already strolling back to his cruiser.

Roy drove—carefully—the rest of the way back to his mom's house. The new house. During his brief visits home, he always avoided the house he'd grown up in. Some people might feel nostalgic about their childhood homes, but not him. His father had built a squatty cinder-block structure that had been a furnace during the summer, a meat locker during the winter, and hideous all year long. After his dad died, his mom had attempted to pretty the place up by painting it yellow and planting a few shrubs, but no matter what, Roy always thought it resembled a Soviet outhouse.

The home Roy had built for his mother, while not deluxe, was in the nicest part of town, the same neighborhood where Jane's parents lived. As a kid, he'd always thought of this as the rich neighborhood, but most of the houses there were pretty simple one- and two-story houses, nothing like the McMansions of modern suburbs. His condo in Seattle had cost twice as much as building and furnishing Wanda's house from scratch.

He parked next to the For Sale sign and went inside, then immediately wished he had somewhere else to go. The silence unnerved him. One thing his mother's house had never been was quiet. She'd always had something on, usually the television. The noise used to drive him nuts, but now its absence was even worse. And what seemed strangest? No Buddy coming in to offer him a slobbery welcome.

Guilt shuddered through him, and he hurried back to the kitchen and sank down into a chair. Why had he done it? Buddy was his mom's best friend. No, he didn't have a place in his life for a big arthritic dog, but maybe he could have managed somehow. There were pet sitters and dog walkers. Yet it still would have meant poor Buddy logging a lot of alone time.

Part of him wanted to get back into the car and drive to the clinic. But if Jane could find Buddy a better home, maybe that would be best for everyone.

A business card lay on the glass-topped kitchen table, letting him know that Lou Barrentine, a local real estate agent, had been by. Maybe that accounted for some of Roy's unsettled feeling. It was strange staying in a house where strangers could tromp through at any moment.

As soon as the thought occurred to him, the front door opened. Roy jumped up, not sure what to expect.

"Roy?"

He tensed. A whole flock of house hunters would have been preferable to a visit from Aunt Ona.

She marched in, offered no greeting, and tossed her purse and keys on the glass tabletop. Ona was a small woman, sparer than Wanda had been, but with a sour personality that fit someone who had worked twenty-eight years at the DMV. "It's so quiet here now!" Her gaze glommed onto the business card, which she scooped up. "Oh! Who did Lou bring through?"

"I don't know."

"You should call him and find out. Maybe we've gotten a

nibble. He could be back at his office drawing up an offer right now."

"Then we'll find out soon, won't we?"

Ona frowned at him. As co-beneficiary of Wanda's will, she would receive half the proceeds of the sale of the house. But his mother had made him executor of the estate, so he had control of when to dispose of her belongings. Ona had nagged him to come down and try to wrap things up sooner than later. She had loved her sister, he knew that, but she wasn't one to dwell on sentimentality when there was money at stake.

"Hey—where's the dog?"

At the mention of Buddy, Roy drummed his fingers. "At the animal clinic."

His aunt's sharp gaze locked on him. "I should've known you wouldn't be able to stay away from her."

"I took Buddy to the animal clinic because you didn't want him." Of course, neither had he. "Like a jerk, I was going to put him to sleep. Dr. Fenton could have done it, for all I cared."

"But it wasn't Carl you saw, was it?"

He shrugged. "He was out."

"Uh-huh."

Oh, for Pete's sake. "Jane's a vet. It was all very professional. She wasn't even very friendly, to tell you the truth."

"That doesn't surprise me. Those Canfields were always too good for everybody else in this town. Or at least *she* thinks so."

She did not refer to Jane, but Jane's mother, Brenda. There had been nothing but hostility between Brenda and Wanda— and by extension, Ona—since they'd all been in high school. Brenda had won the homecoming queen title over Wanda by one measly vote. The enmity that had begun when they were teenagers continued on through marriages—Wanda to the no-good Wade McGillam, and Brenda to that pillar of the community, Doug Canfield. And now, when both Wade and Wanda were gone, Ona was carrying on the feud for her sister's sake.

"Jane said she'd find Buddy a good home."

His aunt snorted. "Who would adopt him?"

He frowned. She was right. Nobody would. Which meant . . .

"It wouldn't surprise me one little bit if she took that dog in just to lure you back," Ona said.

"Ridiculous."

"Is it?" One jet-black eyebrow peaked into her forehead. "You two are on the tips of everybody's tongue today. Jared Evans said that's where you were coming from when he let you off the hook on that speeding ticket."

So she'd already known where he'd been before she asked him. Of course. The grapevine in this town was as fast and tenacious as kudzu.

"I don't know why you look so put out," Ona said. "Jared never lets me off on traffic tickets. But I don't have a building named after me, I guess."

"I made the donation in the name of the whole family. That includes you."

"My name's not McGillam—and believe you me, most of my life I've considered that a good thing."

Roy's face reddened—just out of reflex, though, not because he disagreed with her. His father was a violent lush who had died in a drunk driving accident that miraculously had killed no one else, and not a soul had mourned him, least of all Roy. He'd worked his whole life to be different from his father, to make the name mean something to people. Even if that something was just dancing pretzels in a TV commercial.

"If you won't call Lou, I will," Ona said, dropping the card in her purse. He could have sworn she looked pleased to have irritated him. "Be great if we could get this house sold quick. I haven't taken a real vacation in ten years. I'd like to feel some sunny sand between my toes this summer. Although you might not be in such a hurry yourself, now that Jane's in the picture again " She pierced him with a knowing gaze. "Wanda guessed you only really got over her a year or so ago. Never too soon to start torturing yourself again."

He scowled. Maybe Ona figured if she upset him enough, he'd agree to take the first offer that came along, just to get away from this town, its memories, and Jane.

Maybe she was right.

Jane wasn't in her house thirty seconds before her phone rang. Knowing exactly who it was, she ignored the ringtone as she plowed her way toward the kitchen, through dogs hopping around her, nervous and demanding, and hungry cats weaving around her legs. Buddy had handled the stairs up to the apartment okay—albeit slowly—but now in the strange place with new animals, he seemed bigger and more slobbery than ever, and was evidently only comfortable staying six inches in front of her. His main competition for floor space was her three-legged poodle, Squeak, and two cats. A third cat, Olive, preferred to travel around the apartment doing her fox-stole impersonation around Jane's neck.

The phone didn't let up, so Jane retrieved it from her purse. "Hey, Mom."

"Good, you're home."

Jane laughed. It was so like her mom to pretend they were across town from each other when Jane was just across the driveway in the garage apartment.

"What's so funny?"

Olive purred and nuzzled into the phone, so Jane switched ears. "A, this is my cell phone, and B, you saw me drive up so you knew I was home before you called."

"How do you know *I'm* at home, Miss Smarty-pants?"

"Because I saw your car in the drive a minute ago, and the drapes twitched as I walked past the kitchen window."

"All right, I'm being nosy. But I couldn't help noticing that dog . . . where did it come from?"

"Just a sec." Jane battled her way to the laundry closet, where the food bowls for the cats were kept. She scooped a quarter cup of dry food in each, which served to disentangle her from the feline portion of her menagerie, at least, and also to buy time to decide how much about Buddy she should mention. No topic riled her mom like the McGillams.

"He's a dog I'm fostering until I can find him a better home."

Her mother heard her evasion right away. "What they were saying at the grocery store was true, then. You're seeing Roy again."

At the grocery store? "No, I'm not. He brought his mom's dog in, was all."

"He dumped Wanda's dog on you?" Her mother tsk-tsked. "Isn't that just typical. And I have to say . . . that animal doesn't look in the best of shape."

"Believe me, for ten, he's doing well."

"I guess he'll fit right in with your menagerie," her mother allowed. "Or misfit right in."

Jane smiled. Her poor mom. In a more benevolent universe, Brenda Canfield would have had a tutus-and-tiaras daughter, a pink-loving princess to spend afternoons shopping with. Instead, she'd gotten an animal nut. Starting in elementary school, in the absence of a pet of her own—Brenda hated animals in the house—Jane had started dragging in doomed wildlife: orphaned baby squirrels, birds with broken wings, and anything else slow enough for her to catch and stick in a jar or a shoebox.

"Still . . ." her mom continued, "there's something wrong about a man coming back after all these years and dumping his mother's dog on you. So selfish."

"I volunteered." She couldn't believe she was defending him. But this was her mom. Old habits died hard.

"You always were a pushover," Brenda said, and just as Jane's spine was stiffening in response, she added, "for animals."

Looking around her small apartment, there was no way she could disagree. Especially when she saw the parakeet cage where Luther huddled on his perch, half-bald from overplucking. Jane grabbed a peanut and crossed the room to hand it to him.

"Oh my heavens!" Her mother's whispered shout, followed by a sharp intake of breath, stopped Jane in her tracks. "Don't answer your door," Brenda said.

Jane laughed, imagining her mom still hovering behind a curtain. "Has the ax murderer arrived?"

A knock sounded and the two dogs exploded in barks.

"Just pretend you're not at home," her mother advised.

Jane pulled open the door. Roy stood on the porch. No wonder her mother was so agitated. Jane stepped aside to let Buddy and Squeak attack Roy. "I'll call you back," she told her mom.

"But—"

Jane pressed End Call and leaned against the door, watching Roy get bathed in dog slobber. The only way for him to escape would be to back over the railing and leap fifteen feet to the ground. He cast a glance in that direction, as if he was actually considering jumping, then let his gaze drift across the driveway to her parents' house.

"You live here?" he asked.

"So it would seem." The truth was, from the moment she'd moved back, she'd considered her stay here temporary. Carl's wife and partner, Maggie, had died six years ago while Jane, fresh out of vet school, had been employed at a clinic in Austin. Jane had returned to help out for a while. She'd worked at the Mesquite Creek Animal Hospital all through high school and summers during college, and Maggie Fenton had been her mentor and role model, practically her idol. To Jane, Maggie had had the perfect life. Unfortunately, leukemia hadn't cared about perfect.

When Jane came home, the garage apartment had seemed an ideal short-term solution. All through Jane's youth, it had been a combination storage room, playhouse, clubhouse, and home to both short- and long-term visitors. Jane paid her parents nominal rent, ate dinner with them on Sunday afternoons, and spent Sunday nights thinking she should really make an effort to find another place. Busy weeks always made her forget her resolution.

Roy straightened from petting Buddy and pushed Squeak's snout away from his crotch. "Would you mind if I came in for a second?"

She stepped aside and gestured him in.

"I remember this place," he said.

Of course he did. It had been one of their favorite places to sneak off to during the summers they were home. Their playhouse. Images from those days popped unbidden into her mind, and she felt a blush rising.

"It hasn't changed much," he said, eyeing the haphazard collection of castoff furniture. Much of it had been here in the old days. His gaze halted at the huge cage in the living room, where poor Luther was fluffing anxiously. "That bird looks half plucked."

"He's got a nervous condition. From being abandoned, I think. That's how I've come by most of these guys."

Roy looked down at the floor for a moment before glancing up at her again. "I never meant to fob Buddy off on you."

"I'm just fostering him until I can find a permanent owner."

Roy took in the three-legged poodle, the cat with one eye, Olive hunched on the television, then Luther. "Just like you're going to find homes for all the rest of them?"

"They're none of your business," she said. "Neither is Buddy, anymore. You gave him up, remember?"

"I wasn't thinking what it would mean to you."

"It's okay. It means that I'll have a great dog for a little while."

Roy flopped down on the nearest chair.

"Make yourself at home."

He didn't smile. "You want to know the truth? It wasn't just Buddy that brought me over here. Talking to you today wasn't how I hoped meeting you again would be."

"You'd imagined our big reunion scene, had you?" As the words came out of her mouth, she wanted to retract them. She couldn't seem to get the awful jokey-acerbic tone out of her voice. Her vocal needle was stuck on sitcom.

She couldn't evade his gaze for long. At one time she'd known Roy's face almost as well as her own reflection. It seemed more angular now. But the intense eyes—those hadn't changed a bit. They'd always been her undoing. The eyes and that voice.

"Haven't you imagined it?" he asked.

Just a few million times.

She smiled tightly. "Maybe you should go. We've already set tongues wagging today."

"I know. I'd forgotten how crazy this place is."

"I thought that's why you stayed away."

"I came back," he said defensively. "I came back every year or so."

"Flew in to visit your mom for a weekend. Flew out."

He stood again. "You didn't want to see me."

"I didn't want *not* to see you."

He blinked at that, as if the idea that she would have wanted to spend time with her old boyfriend had never occurred to him.

He lowered his gaze again. "Mom always wanted me to visit for longer. But . . ." He sighed. "I always thought there would be time. That she'd be here."

He looked so hangdog, so mournful . . . but she would

not comfort him. So he'd been given a crash course in Life Is Short. *Welcome to adulthood.* "How long are you staying this time?"

"Oh . . . just till things are settled."

"Things?"

"My mom's stuff. And they're making a big deal of the auditorium. I don't know why."

"You obviously haven't been to the school campus lately. It's half portable buildings. When the auditorium burned down it felt like a town tragedy. Getting a new one up and running so soon is a big deal. You're a hero."

"I'm glad—to have helped, I mean."

"The seniors are doing *Romeo and Juliet* again, breaking the place in before graduation."

" 'For never was a story of more woe.' " He laughed. "Remember? It's woe all over the place in that play. I've never said *woe* so much in my life. In fact, maybe never, since then."

Jane couldn't help smiling, recalling those days. "I have great memories of that play, woe and all. Even if I did want to throw up for an entire week."

He laughed again, no doubt remembering her nerves. She'd gotten the shakes every time she set foot on the stage, to the point that they'd worried the entire audience could see the balcony jittering.

"Anyway, I had a good time," she said. "The boy playing Romeo was really funny."

His eyes met hers. "Was he?"

"Mm-hm. For years he'd acted as if he didn't know I existed, and then one day turned on a dime and decided I was actually his Juliet. Life mirroring art . . . or art mirroring mental illness. Something like that."

"Or maybe just boy getting a clue." He moved closer to her. "I'm not kidding, Jane. When I think of those days now, they really do seem like the happiest days of my life. Back then I wanted to kick myself for all the time I wasted before

I found you. And when I look at you now, I feel I've wasted nine years."

The words worked like a balm on the hurts that had festered since he'd picked up and left Mesquite Creek. She'd sometimes wondered if she'd just imagined their closeness, but now she knew she had meant as much to him as he did to her.

Or at least that he wanted her to think that.

She frowned. "Why did you really come here, Roy?"

She wasn't sure she expected an answer right away, but he had one. "To give you something." He reached into his pocket. Her mind raced, panicking at what he could possibly want to give her. Had he carried some token around all these years and now intended to present it to her? With Roy—the old Roy—there had never been any knowing what he'd do. Once, he'd spent his student loan money on a birthday gift for her. She had to frog-march him back to the store to return it.

"Roy, I don't think you should—"

He pulled out his wallet and fished for a couple of twenties. "Here," he said. "Take some money. For Buddy."

She shrank away from his outstretched hand. "That's not necessary."

"Caring for him is bound to be expensive."

And he thought eighty bucks would cover it? He obviously wasn't a pet owner. Or maybe that eighty dollars was just meant to assuage his guilt. "I don't want your money."

He dropped his hand in frustration. "Why are you being like this?"

"Because I thought you came here to . . . out of friendship. Not to pay me off."

"I'm not paying you off," he argued. "I'm just giving you money."

"And I'm telling you I don't need it. Thanks."

Someone knocked at the door, setting the dogs off again, and Jane couldn't help rolling her eyes in irritation. Her mother trying to rescue her, no doubt. She probably assumed they were all over each other. She crossed to the door and swung it open, not bothering to mask her irritation. "See? No orgy."

But then she looked up and it wasn't her mom standing there. It was Carl.

She gaped at him until she noticed that all his attention was focused, bird dog–like, on Roy. Roy, whose eyes glinted in amusement at the situation.

"I'm sorry, Carl. I expected you to be someone else." She stood aside. "Come on in. Roy was just leaving."

"I was?" Roy asked.

She flashed a glare at him before turning back to Carl. "You remember Roy McGillam, don't you?"

"Sure." Carl walked toward Roy, hand outstretched. As he passed her, she caught a stronger-than-usual whiff of Aramis. The two men shook, and for a moment Jane was struck by the stark differences between them. Roy might have bulked up since his early twenties, but he still seemed slight next to Carl. With his rusty blond hair and ruddy tan, Carl sometimes reminded her of a pioneer man stuffed into modern clothing. Roy looked urban and hip next to him. Jane supposed that was what he was, at heart. He lived in Seattle, worked as an artist. Mesquite Creek probably seemed like the boondocks.

Heck, even she thought of it that way most of the time.

"I don't mean to rush you off," Carl said. "I just came by to talk to Jane about some things." When Roy continued to stand unmoving between them, Carl added, "In private."

Understanding dawned on Roy's face, causing Jane to smile. But at the same time she couldn't help thinking, *This is so weird.* Carl never popped by her apartment. If not for the time he'd given her a ride when her car was in the shop, she doubted he would have known where she lived. Nevertheless, she was comforted to have him here now.

"Thanks for dropping by, Roy." She moved none-too-subtly toward the front door.

He skulked after her. "We'll see each other again."

"Bound to," she answered, "in a town this size."

His face fell and she felt a zing of satisfaction until she shut the door behind him and thought, too late, that the chance existed that she might never see him again.

What am I doing?

Chapter Three

"Are you okay?" Carl asked when her gaze fixed too long on the door she'd just closed.

She nodded, but didn't quite trust herself to speak yet. For a few moments before Carl showed up, it had felt as if she and Roy had some of their old rapport back. But then he'd handed her that money and something in her had snapped. Now she wondered why. Maybe he hadn't meant to seem so impersonal, as if he was buying his way out of something.

"I heard about Wanda's dog." Carl scratched Buddy behind the ears. "Is this going to put a strain on your existing population? I could take him in . . ."

He'd do it, too. She crossed her arms. "It's an occupational hazard, isn't it?" Carl had a menagerie of his own, including a goat that lived in his backyard. "But I've always liked Buddy."

Actually, she'd always liked Roy's mom, and by extension, her dog. Whenever Wanda had brought Buddy into the clinic, Jane had been able to ask her about Roy.

"Marcy told me you didn't like the new couch for the clinic," Carl blurted out. "You left before I had a chance to talk to you about it."

The abrupt subject change required a mental shift of gears. This morning seemed forever ago. Since then, her mind had been filled with Roy.

"I wanted to brighten things up," Carl continued with Jiminy Cricket eagerness. "But maybe I went overboard, huh? I should have asked for your input. What's your favorite color?"

"For a vet's office?"

"For anything. You must have a favorite color."

Did she? No one had asked her to pin one down since third grade. "Maybe green," she said. "But color is . . . well, it's not really the point here. The design of the furniture might not hold up very well at the clinic. Maybe we should just keep the wooden chairs we have and repaint. Paint can lighten a room, and if it gets stained you just paint again."

He listened intently, as if she were conveying priceless pearls of wisdom. As if no one had ever thought of repainting a room before. "That's a great idea. Really great."

"We can send the couch and chairs back, I'm sure."

He snapped his fingers. "Already done. I called as soon as I heard you didn't like it. Shane will pick the stuff up again tomorrow."

Shane will love that, she thought.

"You know," Carl said, hesitating a little, "the clinic's had that other furniture since the beginning. Maggie picked it out."

"I know."

Any mention of his late wife, who'd been Jane's old friend and mentor, usually sent Carl into a funk, but he weathered this moment better than usual. Although his face did grow more solemn. More Carl-like. "Can we sit down and talk for a moment?" he asked.

"Of course." She didn't know where her manners had gone. Out the door with Roy, she supposed. "You want some coffee, or a beer?"

"No, thank you."

She feared something was wrong and settled on the couch, primed for bad news. Maybe he was selling the clinic. Could that explain his sudden mania for redecorating? "Is everything all right?"

He sat down next to her. "Everything's . . . well, it just seemed to me that we need to talk. About how you feel about things."

"Things," she repeated, clueless.

He took a deep breath. "About the clinic, say."

"Is this still about the couch and chairs? I didn't mean any offense. Honest. I just don't think a vet clinic should go too Martha Stewart—"

He cut her off. "What I was wondering was how you feel about the place in general."

It didn't take her more than a second to respond. "I love it. I always have. It's been like a second home to me."

He drank in her words but looked as if he didn't quite trust them. "For instance, where do you see yourself in five years?"

The classic interview question. "Working in the clinic," she said without hesitation.

"And in ten years?"

Ten years. That number struck her more forcefully. In her mind, she tried to stare down the next decade. A lot could happen in ten years. Then again, a lot could *not* happen, and that might be even worse. Here she was, living in her parents' garage apartment and working in the same clinic where she'd had her after-school job in high school. Time hadn't changed much except for the first gray hairs she'd noticed making their unwanted appearance, and the way her knees felt crunchy after she exercised.

In ten years, she'd be creakier and grayer. Aging was inevitable. But would she still be living above her parents' garage? Still working in the same spot? Those last two possibilities spooked her.

"Jane?"

Ten years. She surveyed her cramped apartment, her little herd, the hand-me-down furniture. She actually had a plump bank account, but she lived as if she was trying to get a jump on being the town's cat-lady kook. At the very least, her life seemed to be showing a failure of imagination, or initiative. "I'll probably be exactly where I am now." The words emerged as gloomy resignation. "The triumph of inertia."

"Or proof that you love what you're doing," he pointed out. "But if you're unhappy . . ."

She snapped out of her own thoughts and studied his face. What was he getting at? Did he not want her to stay? Or did he believe, not unreasonably, that someday she might actually go somewhere else.

Perhaps Roy's sudden appearance had set him to thinking.

She half blamed Roy for her own funk. His showing up had pulled a rusty lever in her brain and set her to wondering what would have been different if she'd run away with him to Seattle all those years ago . . .

Well, that train had left the station.

"If you think that just because Roy was over here that I'm considering running off to Seattle," she said, "believe me, that's not in the cards."

The lines in his brow smoothed in relief.

A laugh burbled out of her. "God, you *didn't* think that, I hope."

"You hear all sorts of things," Carl said. "And Kaylie was jabbering all about that *Romeo and Juliet* stuff this afternoon when I got back. Of course, that was all a lifetime ago."

It hadn't been *that* long. Still . . .

"Roy's done a great job making himself scarce all these years," she said. "I imagine now that Wanda's gone, he'll go back to Seattle and we'll never hear from him again."

"Good." When he caught Jane's look of surprise, he explained, "I mean—well, it's not like there's much for him to stick around for . . . is there?"

"No, there's not." Why did that thought depress her? Roy hadn't been around for nearly a decade. Twice the time they'd been involved. And it wasn't as if they'd hit it off today, except for those few fleeting moments.

"Jane?"

Her attention lurched back to Carl. She'd obviously missed something. "What?"

"I was just asking about the Jam. If you had plans to go."

The Blackberry Jam, Mesquite Creek's May festival, was an excuse to celebrate all things blackberry and for regional musicians to play in front of the courthouse. Skipping it wasn't an option. Jane could open up her windows and hear the thing happening a few blocks away, and the traffic usually backed up to her street.

Not that she would willingly miss the one time a year the town really came alive. "I'm always there. But if you need me to work late Saturday, that's no problem," she offered. "Just let me know."

"I was only wondering whether I'd see you there. I was thinking about going myself."

She was glad. Despite being a much-beloved figure in the town, Carl had kept to himself since Maggie had passed away. "It's great that you're going, Carl. You'll have fun. I'll see you there."

"You will?"

"Of course." She laughed. "It's not *that* crowded—and that hair of yours makes you easy to spot."

He swiped a hand self-consciously over his rusty hair, which managed to defy classification as brown, blond, or red. He seemed on the verge of speaking, stopped himself, then a split second later managed, "I should probably go home now."

"Okay," she said.

After he'd left, she counted to three slowly and was able to pick up her mother's call before the first ring had ended.

"What did Carl want?" Brenda asked.

She thought for a moment. "Not sure, actually."

"Don't be naïve. Carl is an eligible bachelor."

"He's also my boss."

"You work together—there's a difference. Remember, he and Maggie were partners, too."

Jane shuddered. That was the problem. She had come back to Mesquite Creek to help out after Maggie's death, not to take Maggie's place. And she couldn't help thinking of Carl primarily as Maggie's husband. Besides, he'd been an adult when she'd first known him as a teenager, a fact that formed a mental barrier that kept her from imagining Carl as a romantic object. "No, Mom." She couldn't imagine going out with him any more than she could imagine going out with her junior high math teacher. "Just . . . no."

"I could give you the e-mail addresses of ten women in this town who would date Carl Fenton in a heartbeat."

Jane laughed. "Give them to Carl, not me."

"But what would he do with them? He wants you."

"Mom, you're a trip. First you think that Roy is carrying a torch for me, and now you're convinced Carl has the hots for me or something. Is there anyone else I should know about?"

"I don't see what's so funny."

"Well, for one thing, for the past few years I've been lucky if I could scrounge up a date every six months or so. Now you're acting as if I'm Mesquite Creek's number-one bachelorette."

"You could be, if you put a little effort into it."

With that, her mother's conversation threatened to veer down the well-worn path of if-only-you'd. *If only you'd dress better . . . wear more makeup . . . take ballet . . . flirt more . . . bleach your teeth . . .* It had been going on for years. "Mom . . . I've got to go. These pups need to get out for a walk."

"I walked Squeak at lunch."

Her Mom always complained about how hideous Squeak was . . . but then she always came in around noon to check on him. "Thanks."

"How are you going to handle two dogs at once?" her mother asked.

Jane stared down at big brown eyes and two thumping tails and felt a smile tug at her lips. "It'll be easier than juggling all the gentlemen callers you're imagining beating down my door."

"Well . . . but it seems like I ought to get to know the new guy a little. He's a purebred, isn't he?"

She smiled. Her mom was a snob even when it came to canines. "He is."

"Could you use a hand? I just happen to have my tennies on."

She could just imagine her mom in the breakfast room, ready to go. Sometimes she wondered if it was normal for people to communicate by phone when they lived only fifty feet apart. They both probably could have traded in their calling plans and just used walkie-talkies.

"I can always use a hand," Jane said.

"I'll be right over!"

The next morning, Kaylie was lying in wait for her. "Can we talk at lunch?"

"What about?"

The receptionist's face fell. "The article? You're the last Juliet I have to talk to . . . and frankly, I hope you have something interesting to say, because Kelli Owens and old Miss Tatum sure didn't."

Jane bit her lip. She'd been hoping Kaylie wouldn't follow through with that. "Maybe that's a sign you should write about something else."

"Too late now. I promised *The Buzz* I'd have something for them tomorrow."

"Well, okay," Jane said reluctantly. "I have a short breather at twelve thirty. I could squeeze in a sandwich and a chat."

"Great! And don't forget the photographer's going to be here at three."

"Photographer?"

"Carl's idea. He wants a picture of the staff. You know—one big happy family."

That was weird. Carl had never had picture day before. Then again, he had never shown any interest in decorating before. Or come over to her house in the evening. Or asked about her future.

Jane hurried into an exam room and was brought up short by the sight of her friend Erin standing across the room from her long-lost cat, Smudge, who was draped across the stainless steel exam table.

Jane let out a whoop of surprise and joy. Erin, who ran a salon downtown, had been depressed for months because Smudge had disappeared. "When did he come home?"

Erin looked considerably less excited than Jane felt. "He showed up on my doorstep yesterday morning." Her mouth quirked. "I hear someone showed up on your doorstep, too."

Ignoring that topic, Jane petted Smudge and then started giving him a going-over. "Has he actually *gained* weight?" He'd never been small to begin with, but now he seemed even puffier and sleeker than ever. His white fur shone, and the single dark gray tabby mark on his back stood out even more.

She leaned over to the counter and read the notes Marcy had made on his chart after checking him in. "Says here he's put on over a pound."

Erin grunted. "All these months, I've been crying my eyes out because I imagined him lost and starving. He was obviously whooping it up somewhere."

Jane listened to his heart, which sounded fine except that it was hard to hear over his loud purring. He was such a sweetie, she had a hard time not making cooing noises at him.

Her friend crossed her arms. "There's something not right about him."

"Well, there's no telling what he's been up to. I'll run a blood test on him and check him for FIV."

"It's like that old movie," Erin said. "You know—the one where the guy comes back from the war and no one knows if he's who he says he is?"

Jane laughed. "This is Smudge."

"Yeah, but he's not exactly Smudge. He isn't playful like I remember. He's just a lump. And he won't eat dry food. I had to break down and open a can of tuna."

"What are you saying?"

Erin shifted and after a moment's hesitation admitted, "I think I've fallen out of love with my cat."

"Oh no," Jane said.

"It's true," she insisted. "I'm over him. I'm even thinking about trying to find someone else to take him, or seeing if the animal shelter—"

"No—you will not take him there." What was it with everyone? Had someone declared this Give Up On Your Pets Week and not informed her?

"You volunteer there," Erin pointed out.

"I don't care. You can't take him there. They do their best, but it's animal Auschwitz. You'd be dooming Smudge to die." Or dooming Jane to owning another cat. She took in Erin's implacable expression. "You're really serious, aren't you?"

"How would you feel if you'd been abandoned for months and then the guy just showed back up again looking fat and happy, and with completely new appetites?"

Hmph.

"He's a cat, not a guy," Jane argued. "Besides, we don't know what happened to him. Maybe his disappearance wasn't his fault. Maybe he got snatched, and was force-fed tuna until he made a valiant escape to get back to you."

"Oh sure—take his side," Erin said, joking.

At least, Jane was pretty sure she was joking. There needed to be relationship counseling for pet owners. "Promise me you won't do anything rash."

Erin hesitated only a moment before relenting. "Okay— I'll give him time." She aimed a pointed look at Jane as she took two blood samples. "What about Roy?" Erin asked. "Any change in his appetites?"

"I wouldn't know."

"I can't believe you didn't call me last night."

"I ended up at Mom's. Roy's return has made her a little frantic, so I let her beat me at canasta. But I'll come by soon and fill you in on all the details about what didn't happen."

Erin looked disappointed. "You'll probably soon take off for parts unknown, too."

Jane laughed. "Not likely."

"Why not? You never meant to live here permanently, did you?"

"No, but . . ." She was about to talk about all the things that made her heart clench up at the thought of leaving. Her parents. Her friends—primarily Erin and all the people she worked with. Even the town—a place she could have traveled through blindfolded. There was something comforting about running weekend errands and recognizing most every face she encountered. Sure, sometimes the town felt a little stifling, a trifle dull, but there was a safe feeling about it, too. "I seem to have become a Mesquite Creek lifer."

Erin scooped up Smudge and put him in his carrier. "Well, as one lifer to another, come by the salon and let me cut your bangs. Roy could be sending you come-hither looks, but you'd miss them for all the hair in your eyes."

The clinic was busy enough that morning that Jane managed to forget about lunch until Kaylie buttonholed her as she was staggering to the back room for a Diet Coke.

"Roy's been calling you," the receptionist informed her. Jane grunted.

"Your mother, too."

"Did she say what she wanted?"

"She wanted to know if Roy had called you."

"Maybe I should give them each other's numbers," Jane mused.

Kaylie laughed. "Ready for the interview?"

They sat at a picnic table that was set up next to the dog-walking area. No one else was there, and Jane was glad for the privacy. She wouldn't relish taking this stroll down memory lane in front of the rest of the staff. In fact, she'd rather not be taking it at all.

To begin, Kaylie read questions from a notebook she had brought with her. "What do you most remember about playing Juliet?"

Jane didn't have to ponder that one long. "Stage fright. We gave three performances, and I was terrified the whole time."

Kaylie twiddled her pen, unsatisfied. Jane felt as if she'd already bored her audience of one. "Yeah, everybody's talked about stage fright already. My question is, if you were so nervous, why did you try out?"

"I didn't. The speech teacher, Mrs. Humphrey, asked me to be the stage manager. I was really happy to do that. I loved going to all the rehearsals, figuring out what props needed to be where, and cuing the lights. Plus I ran lines with the actors. That was a blast. But then our Juliet, Lacey Butler, got sick at the last minute. And since I'd been running lines and going to all the rehearsals, I knew the part. So Roy told Mrs. Humphrey that I should do the role."

Interest sparked in Kaylie's eyes. "Roy McGillam asked for you to be his Juliet? Weren't y'all going out?"

"Not really. That happened . . . well, during the show."

"You mean you *fell in love* with your Romeo?"

God, that sounded so corny. "I guess we'd sort of been,

you know, attracted to each other for a while before that. But, yeah, we started dating during the show, and then for the rest of senior year. Back then, we had the senior play earlier in the fall, not the spring."

From the rapturous look on Kaylie's face, she could tell that Kaylie didn't care if the play happened in November, May, or Whenevuary. The story was now all about sex. "So basically, Roy was swoonworthy even back then?"

"Oh yeah. He always was, from first grade on. I'd always thought he was too cool for me. I'd always been a geeky study wart. I was really shocked when I figured out that he liked me."

"When was that?"

Jane tried not to blush. "Well, we had to kiss onstage a couple of times. The first time was in rehearsal, and even though I really wasn't that experienced, I knew it wasn't a playacting kind of kiss."

"That's so sweet. What else do you remember?"

Encouraged, Jane rambled on with a few more anecdotes. She talked more about Roy, and dating Roy, and the friction it caused because their mothers had been rivals for homecoming queen. And she mentioned a few incidents involving other people in the cast, like the time Jared had a costume malfunction and the crotch of his leggings kept falling around his knees, to the point that he toppled off the edge of the stage one night.

"But the audience just thought it was part of the fight scene," she explained, remembering too late that some of this might find its way into print. She didn't want to embarrass Jared. "He really did a great job."

"So you and Roy kept going out after the play, right?"

"All through college. We broke up just after we graduated. I mean, we didn't really break up, but we went separate ways—him to Seattle, me to vet school at College Station."

"Star-crossed lovers," Kaylie said.

"There was never any big scene. No poison or daggers."

"So you two never really fell out of love?"

"No, not really. I mean—there was never a breakup."

"And neither one of you has married?"

"No." Jane's brows knit as she watched Kaylie scribbling on her pad. "But we're definitely not involved now. That's clear, right?"

"Oh sure."

"I probably shouldn't have rambled on so much about Roy. Everybody has their experience with young love, right?"

"Exactly." Kaylie smiled brightly at her. "Thanks so much for talking to me, Jane. This has given me *a lot* to work with."

Jane tilted her head doubtfully. "It has?"

"Definitely."

Jane wasn't so sure that was a good thing.

Chapter Four

When Jane got home from work on Saturday afternoon, she changed into shorts and sandals and walked to the convenience store near her house on her way downtown. Driving anywhere today was ill-advised. Disgruntled locals spoke of the Jam with a double meaning, since it was the only time of year Mesquite Creek ever had a problem with traffic.

The Jam was a family-friendly event—which in Mesquite Creek meant that alcohol would not be sold. Which in turn meant that everybody brought their own. Jeff Sims, the owner of the Quik Stop, was probably the happiest person in town that day. He took note of Jane's six-pack with a grin.

"Meeting your sweetheart at the Jam?" he asked.

She laughed. "Not unless I manage to scrounge one up while I'm there. You know I'm footloose and fancy-free."

"I might, but *The Buzz* don't."

She looked down at the papers stacked in the wire rack by the counter. There was a picture of a new police vehicle taking up most of the front page, but right above the fold she glimpsed the headline "Star-Crossed Juliet Haunted by What Might Have Been." Next to the words was a smaller picture, very familiar to anyone who'd been in Mesquite

Creek High School during the past fourteen years, of her and Roy, their mouths centimeters apart. Beneath the picture was her truncated quote, "We never fell out of love."

"Oh no," she said, taking a copy.

Jeff added it to her total. "And here all these years I thought you'd dumped the guy. I don't see why a pretty thing like you should pine away half her life."

"I haven't been!" She skimmed and realized that the article made it sound as if she'd been doing exactly that. Her quotes were familiar to her, but they seemed to have been put through a filter that shifted their meaning from what she'd intended when she'd spoken them.

"I'm going to strangle Kaylie."

"Why? If Roy reads this, maybe he'll see you're still in love with him."

"But that's just what I *don't* want."

What a nuisance. She dreaded going to the Jam now. This stupid article would be fresh on everyone's minds.

"Have you sold many of these today?" she asked Jeff.

"Yep. Lots of people looking at that article. There's the bit with you and Roy, but it continues on page six, where there's another picture of old Miss Tatum as Juliet back in the fifties." He whistled. "Man, she was *hot*. Who knew?"

Jane paid for her things and left the Quik Stop, catching herself casting furtive glances around to see if anyone was coming before scurrying to the sidewalk.

She was acting so ridiculous. Over what? Just a little article. Who read *The Buzz* anymore, anyway? And, despite what Jeff said, who really cared?

Her phone rang, and she pulled it out of her purse. "Hi, Mom."

"Have you seen it?"

"Just now. I'm on my way to the Jam."

"You're going?"

Jane laughed. "Yes." Somehow, her mother's horrified

overreaction shrank her own down to a bearable feeling of rueful amusement.

"I don't know what made you go on like that in front of a newspaper reporter. You're usually so much more diplomatic."

She made it sound as if Jane gave interviews all the time.

"It was just Kaylie, from work, and I don't remember saying half those things. Or I don't remember them sounding so . . . pathetic."

"Why don't you come over to the house? I'll break out the *Mamma Mia!* DVD and some chardonnay and you can forget all about it."

As plans went, it wasn't a bad one. If she wanted to hide away and let people assume the newspaper story was true.

"Mom, I'm thirty-one, not fifteen. Being the object of gossip, even a few sneers, isn't going to kill me."

"But what if you see Roy? What if he thinks it's true that you're still pining away for him?"

Clearly, she didn't want him to have that satisfaction.

Jane tried to keep her phone to her ear as she shifted her beer to her other hand. "I'm pretty sure he won't believe it. It's not as if I welcomed him with open arms the other day. And I've been too busy, tired, or indecisive to return his calls. So don't worry—and don't drink all that chardonnay by yourself. I might need a few slugs of it when I get home tonight."

Silence crackled over the line. Jane knew her mom was dying to tell her how to run her life, and she loved her for fighting the impulse.

"You're coming over for lunch tomorrow, aren't you?" Brenda asked her. "I'm making a roast."

"Wouldn't miss it," she replied before signing off. She was probably the last thirty-something in America who still had pot roast lunches with her parents every Sunday.

Her stomach fluttered a little as she approached the

downtown square where the Jam was held. Bunting had been hung between light poles, and the open area had been converted into something resembling a Bedouin blackberry bazaar. Different vendors sold blackberries, blackberry goods, festival souvenirs, and crafts. There were also carts and card tables set up on the sidewalk by people offering ice cream and other treats. The first person Jane ran into was Marcy, who she had just parted company with at work an hour ago.

"Howdy, stranger," Marcy said. "After I saw Kaylie's story, I expected your mother would have you hidden away."

"Oh . . . so I guess people have read it?"

"Read it? Devoured it, from what I've heard around here. I had no idea you were still in love with him after all these years. You hide it pretty well."

Jane clucked in frustration. "I only intended to say that there was no big breakup, no moment when we decided to call it off or . . . you know, stop being in love. But that doesn't mean we still are."

"Uh-huh." Marcy looked confused by the distinction. "Well, maybe if I tell Keith your sob story, he'll decide it's time to seize the day and get off his ass and propose. You think?"

"I'm not the best person to be asking for advice on happily-ever-aftering." Jane looked around. "Where is Keith?"

"He said he'd be showing up later. You know how the afternoons are. It's all the lame music, blackberry-jam prizes, crowning Little Miss Blackberry, and kids getting sick on too much cobbler."

Jane had hoped to see Erin, but she probably couldn't get away from the salon yet. On a stage, about ten women with a sign proclaiming themselves to be the Mesquite Creek Flute Choir were doing a peppy rendition of "Wimoweh."

"I saw Roy around here not too long ago," Marcy said, perusing the crowd. "Look—there's his aunt."

Oh heavens. Jane turned and caught Ona's glare seconds before the woman began chugging toward her.

Maybe she should have opted for *Mamma Mia!* and chardonnay, after all.

Ona resembled Roy's mother, only she was twice as vigilant about guarding her size four figure. She wore pink pedal pushers and a white shirt that showed off her midriff, and her makeup was carefully done, if a little on the heavy side.

"Where's Roy?" Ona's tone suggested Jane had the man bound, gagged, and hidden away somewhere.

"I don't know. I just got here."

"But y'all have plans to meet." She stated it as a foregone conclusion.

"No," Jane said. "We don't."

Ona grunted. "I didn't just fall off the turnip truck. I read the paper. If you think you're going to convince him to keep Wanda's house—"

"I don't know anything about that," Jane said, cutting her off. She was angry enough at the woman now, that she felt her chest rising and falling in heavy breaths.

Ona studied her for a moment before backing down. "Well, if you do just so happen to bump into my nephew, tell him to call me."

She huffed away.

"Aren't you sorry you didn't marry Roy?" Marcy asked as they watched the older woman's departing figure. "You'd have the awesomest in-laws."

As Jane scanned the crowd, she caught several huddles of people staring back at them.

Marcy tugged on her sleeve. "Oh boy—look who's up next." The flute choir cleared off, making room for Doug Sims and his guitar. People gathered round. Doug wasn't the greatest singer, but his standard opener was "American Pie," which was a crowd-pleaser. Everyone always sang along, so by the end his voice was mostly drowned out anyway.

He thumped the mike to test it, and the reverb screeched through everyone's spines. He had the crowd's attention now.

"I'd like to dedicate this song to a gal I went to school with," he said. "In fact, I'd never have gotten through biology without her helping with homework during study hall." Doug's gaze zeroed right in on Jane, causing the crowd to pivot toward her. "Jane, this one's for you. Keep your chin up, babe."

A few whoops and catcalls echoed in response. Jane hoped she was smiling—whatever expression was on her face, she was sure it was going to be frozen there for the entire length of the song.

Luckily, nothing kept people from wanting to sing along with the Don McLean classic, and she was able to back away from the crowd and slip around the side of the courthouse, where there was a concrete bench next to the recessed rear door. Most of the time it was where county employees came out to smoke during business hours. During the Jam, it was a secluded spot where kids usually hung out. She rounded the corner and found it almost empty.

Except for Roy.

Roy smiled when he saw Jane's hunted, surprised look. "Escaped from the wolves and ran smack into the bear," he guessed. Her brows lifted and he explained. "I read the article."

She hitched one hand on her hip. "Who are you hiding from?"

"Aunt Ona."

He'd also been wallowing in a little self-pity. He'd hoped the Jam would be his best chance of seeing Jane. When he hadn't found her in the crowd, he'd wondered if he should go back to the house and do some work. A crisis was brewing and he wasn't sure Evan, his second in command, was handling it well. But he hadn't relished spending the afternoon thinking about contracts.

Now his mood lifted considerably.

"Coming here I expected I might roust some teenagers making out or sneaking a beer," she said.

"Why should teenagers have all the fun?" He angled a

look into the sack she was carrying. "Speaking of beer . . . are you sharing?"

She appeared to debate the question for a moment, then sat next to him on the bench. "Better to hang out with you than people who think I'm obsessed with you." She handed him a can and popped one open for herself. "At least you know better."

"Or I thought I did, till I read the morning paper," he said.

Her expression flashed a warning. "Watch it—or I'll give your location away to your aunt."

He laughed. "Do you have anyone specific you're trying to avoid today, or was I it?" he asked. "You did a great job dodging my calls yesterday."

She expelled a long breath. "Today is a whole new ball game."

"The article," he guessed.

Jane might not want to talk about it, but it was out in the open now. Pointless to avoid it.

"Kaylie made it sound as if I'm a love-obsessed spinster," she said. "Old Miss Tatum came off way better."

"Could you believe that picture?"

Jane leveled an amused glance at him. "You and every guy in town." She took another sip of beer. "It sounded as if I'm a kook, saying that we hadn't ever fallen out of love. But you know what I meant, right?"

"Exactly."

She looked relieved until she caught him staring at her. He couldn't help it. The article was one hundred percent right, as far as he was concerned. He hadn't fallen out of love with her, forgotten about her, or stopped wanting her. Yes, he'd felt stung. He'd dated other women and worked his heart out. But sometimes the only way he'd made it through the years away from Jane was by imagining that fighting the good fight against rabies, mange, and boredom in Mesquite Creek had aged her like Miss Tatum. But no, here she was, almost as if she'd been preserved in amber. And with all the personality quirks, expressions, and the voice that made the ache in his heart tear right open again.

Maybe if they'd had a big blowup, it would have been easier to move on. Instead, he'd dragged the memory of her with him wherever he went. And the possibility that someday . . .

"Every time I've seen you since I moved away, you've always put up a great show of indifference," he said. "I assumed you didn't care for me at all. I'd decided there was no hope."

She angled a distrustful look at him. "Are you between girlfriends or something?"

"As a matter of fact, yes." He smiled.

"How long does that usually last? I don't remember you ever being dateless back in school. In fact, I do remember a time when you had one date too many."

Her harsh glare made him wince. Once, when they were sophomores in college, he had taken a girl from his drawing class to a movie and had bumped into Jane in the ticket line. The incident had exploded into a breakup for the rest of the semester, although they'd gotten back together in the summer, after they ran into each other at their favorite swimming hole on the creek.

"Do you remember making up over the break?" he asked.

She took another sip, avoiding his eyes. Avoiding the question. "About the article . . . it really was just a case of diarrhea of the mouth."

"Of course. Everyone knows you're a chronic babbler."

"I only meant to say that we had never formally broken up," she continued. "We just went our separate ways. Which was a good thing, considering how things worked out. We've both found success in our work. And isn't that the best thing that can happen to people—to love what they do?"

"There are other good things that can happen, too."

She scrutinized him for a moment. "I can't believe you haven't gotten married. Your mother always made it sound as if you were the Rudolph Valentino of Seattle."

"Consider the source," he said. "Also, how many times did Rudolph marry?"

"Are you saying you never found the right woman?"

Might as well tell the truth. "Actually, I did find the right person. Once. I just didn't think she returned my feelings."

Jane kept her gaze focused on the ground, her expression thoughtful. "That's too bad."

Did she truly not understand who he was talking about? "I guess I always assumed that when my mind was made up, the moment would arrive and the words would just come," he confessed. "Spontaneously."

She laughed. "Well, who knows? It could still happen — you're only thirty-one."

"Is that all? This project I'm working on with a company in Los Angeles is making me feel more like eighty-one."

"Stressful art work?"

"Sometimes it doesn't feel like I'm an artist at all," he admitted. "It's not what I expected when I was in college and imagined working on my own in a basement somewhere. This business snag today is over licensing a video game. A video game—creative, maybe, but not the masterwork I was expecting to pour out my lifeblood for. And it *is* a business. A big part of my life is dealing with the nuts and bolts—tax questions, and benefits. Even though I have great support staff, most days leave me feeling as if I should have taken business courses, and accounting. And plumbing—McG Studios is in an old warehouse building."

"It still sounds pretty fun," she said.

"It is. Even on a bad day, I can't imagine doing anything else."

"Then you're a success."

They sat sipping and listening to the sounds of the guitar strumming in the distance. "So to get back to topic A," he said. "If we never broke up, doesn't that mean we've technically been together all these years?"

"You'd better hope not. It sounds as if you've been cheating on me quite a bit."

He stretched out his legs. "As if you haven't been stepping out yourself." When she opened her mouth to deny it, he decided to jog her memory. "Stu Lunsford?"

She eyed him sharply. "How did you find out about Stu?"

"I have my stooges."

The memory of his mother, who'd always kept him apprised of the goings-on about town, sent a jolt of sadness through him. He wouldn't have that anymore. Once he sold her house and left town this time, he wouldn't have much of a connection left to Mesquite Creek. Or Jane.

"Stu's very nice," she said, a little defensively. "He's a pharmacist now. Our moms set us up."

"And you were how old?"

She ducked her head. "Twenty-eight. He's very interesting, but when he wanted to go to a gun show for our second date, I broke it off. Something about the combination of pharmaceuticals and firearms made me uncomfortable."

"No regrets about the one that got away, then?"

"No, not with Stu."

As soon as the words were out, her eyes widened. Roy's heartbeat kicked up a notch, but before he could react in any other way, someone came around the corner. Roy suppressed a groan. It was Carl. The man smiled—an expression that dimmed slightly when he noticed Roy.

"I was beginning to wonder if I would ever run into you," he said to Jane.

What did that mean? Roy looked over at Carl and tried not to let his consternation show. He'd never considered the vet as a rival, even after he had interrupted them at Jane's apartment. Carl was a good fifteen years older, for one thing. But he supposed that age difference didn't mean much now.

"I'm actually glad to see you here, Roy," Carl said, catching him off guard.

"You are?"

"Do you know anything about design?"

Jane laughed. "That's sort of his life, Carl."

Carl's red brows drew together. "Yeah, the dancing food and stuff. But I've been wondering about lettering. See, I'm trying to figure out a new sign for the clinic . . ."

With dismay, Roy watched Jane toss her half-finished can away and slap her hands together. "I'm going back to the Jam."

Carl looked over at her, clearly dismayed. Roy felt the same way. "Really? We could—"

"No," she insisted. "You two talk shop awhile. I want to track down Erin. I'll leave the refreshments with you."

Roy's instinct was to run after Jane. Then again, this was the second time he'd bumped into Carl and Jane together. That had to mean something. Maybe it would be useful to know what the man's intentions were. And to keep him out of Jane's path.

When she was gone, he turned back to the other man. "Have a beer?"

Jane hurried away, discombobulated by her encounter with Roy. The conversation had seemed half flirtation, half elegy to their dead romance. And asking him about his love life—how nosy and masochistic was that?

Masochistic, because she found herself fighting jealousy against these women that he'd mentioned he'd been seeing. Which was crazy.

Leave it to Roy to unsettle her this way. As a teenager, she'd prided herself for having her feet firmly planted on the ground. Then Roy had come along. The fun times—driving to Mexico and back on the spur of the moment, bungee jumping, skinny-dipping, staying up all night just to watch the sunrise—had all been at Roy's instigation.

Maybe that had always been part of Roy's allure. All through school she'd kept her head down, doing what she was told, studying hard, knowing she was destined to be one of the soldier ants of the world. And then Roy had suddenly made her feel as if she had a spark of something special inside her, as if she might actually have possessed a hint of Juliet. Someone who had "taught the torches to burn bright."

But of course he'd probably made a lot of women feel that way. He was a man who made pretzels dance.

She bumped into Marcy again near the blackberry-lemonade stand.

"Where did you disappear to?" Marcy asked. "You've missed the Chamber of Commerce Barbershop Quartet and the awarding of the blue ribbon for blackberry preserves."

"Mona Breyer," Jane guessed. Mona always won.

"Well, yeah," Marcy said. "But you still missed it."

Shane approached them. "Hi, y'all," he said, although he was looking only at Marcy. "I'd ask you to dance, but there hasn't been anything played that has a beat to it. Creek Fire is slated to play after the Methodist Sunday School Choir, though. Maybe then . . . ?"

Marcy's mouth set in a fierce line. "If Keith hasn't shown up by then, I'll be at home drowning my sorrows in a tub of Haagen-Dazs."

"Oh," Shane said. "Well, I guess . . . See ya Monday, then."

Marcy nodded. "Sure."

When he was out of earshot, Jane said, "That wasn't very nice."

"What?"

"The way you blew off Shane just now."

Marcy looked confused. "He was just talking."

"He was trying to ask you for a dance."

"Four hours into the future? What kind of guy does that? We're not living in a Jane Austen movie." She lifted her chin. "Besides, everybody knows I'm as good as engaged to Keith."

"Everybody except Keith." Jane prepared herself for Marcy to start yelling at her.

Instead, Marcy listened to the choir for a minute before turning back to Jane. "Are you saying that the reason Keith hasn't proposed is because he doesn't want to get married?"

Jane shrugged. "I don't know. What does Keith say?"

"He's never mentioned it."

"Have you?"

Marcy goggled at her. "Of course not."

"Well, why not?"

"Because a guy likes to pop the question, right?"

"Oh, for heaven's sake. You're an adult, not a damsel in a fairy tale. Just talk to him. Maybe he never wants to get married. Wouldn't that be good information to have? Or maybe he just needs to know that's what you want, too. Either way, you're better off speaking your mind."

Marcy looked dazed. "You're right. I've been acting as if Keith were Prince Charming." She lifted and dropped her arms. "Why? The man needs to be nagged into doing everything from asking for a raise to clipping his toenails. Why have I been expecting him to show the initiative in proposing? For that matter, maybe *I* should propose to him."

Her determination brought out Jane's inner ditherer. "Oh, I don't know if I'd go that far . . ."

"I do," Marcy said, cutting her off. "In fact, I'm going to hunt him down right now and ask him."

She pivoted and practically sprinted away. Jane watched her, torn. Part of her wanted to call her back.

But at least she'd struck a blow for plain speaking. For rationality over romanticism. And maybe in ten years Kaylie wouldn't be writing crazy interviews for the newspaper about how Jane didn't know what happened to the one big romance she'd had in her life.

Chapter Five

That night, an explosion of barking rousted Jane out of a nearly sound sleep. From the full-throated cries the dogs were unleashing at the door, she expected an intruder to come bursting through any second. She jammed her feet into scuffs, shushed the animals, and attempted to clear her head of sleep.

Then a spray of something hit the window in the living room. The dogs went nuts.

Jane grabbed her robe and sprinted into the next room to make sure the window was locked. Mesquite Creek prided itself on being the kind of place where you could still keep your windows open at night, although it was warm enough already that Jane had been using the air conditioner.

She pulled back a curtain to peek out just as another blast of rock hit the glass. Her bleat of surprise sent the cats racing to their safety spots. Jane squinted through the pane and spied someone pacing down below.

Roy.

She ran to the door, nearly tripping over Squeak. Once again she shushed the dogs before opening the door and stepping onto the landing. She peered down at Roy's barely visible form in the darkness.

He raised an arm dramatically. "Hark, what—"

"What are you doing?" she said, cutting off the theatrics. "It's after one!"

"I know—the night is young, and the town is dead. And there's something I've been wanting to do since I saw this balcony the other day."

"It's not a balcony, it's a staircase landing, and you can't—"

But he could. He disappeared and she leaned over the railing, watching him trying to get purchase on the morning-glory trellis attached to the pole supporting the landing. "The stairs are so much easier," she told him.

"That's the trouble with you, Jane. No sense of—*ouch!*" Gasped curses floated up from below.

"What happened?" she said, squinting down at him.

"Splinter."

"Would you please jump down?"

"Nope. I've come this far . . ." Grunting, he kept climbing until they were face-to-face. He breathed a sigh of relief. "Made it."

And then something cracked, and he was gliding away from her—as was the entire top of the trellis. He reached out to grab the railing, missed, and clasped her arm instead. For a horrifying moment, she worried she was going to be yanked down with him. Instead, she dug in her heels, trying to ignore the cacophony of dogs and shrieking parakeet in the apartment behind her, and tugged as hard as she could, pulling him and the trellis back to the landing.

When he was close enough, Roy let go of her hands and clutched at the railing for dear life. She helped haul him over, and they collapsed against the door, which hadn't latched properly and fell open unexpectedly. In the next moment, they tumbled in a heap on the floor of her apartment, laughing hysterically.

"That was really stupid," Roy said, catching his breath.

"Yes." She kicked the door closed. "And really not good for Luther's nerves." She would probably have a one-hundred-percent-bald bird by morning.

"*Luther's* nerves?" he asked. "What about mine? I need a drink."

"I'm guessing you've already had a few." She stood.

"I mean, something to drink like water. I had three beers with the good doctor."

"Which doctor?"

"Carl," he said.

"You two were together this whole time?" She had waited around the Jam for them for a while but had finally given up and sought out Erin at the salon. They'd gone out for dinner and then returned to the gathering to listen to one of the later bands. But Roy had never shown up again. She'd just assumed he'd gone home to work on the project he'd been talking about.

"We went to the clinic so he could show me his sign idea," Roy explained. "By the time we got back downtown, you must have already left." He smiled, all innocence. Which made her suspicious. "Carl's a really nice guy."

She got up off the floor, opened the fridge, and grabbed the iced tea pitcher. What wasn't he telling her? Plus, he was wearing different clothes than he had been this afternoon. Also . . .

She studied his head. "What's in your hair?"

He looked up, his eyes almost crossing.

"You've got light green streaks in your hair," she pointed out.

He laughed. "Oh. Probably from when I was doing touch-up work around the house."

"And what were you and Carl up to that took so long?"

"We talked about all sorts of things." He gave her a significant look. "Including you."

She took a long swig of tea, forgetting that she'd poured it for Roy. She got another glass down for him.

"You know what conclusion I've drawn about the good doctor?" Roy asked, stretching out and scratching Buddy behind the ears.

"You made a psychological assessment?"

"No—just gut reaction. I like him."

She went to hand him the glass, but he was surrounded by dogs who looked as if they might nose it right out of his hand. "You'll never be able to drink in peace while you're on the floor."

He lifted his hand to her, and she pulled him up. He came to standing about an inch from her, so close that she could feel body heat coming off of him. She stepped a safer distance away and held out the glass.

"Of course you like Carl," she said. "He's a nice guy—always has been. Why do you think I came back to help out?"

He shrugged. "When Mom told me you'd moved back here after vet school, I just assumed that you wanted to be close to your family, to what was familiar."

"Because I was unadventurous, or lacked imagination to do anything else," she translated.

"I never said that."

"I came back because when I talked to Carl he was so distraught, and he wanted to take a few months off to grieve for Maggie. And after that . . . well, so far I've just never found a good reason to leave."

"He's not grieving for Maggie now," Roy said.

"No, I think he's finally coming out of it. I'm glad."

Roy moved closer to her again. "I guess what I'm saying is that I can see why you'd like him." He swallowed. "Why you might love him, even."

The words took a few moments to absorb. "I could see how some woman might love him," she corrected. "But I don't."

"I know from talking to him that you two aren't involved. But I don't want to step in and ruin anything that might be brewing."

She laughed. "Nothing is brewing, believe me."

His eyes clouded, troubled. "I don't know . . ."

What on earth had Carl said to him? Before she could voice the question, another oddity struck her full force. "Wait a second . . . what do you mean by stepping in?"

"Isn't it obvious?"

"By your antics on the trellis? All I gleaned from that is that your Romeo days are probably behind you."

"Why do you think I'm in Mesquite Creek, Jane?"

She tried to ignore the huskiness in his voice. "To sell your mother's house."

"I could go back to Seattle and let Lou and Aunt Ona handle it. I stayed because I saw you and realized I didn't want to leave without trying again. Because after the house is gone . . ."

He might not be back.

"All these years you would breeze in and out of town during your visits and you barely acknowledged me," she said, surprised by the anger that bubbled up.

"I know. I felt stung when you decided to choose vet school here over me."

"It was what I'd been working for all through school. Weren't you paying attention?"

"You could have gone to school on the West Coast."

"And you could have stayed—just waited two or three years for me to finish," she said.

"Years!" He shut his mouth and shook his head. "Okay. We're back in the old argument."

"Exactly."

He took her hands in his. "But things are different now for both of us. We're both who we wanted to become. My pride was hurt when I left, but maybe it was good for me.

And you were always in the back of my mind as the ideal, Jane. I swear. No one else has measured up."

Even now, when every atom felt electrified as she stared into those gorgeous blues, a corner of her mind shouted at her to be sensible, not to make a misstep.

And then he was pulling her closer, wrapping his arms around her, and she sank against him, ignoring her inner good girl shrieking warnings. When Roy's lips touched hers, it felt so right. He'd always been a great kisser, and now she remembered why. Men since had been too aggressive, or their technique too slurpy. Roy's mouth fit perfectly against hers; his tongue felt natural, not like a probe. They had taught each other to kiss, and their bodies hadn't forgotten. Whatever was between them felt instinctive now, almost primal.

Her hands roamed up his chest, twining around his nape. Where in the old days there had been more hair, there was now just a soft bristle of close-cut fuzz. She stroked it and he groaned, pulling her closer, hands roaming down her hips so that she could feel him pressing against her belly. A sharp yearning hit her, and she could feel them moving toward the Herculon couch, a place that knew them well.

Someone knocked at the door.

The dogs barked and Roy pulled back with a ragged curse. She swallowed, trying to still her heartbeat, to clear her thoughts.

"Were you expecting anyone?" he asked, almost in a whisper.

She shook her head. Could her mother have seen Roy and decided to come over and break up whatever was going on? It was so like her to jump to conclusions—

Another knock sounded. Of course, this time her mother's conclusion would have been completely accurate.

She stumbled to the door, retying her robe and praying she looked somewhat composed. Prepared to face her mother, she was completely caught off guard to find Jared standing on her doorstep in his police uniform, one hand on his weapon.

He looked surprised, too—which was strange, since he had to know who lived here. Then she realized he wasn't looking at her, but beyond her, at Roy. He stepped inside the apartment. "We had a call from one of your neighbors about a possible intruder . . . said there was a lot of barking."

Jane rolled her eyes. "Cora Philpott? She's always complaining about the dogs. I don't know how she can hear them when they're inside."

"She also said she saw some suspicious activity outside the apartment."

"That was probably me," Roy said, smiling.

Jared laughed. "Trying to make a big entrance?"

"Sort of. Though I swear I wasn't going to break in."

The policeman shrugged. "Well, don't worry about it. If I'd known it was you, I wouldn't have come rushing over."

Jane frowned. "He's been here twenty minutes. You couldn't have been rushing too quickly."

"It's Jam weekend. We get lots of calls." Jared put his hands on his hips. "Not to mention, I spent part of the evening with my sister, trying to deal with the fallout from all the trouble *you* started."

Jane flinched. "Is something wrong with Marcy?"

"Wrong? She's a wreck! Said you told her she ought to propose to Keith, which she did. Where did you come up with such a cockamamy idea? Scared the guy so much that he dumped her outright."

Jane's jaw dropped. "Dumped her?"

"Told her that since she was so antsy about getting married, he didn't want to lead her on. Said he didn't know she had expectations."

"Oh no," Jane said.

"Poor thing spent the whole night crying herself sick. You know how many times I've seen my little sister cry, besides funerals? Zero. If I weren't an officer of the law, I'd kill him."

"I'm sorry. That's terrible for her."

"If you'd just left well enough alone, Keith might have come around eventually. Guys don't like to be cornered, you know?"

"I only meant for her to talk to him . . ."

"Well, mission accomplished."

Footsteps clattered up the stairs, and in the next second her mother appeared in her short-sleeved terry cloth bathrobe. "What's wrong? What happened to my trellis?"

"There was a little accident," Jane said.

"An accident?" Her father, who'd come in on the heels of her mom, stood in his old plaid robe. He looked a little stooped, as he always did in the apartment, as if he feared his head would scrape the ceiling.

Roy stepped forward. "It was my fault," he confessed. "I unintentionally damaged the trellis."

Her mother blinked. "How?"

"By climbing on it."

Her mother's cheeks flooded with red, but it was her father who spoke. "Are you drunk?"

Jane tried to ease the tension with a chuckle. It was so ridiculous. She felt as if she was in high school again and had been caught out after curfew. "We were just horsing around."

"Why were the police called?" her father asked.

Jared assured them, "Mrs. Philpott said it looked like breaking and entering, but it was just Roy."

This only agitated her mother more. "Oh, for heaven's sake! What do you—"

"Now, we can all talk about this tomorrow," Jane's father said, putting his hands on his wife's shoulders to try to calm her. Jane could have hugged him. "For now, there's probably no harm done that some staples and a little Gorilla Glue won't set right."

"Sure." Jared shot a quick glare at Jane. "Well, except for poor Marcy. You can't Gorilla Glue that right again."

He turned and left.

Jane smiled weakly. "I gave someone at work a little bad advice," she explained to her folks.

They nodded. Then they transferred their gazes from her to Roy.

Neither of them budged.

For Pete's sake. Did they really intend to stand there all night and protect their little girl's virtue?

Evidently.

Roy finally took the hint. "I should be going. Guess I've caused enough problems for one night."

"Yes," Brenda said.

"Mom . . ." Jane hurried after Roy to the porch.

Out of their hearing, he turned back to her, grinning. "I'll call you tomorrow and we can get together."

"Great," she said.

He took her hand and gave it a firm squeeze.

When Jane went back inside, her mother's fierce, protective look had changed to a more searching gaze. She examined Jane's face so intently that Jane drew back a little, disconcerted.

"What's the matter?" Jane asked.

"I just thought I saw something," her mother murmured.

Jane's father seemed more amused than anything else. "Roy's looking good, isn't he?" he said. "I thought so the other day when we were touring the new auditorium at the school. He hasn't changed a bit."

"No, he hasn't," her mother grumbled. "Still acting like a teenager."

Jane crossed her arms. "No, you're still acting as if I'm a teenager—chasing my friends away as though I had a curfew."

"Did you want him to stay all night?" her mother asked.

Did she ever.

Her father began to tug her mother toward the door. "Maybe we should leave this for tomorrow, Brenda. In the light of day, this will all seem like nothing. After all, Roy's just going to be here a few more days. He told me himself that the only reason he was sticking around was for the opening of the auditorium."

"When did he say this?" Jane asked.

He thought for a second. "Day before yesterday? Well, he's giving a speech Thursday, so of course he's going to stay. But after that . . ."

Of course. She'd even known about the auditorium dedication. And yet she'd fallen for Roy's I'm-here-because-of-you patter—hook, line, and sinker.

Her father smiled encouragingly at Jane before they left the apartment. "Don't worry. Incidents like this blow over. Soon, Roy will go back to Seattle, life will return to normal, and everyone will remember how sensible you are." He winked. "Good night."

When they were gone, Jane stumbled back to bed and flopped back against the mattress.

Maybe Roy had wanted to rekindle their romance. Why not? He was breezing through town, bored, avoiding work . . . Probably he was still feeling sad because of his mom. So he'd reached out to the old and familiar. Old, familiar Jane.

Damn.

And the saddest part? She wasn't sure whether she cared if he was sincere or not.

Everything will get back to normal. That was supposed to be comforting. The trouble was, Roy had come back, and now normal seemed lackluster.

Chapter Six

On Sunday morning Jane waited for the promised call. During lunch with her parents, she stayed within grabbing distance of her phone, like a teen in an Annette Funicello movie. During the middle of the meal, she received a text from Roy.

Sorry haven't called. On my way to California. Could you assure your dad I'll be back for aud dedication? Thanks! xoxo, R

So. Back to normal had arrived even sooner than she expected.

As she came through the clinic's front door Monday morning, the sharp odor of fresh paint brought her up short.

Jane gaped. The room was no longer its old faded eggshell white, but an eye-peelingly vivid minty green. Clutching the bag containing her lunch and the book she always read on her short lunch break, she completed a full turn.

"What do you think?" Kaylie asked. "Really brightened the place up, huh?"

"It's . . . minty." In fact, it felt as if she were inside a toothpaste tube. "Who did this?" But even as she asked the question, she knew. The weird streak in Roy's hair Saturday night. The hours during which he and Carl had disappeared. All his hints about how Carl felt about her.

Of course. She'd told Carl she liked green. Carl had probably mentioned her preference to Roy as a reason for his choice of color. (Not that she'd had *this* in mind.) With his usual enthusiasm, Roy—or R, as she liked to think of him now—had probably thought helping Carl would be a lark.

"I think Carl did it himself—if you look closely you can see the sploops," Kaylie pointed out. "He's on the phone right now, but he's been impatient for you to get here. He's like a little kid with a huge secret." She lowered her voice. "I guess a lot of people had interesting weekends."

Jane leaned on the reception desk, remembering she'd intended to give Kaylie a piece of her mind. There had to be some repercussions for a receptionist who practiced yellow journalism on the side. "That's the last time I'm ever speaking to you while you've got your press hat on."

Kaylie laughed. "Oh, come on. I thought the article turned out great. Everybody was talking about it."

"Were they? I guess I was too busy hiding in my apartment to notice." After Sunday lunch, Jane had decided to put Roy out of her mind and had turned off her phone while she did furious housework. Periodically, she would check messages and feel even more aggrieved to see that there were no missed calls. No more wildly effusive text messages, either.

"I did some spring cleaning," she added.

One of Kaylie's blond brows darted up. "Uh-huh. Was this before or after Roy was hanging out at your place?"

"Who told you that?"

"It's practically public record, thanks to my brother," Marcy grumbled from the hallway. She was mopping outside the exam rooms.

Remembering Marcy's troubles, Jane took a deep breath

and strode over to her. "Jared told me what happened with Keith. I'm so sorry."

The vet tech didn't look up. When she spoke, it was in a monologue muttered at her broom handle. "Dear Miss Lonelyhearts, I've been in a long-term relationship and would really like it to go to the next level. What should I do?" She answered herself, drawling sensibly, "Dear Marcy, why not pinpoint someone you know who's barely been able to scrounge up a date for years and ask her? You might get lucky. This love expert and so-called friend of yours might advise you to corner your commitment-phobic boyfriend and ask him to marry you, and maybe you'll even be dumb enough to take her advice. He might drop you like a greased watermelon and run as far and as fast as he possibly can."

Jane shuffled uncomfortably. "I can't believe Keith reacted that way."

"Believe it. Said he just wasn't ready to settle down—or maybe he just said settle. Then he told me that if marriage meant so much to me, it would be better for both of us if we went our separate ways."

"That's so awful. But at least—"

Marcy broke off her words with a bray of irritation. "Oh yeah! At least I know what kind of guy he is now. And at least there's no uncertainty. Yup, thanks, figured that out. Glad to know." She slopped the mop back into the janitor's bucket and then rung it out within an inch of its life. "I'd invite you for a single-girl night of *Glee*-watching or something, but I hear *some* people's weekends turned out better than others'."

If misery loved company, at least she could give Marcy some consolation. "You might have been misinformed. Roy's already flown the coop again."

Marcy frowned. "What, already? Why?"

"Business. That's what he said in the one brief message he deigned to send."

"After breaking your mom's trellis and stirring up a hornet's nest of gossip about you?"

God, people even knew about the trellis. "Yup."

"What is it with guys?" Marcy asked. "Do they all see their lives as having limitless romantic possibilities? There has to be some reason why they scoot out the door—or leave the state—as soon as things get complicated." She angled a sympathetic look at Jane. "Is he gone for good?"

"Well, he does have a history of disappearing for a decade. But it's not like we had actually gotten involved." When Marcy and Kaylie exchanged a skeptical glance, she added, "Really."

Kaylie sighed. "Better to have a broken trellis than a broken heart."

Jane shook her head. "Never any risk of that. He was just here for a few days. And he's obviously no good at long-distance relationships. Ten years ago, we didn't bother to attempt one, and now . . ."

Marcy's lips twisted into a disgusted frown. "So all that *Romeo and Juliet* stuff was still just playacting on his part. And Jared's been talking him up for days as if he's some kind of town hero. Town jerk, more like it."

Jane felt uncomfortable vilifying him. "Well, there is the auditorium, and the police cruiser."

"You don't have to defend him," Marcy said, looping an arm up around Jane's shoulders. She looked up and gave her a bracing squeeze. "Single solidarity. I'm sorry I gave you crap for wrecking my relationship and maybe my entire future. If I'd known you were in the bleak corner, too, I'd have kept my yap shut."

"That's okay," Jane said as the office door opened.

Carl came out, his face expectant. "You're here!" He looked as if he was about to say more—probably to ask her opinion about the paint. At that moment, however, Kaylie let out a gasp, directing their attention to the clinic's front door.

They all turned, expecting an early arrival or an emergency. But instead of anything on four legs or an owner toting a cat box, Ann from Buckets of Blooms appeared—or at least Jane assumed it was Ann. Her face was hidden by an enormous spray of spring flowers with a Mylar balloon sprouting out the top that announced *I'm Sorry* in script.

"How beautiful!" Kaylie exclaimed.

Marcy dropped her hand from Jane's shoulder and raced to the front. She practically tackled the florist. "Who's that for?"

Ann heaved the arrangement onto the counter. "Jane."

At her name, Jane felt an absurd flush of excitement. She approached the flowers, which seemed even larger close-up, and picked the pale yellow card off its plastic holder. Aware of all eyes on her, she quickly opened it and read. *Sorry for the radio silence. Things are crazy here. Back soon!*

"They're from Roy, right?" Kaylie asked.

Jane nodded, trying not to smile.

"He's sorry because it's over?" Marcy asked.

"I think he's sorry because he didn't call," Jane explained.

Marcy's face fell.

"I was so excited when I came in this morning and saw the order online," Ann said, standing back to take a last look at her handiwork. "Hardly anybody ever orders the Tower of Flowers. It's only the second time I've done it. Lucky I had enough gladiolas!"

"You did an incredible job," Kaylie said.

"Isn't it a little much?" Marcy pursed her lips. "I mean, geez, couldn't he have just sent an e-mail?"

"Flowers are a tangible manifestation of sentiment," Ann said, as if reciting from the United Florist Association handbook.

"Yeah, and they wilt and have to be tossed out." Marcy turned to Jane with an expression showing a lot less solidarity than before. "You might want to check with Carl to see if it's okay to leave them there. Some people are allergic." She skulked away to finish the mopping.

To get Carl's verdict, Jane twisted to where he had been standing earlier. But he'd already disappeared.

There were days when she wished she'd never read *All Creatures Great and Small*. Though she'd always loved animals, it wasn't until her father had given her a boxed copy of James Herriot's books that her obsession had coalesced into an ambition.

Why? she wondered now. She'd started her day with an operation on a dog with a broken leg tendon. That had been followed by the usual parade of veterinary woes, including a dachshund with a disc problem, an adorable stray with feline leukemia, and a cranky cockatoo who was even more ornery when he had a cold. Around noon she'd driven out to the county animal shelter where she volunteered two afternoons per month. She was happy to do the work, but the shelter always left her feeling low. The bottom of the food chain when it came to county funds, it survived on a shoestring thanks to volunteers. But the animals who appeared in the old, crowded cages were the flip side of the animals with devoted owners she saw every day—these were the abandoned, the abused, the lost. Most people had no idea how many the shelter processed, how many healthy adorable animals were put down because there were simply not enough homes. And there was a never-ending stream of them.

Before leaving the shelter, she was called out to a farm where there was a sick horse. The problem was colic, and a dose of Banamine seemed to help the animal, an appaloosa beauty named Zelda. Just to make sure the horse was reacting well to the medicine, Jane stayed and walked her on a lead. The owner—actually the owner's father, since Zelda's rider, a scrappy young barrel racer, was in school—dogged Jane's steps.

"I was expecting Carl to come out. He usually did the serious work, I thought."

She rarely got this, but Jack Lewis was the old-fashioned type. Maggie used to joke about the expectations ingrained in old-school types when it came to veterinary medicine—the assumption that female vets were supposed to minister to kittens and hamsters. "Carl was tied up," Jane explained.

Jack grunted. "Maybe the next time, he'll hire a man."

"Next time?" Jane's head turned so sharply, she startled Zelda. She reached up to pat the horse's neck and calm her. "I didn't realize I was on the cusp of unemployment," she joked.

"Well, how long are you going to last out here now that the McGillam boy's back in town?"

She frowned. As far as she knew, Roy *wasn't* back. She'd expected to hear from him Monday night, but again he hadn't called. And she'd been too busy today to check messages. Not that it made any difference. "I'm not seeing a connection," she said. "Besides, Roy and I aren't even . . . involved." One little kiss, that's all there had been.

Jack snorted. "Sent you the Tower of Flowers, didn't he?" While Jane, struck dumb, led the horse, he shook his head. "No, I imagine Carl'll be looking for somebody else pretty soon. Or maybe he'll go it alone. That's what I'd do, probably, if I was him."

Ah yes. The old "what I would do if I were a vet whose partner had run off with an old flame" scenario. A body just couldn't help ruminating about that sometimes.

After leaving Zelda on the road to recovery, she got back in her car and started the drive back into town. It seemed half the town already had her paired off with Roy, while her mother was certain that *Carl* was in love with her. The story of the green paint—which Jane had only mentioned to her mother to get her to stop fretting about Roy's flowers—had nearly short-circuited the maternal unit.

"Isn't that sweet, Jane?" Brenda had gushed. "He's like one of those little bowerbirds, making his nest appealing to you."

Actually, the idea made Jane uncomfortable in all kinds of ways. "Why should he have to appeal to me?" she asked. "I already work there. Of course I like the place."

"But I bet he wants to make it more attractive to you."

"Or maybe he finally noticed that the other paint had faded to a hideous khaki color and was chipped everywhere."

Besides, Jane had been observing Carl closely in the past day, and he had been nothing but his usual professional self toward her.

"And don't you think if Carl and I had any kind of chemistry, we would have found that out by now? We've been alone together a lot, and I can swear to you that he's never been anything less than a gentleman."

"Well." Her mother had sounded indignant. "I would hope so. Although, maybe if you'd give him a little encouragement . . ."

As Jane went over the conversation in her head once again—the many conversations she'd had with her mother on this perplexing topic—she began to feel weary. And hot. Afternoon temperatures were already spiking into the nineties, and she'd been going all day. She should tag the clinic and then go home and take a shower, although neither the clinic nor home seemed very welcoming.

Out of the corner of her eye she spotted the blacktop road that branched off to a smaller dirt road that led to the creek. She hadn't been there in years, but suddenly staring at water appealed to her more than going back into town. The two-lane was empty and she hit the brake and then U-turned, looping back to the blacktop road and then bouncing down the rutted lane that dead-ended at Mesquite Creek.

She was in luck. Only one other vehicle, a shiny SUV,

was parked nearby. Probably a guy fishing somewhere on the creek. Or a serial killer dumping his latest victim. Whoever it was, hopefully they would leave her alone.

She got out, grabbed a blanket from the trunk, and took a deep breath. The temperature seemed to have dropped ten degrees since she was at the ranch, and the spring air held a hint of honeysuckle. In the area along the bank, patches of purple thatch and Indian paintbrush provided splashes of color. This section of the creek wasn't the most popular swimming hole—on the other side of town there was a wider spot with a more beachy area where teenagers liked to hang out. But this had always been her favorite place. A couple of flat gray boulders jutted out of the water like humps of a sea monster, providing a good place to sunbathe or just sit and meditate.

She didn't see him at first when she entered the clearing. She'd kicked off her shoes, rolled up her jeans, and was in the water already. But when she did spot him, her heart lurched twice in her chest—first out of surprise, and then because it was Roy. Why hadn't he told her he was back?

And why did she feel so absurdly happy to see him there?

He was lying on his back on the rock she'd intended for her own use, one arm flung over his eyes. He was wearing a T-shirt and baggy jean shorts, but he still managed to steal her breath. From the definition in those muscles, he hadn't been spending his entire life behind a desk.

She was torn between creeping furtively back to her car or sneaking up on him when he jolted up to sitting. Startled, she shouted, and when his face broke out in a broad smile, she reached down and splashed him with water.

"Hey!" he yelled. "You're getting my rock wet."

"That's *my* rock."

"There's room for two." Even from several yards away, his eyes seemed bright. "Remember?"

Visions of their former selves came to mind, during summers when there always seemed to be time to spend a lazy afternoon hanging out at the creek. It's where they had re-united after their one breakup during college. The miracle of the rock.

She bit her lip. "The prodigal slacker returneth—and I didn't even get a text. What are you doing here?"

His head tilted. "What are *you* doing here? And why are you just standing there in the mud?" He scooted over to make room for her.

She stood, torn, her toes squishing on the creek bottom as she curled them in her indecision.

"I chased off the water moccasins for you," he said.

At that reminder, she hopped gingerly toward the rock. It was spring, so the water was higher than she remembered. She nearly lost her balance when her foot hit a dip, but she managed to keep hold of the blanket. Roy offered a hand to help her scramble onto the rock. His grip was strong.

She spread the blanket out and sat on it, bending her knees so she didn't get the blanket soggy. "I wish I'd brought a towel, too."

Roy smiled at the fussy way she settled herself. "Where did you get that blanket?"

"I keep it in my trunk for emergencies." It smelled vaguely of horses and WD-40.

"Like a good Girl Scout. Always prepared."

"You're thinking Boy Scouts."

He lifted his shoulders sheepishly. "I was a Boy Scout dropout. Didn't make it that far."

She laughed. "As far as the part where they talked about the motto . . . wouldn't that be the first meeting?"

"My dad forgot to show up for the orientation," he explained. "I ended up having to be driven home by the troop leader, Mr. Bernie. Dad was at the bottom of the bottle then, I guess. Anyway, he ended up slugging poor Mr. Bernie. I never joined, obviously."

The story didn't surprise her. She and Roy might have grown up within a mile of each other, but their experiences had been worlds apart. When she was a girl, her every activity had been guided, monitored, and usually applauded. Roy had raised himself, to a certain extent.

"I'm sorry," he said. "I didn't mean to go down that path. Coming back always hits me in unexpected ways. It's supposed to feel like home here, but it's not always the good stuff that surfaces. It's unsettling."

"I understand." She was feeling a little unsettled herself, just being in this place with him. The irritation she'd felt while he was gone seemed to melt away in his presence.

He studied her. "Can you? I would have guessed that you couldn't believe anyone could have mixed feelings about Mesquite Creek."

"Why? Do you think you're the only person who can see two sides of a coin?"

His expression collapsed into something like contrition. "No, of course not. But come on, with the exception of college, you've spent your whole life here. I've had a decade now to work it out, and I think I understand. You were always happy here, and why not? Your family was respected, and you were a town darling. The good girl. Little Miss Blackberry, 1988. The town made a place for you."

"Wow." She took a moment to absorb his words. His misconceptions. "How many years did you say your brain's been mulling this over? Because, first of all, you need to get your facts straight. I was never Little Miss Blackberry. I was second runner-up."

"Excuse me," he said.

"And yes, I always had a lot of support here that you didn't, but do you think that didn't have its drawbacks? You think this place felt claustrophobic for you? Try growing up as a school superintendant's daughter. My folks put a lot of pressure on me to do well, and I put pressure on myself, worrying I would shame them. I hung my head for weeks over missing my final word in the regional spelling bee. I was ten years old and wanted to die because I couldn't spell *vacillate*."

Roy frowned. "I'm not sure I could spell it now."

"One C, two L's," she said automatically. The word had featured prominently in her nightmares for twenty years. "I'm a naturally shy person, but all my life here I've felt like public property. And when I excelled at something, I always heard grumbles from kids who thought I was just a teacher's pet because of who my dad was. That sucked, frankly."

"But you never rebelled." His gaze met hers. "Till me."

"That wasn't rebellion. That was just"—she ducked her head—"what I wanted. They didn't come into it. So if all these years you've been thinking that I was only using you—"

"I haven't. I just thought you were happier here. That's why you came back, right? To be where it was safe?"

"You mean I fell back into my comfort zone instead of following you to the rough wilds of Seattle?"

"It is your comfort zone," he insisted.

Her lip curled. "If it's so comfy for me, why couldn't I face going back there just now?"

He tilted his head. "You mean this isn't part of your normal routine?"

She scooted forward and dipped her feet into the cool water. "I haven't been back to this spot since you and I were here last."

His eyes widened. "Seriously."

"Seriously."

"I knew it—kismet!"

She would have laughed except for the look in his eye—the conviction of a true believer. A true romantic. She hated to encourage him, but she had to be honest. "I pass this way all the time. I just happened to stop today because I needed time to think."

"You noticed it because of us. Because the memories have been bubbling up. Am I right?"

"Maybe . . ."

He took her hand, which she snatched back. "Thank you for the flowers," she said. Then she added, "Way to get tongues wagging."

"Did you like them?"

"Of course. I just would have preferred a phone call. You know—something private."

"I thought you might appreciate a little space to think over all that's happened."

"*Nothing's* happened." She looked into his face, felt a clamping sensation around her heart, then looked away. "A kiss. We're two adults. There's no reason to make a big deal out of such a little thing."

"We're not just any two adults. We were in love."

"When we were seventeen to twenty-two. Practically children. People that age fall in and out of love all the time. They—"

"You didn't," he said. She couldn't help looking in his eyes again. Couldn't resist the way her body leaned toward his. He reached out for her arm again. "I didn't," he added, pulling her to him.

It would be so easy to throw herself into his arms, to lose herself there. Instead, she planted her hands against his chest. "But we drifted apart for a reason."

"What was the reason?"

Before she could answer, he bent down and nuzzled her ear. A gasp escaped her lips, and her mind blanked for a moment before rational thought broke the surface again. "We went our separate ways," she said.

"And now our paths have crossed again," he murmured. "Happens all the time. It happened once before, remember?"

She remembered. Vividly. They'd split up briefly in college. But then, over the summer, she'd found him here. One thing led to another, and . . .

The memory of their bodies intertwined in this very spot on that hot July day was one part incendiary, one part dousing of cold water. That reunion hadn't lasted but one more year.

Roy pulled her up against him. There was no mistaking that the memory had been all incendiary for him.

"Roy . . ." He kissed her temple, and it was all she could do not to turn her head toward him. "We're on a rock in the middle of Mesquite Creek."

"Our rock," he said.

She laughed, looking up at him.

His answering smile faded and he dipped to brush his lips against hers. But once their mouths touched, pulling apart was impossible. *Think* had nothing to do with it. Her senses crowded out all thought—the taste of him, the definition of his muscles beneath his T-shirt, the light cedar scent of after-shave.

Their tongues intertwined as if they belonged together. It felt so familiar and so . . . different. Her hands explored his body, filled out but the same as ever. They roamed over pectorals that had been to a gym since the old days, then the scar where he'd fallen on a piece of broken glass, across shoulders that were as broad and firm as ever.

The kiss was too absorbing for just nostalgia. Reeling senses combated reason—she pushed away, hoping to take a last swing for rationality. The crazy thump of her heartbeat made it difficult to draw a breath. "We really shouldn't . . ."

She couldn't help but look into his eyes, eyes burning with hunger. They mesmerized her, battering her crumbling defenses.

When he took a breath, it seemed to take as much effort as her own had. "Jane."

No one could make her name sound like he did. When he locked his gaze on her and spoke to her in that voice, she became some impossibly desirable creature, someone longed for and cherished.

"This is insane."

A hint of a smile, a challenge, touched his lips a moment

before he pulled her to him again. "That's what makes it amazing. I'd given up hope I'd ever hold you like this again. That I'd ever have the chance to tell you that I love you."

"But we're . . . out here."

"The best spot in Mesquite Creek. Besides, I can't invite you back to my place—every real estate agent in town could barge in on us. And your place . . ."

Her mother could barge in. And often did.

But the rock wasn't the problem. She closed her eyes and leaned against him, listening to his heavy heartbeat. With each thump, her reason crazed and cracked and fell to shards. *Unless you're not sure*, Roy had said to her the first time they'd made love, back in high school. It had been so unlike him to allow for doubt, for turning back, but he'd been giving her that out in case she wasn't ready. And what had she said? *Nothing's ever sure, is it?*

Wiser at seventeen than at thirty-one. Because at this moment she was so blinded by wanting Roy that she didn't see any downside to lifting her head, drawing herself as close to him as humanly possible, and agreeing that there had never been a more perfect place to rip off their clothes and let one thing lead to another.

Chapter Seven

"You poor thing—it looks like you just fell off a cliff."

It felt that way, too, especially when Jane had found her mother in her apartment when she came home. Throwback questions darted around her mind—*Did she find out? Am I in trouble?* Then she looked down at herself and noted that one of her pant legs was sodden with creek water . . . and her shirt was a dusty, dirty mess. Scrapes showed on her arms, and she hadn't had a comb in the car, so no telling what her hair was doing. Olive landed on her shoulder, and Jane arranged her like a stole as she reached down to scratch dog ears and began to stammer out explanations. "I had the longest day, including the animal shelter, and then—"

"I know all about it," her mom said.

The blood drained from Jane's face. "You do?" Had she and Roy been spotted? They hadn't seen anyone, or heard a car.

"I called the clinic," her mother said. "They told me."

Her forehead tightened. "Told you . . . ?"

"That you were out at Jack Lewis's ranch. I called your cell but you didn't pick up, so I figured you were busy." Brenda huffed. "Jack! He was exasperating even as a child.

Did I tell you I used to babysit him and his brothers? Worst. Behaved. Children. Ever. One time while I was tidying up after supper they brought their Shetland pony into the living room. Nearly screamed when I saw the thing in front of the television watching *Eight Is Enough*."

Breathing again, Jane managed a chuckle. She dropped her purse on her Formica-topped table, then tilted her head in puzzlement. "What made you call the clinic?"

"I was worried about Buddy."

Jane pivoted toward the dog. "What's wrong?" He had seemed quiet when she walked in, not trying to nose through and steal attention from Squeak. But in truth, since her mom had taken him to the groomer's earlier in the week, she hardly recognized him. The mats were gone, his fur shone, and he actually smelled good.

"He didn't do his business at noon," her mother said. "Seemed suspicious to me. Squeak's like clockwork."

Jane examined Buddy as his tail flicked in a nervous thump. "All dogs are different." Still, she felt his abdomen and figured out the problem. "You should be a diagnostician, Mom."

Her mother nodded, but her face was tensed. "What's wrong? Is it a tumor?"

"No—I think this dog needs some Metamucil. Probably all the moving and change of diet has stressed him out."

Brenda collapsed on the couch. "Thank God! I've been so worried."

"About Buddy?"

"Well, of course. First losing his owner . . . then getting dumped with Ona for two months. And now living with his doctor—and you're never home."

Guilt pinched at Jane as she went and rummaged through the kitchen cabinets.

"Plus he has to go up and down those stairs," her mother said, practically cooing at Buddy. "Poor thing."

The big animal lifted his paw and placed it gently on

Brenda's leg, and she didn't flick it away. And those were white pants.

"Buuuuunddy," Brenda drawled in a tone of voice that Jane couldn't remember hearing since she was four years old. Maybe the universe was finally giving her mom the child of her dreams after all. In canine form.

"I don't have any Metamucil here," Jane said. "I'll have to go to the store."

"Never mind," her mom answered. "I have some. Your father couldn't survive without it." She put her hands on her hips. "In fact, why don't I just take Buddy with me? He'll be closer to the yard that way, and I can keep a close eye on him for the next day or so."

"Okay . . ." Jane frowned, especially when she saw that Buddy was ready to go. Eager, in fact. "But your floors—"

Her mother waved away that objection. "I've got a little bed set out for him in the living room. Confession time—I've been sneaking him over. He's very well behaved."

Jane would have thought Buddy's former human connections would have overshadowed his behavior or purebred canine cred. "You know he's Wanda McGillam's dog."

"I know. Poor woman."

"Poor woman! You two hated each other."

"I never did," her mother said, as if shocked that Jane could even think such a thing. "Yes, Wanda was just a teensy bit jealous of me because Wade McGillam had a crush on me junior year. We only went out on two dates, but Wanda spent the rest of her life in a snit about it. As if I was always on the verge of stealing her man. Even after the man became a disgrace!"

"Wait." Jane's mind was spinning. "You went out with Roy's dad?"

"Two dates," her mother said. "A little youthful indiscretion. But if you could have seen him back then . . . he looked just like Robert Redford as the Sundance Kid." She eyed Jane pityingly. "Much cuter than Roy."

"Then why . . . ?"

"Why did I break it off after two dates? Because he was a devil, that's why." She sighed. "I guess every girl wants to have a fling like that. But then you snap out of it and grow up—like you did." Her gaze cleared and homed in on Jane's face, watching her closely. "You were just slower."

Jane felt dazed. "Much slower."

She drove over to Roy's place after dark, when the chances of a prospective buyer wanting to look at the house, or Ona walking in on them, were slim to none. Not that she and Roy were sneaking around, she assured herself. They were just being gossip-conscious.

Jane hadn't known she was going to bring up the subject of their parents, but as soon as she'd tossed her purse on the glass-topped table in the kitchen, the question popped out. "Do you know why our mothers really hated each other?"

His eyes widened in surprise. Probably not what he'd expected to hear first thing after their encounter this afternoon. Still, he was curious. "No. Do you?"

"It all went back to high school . . . when Mom *dated* your dad."

For a moment, his jaw hung slack. "Your mother told you this?"

Admitted it, he meant. No one had a lower opinion of his dad than Roy did.

"She said he was her wild fling." Jane couldn't help smiling. "She also said he was a lot better-looking than you."

"I don't doubt that." He frowned. "There's not a Greek tragedy buried in this, is there? My father and your mother . . . and then seventeen years later . . ."

She shook her head. "I wondered that, too. But they only dated twice, junior year."

"Of course—they probably weren't real dates, either. Did

she sneak out to meet him? Your mother would never be seen actually going out with a lowlife like my dad."

She looked down, wishing now she hadn't brought it up. The subject of his father always rattled him. No matter how successful he became, while he was in Mesquite Creek a class war would always rage in his head. "Anyway, no worries. The math doesn't work out. We were both born years after those two dates."

"Good." Roy sighed and took her in his arms. "Let's stop thinking about the past for a while. You want something to drink?"

She shook her head and wrapped her arms around his middle, burying her head on his chest. He smelled so good. "Mom said I looked like I'd fallen off a cliff."

His chest rumbled in a laugh.

She cricked her neck to look up at him. "Oh—and weird thing. Mom seems to have taken a shine to Buddy."

He smiled, then said, "Are we ever going to stop talking about your mom?"

She was about to chuckle in agreement, then stopped herself. "I don't know. She's been my friend these past years. She's my mom still, of course, but we're next-door neighbors. She's sort of my Kramer, my Millie Helper."

He took this in, then nodded in understanding. "Your Tray."

She shook her head. "My what?"

"Tray's a guy who lives in the basement apartment of my building. He pops in for a lot of visits, especially during baseball season."

"Baseball?" Since when did he like baseball? He'd been a hoops guy.

He shrugged. "I started watching it when I moved up there. We've got a great stadium. I can't wait to show you Seattle—Pike Place Market, the neighborhoods, McG Studios . . . even with all the headaches of traveling, I love where we are. You'll love it, too."

She frowned. What was he talking about? "Love . . . ?"

"Seattle—everything." He beamed at her. "When you come . . . for a visit. I'm hoping you will. Soon." He cleared his throat. "A long visit."

"That sounds so nice. I haven't taken a vacation in . . ." Three years. That was too embarrassing to admit. "Well, the last time I was gone for any amount of time was when Carl and I went to a convention in San Antonio."

"You and Carl?" Roy asked. "Together?"

She laughed. "Yes. We had separate hotel rooms. In fact, we weren't even in the same hotel."

He actually looked relieved.

"Roy, whatever you suspect about Carl is not true. There's never been anything going on there."

"He likes you. In fact, I could swear he thinks I'm a rival or something."

"He might be worried that I'll leave. But that's just crazy." Roy's eyes widened. "Is it?"

She laughed. "Well, yeah." When he didn't laugh with her, not even a chuckle, her own laughter died out. "Isn't it?"

He pulled her to him. "I thought we were rekindling something here."

"Well, yeah." *Here*. "But there's no rush, is there?" She put her arms around him again, playing with the soft fuzz at his nape.

He kissed her then, and it felt as if there was a rush. A rush of desire to be against him, naked. He broke apart only briefly, to take her hand and lead her upstairs.

The next day when she took off on her lunch hour to visit Roy, everything had changed at Wanda's house. The furniture was all gone. Jane stood in the middle of the living room, stunned.

"The estate sale place picked it all up this morning," Roy

said as he showed her through several rooms. "Except for a couple of boxes for me and Ona in the garage."

He said the words with satisfaction, but she couldn't help thinking about Wanda, and how the treasures of an entire lifetime could be packed away in a couple of boxes.

"The cleaners are coming Friday," he said. "I think the place will show better then. Although . . ."

"What?"

"Well, we've got an offer on the place now. It's low, but Ona wants to take it."

"And you don't?"

"I don't see why we have to be in a hurry to accept a low-ball offer."

Jane nodded and began to breathe normally again. She knew nothing about real estate transactions, but it had to be a good thing that Roy wasn't chomping at the bit to get out of town. Although . . . "An empty house isn't a great place to stay."

"There's still the box spring and mattress in the guest room upstairs. It's like camping out, but comfortable."

"You could stay at the garage apartment."

He put his arms around her. "That sounds good." They kissed, and for a moment she indulged herself in the fantasy of having Roy waiting for her at the end of the day. Greeting her at the door next to Buddy and Squeak.

He broke the kiss, leaning his forehead against hers, his hands still looped around her waist. "It also sounds crowded. Besides, I can't come over tonight." He gestured to the Mac set up on the kitchen counter. His workstation. "I need to figure out some kind of speech for the auditorium opening tomorrow. I'm so dreading it. I have to give speeches for work sometimes, but this . . ."

She knew from her dad that it was going to be a big to-do. Their congressman was going to be there. "You haven't prepared anything?"

He shook his head. "I could wing it, but then I risk the chance of going into a Don Knotts nervous meltdown."

She laughed. "I can't imagine that."

When she got back to the clinic that afternoon, everyone was buzzing about the new ultrasound machine that had been delivered at noon. Though Marcy told Jane that Erin was waiting for her, Carl whisked her into the other exam room, where they'd wheeled the machine, and went over all the new features as excitedly as a guy in a showroom demonstrating a new Mercedes.

"Do you like it?" he asked her.

Given his enthusiasm, it was hard not to catch the fever. "It's great, Carl. Big improvement." That wouldn't have been difficult. Their older one had gone on the fritz several times. A couple of times they'd even had to send patients to a clinic in another town.

But his eager expression and the hopefulness in his voice suddenly made her remember her mother's words. *Like a bowerbird.* Was this really a machine for taking sonograms, or another twig in his fastidious nest building?

She took a deep breath; the air still smelled of fresh paint. "I need to go look at Erin's cat. But this is terrific, Carl. Excellent purchase."

She hurried to the next room and greeted Erin, who was in the middle of blowing her nose. "Is something the matter with Smudge?" Jane asked.

The big white cat seemed perfectly calm—his green eyes were certainly clearer than Erin's red-rimmed ones. "I came home for lunch and as I was about to leave, I found him like this."

"Like what?"

"Covered in blood!"

Jane carefully turned the animal so she could see the angry

red splotches underneath. At the sight, Erin began to quiver. She looked way more traumatized than Smudge did.

At least she wasn't threatening to take him to the shelter anymore. The two must have bonded again a little bit.

Erin collapsed into the plastic chair and honked again into a Kleenex. "I don't see how he could have cut himself. But he must have, even though there wasn't a trail of blood around the house. Just a few"—her voice began to crack, and she barely wheezed out—"little red pawprints."

The animal's abdomen and two of his feet were red. Jane frowned. She put on gloves and then rubbed the area on his abdomen gently. Smudge purred and flopped over as if he were on a sunny windowsill instead of an exam table.

Jane lifted the glove to her nose and sniffed. Smudge's blood had a pleasant garlicky-oregano aroma. "What did you have for lunch today?"

Erin sniffed. "Pizza. I had some left over from last night, so I got the box out of the fridge and put it on the table, grabbed a piece and . . ." Her face fell as a possibility occurred to her.

"And left it on the table while you watched television, maybe?" Jane prompted.

Erin's eyes widened, and a flush crept into her cheeks. A tomato-colored flush, appropriately enough.

"You'll probably find little paw prints in the remaining slices in the box. But I think all Smudge needs is a bath."

"I'm so sorry," Erin said. "And y'all are so busy!"

"Never so busy that we don't like a happy ending," Jane told her as she wiped more sauce off Smudge with a towel.

"I guess I just got so upset that I didn't stop to think. I was so worried that something was really wrong, and that I'd be . . ."

Her voice broke off and Jane didn't press her to finish. She knew . . . *and that I'd be alone again.*

After she'd returned Smudge to his carrier and collected

herself, Erin touched her hand to Jane's arm. "I don't know how I'm going to get through these crises without you."

Jane rolled her eyes. "Not you, too."

"Isn't it true, then?"

Sadly, she didn't have to discuss what "it" was. "*It* hasn't been discussed."

Erin looked relieved. "Oh good." Then she looked guilty. "I mean, that's good for me. You're practically my last friend from school still around. And we were just talking at the salon about how we'd all miss you."

"So many people have me moving, I'm already beginning to miss me, too."

Erin laughed. "We need to have a night out. Paint the town red—or at least a dusty pink. After Roy leaves, let's get together."

Jane seconded that motion, even as her heart constricted a little. *After Roy leaves.* Her brain just didn't want to wrap itself around that.

It felt as if every person in Mesquite Creek had turned out for the opening of the new auditorium. The high school marching band, decked out in full uniform, marched up Main Street from the Food Saver to the campus, followed by a caravan of cars carrying local dignitaries. Along the way, people sat in folding chairs or stood outside the smattering of businesses, watching. Jane was among them. Her father had told her about all the plans for the day. Still, she couldn't hold back astonishment when Roy drove by in an open convertible next to the congressman.

Jane had taken the afternoon off to see Roy give his speech, and Kaylie was covering the event for *The Buzz*. They'd had to park a little ways from the school, since Jared and the other policemen had closed off Main Street to parking. By the time they arrived at the auditorium, it was almost full.

"Oh! I see someone." Kylie waved at Tom Anderson, editor of *The Buzz,* who was sitting on the other side and had an empty seat next to him. "I can probably get a ride when this is over, Jane."

Jane nodded and hung back. The new auditorium was twice as big as the old one, with a real stage and curtains, instead of a narrow raised platform. The seats were nice, too — like theater seats instead of the old, hard folding wood seats that had made long assemblies and ceremonies a torment. She would have liked to try out one of those seats, but the place was full. All the students and faculty were in attendance, and just a small section had been saved for visitors.

Onstage, the Skeeter choir was singing "Wind Beneath My Wings." In front of them, a podium awaited. To the side of it was a line of chairs that started filling up with the speakers for the day.

She scanned the crowd until she saw a cluster of men working their way up to the stage. Her father was among them, as was Roy. She felt absurdly impressed by the fact that he was wearing a suit—a really nice one, dark with a striped tie. She'd seen him dressed up before, but never looking so like a grown-up. So like what he was. A man who could get an auditorium built.

Her father was first to the podium, to welcome everyone. He talked about the importance of having a place to gather—to commemorate, to celebrate and entertain, to honor and remember. He reminded them that in the next two weeks alone, the auditorium would be the venue for the year's senior play, and then the very next week would witness members of that class graduate. Someone from the audience shouted out a joke about june bugs, and it took her father a few seconds to stifle the laughter and pass the mike to the congressman.

The congressman talked and talked, praising the building and its primary funder so lengthily that Jane was pretty sure he'd lose votes in the next election for sheer windbaggery. She took advantage of the time he was droning on to look at Roy again. How far he'd come in the world had never struck

quite so forcefully until now, seeing him back here where
he'd started. Where they'd both started. Once or twice she
thought he caught her eye, but she couldn't be sure. There
were a few stage lights on, so it was possible that people up
there couldn't actually pick out individuals in the crowd.

She was relieved and—she had to admit—a little nervous
when the congressman wound up the speech and started in
on a long intro to Roy, sketching out his modest beginnings
and listing his big achievements, including a Clio, various
other business awards whose names meant nothing to Jane,
and finally, this auditorium. The crowd clapped and rose to
their feet as Roy stood, shook the man's hand, and took his
place at the podium.

Jane wished she'd found a seat, because her legs jittered
with nerves. She crept along the side of the auditorium, as
much from restlessness as from the need to get a little closer.
She missed the first line of Roy's speech, which got a laugh.
He seemed to be looking down at notes; obviously he hadn't
wasted his time the night before.

But he sounded wooden—even though she knew he
meant every word about his gratitude toward the town, and
how he wished his mom could be there. If there was a
heaven, Wanda McGillam was the happiest person in it
today. Jane glanced around the audience to see if anyone else
noticed that Roy seemed a little stiff, but all the faces turned
toward the stage appeared rapt. She finally picked her mom
out in the crowd. Even Brenda seemed entranced. But none
of these people knew Roy like Jane did. They couldn't have
heard the slight tension in his throat, the hesitation as he
tackled the next bullet point on his note cards.

Finally, it seemed as if his speech was heading for the finish line. He addressed the students, and at once his voice
changed, became more natural and conversational. He no
longer even glanced at his notes. "I especially appreciate
your being here, not just because the building is for you, but

because I know it might not seem like that big a deal to you. What's an auditorium? What's it to me? you might be asking. Until I was seventeen, I would have been scrunched down in my seat toward the back row, probably doodling, only half paying attention. Because I didn't know that the next year I'd be cast in a play, and that play—*Romeo and Juliet*—would change my life. Not just because I got the chance to recite Shakespeare. I wasn't that good at that, frankly. And I didn't look so hot in the costumes, either."

Chuckles rippled through the audience, and it felt as if the entire audience leaned forward a little in their seats.

"Up till then, I didn't understand how full of possibilities life really was," Roy continued, more eagerly. "I had dreams, sure, but I didn't have a lot of confidence. The play gave me that." He frowned. "No, *Jane* gave me that."

For a fraction of a second, she wondered if maybe she'd just imagined that he'd mentioned her name. Maybe it had just been an aural hallucination. But then Roy turned toward her, picked her out with his gaze as if she were the only person listening. The only person who mattered. The audience tracked his gaze and pivoted toward her.

"Jane," Roy repeated.

Heat rushed to her face.

"I know you don't trust this," he said to her, as intimately as if there weren't several hundred people looking on. "We took separate roads—but that doesn't mean we can't go back. No"—he shook his head—"not back. Forward. Life is still full of possibilities for us. And one of them is us, together. Jane—"

Is he really doing this? Panic coursed through her. In that moment between sentences, Roy was a man stepping off a curb into the path of an oncoming bus. She wanted to wave her hands at him, shake her head, yell at him to stop. She had a horrible feeling that he was going to—

"—I love you. Will you marry me?"

A collective gasp went up, and she could have sworn she heard something drop. Probably her mother hitting the floor in a dead faint.

She'd never been so close to passing out herself. Her face was on fire, and though she couldn't look out at the people sitting in the seats—that would have been death—their gazes felt like a force field. She was frozen in place, fighting off successive waves of love, anger, panic. Could she marry Roy? Was this really the place to figure that out, right this moment? Did he actually expect her to answer *now*?

Apparently, he did. He was waiting for her answer. So were a few hundred other people.

Seconds ticked by. Dragged by like centuries. Someone cleared their throat.

Love. Anger. Panic.

Panic won.

Jane turned and fled the auditorium as fast as her legs would move.

Chapter Eight

Aunt Ona exhaled a dragonlike stream of smoke. "That was seriously weird."

Roy half expected her to laugh at him, but she didn't. She just stared fixedly at the cloud she'd created, her mind no doubt replaying those indecisive moments in the auditorium—agonizing to Roy, then and now—before Jane had pivoted on her heel and sprinted for the door.

She shook her head in amazement. "I never thought of her as the athletic type, but she can move pretty fast when she needs to, can't she?"

If only he had been able to escape as quickly. Instead, he'd been trapped onstage, frozen in shock and disappointment. Eventually the four hundred pairs of eyes that had been focused on Jane's crazed dash turned back to him. Including the school superintendant's harsh glare. Amid a rising buzz of chatter, Mr. Canfield finally pushed Roy aside at the podium and thanked everyone for coming. He then directed the choir to sing their planned closing song, which was a distracted rendition of "Let the River Run." Roy winced every time the solo singer had drawn out the phrase about her heart aaaaaaaaaaaching. When the speakers stood to go, he hadn't been able to get out of there fast enough.

"You know," Ona said, "even if you hadn't donated a truckload of money, this town might have named that auditorium after you just for coming down and giving that speech. Bet they'll be talking about it longer than they talked about Liston Pruitt scoring the goal on the buzzer at the state championship in '56."

"Too bad they don't give out trophies for being an ass," Roy grumbled. "They could give me one and show it off as an example of how not to propose to a woman."

"Ha. Consider yourself dipped in bronze, because right now you're pretty much a walking example." His aunt clucked at him. "Have you talked to her since?"

"She wasn't at the clinic today, and she's not answering my calls." He let out a long breath. "But why should she? She gave me her answer."

"You can say that again."

"Look," Roy said, "the reason I called you over here is that I talked to Lou. I told him to go ahead and accept the offer on the house."

Ona's jaw dropped. "I thought you said it was too low."

He shrugged. "A house is worth what someone's willing to pay for it. Besides, it's some family moving in from out of town. I'd like to think of a family living here."

"And you just want to get it over with." Ona stabbed her cigarette onto an old chipped saucer that hadn't been deemed sale-worthy. "Well, sounds good to me."

"I figured it would," he said. "The cleaners are still scheduled for tomorrow. Could you let them in?"

Ona's eyes widened. "You're leaving that quick?"

"Tomorrow, around noon. I don't see any reason to stick around. I can handle all the details of the sale by fax."

"What about the details of getting Jane back?"

Roy tensed and felt his lips turning down into a frown. "I don't think there's any *back* about it. For a while I thought . . .

But maybe we were just clutching at something out of nostalgia."

Ona looked as if she was going to give him an argument, but then she let out a long breath. "I'm glad we're selling this place, at any rate. It seemed stupid to pass up a decent offer."

When Ona left, he felt a crazy kind of sadness. His aunt was his closest living relative right now, and the only tie left to his mom. And Mesquite Creek.

Maybe he would invite her to visit him. She'd have fun in the city—his mom had always gotten a kick out of it—and surely he and Ona could stand each other's company for a few days.

When he heard someone walking up to the porch just after Ona had left, he opened the door, expecting she'd come back for something she'd forgotten. The invitation was on the tip of his tongue, but died when he saw Jane beneath the porch light, her hand raised to knock.

He felt speechless. Too bad he couldn't have felt that way this afternoon.

"Can I come in?" she asked.

"I've been calling you." He shifted his feet. "Also went by your house."

"I hung out at Erin's for a while."

He stepped aside, allowing her to pass through. In the small foyer they almost brushed one another, and for a moment he caught the faint scent of a flowery perfume. He closed his eyes a moment, then followed her into the empty living room. A stubborn optimism rose in his chest, but he didn't want to get his hopes up too high. Also, he couldn't help feeling a trace of bitterness. Maybe he had instigated the awkward incident at the auditorium, but she hadn't smoothed things over any.

"I came to apologize," she said. "I guess I looked pretty silly this afternoon . . ."

"Not as silly as I did, according to Ona," he assured her.

The words didn't appear to comfort her. "You just surprised me. If I'd had any warning . . ."

"I surprised me, too. I don't know what happened—one minute I was talking about the auditorium, the next I was proposing. I guess I should have practiced my speech more."

"Then you didn't mean it. I didn't think you could have."

"No," he said, making sure that she was looking him in the eye. "I meant every word."

He felt that strong tug between them, pulling them toward each other.

She broke the connection with a toss of her head. "But that's just crazy. Marriage? We've only talked to each other—what?—ten times in the past nine years?"

He smiled. "Are you saying we don't know each other well enough yet?"

"There's knowing and there's *knowing*," she said.

"Jane, we're as close as two people can be already. We might have spent too much time apart, but I've been alone most of that time. And why? Because you set the bar high, Jane. You're smart, and funny, and compassionate, and an incredible lover—"

She raised her hand, traffic cop–style, stopping him. "Those are words."

He closed the distance between them. "What else is there? We fell in love over words, remember?" He lifted her hand to his cheek, as he had all those years ago. " 'For I ne'er saw true beauty till this night.' "

She stepped back. "Roy, we're not seventeen anymore. We're talking about living together. Marriage. And just seeing each other this past week has been bumpy. We're grown-ups, with different lives."

" 'For you and I are past our dancing days,' " he said.

She practically hopped, in a Yosemite Sam stamp of frustration. "Will you stop quoting at me? It's irritating! I can't think."

"I don't want you to think. I want us to run away together, like we should have years ago."

"Okay—there you go again. You think I should have run away with you to Seattle."

"It's a great city."

"Sure, but it's a thousand miles away from my home, my parents, and my friends—not to mention the clinic."

"We'll work something out."

"How?" she asked. "Are you going to move your studio to Mesquite Creek?"

"I have forty people to think of, remember?"

"So what you mean is, *I'll* work something out. I'll pick up and follow you."

He took a deep breath. He couldn't tell if they were making progress or not. "Is that your only objection? Geography?"

"It's a big objection. And . . ." She bit her lip.

"What?"

She hesitated, then blurted out, "I don't trust you. You left. For years. No phone calls, didn't seek me out when you visited. Just cut me out of your life. And now you're back—and you've decided in a week that you want me to go back with you. Just like that."

"I was wrong. I was twenty-two, and hurt by your decision. We'd been going out since we were seventeen. I didn't realize what not having you in my life forever would be like."

"But you never called, never wrote."

"Neither did you. I thought you were choosing here over me."

She gnawed this over for a moment. "I guess I was."

Maybe she still was.

Her gaze focused on the carpet. "You blurt out things and make snap decisions. I can't do that. I know it might not seem like much to you, but I have a life here. I need time."

"I know, but . . ."

She glanced back up at him. "But what?"

He swallowed, sure this was going to be the wrong thing to say. But he couldn't lie. "I'm leaving tomorrow."

Her glance turned into a gape. "*Tomorrow?* You're just taking off?"

He nodded. "I got a one o'clock flight."

"But what about your mother's house?"

"We're selling it."

"When did you decide that?"

"This afternoon. When I got back. Ona's happy."

"I'm sure she is." She tilted her head. "I bet you are, too."

"Believe me, right now I'm the opposite of happy." He reached out, but she darted away before his hand could clasp her arm. If he could just touch her, kiss her . . . they could work everything out somehow.

She edged around him and started for the door. "I'm sorry, Roy. I can't make the kind of jackrabbit life decisions you do. It's not even fair of you to want me to."

She left him before he could argue that he didn't, which wouldn't have been entirely truthful anyway. He *did* want her to go back with him. He did see them galloping off into the sunset together . . . or flying off into the wild blue yonder.

Roy closed the door behind her and then sank against it, depressed. He tried to look on the bright side—she had come to talk to him. On the other hand, she'd didn't appear about to budge.

Maybe, given time . . .

He sighed. He felt woeful.

"It was romantic, you have to admit." Erin twirled the last of her red wine around the bottom of her glass.

It was a water glass, Jane noticed. *I'm almost thirty-two, I make good money, and I don't own any wineglasses.* She sank against the cushions, considering that fact. Roy took off, started a business, made millions. She bet his condo was loaded with wineglasses. Or at least enough of them to entertain. Meanwhile, here she'd been, living as if she was camping out waiting for Prince Charming. She'd had a lot of crust to lecture poor Marcy.

She straightened.

"You know what I'm going to do tomorrow?" she asked Erin. "First I'm going to rent a truck. Then I'm going to load up all this stuff and take it to the Salvation Army or someplace like that. And then I'm going to drive to Dallas this weekend and I'm going to shop till I drop. I'm going to buy wineglasses, and furniture—heavy furniture—and new silverware that isn't just mismatched stuff that my relatives don't want anymore. I'm going to buy a whole set of china—something beautiful and permanent that most people only expect to receive as wedding gifts. Eight place settings, along with all the extras. Gravy boats and soup tureens . . ."

Her friend studied her worriedly and then proceeded to cork up the wine bottle. "Maybe I shouldn't have brought this over."

It was nice of Erin to come check on her after the visit to Roy's, especially since she had already spent part of her afternoon listening to Jane's Roy lament. Erin hadn't been at the auditorium, but she'd been appropriately dismayed by what had happened—and sympathetically indignant on Jane's behalf. But it was she who had encouraged Jane to go see Roy this evening, pointing out that she couldn't avoid the man forever.

Although apparently if she had waited another day to confront him, she could have. Because he would have been gone.

Because that's how Roy operated.

Jane drained her glass. Not that she was drunk. In fact, she was finally seeing things clearly. "My life's been in a holding pattern. But no more."

"Gravy boats? This is a solution?" Erin's brows arched. "Buying the trappings of a life for yourself. Sounds great."

"It's a start."

"It's a distraction. But you'll probably figure that out after you've drained your savings account." Erin stood and stretched. "It's late. I'll talk to you tomorrow." She looked at her watch. "Which is actually already today."

"But you want to come with me?" Jane asked her. "Sunday?" They both worked Saturdays.

"Oh sure. When have I ever passed up an invitation to go soup-tureen shopping?"

After she left, Jane intended to go to sleep but ended up gathering all the boxes she could find in the apartment and in the garage below and tossing things in. Chipped bowls and ratty towels, clothes she hadn't worn for ages or ever, videocassettes and college textbooks. She filled box after box, amazed at how little connection she felt to things. Then she ran across a shelf with her old yellowed copy of *Romeo and Juliet*.

She flipped through it, impressed by the exhaustive margin notes overlaid with stage directions in green pen. Had she really been that obsessive about a school play, and that organized? On the inside of the back cover Roy had sketched her—relaxed, with her head resting against her hand. It was a good drawing, if way too flattering. Around the picture, he'd written in careful calligraphy, *O, that I were a glove upon that hand, that I might touch that cheek!*

She could hear his voice saying the words, like a caress in her ear.

The letters blurred. She let out a strangled cry and tossed the book in a box next to a CD she barely remembered owning. It was as if Roy were trying to romance her retroactively.

To get the voice out of her head, she decided to vacuum.

Sometime around three, she fell into bed, exhausted.

Her six-thirty alarm went off like a firehouse bell in her ear. She careened out of bed and got ready as fast as she could, downing a coffee and two aspirin on the hoof. Maybe she'd had more wine than she thought.

Her mother was surprised to see her. "You poor thing! I saw your light on till all hours."

Jane headed automatically to the fridge. She pulled out a container of orange juice and poured a glass. "Will you do me a favor? I need someone to take me to the rental-car place."

Her mother's brow furrowed. "What happened to your car?"

"Nothing, I'm renting a moving van."

Brenda sank into a chair at the breakfast table, tears in her eyes. Buddy hurried over to rest his head on her lap. He wore a bright green bandanna now, and smelled of rosemary-lavender pet shampoo.

"I always knew it," her mother said on a sigh.

"Knew what?" Jane gulped down some juice.

"That you'd want to be with him eventually."

"Mom, I—"

"I don't want to be clingy. I just want to know you're happy."

"I'm renting a van to run errands with. Why would you think that I was running away?"

Her mother breathed easier but didn't look entirely convinced. "Because I can still see the gleam."

"The what?"

"That something that was always between you and Roy when you were together. I used to think it was just mischievousness, like me when I went out with Wade McGillam. Later, I never had a gleam. You've still got it. You've had it for days."

"A gleam? Mom, that's whacked. Now, get your keys and let's go to the rental place. Otherwise I'm going to be late."

Her mother stood up. "If you do go, what are you going to do with Buddy?"

"I'm not going anywhere but to work," Jane insisted.

All the way to the car place, however, she had to force herself not to stare into the vanity mirror to see if she could detect the gleam.

Floating on her overnight resolution to reboot her life, she almost forgot how fresh in people's minds the events of yesterday would be. The clinic was an instant reminder.

Even Kaylie wasn't smiling at her this morning. She was on the phone when Jane walked in, and looked harassed. "Oh good—you're finally here. Could you check and sign for this drug delivery Shane has? Carl's holed up in his office and I've been calling Marcy, but . . ."

Jane frowned, disconcerted by the chilly reception. But she put her things down and turned to where Shane was waiting.

"I heard you'd gone into hiding," he said.

"I had yesterday afternoon off," she corrected, skimming her eyes over the delivery order. "Besides, why should I go into hiding? I didn't do anything wrong. I was just there to watch his speech, and then, *wham*. Gruesome public situation."

Kaylie hung up the phone and looked at her. "But it was so sweet, so romantic—or at least it was until you freaked out and ran. Then it was just sad. If you could have seen Roy standing up there . . ."

The mental image of Roy left standing at that podium after she'd run was horrible, but . . . "What about me standing up there in shock while my boyfriend from a decade ago proposed to me in front of my parents, the entire town, and my congressman? *That* was awkward."

"Awkward, but not insulting," Kaylie said.

"It was not the right moment for a rational discussion," Jane argued. "For one thing, I didn't have a microphone. I would have had to shout my reasons across the auditorium."

Marcy drifted in. "If you've thought over such a sweet, impulsive gesture in such a cold, reasoned way, then it's clear you have no heart."

Jane was starting to feel cornered again. "How would you have reacted?" she asked Marcy. "Would you have said yes just because you were backed into a corner?"

"No," Marcy said, "I would have said yes because I'd know someone who had put himself on the line like that must be really in love."

"Seriously?"

Jane was still processing this insane pronouncement when Shane walked over to Marcy and dropped to one knee. For a moment, her heart stopped—almost as completely as it had in the auditorium.

Kaylie vaulted to her feet and leaned over the reception desk for a better view.

"Marcy, I've loved you since you knocked me off the monkey bars," Shane confessed. "I just have to ask if—"

Marcy's stunned, panicked look as she stared into Shane's eyes probably mirrored Jane's expression the day before. Jane was about to rush forward and intervene when Shane caught Marcy's look. His throat hitched, and he swallowed, apparently thinking twice about going for the whole enchilada.

"—ask if you'll go out with me tomorrow night."

Marcy exhaled in relief. They all did.

"Tomorrow night? Of course."

Shane straightened up from the floor, almost looking as if he didn't trust her. "Really?"

"Yes," Marcy said.

Shane beamed. "It only took me twenty years to ask."

Marcy turned to Jane. *"See?"* Almost smug, she strolled away past Carl, who was standing among them now.

"What's going on?" he asked. When no one volunteered to explain, he beckoned Jane toward his office. "Can I speak to you for a moment?"

Uneasiness took hold of her. He never called people into his office except on the rare occasions when he'd had to fire someone. He wasn't going to do that, was he? She flashed back to the couch and chairs arriving, and the awkwardness when he'd popped up at her apartment, and the surprise of the new paint. Could her mother's spin on these events have been completely wrong? Maybe he was hoping to make a clean sweep by getting rid of her.

Catching his nervous expression as he settled himself in his desk chair, she was sure something terrible had happened, or was about to happen.

"Take a look at this," he said.

He leaned forward and swung his computer monitor so she could see it. Jane nearly jumped back in horror. There on the screen were she and Carl, standing back-to-back in white coats, all smiles. Huge smiles, like you'd see on billboards for morning news teams and real estate agents. She leaned forward, amazed at the amount of Photoshopping and airbrushing that must have been involved to create this image. Her teeth hadn't been that white or her skin that clear since she was four years old. Carl had been cleaned up, too. His burnt-orange hair appeared to have been toned down to a more palatable auburn. Underneath their cutoff torsos was a line of cats and dogs in various frolicking poses, sitting atop the words *Mesquite Creek Animal Clinic*.

"What do you think?" he asked. "We make quite a team, don't we?"

A shiver went through her. "Like a demented Donny and Marie. In lab coats."

He frowned. "You don't like it?"

"What *is* it?"

"It's the new sign for the clinic. Or it will be, once I send in the order. I want to offer you a partnership, Jane." His face darkened a little. "I want to offer you more, if you're interested."

She thought of the old rustic woodcut sign in front of the

clinic, there since the eighties or maybe earlier, from before Carl and Maggie had taken over the clinic from old Dr. Spaulding. Coming here after school, turning up the walkway at that sign and looking forward to a couple of hours of being around the vets and the animals, had been one of the highlights of her childhood. Seeing the old sign go would be sad, but replacing it with this would be a travesty. It was wrong on so many levels.

"Roy suggested the lettering," Carl said.

That name made her even more wary. "Carl . . ."

"You don't like it, do you?" He swerved the monitor back to inspect it some more. "Is it the composition"—he lifted a brow—"or is it you and me?"

"It's all of it. This is your clinic, Carl. The business you built up with Maggie. I've never thought I was doing any more than filling in."

"But that's what I'm saying. I want you here permanently. I was hoping there might be a chance that you'd—"

She cut him off. "I'd still be filling in, Carl. It's been so great to see you springing back recently, more like your old self. Maggie would want that. But I'm not the right person to turn to." She smiled. "My mom says she could give a list of ten women who are half in love with you already."

Carl drew back, and she worried she'd made a blunder mentioning the list.

"But you're not on the list, obviously," he said, his mouth turned down. "I thought you'd see things differently. I know you're younger, but you had your big romance already, and I had Maggie. That doesn't mean that we shouldn't be happy. And this is a perfect setup—we work together, have similar interests. What could be more reasonable, more practical?"

Those words chafed. He made it sound as if she should be settling in for life's evening already. And why not? She had been on the verge of making a similar decision for herself, keeping herself earthbound with heavy furniture and soup tureens. What was the matter with her?

"That's just it," she said, thinking aloud. "I've worn myself into a reasonable, practical rut. We shouldn't have to settle for practical. Love shouldn't be reasonable, or convenient, should it?"

He continued to look at the screen.

"It's the messiness, the irrationality, the impulsiveness that's what's so beautiful about people finding each other." She swallowed. "Or re-finding. It can turn the second runner-up Little Miss Blackberry of 1988 into a Juliet. Twice."

They remained silent for a moment, but her thoughts weren't quiet. Her brain sizzled and snapped with ideas, plans, urgency. Roy was leaving today. She couldn't let him go. Or maybe . . .

Carl finally released a long sigh. "Well, this is a big fat pile of awkward. Maybe you'd like to—"

"Would it be okay if I took a vacation?" she asked at the same time. "A long one?"

"As in . . . a permanent one?" He considered this. "Roy?"

"I'm afraid so."

He thought for a moment. "Maybe it would be the best thing if you did," he said. "You want to go now?"

She nodded, already antsy to leave.

"E-mail me when you get to Seattle," he said. "I'd like to know how you're getting along . . . and whether I should be advertising for a new vet."

She headed for the door. "Thank you, Carl."

"Good luck." He smiled back at her. "Oh, and when you e-mail me, could you include the names of those ten women?"

She laughed.

"You're taking them all with you?" her mother asked, exchanging a doubtful look with Erin.

"Roy might as well know what he's getting into." Jane loaded the third cat box into the van. Squeak could ride up front. The last thing she had to do was secure Luther's cage and then load up her own belongings, some of them stuffed haphazardly into Hefty bags for the voyage.

"When worlds collide," Erin said.

Brenda held tight to Buddy's leash. "But you can't uproot this one again," she said. "You'd better leave him with me."

Buddy looked up at her and wagged his tail.

He had started life keeping Wanda company after Roy left home. Now . . .

Jane swallowed. She wasn't going to cry. This was the beginning of an adventure. Maybe a foolhardy one, maybe even the craziest, worst decision she would ever make in her life, but it would not be launched with tears. She stopped and hugged her mother.

"Take good care of him, Mom," she said. "And take care of yourself."

Her father came down with her big suitcase and put it in the back. "Be careful driving. Do you have enough money to handle an emergency?"

Jane couldn't help laughing as she gave her dad a squeeze. "I'll be fine. Don't be a worrywart."

She and Erin got in the van while her parents stood in the drive and waved her off.

"I knew she was a goner the minute I saw the gleam," she heard her mother say.

"Thanks for helping me," Jane told Erin when they'd rounded the corner. It was only a minute's drive to the salon, thank goodness. Squeak was squirming and panting in Erin's lap.

"Are you sure you'll be able to catch Roy?" Erin asked.

"I hope so. He didn't pick up the phone, but I texted him to wait for me in front of the airport." She intended to breathe deeply, but struggled to take a shallow breath. "I hope he does."

"I know he will," Erin assured her.

"I'll miss you."

Erin smiled. "I just wish I'd had time to cut those bangs."

After dropping Erin off, Jane sped the rest of the way to

the regional airport. Alone for the first time since making her decision, with Squeak shivering unsteadily next to her and intermittent outraged meows and squawky chirps sounding off behind her, she began to sense doubts crowding in. *This is insane. You've never been to Seattle. Living with Roy might be a disaster. You might never find another job . . .*

At a stoplight at the turn-in to the airport, she reached for her phone. No messages. The man definitely needed to work on his telecommunication skills.

Or maybe he'd taken an earlier flight.

The light turned green, and she stepped on the gas. Her heart thumped nervously as she approached the passenger area. It was deserted.

She crawled past slowly, glancing often in her rearview just to make sure she hadn't missed him standing beside a pole or something.

But he wasn't there. The one-way corridor forced her to keep going, and as she approached the fork where one lane led to the exit and one led to the turnaround to circle back to the terminal, she hesitated. The last shred of her sensible self was still trying to dig in its heels.

I've been happy here. Mom and Dad are getting older, too. And all that Northwest rain . . .

The van hovered between lanes.

It's a nice town. And safe.

Safe.

She wrenched the wheel to the left and took the turnaround, speeding back to the airport. At the entrance, she squealed to a stop, flipped on the emergency lights, and hopped out. Just then, the terminal's sliding doors opened and Roy stepped out with his laptop bag slung jauntily over his shoulder, rolling a suitcase behind him. His doubtful look morphed into a huge smile when he saw her. He hurried over.

"I saw the van go by earlier," he said. "I didn't know it was you."

"It was." She felt ill at ease standing before him, grinning like an idiot. But she didn't care. "Can I give you a lift?"

His eyes narrowed on the van. "What have you got in there?"

"Three cats, a dog, a bird, and all my worldly belongings."

If the menagerie worried him, he didn't show it. In fact, it seemed to delight him. He dropped his case and wrapped his arms around her. A long kiss turned into a joyful hug that lifted her off her feet. The last fleeting doubts seemed to be squeezed out of her as he swung her in a half circle. "When do we start?" he asked.

A start. A fresh start. Nothing had sounded so wonderful to her ears in a long time. They'd waited so long to get to this moment.

"Will there ever be a better time than now?" she asked, taking his hand.

THE DEVIL AND
MR. CHOCOLATE

Janet Dailey

Chapter One

Kitty Hamilton, owner of Santa Fe's renowned Hamilton Art Gallery, lolled in the expansive tub, surrounded by mounds of scented bubbles. Her long chestnut hair was pinned atop her head, no longer contained in its customary severe bun.

Scattered about the spacious bathroom were pillar candles. Their wavering yellow flames created a certain ambience to accompany the first movement of Mozart's Serenade No. 13 playing softly in the background.

A bottle of champagne poked its neck out from the bucket of ice sitting on the tub's ledge. On the opposite side sat a plate of chocolate-dipped strawberries. Kitty selected one, took a bite, and moaned in her throat at the delicious combination of juicy sweet berry and decadently rich chocolate. A sip of champagne provided the perfect complement to the treat. She dipped the partially eaten strawberry into the champagne and took another bite.

"Perfect," she murmured with her mouth full.

Beyond the bathroom's long window, with its view of the high desert mountains, a crimson sun hung on the lip of the western horizon. The sky was a wash of magenta, rose madder, and fuchsia bleeding together. Its flattering pink light spilled into the bathroom, but Kitty took little notice of it.

Having lived in Santa Fe most of her life, she had grown used to the spectacular sunsets and sharp clear air for which the city was known and with which artists were so enamored. At the moment she was much too busy luxuriating in her sensuous bath to admire the view. It was too rare that she had the time to indulge herself this way. But tonight was a special night. Very special.

Remembering, Kitty smiled in secret delight and sank a little lower in the tubful of bubbles, convinced she had never been this happy in her life. Perhaps the world always seemed this glorious when one was in love; Kitty honestly couldn't say. But she knew she wanted to revel in this giddy contentment she felt. It was a thing to celebrate—and an evening to celebrate. Hence the strawberries and champagne, the music and candlelight. She wanted everything about this evening to be special, from beginning to end, with nothing to spoil it.

On that note, she splashed more champagne into her glass and plucked another chocolate-dipped strawberry from the plate, then alternately sipped and nibbled. She silently vowed again that, for once, she was not going to be hurried. She wanted the evening to begin with sensuous pleasures and end with sensual ones.

Suddenly the bathroom door swung open, startling Kitty. Surprise quickly gave way to annoyance when Sebastian Cole walked in, all six feet two inches of him. He was dressed in his usual T-shirt, jeans, and huaraches, but for a change he didn't reek of turpentine and oils. Judging from the wet gleam that darkened the toasted gold color of his hair, Kitty suspected he had come straight from the shower.

"Sorry. I didn't realize you were in here." He threw her an offhand smile and walked straight to the vanity table.

"Now that you do, you can leave." Irritated by the sudden sour note in her evening, Kitty set her champagne glass down and reached for the loofah sponge. Having known Sebastian for nearly twenty years she was well aware that even if he had known she was in there, he would have walked in anyway.

"First I need to borrow your razor." He began rummaging through the contents of the top drawer. "Don't you usually keep your spare ones in here?"

"It's the drawer on the other side." She rubbed the soap and sponge together and wished she was rubbing the lathered bar over his face. "With the fortune your paintings are bringing, I should think you could buy your own razors."

"But with the commission you make from selling them, you can afford to supply me with a razor now and then. Besides, I ran out." He opened the other drawer and took out a disposable razor. "Why should I go all the way to the store for one, when you live right here in my own backyard? Correction, my front yard."

"You really need to find a larger studio, Sebastian. That one is much too small."

"It suits me." Razor in hand, he turned to face the tub and sat down on the vanity, stretching out his long legs and giving every indication that he intended to stay awhile.

Stifling the urge to order him out, Kitty struggled to ignore him. But Sebastian Cole was much too compelling to ignore. She had never quite identified the exact cause of it. At forty, he still possessed the kind of leanly muscled physique guaranteed to draw a woman's eye. His rugged features stopped just short of Hollywood handsome. And there was something striking about the contrast of golden blond hair and dark, dark eyes. Or maybe it was all in his eyes, and that devilishly lazy way he had of looking and absorbing every minute detail of his subject, not with an artist's typical dispassion but with a caress.

And he was doing it to her now. Kitty could feel his gaze gliding along her outstretched arm, the slope of her shoulder, and the arched curve of her neck. Her nerve ends tingled with the sensation of it.

She flicked him a glance, feigning indifference, although, of all the feelings Sebastian had ever aroused in her, indifference had never been one of them. "Was there something else you wanted?"

"Thanks. Don't mind if I do," he said in response, and pushed away from the vanity table, crossed to the tub, reached across its width to lift the champagne bottle from its icy nest. Taking the water glass by the sink, he filled it with the bubbly wine, then returned the bottle to its bucket. "And strawberries drenched in chocolate, too. Perfect."

He popped one into his mouth while somehow managing to extricate the cap from it, and chewed with relish. "Mmm, good," he pronounced, and washed it down with a big swallow of wine. "The chocolate is obviously from La Maison du Chocolate. Had another batch flown in from Paris, did you?"

"Wrong," Kitty replied with some pleasure. "The chocolate is Boulanger's."

"Boulanger's?" Sebastian frowned in surprise. "That's a new one."

"It's Belgian."

"Ahh." There was a wealth of understanding in his nod. "In that case, I'll have another."

Kitty watched in disgust as he consumed another chocolate-covered strawberry in one bite. "How can you devour it like that? It's a treat that should be savored."

"My mistake. Let me try again." He picked up a third and nipped off the end, the gleam in his eyes mocking her.

"Oh, eat it and be done with it," Kitty declared with a flash of impatience. "That's what you want to do anyway."

A blond-brown eyebrow shot up. "My, but you are in a bad mood tonight."

"I was in a glorious mood until you showed up," she retorted, and switched from lathering her arms to soaping her legs.

"Of course you were," he replied dryly. "That's why

you're here lazing in bubbles, surrounded by candlelight and music, sipping champagne and eating strawberries dipped in chocolate. Consolation, I imagine, for spending another lonely evening all alone. If I had known, I would have asked you to join me for dinner."

She hated that smug look he wore. "For your information, I already have a date."

"Johnny Desmond's back in town, is he?"

"I wouldn't know."

"Not Johnny, huh. Then it must be—"

Kitty broke in, "It's no one you know."

"Really?" The curve of his mouth deepened slightly. "Something tells me you've been keeping secrets from me."

"I wouldn't call it a secret," Kitty replied smoothly. "My private life is simply none of your business."

"Then, this isn't a business dinner," Sebastian concluded.

"Not at all." This time it was her smile that widened. "It's strictly pleasure. Wonderfully glorious pleasure."

He released an exaggerated sigh of despair. "Don't tell me you've fallen hopelessly in love again."

She paused, staring off into space with a dreamy look. "Not again. For the first time."

"That's what you said about Roger Montgomery and Mark Rutledge," Sebastian reminded her, naming two of her former husbands.

Doubt flickered for a fleeting second. Then Kitty mentally shook it off. "This time it's different." Lifting a leg above the mound of bubbles, she reached forward to run the loofah over it.

"You have beautiful legs," Sebastian remarked unexpectedly, studying her with an artist's eye. "It's a pity I don't have my sketch pad with me. You would make a marvelous study with the soft froth of the bubbles, the porcelain-white gleam of the tub and tiles, and the cream color of your skin. The darkness of your hair, all tumbled atop your head, and the

flaming sunset behind you adds the right shock of color."
His eyes narrowed slightly. "But I would need to move a
couple of the candles closer."

She could see the painting in his mind and knew exactly
where he wanted the candles placed. It was something she
took for granted, dismissing it as the result of the two of
them working so long and so closely together over the years.

"Stick to landscapes. They sell," was her response.

"So speaks Kitty Hamilton, art dealer," Sebastian replied
with a bow of mock subservience.

"Well, it's true. The painting you described might be appropriate for the cover of a romance novel, but for something more artistic, it needs to be midnight-black beyond the
window, creating a reflection in the glass, with a vague scat-
tering of stars and a pale crescent moon. Now, *that* would be
a great study in blacks and whites."

"Probably." Sebastian was clearly indifferent to the suggestion. "But any artist can do a black-and-white. I'm talking red-and-white."

Kitty was momentarily intrigued by the thought. "You
would need a redhead for that."

"The glow of the sunset has given your hair a red cast."

"Really?" She looked up in surprise, then curiosity. "How
does it look? I've been toying with the idea of having Carlos
add some red highlights. It's so in right now."

"Don't." He drank down the last of the champagne in his
glass, set it aside, and reached for the loofah sponge in her
hand. "Here. I'll wash your back for you."

Distracted by the shortness of his answer, Kitty automatically handed it to him. "Why?"

"Why what?" He soaped the sponge into a thick lather
and rubbed it over her back in slow, massaging strokes.

"Why wouldn't I look good with a few red highlights
streaked through my hair?"

"I know you too well. You wouldn't be content with a few.
Before it was finished, you'd be a flaming carrottop."

"Not necessarily."

"Everything is always whole-hog or die with you." His voice had a smile in it. "It can be love or business; it's always both feet. Speaking of which, who is the new love of your life?"

The hint of ridicule in his voice made Kitty loath to answer. Which was childish. After tonight, it would be public knowledge.

"Marcel Boulanger."

"Sounds French."

"Belgian."

"My mistake." The drollness of his voice was irritating, but the kneading pressure along the taut shoulder muscles near the base of her neck made it slightly easier to overlook. "Boulanger," he repeated thoughtfully. "It seems as though I've heard that name before. What does he do?"

"His family makes chocolate. In fact, many consider it to be the finest in the world."

"Ah," he murmured in a dawning voice. "The strawberries."

"Dipped in Boulanger chocolate," Kitty confirmed, and sighed at the remembered taste of it. "Even you must admit, it's absolutely exquisite chocolate. And it's no wonder, either. Marcel regularly travels to Central and South America to select only the best cocoa beans."

"I'm surprised he hasn't been kidnapped and held for ransom."

Kitty stiffened in instant alarm. "Don't say that. Don't even think it!"

"Sorry. So, when did you meet Mr. Chocolate?"

"Almost three weeks ago. He came by the gallery with the Ridgedales. He's staying with them," she added in explanation. "So of course, I saw him again that evening at the Ridgedales' pre-opera cocktail party."

"And you were smitten?" Sebastian guessed.

"Instantly." She almost purred the word as that deliciously exciting feeling welled up inside her again.

"Love at first bite, you might say."

"Very funny, Sebastian," she replied without humor.

"I thought it was. Obviously you're in love, since you seem to have lost your sense of humor."

"I'm very much in love," she declared with feeling.

"And how serious is Mr. Chocolate?"

"Very. He's asked me to marry him."

"And you said yes, of course."

"Naturally."

"A man who makes chocolate—how could any woman refuse?" Sebastian murmured.

But Kitty was too wrapped up in her memory of Marcel's proposal to pay any attention to Sebastian's sardonic rejoinders. Besides, she was too used to them.

"It was such a romantic setting. Dinner in the courtyard, just the two of us, crystal gleaming in the candlelight, the air scented with gardenias in bloom. There at my chair was a single red rose and a small gift. I opened it, and—do you know what I found inside?"

"An engagement ring. Not really very original."

"Oh, but it was," Kitty insisted smugly. "Maybe the ring part of it wasn't original, but the box it came in definitely was. It was made out of chocolate. Perfect in every detail, too, right down to the slot to hold the ring."

"Milk chocolate or dark?"

"Dark. It even had the Boulanger family crest embossed on top of it."

"On top of the ring?" Sebastian feigned shock.

"No, on top of the box."

"I hope the ring wasn't made of chocolate, too."

"It's one hundred percent diamond." She held up her hand, wagging her fingers, letting the stone's facets catch and reflect the light. "All three carats of it."

"That's as bright as a spotlight. Be careful. The glare from it can blind you."

"It is eye-catching, isn't it?" she murmured, admiring its fiery sparkle.

"That's one word for it," he responded dryly, and dipped the loofah in and out of the water. "Hand me the soap, will you?" She slipped the scented bar off its ridged ledge and passed it to him. "I'm not surprised you fell madly in love with him. Chocolate's a turn-on all by itself. Who needs foreplay when you have chocolate, right?"

She threw him a look of disgust. "You can be so crude sometimes, Sebastian."

"That's not crude. It's the truth. It has something to do with endorphins. Oops, I dropped the soap." He groped underwater for it, his hand sliding along the curve of her hip to her thigh.

A second later, Kitty felt the bar squirt under her leg, and his hand immediately came over the top of her thigh to search for it between her legs. He quickly became dangerously close to areas she didn't want touched by him.

She pushed at his arm. "Stop it. I'll get it myself."

"Wait. It's right here. I can feel it."

"Don't! That's not it!" As she squirmed to elude his playful fingers, she slipped in the tub. She yelped in alarm as she started to slide under the bubbles. "Stop! I don't want to get my hair wet!"

"I've got you." His muscled arm was a band across her breasts, hauling her back upright.

Suddenly everything about this scene seemed much too intimate. There she was naked in the tub with his hands all over her. And Kitty realized that at some point she had lost control of things. Worst of all, Sebastian knew it.

"You bastard. Let me go!" She tugged to free herself of his hold, but between her wet hands and his wet arm, she was hardly successful.

"I'm only trying to help," he protested.

"Help, my foot. You're copping a feel, and you know it."

Abandoning the useless struggle, she located the loofah sponge and slapped at him with it.

"Hey!" He jerked back to elude contact with it, but he couldn't elude the splattering of water droplets and bits of foamy bubbles. As he reached up to wipe at his face, he accidentally bumped the plate of strawberries, knocking them into the tub.

"My strawberries," Kitty wailed.

"Let me get that plate out of there before it gets broken." He plunged both hands into the water.

"Just leave it alone," she exploded in anger, and pummeled him with her fists. "Get out of here! Out! Out! Out!"

"Will you stop it?" he yelled above her shrieks of outrage, hunching his shoulders against the raining blows.

The bathroom door burst open. Kitty squealed in dismay at the sight of the thunderous look on the face of a tall, dark man with distinctively Gaelic features—the man who was her fiancé.

"You! Get away from her," Marcel Boulanger ordered in that gorgeous accent of his.

Sebastian started to rise, then lost his footing on the wet floor and slipped halfway into the tub.

"It's all right, Marcel," Kitty rushed. "It's not what you think."

"Who is this man?" he demanded, his accent thickening noticeably.

Half in and half out of the tub, Sebastian replied. "I'm her husband. Who the hell are you?"

"Your husband?" Marcel scowled blackly at Kitty. "What is this he is saying?"

"He's my *ex*-husband." She hurried the explanation and pushed Sebastian the rest of the way out of the bathtub, while trying to hide her own self among the bubbles. "We've been divorced for years."

Whatever comfort Marcel found in that, it was small. "What is he doing here now?"

"I live here," Sebastian answered, rising to his feet.

Kitty hastened to correct that impression. "Not here, precisely. At least, not in the house. He has a studio out back. He lives there."

"A studio? This man is an artist?" He eyed Sebastian with considerable skepticism.

In all honesty, Kitty had to admit that Sebastian didn't fit the popular image of an artist. He certainly didn't possess the temperament of one. He was much too easygoing.

"This is Sebastian Cole. The Ridgedales have two of his landscapes hanging in their Santa Fe home." Conscious of the rapidly dissipating bubbles, Kitty reached for the oversize bath towel lying on the tub's tiled ledge.

The doubtful look vanished as Marcel smiled in recognition of the name. "Ah, yes, you are—"

"Please don't say the great Sebastian," Sebastian interrupted, his mouth slanting in a wry smile. "It makes me feel like a trapeze artist in a circus. Plain Sebastian will do. You must be Mr. Chocolate."

Confusion furrowed his brow. "*Mais non*, my name is Marcel Boulanger."

"He knows that . . ." Kitty gave Sebastian a dirty look as she maneuvered closer to the side of the tub. "It's just a nickname he gave you. It's his idea of a joke."

"I sampled some of your family's wares earlier," Sebastian remarked. "Kitty had a plate of strawberries dipped in your chocolate. Unfortunately I knocked it into the tub."

"That's what he was doing when you came in—looking for the plate." With one arm holding the towel high above her breasts and the other hand trying to hold the ends together behind her back, Kitty attempted to stand.

"Let me give you a hand." Sebastian moved to help her out of the tub.

"I can manage just fine." As she drew away from his outstretched hand, she stepped on a strawberry, slipped, and pitched forward with a yelp.

Sebastian caught her, swept her out of the tub and into the cradle of his arms, towel and all. Kitty was stunned to find herself in such a familiar position, and not altogether sure how she had gotten there. But the memories were much too strong of all the times their arguments had ended like this, with Sebastian sweeping her off her feet and carting her off to the nearest soft or flat surface and there making love to her. Most satisfactorily, she recalled as color flooded her cheeks.

"Put me down," she snapped.

"Whatever you say, kitten." He released her legs with an abruptness that took her by surprise.

She managed to retain her grip on the towel as she hissed an irritated "Don't call me that. You know I hate it."

Sebastian simply smiled with infuriating ease and turned his attention to Marcel. "Since I understand congratulations are in order, you might as well know she has a temper."

"I do not!" She stamped her foot on the plush bathroom rug. The muffled sound didn't add much emphasis to her denial.

Sebastian ignored her. "I wouldn't worry about her temper, though. I'm sure you already know about her secret passion for chocolate. It doesn't matter how mad she gets, just pop a piece in her mouth and she'll melt in your arms."

"That is not true." Kitty pushed the angry words through her teeth and hurriedly wrapped the towel around her. "You're making me seem like some foolish female, or worse."

"Well, you're definitely female." His twinkling glance dipped to her cleavage.

Kitty wiggled the towel higher. "You came in here to borrow a razor. Take it and leave."

"She's a little upset about the loss of the strawberries," he explained to Marcel. "She hates to waste good chocolate."

"Go." She pointed a rigid arm at the door.

He cocked an eyebrow. "Now, you know you don't want me dripping water all through your house." He pulled at the side of his T-shirt, reminding her that half of his clothes were soaked. She hesitated fractionally, visualizing the trail of water through her beautiful home. "You still have that spare terry-cloth robe hanging in the closet, don't you?"

She hated the way Sebastian made it sound as though he knew where everything was. Of course, the truth was he did. She shot an anxious look at Marcel, worried that he might put the wrong construction on that.

"Yes, it's hanging—"

"I'll find it," Sebastian assured her, and he headed for the bedroom, a faint squelch to his woven-leather sandals.

Kitty didn't draw an easy breath until he was out of the room. Even then, she was a little surprised that he hadn't lingered to make a further nuisance of himself. Fixing the warmest smile on her face that she could muster, she crossed to her fiancé.

"I am so sorry about this. It must have looked awful when you came in—a strange man in the tub with me. Thank God, he was fully clothed, or—" She broke off the rush of words and allowed chagrin to tinge her smile. "It's absolutely impossible to explain any of this. You would have to know Sebastian to understand." Then it hit her that she hadn't expected Marcel to arrive until much later. "What are you doing here anyway?"

He seemed a bit taken aback by her question. "Your maid let me into the house as she was leaving. I heard your cries and thought you were being accosted by some thief."

"No." She shook her head. "I mean—I thought you weren't going to be here until eight o'clock."

From the bedroom closet came Sebastian's muffled shout, "I found it!"

Deciding it was best to simply ignore him, Kitty bit back the impulse to shout back at him to put on the robe and get out. "Pay no attention to him." She laid a hand on Marcel's arm, drawing his attention back to her when he half turned in the direction of Sebastian's voice.

"Yes, that is best," he agreed, then explained, "I came early to your house because I received a phone call from home this afternoon. My *maman* has taken ill. Nothing too serious," he inserted when Kitty drew a quick breath of concern. "But I must fly home to Brussels tomorrow. It is my desire that you come with me. I wish to have my family meet with you."

"You mean . . . leave tomorrow?" she asked in shock, her mind exploding with hundreds of problems that would create.

"But of course. We would leave in the morning."

"Marcel, it simply isn't possible for me to fly off at the drop of a hat. Not with everything that's going on at the gallery. This is one of our busiest times of the year. I—"

"Surely your assistant is able to take charge while you are gone."

"Harve is very competent," she agreed. "But I have a special exhibit scheduled in two weeks—actually less than that. The shipment should be here in two or three days. And there are so many other things that must be coordinated. Honestly, it just isn't possible. I'm sorry, Marcel, but—"

A bare-shouldered Sebastian stuck his head around the bathroom door. "Sorry to interrupt, but I need a towel to wrap my wet clothes in."

Teeth gritted, Kitty snatched a towel off the bar and shoved it into his hands. "There."

"Thanks." With a smile and a nod, Sebastian was gone.

Struggling to regain her calm, she faced Marcel once again. "All things considered, I think it would truly be best if I met your family another time, especially since your mother isn't well."

"Perhaps it would be," he conceded, then reached out to grip her upper arms, his gaze burrowing into her with intensity, his eyes darkened with a passion that so thrilled her. "But it pains me to leave you even for a day."

"Me, too." The agreement came easily.

With a groan of desire, he pulled her against him and his mouth came down to claim her lips. But Kitty found it difficult to enjoy the devouring wetness of his kiss when any second they could be interrupted by Sebastian again. After a decent interval, she drew back from his kiss.

"We still have tonight, don't we?" she murmured, one hand on the lapel of his suit jacket and the other pressed against the front of the towel to keep it in place. "After all, we do have an engagement to celebrate."

"Indeed, we have much to celebrate. It may require all night."

"I certainly hope so," Kitty replied, then stepped away when he would have kissed her again. "Why don't you go fix yourself a drink while I finish up here? I promise I won't be long."

As Marcel released a sigh of regret, Sebastian rapped lightly on the door, then looked around it, this time bundled in a white terry robe. "I don't mean to keep busting in on your little tête-á-tête, but I thought I should let you know I'm leaving."

"Promise?" Kitty retorted with a touch of sarcasm.

"Cross my heart."

She didn't believe him for one minute. "Marcel, why don't you go with him and make sure he actually does leave?"

"With pleasure," Marcel declared, clearly as eager to be rid of him as Kitty was.

"Something tells me Kitty doesn't trust me." Sebastian's grin was wide with mischief.

"I wonder why," she murmured, and followed both men into the bedroom, then ushered them out the bedroom door and closed it behind them.

Alone in the bedroom, she stood there a moment and struggled to regain that gloriously happy feeling she'd felt earlier. At the moment, she was much too annoyed with Sebastian. The man had an absolute talent for getting under her skin.

Determined not to let him spoil any more of her evening, Kitty stalked to the huge walk-in closet. The plush throw rug was damp beneath her feet, a reminder that Sebastian had been there before her. As if she needed one.

"Put him out of your mind, Kitty," she muttered to herself, needing to hear the words.

Chapter Two

Sighing, Kitty scanned the clothes in her closet. Now that Marcel had arrived early, she no longer had the luxury of dressing at her leisure. She told herself that she truly didn't mind. It was better to look on the positive side of things; this much-anticipated evening would simply begin earlier than she had expected. Now that she had finally gotten rid of Sebastian, everything was going to be as wonderful as she'd thought.

In the closet, she loosened the towel and used the drier portions of it to wipe the remaining moisture on her skin, all the while surveying her vast wardrobe, regretting that she hadn't already decided on something to wear. Until now, it was a decision that hadn't needed to be hurried.

"Too bad Picasso isn't around to do an abstract of this—Woman's Derriere Amidst a Swirl of Clothes."

At the first sound of Sebastian's familiar voice, Kitty wheeled in fury, snatching the towel back around her. "Don't you ever knock?" she hurled angrily.

He stood in the closet doorway, clad as before in the white terry robe, a portion of his wet jeans sticking out of the rolled-up towel under his arm. "It's a bad habit I've got, I'm afraid," he replied without a smidgeon of remorse.

"It's one bad habit you need to concentrate on breaking," she retorted, then demanded, "What are you doing here again? I thought you'd left."

"I forgot the razor." His expression was much too benignly innocent to be believed.

"On purpose, I'll bet," Kitty guessed, eyes narrowing on him. Careful to keep her bottom covered, she turned back to face the racks of clothes. "Get your razor and leave. Better yet, forget the razor and grow a beard. It would fit the public image of an artist."

"You wouldn't like it," Sebastian replied easily. "I tried growing one before, and you didn't care for the way it scratched, remember?"

"That won't be a problem anymore."

He snapped his fingers as if only recalling their divorce at that moment. "That's right. You're engaged to someone else now, aren't you?"

"As if you didn't remember." She let the sarcasm through.

"Have you decided what you're wearing for the big dinner tonight?"

"That's what I'm doing now."

"I recommend the cranberry silk number."

"Good. That's one I definitely won't choose," Kitty retorted.

"You should. I have to swallow a groan every time I see you in it."

There was a part of her that was secretly pleased she could still turn him on. But only a small part.

She cast a challenging look over her shoulder. "The razor?"

"Right. That's why I came back, isn't it? I'll just get it and leave."

"That would be an original idea," Kitty muttered as he turned to leave.

Sebastian swung back. "Did you say something?"

"Not to you. Go." She waved him out of the closet.

This time when he left, Kitty wasn't convinced he was gone for good. And she was determined that he wouldn't catch her again without a stitch of clothing on. Hurriedly, she discarded the towel and donned a set of nude lingerie from the drawer. After quickly riffling through the rack of dresses, she selected a simple but elegant sheath of white lace with a plunging keyhole back. She removed it from its padded hanger and wiggled into it.

Still there was no sign of Sebastian, no sound at all to indicate he was anywhere in the vicinity. Kitty wasn't sure whether that was a good thing or a bad thing. But she couldn't help being suspicious of the silence.

Crossing to the built-in shoe caddy, Kitty considered the possibility that he might have actually left. A second later, she stiffened, panicked by the sudden thought that he was out there talking to Marcel. Heaven only knew the sort of things Sebastian might be telling him. Sometimes the man was a devil in disguise with an absolute knack for making the simplest thing sound outrageous.

She bolted out of the closet and stopped abruptly as Sebastian came out of the bathroom. "You're still here." It was almost a relief.

"As usual, you forgot to let the water out of the tub. While I was at it, I went ahead and retrieved the platter and the strawberries." He showed her the plate of sodden strawberries and partially melted chocolate.

Recovering some of her former annoyance, Kitty retorted, "When did you appoint yourself to be my maid?"

"I could have left it, I suppose. But I don't think it would have been a very pretty sight come morning. You need to tell Mr. Chocolate that the flavor combination of bathwater and his chocolate is a poor one."

"Will you stop calling him that? His name is Marcel."

"Whatever." Sebastian shrugged off the correction. "Actually the strawberries didn't fare too well in the bath either. Their flavor got pretty watered down. Here. Try one." He picked up a limp berry that dripped a mixture of brown and pink juice.

Kitty was stunned he would offer her one, even as a joke. Well, the joke was about to be on him, she vowed, and took the berry from him and squished it against his mouth.

Laughter danced in his eyes as he scraped the remains of it off his face and onto the plate. "I'll bet that felt good," he observed.

"Actually I got a great deal of satisfaction out of it."

"I thought you looked like you wanted to hit something," he observed.

"I wouldn't if you would just leave."

"Is that what you're wearing tonight?" he asked, ignoring her broad hint.

"Please tell me you don't like it. Then I'll know I have chosen the right dress."

"You look fabulous in it."

She heard the hesitation in his voice. "But what?" She was furious with herself for seeking his opinion. She blamed it on her respect for his artistic eye.

"I was just thinking—don't you think virginal white is a bit of a stretch?"

Glaring at him, Kitty demanded, "Give me that plate of strawberries so I can shove the whole thing in your face."

When she made a grab for it, Sebastian held it out of reach. "I don't think so," he said. "Something tells me you'd break it over my head. What do you say we call a truce, and I'll stop teasing you."

"I have a better idea. Why don't you go home?" Kitty suggested, then remembered, "You did get the razor."

He set the plate on a dresser top and patted the pocket of his robe. "Right here."

"Then leave, so I can get dressed in peace."

"Let me fasten that hook in back first. You know you'll never be able to reach it yourself."

To her irritation, Sebastian was right. Against her better judgment, Kitty turned her back to him, giving him access to the hook.

"I could have had Marcel fasten it for me." She could feel the light pressure of his blunt fingers against her skin as he drew the two ends together.

"I have no doubt he would have been delighted to do it."

"As long as you understand that."

"You need to wear your silver shawl with this, and those silver, strappy heels you have."

"That's probably a good choice. Silver is in this season," she recalled thoughtfully. "And I will need something later this evening to ward off the chill. What about jewelry? How about the necklace of turquoise nuggets?"

"Everybody will be wearing turquoise. And it would be too chunky with the lace. Try that slender silver choker with the cabochon pendant of pink coral."

Kitty didn't need to try it. She could already visualize it in her mind and knew it would be perfect.

"Have you set a wedding date yet?"

"No. We planned to talk about it tonight." But with Marcel's mother being ill, she wasn't sure it would be an appropriate subject. "It will be sometime soon, though. It's what we both want."

"I guess that means I'll have to start looking for a new art dealer. It won't be easy. You've spoiled me."

"What are you talking about?" She twisted around, trying to see his face.

"Hold still. I almost have it fastened."

"Then explain what you meant by that." She squared around again. "Just because I'm getting married doesn't mean I can't still represent your paintings."

"True, but it might be a little difficult trying to do that from Brussels."

"Brussels?" She turned in shock, not caring that he had yet to fasten the top.

"That's right. According to Mr. Chocolate, that's where you'll be living after you're married. I suppose you could keep the gallery here in Santa Fe and find someone to manage it for you. Although it would probably be simpler just to sell it."

"Sell the gallery? After I've worked so hard to build it to this point?"

Tilting his head, he scanned the bedroom's ceiling, exposed beams spanning its breadth. "I don't remember this room having an echo."

"Will you be serious?" Kitty demanded impatiently.

"I am serious." He brought his gaze back to her upturned face, a new gentleness darkening his eyes. "I take it you hadn't thought about where you would be living?"

Truthfully, she hadn't given any thought to it at all. The realization made her feel utterly foolish.

Once again, she turned her back to him, aware that those sharp eyes of his saw too much. "I more or less assumed we would be dividing our time between Brussels and Santa Fe. That's what is usually done when two people have separate careers."

"I suppose that could work."

Reassured, Kitty relaxed a little. "Of course it could."

"I guess that means you'll be keeping the house, too."

"Naturally. I'll need somewhere to live when I am here."

"Mr. Chocolate thought you would prefer to sell it and avoid the financial drain of maintaining two households. I told him that you didn't have to look for a buyer. I'll be happy to take it off your hands. We could even work out some sort of arrangement where you could stay here whenever you do come back."

"That's very generous of you, but I'll keep it, thank you," she stated firmly.

"It was just a thought." The tone of his voice had an indifferent shrug to it, but Kitty wasn't fooled.

"You've had a number of thoughts. It almost makes me think that you're trying to put doubts in my mind about my engagement to Marcel."

"Would I do that?"

"In a heartbeat," she retorted.

"Honestly, I'm not trying to create doubts—"

"And just what would you call it?"

Sebastian finished fastening the hook and turned her around to face him, both hands resting lightly on the rounded curves of her shoulders. "I'm only trying to make sure that you've thought things through a little before committing yourself to this engagement. You tend to be a bit impulsive where your heart's concerned. It certainly wouldn't be the first time. You have to admit that."

"Oh, I do. And the first time was when I married you." Standing this close to him, Kitty found it difficult not to remember how madly in love with him she had been.

"As your first husband, I think I have the right to vet any future replacement."

Kitty bristled. "That is the most arrogant statement I have ever heard you make. And you have made quite a few."

"Why is that arrogant?" Sebastian countered in a perfectly reasonable tone. "You have to know that I still care about you a lot, even if we aren't married anymore. I don't want to see you get hurt again. Believe it or not, I hope Mr. Chocolate makes you very happy."

"Well, I don't," she stated flatly.

A frown of disbelief swept across his expression. "You don't want him to make you happy?"

"Of course I do," Kitty replied in exasperation. "But I don't believe that you do. And his name is Marcel."

"My mistake." He dipped his head in mild apology, a smile tugging at the corners of his mouth.

"You've made a lot of them." Kitty needed to get a dig in to negate the effects of that near smile.

"I have, but you were never one of them, kitten."

"Don't call me that. You know I hate it."

"You used to like it."

"Don't remind me, please. That was long ago. And I was very young and very foolish."

"And very beautiful. You still are." With his fingertip, he traced the curve of her jaw.

The featherlight caress made her skin tingle. "Don't start with the flattery, Sebastian. It doesn't work anymore." She did her best to ignore the rapid skittering of her pulse.

"It's not flattery. It's the truth."

"Then keep it to yourself."

"I will, on one condition."

"What's that?" she asked, instantly wary.

"You see, something tells me that I won't be invited to the wedding—"

"It's a wise little bird that's whispering in your ear."

Sebastian pretended not to hear that. "—So, this may be my only chance to kiss the bride."

"Not on your life." Kitty took an immediate step back.

"Why not?" He looked genuinely surprised.

"Because it's just another one of your tricks. You know there's a physical attraction that still exists between us. You want to use that to confuse me."

"Do you think I could do that with just one little kiss?"

"I am not going to find out," she stated.

"Don't tell me you're afraid? You, Kitty Hamilton?" His look was one of mocking skepticism.

She shook her head. "That's not going to work either. You aren't going to dare me into it, so you might as well give up."

"Now you've hurt my feelings." But his smile mocked his words.

"You'll get over it." Determined to bring this meeting to an end, Kitty stated calmly, "Thank you for hooking my dress. Now, if you don't mind, I would like to finish getting ready. And you, as I recall, were on your way back to the studio to shave—with my razor."

He started to sing, " 'You go your way. I'll go mine.' "

"Don't." Kitty covered her ears. "Singing is not one of your talents. Stick to oils."

"Kiss me and I'll go."

"Not a chance. With my luck, Marcel would walk in to see what's taking me so long. It was awkward enough when he found you in the bathroom with me."

"All right, I'll go. But it's under protest."

"Under, over, I don't care. Just go."

The minute the door closed behind him, Kitty rushed over and locked it. The sense of relief didn't last though. She had the uneasy feeling that Sebastian had given up a little too easily. She wouldn't feel safe until she and Marcel were out of the house.

As much as she would have liked to tarry, Kitty put on her makeup and fixed her hair in nearly record time for her. Taking Sebastian's advice, she wore the coral pendant and matching earrings, slipped on the strappy heels, and draped the silver crocheted shawl around her shoulders. After a satisfactory check of her reflection in the tall cheval mirror, she unlocked the door to the hall and walked swiftly to the living room.

But Marcel wasn't there.

The feeling of alarm was instant. It only intensified when Kitty heard Sebastian's voice coming from the kitchen. The high heels were the only thing that stopped her from sprinting there.

As she entered the kitchen, she saw Marcel comfortably seated at the table. Her glance ricocheted off him straight to Sebastian, leaning negligently against the tiled countertop, his hands wrapped around a toweled wine bottle, his thumbs gently easing out the cork. Marcel rose when she entered.

Her patience exhausted, Kitty snapped, "Haven't you left yet?"

"Really, Kitty," Sebastian said with a mocking *tsk-tsk*. "I credited you with having better powers of observation. Here I am, freshly shaved, wearing dry clothes, and you didn't even notice."

As he took one hand away from the wine bottle to gesture to his change in attire, the cork shot into the air with an explosive pop, caromed off a ceiling vega, sailed past Kitty's head, and bounced onto the floor. Foam bubbled out of the bottle and spilled down its side. Hurriedly Sebastian swung around to pour the effervescent wine into the tulip-shaped champagne glasses on the counter.

"Don't you know you are supposed to ease the cork out of the bottle?" Bending, Kitty retrieved the wayward cork, certain she would step on it if she didn't pick it up.

"That's what I was in the process of doing when I was so rudely interrupted," Sebastian countered smoothly.

"What are you doing back here anyway?" Kitty demanded, unable to rein in her irritation with him.

"I was just telling"—he paused, his eyes twinkling devilishly when she shot him a warning look—"your fiancé that I thought the occasion of your engagement deserved a celebratory toast. So I brought over a bottle of champagne."

Kitty's suspicion warred with her curiosity, but curiosity won. "Why do you have champagne on hand? I thought you didn't like it."

"Ever since your last divorce, I've always kept a bottle in the fridge. That way, the next time you show up at my door in the wee hours of the morning, wanting to drown your troubles in some bubbly, I won't have to go all over God's creation trying to beg, borrow, or steal one." After filling the last glass, Sebastian set down the bottle, then turned with a sudden look of regret. "Sorry. That was bad taste to mention your last divorce, wasn't it?"

Marcel turned to her in confusion. "Your last divorce? What does he mean by this?"

"Don't pay any attention to him. He's just being Sebastian." She directed a careless smile at Marcel and glared at Sebastian when she walked over to pick up two of the champagne glasses. "A name that sounds distinctly like another one," she murmured for Sebastian's ears only.

He merely smiled and picked up the remaining glass. "A toast," he began, and waited until Marcel had a drink in his hand, "to the woman who can still take my breath away, and to her future husband. Happiness always." His gaze was warm on her as he raised his glass to his lips.

Kitty did the same, a little of her own breath stolen by the unexpectedly sincere compliment. But she was careful to direct her tremulous smile at Marcel.

"I must agree with you, Mr. Cole." Marcel flicked him a glance, then smiled lovingly at her. "She is quite beautiful. And never more so than tonight."

Marcel lifted her hand and kissed the back of her fingers, a gesture that came very naturally to him. She didn't have to glance at Sebastian to know that he was observing it all with a droll little smirk.

There was no sign of it, however, when he asked, "Have you already made dinner reservations for this evening?"

"Of course." Truthfully it was an assumption on Kitty's part.

"Somewhere special, I hope." Sebastian took another sip of his champagne.

"Very special," Marcel assured him. "I have arranged for us to dine at Antoine's."

Sebastian cocked a blond eyebrow at Kitty. "Is that wise? First me, then Roger, then Mark. With a track record like that, are you sure you want to go there with him?"

If looks could kill, Kitty would have been staring at Sebastian's gravestone instead of him. "Of course I'm sure," she stated, and fervently hoped that Marcel hadn't followed any of that.

"Antoine's, it is your favorite place, is it not?" Marcel darted confused glances to first one, then the other.

"It's very definitely her favorite," Sebastian replied before she could answer.

"And why shouldn't it be?" She slipped an arm around the crook of Marcel's and snuggled a little closer to him. "The food there is superb."

"You have dined there before with these other men he has mentioned?" Marcel was clearly troubled by that. "They were special to you?"

"I think it's safe to say that," Sebastian inserted. "She married all of us. Not at the same time of course," he added for clarification, then feigned surprise. "Didn't Kitty mention that she's been married three times before?"

"She tells me she is divorced, but I did not know it was from three different men," Marcel replied stiffly, a coolness in the look he gave her.

Kitty struggled to defend the omission. "I thought you knew. It's common knowledge to nearly everyone in Santa Fe."

"That's hardly surprising," Sebastian said, coming to her rescue. "From the sounds of it, you two have had such a whirlwind courtship you haven't had a lot of time to exchange stories about any skeletons in the closet, or—in Kitty's case— ex-husbands. I guess that's the purpose of engagements. Kitty and I never had one. Two days after I proposed, we were married. With the logistics of each of you having careers in different countries, I imagine you're planning a long engagement. Have you decided where the wedding will be? Here or in Brussels?"

"In Brussels, of course," Marcel stated with a certainty that irked Kitty, considering it was something they hadn't gotten around to discussing. And it was, after all, a decision the bride was supposed to make, not the groom.

"Brussels, you say," Sebastian said and sighed. "That's a shame."

"Why do you say this?" Marcel wondered, a puzzled knit to his brow.

"I do all my traveling on the ground. I don't fly, certainly not across an ocean—not even for Kitty," Sebastian added with a smiling glance in her direction. "As much as I would like to be there to see her walk down the aisle, I won't be coming to the wedding."

"You're assuming you would even receive an invitation." Her own smile was on the saccharine side.

"You know you'd invite me, kitten," Sebastian chided. "For business reasons, if nothing else," he added, then chuckled. "I can see the wheels turning already, trying to figure out a way to arrange an exhibit of my works on the Continent. Go ahead, but don't expect me to attend."

"But you wouldn't have to fly. You could go by sea, rent a first-class cabin on some luxury liner and travel that way." Recognizing the value of having the artist in attendance, Kitty chose to work on that hurdle first.

"What if I get seasick?" he countered out of sheer perversity.

"They have a patch you can wear now to take care of that. It won't be a problem."

"And go around feeling all doped up, no thank you."

"Don't be difficult, Sebastian."

He just smiled. "You know you love a challenge. Think how dull your life will be when I'm not around."

"Where are you going?" Marcel struggled to follow their conversation.

"Me? I'm not going anywhere. It's Kitty who will be moving to the other side of the world when you two get married."

She was quick to correct him. "I'll only be there part of the time."

"Why do you say this?" Marcel drew back, again eyeing her with faint criticism. "We will be living in Brussels. It is the place of my business. It is where our home will be."

"Of course, but I do have my gallery here—"

"We will make arrangements for that." He dismissed that as a concern. "Art is better pursued in Europe. Although, after we are married, you will discover that you are much too busy to run some little shop of your own."

For an instant, his attitude made Kitty see red. But she was much too aware of Sebastian and the delighted interest he was showing in their conversation to unleash her temper. She was also aware that the blame for all of this belonged directly at his feet. Sebastian had deliberately brought up this subject to cause trouble between her and Marcel. Therefore she wasn't about to give him the satisfaction of succeeding.

Instead of objecting, Kitty smiled serenely. "It's quite possible you are right, Marcel."

"Spoken like a dutifully submissive wife," Sebastian murmured tauntingly.

Angered that he knew her much too well, Kitty resisted the urge to empty her champagne glass in his face. With an effort, she replied, "You should know."

"Believe me, I do know."

"What is this you know?" Marcel frowned. "I hear the words, but it is as if you are speaking in another language."

"I can guarantee Kitty will explain it all to you later." A smile deepened the grooves on either side of Sebastian's mouth. "I imagine there are a lot of details you two need to thrash out—without a third party listening in. So I'll be going and let you have some privacy."

"That's the nicest thing you've said today," Kitty declared. "The only thing better would be if you actually left."

"Oh, I'm going." He slid his champagne glass onto the tiled countertop, then squared back around. "But before I do—"

She sighed in annoyance. "Somehow I knew you'd come up with something."

"Since I won't be coming to the wedding, with your permission"—he inclined his head toward Marcel—"I'd like to kiss the bride-to-be. I don't know when I'll get another chance. And it's only kosher that I do it in your presence so you don't get the idea there's any hanky-panky between Kitty and me."

"I know not this hanky-panky of which you speak," Marcel admitted, then gestured to Kitty with a flourish of his hand. "*Mais oui*, you may kiss the bride."

Left without an objection to make, Kitty fumed inwardly as Sebastian stepped toward her, eyes twinkling. When his hands settled on the rounded points of her shoulders, she obligingly tilted her head up. His head bent slowly toward her as if he was deliberately prolonging the moment of contact.

At last his mouth moved onto hers with persuasive warmth. Her pulse raced, but she reasoned that it was strictly out of anger and the awkwardness of having Marcel standing so close, observing it all. She held herself rigid, refusing to kiss him back. And that was harder than she had expected it to be. Sebastian was in that familiar, slow lovemaking mode. It had been her undoing countless times in the past.

His lips clung to hers for a moistly sweet second longer, then they were gone. She immediately missed their seductive warmth. It was a vague ache inside, one that prevented her from being glad that he had kept the kiss so brief.

"I honestly want you to be happy, kitten," he murmured.

Determined to break the spell of his kiss, Kitty reached for Marcel's hand. "We will be very happy together."

There was something mocking in the smile Sebastian directed her way before he turned to shake hands with Marcel. "Congratulations."

"*Merci.*" Marcel made a slight bow in response.

"I'll be going now. Enjoy your dinner." With a farewell wave, Sebastian moved toward the back door.

"I'll show you out." Kitty moved after him. "I need to lock the door anyway after you leave." When he opened the door, she was right behind him. The instant he stepped outside, she muttered a warning, "So help me, Sebastian, if you show up at Antoine's tonight, I swear I will take a knife to every one of your paintings."

He grinned. "Actually I plan on spending the entire evening at home. Alone, I might add. Does that make you feel better?"

"Good night," she said in answer, and closed the door, turning the lock with great satisfaction. Turning back to Marcel, she smiled with genuine pleasure. "I'm ready if you are."

Chapter Three

The Sangre de Cristo Mountains were a black silhouette that jutted into the night sky's star-crusted backdrop. But Kitty took little notice of it as the taxicab moved in and out of the glow from the streetlights that lined the road. She sat silently in the rear seat, her face devoid of all expression.

The driver slowed the vehicle as they approached the tall adobe wall that enclosed her property. Recognizing it, Kitty opened her slender evening bag and took out the fare. When he pulled up to the gated entry, she passed him the money and climbed out.

Using the key from her purse, she unlocked the wrought-iron pass-through door, stepped through, and locked it behind her. Soft landscape lighting lit the flagstone walk that led to the low adobe house. But Kitty didn't take it. Instead, she struck out on the side path that swept around the house to the studio located in the rear courtyard.

Light flooded from its windows in wide pools. She wasn't surprised. Sebastian had always been late to bed and late to rise. She paused outside his door long enough to slip off a silver shoe. With great relish, Kitty proceeded to pound the shoe against the door as hard as she could. The heel snapped off, but she kept pounding until the door was jerked open by Sebastian.

"Kitty," he began.

But she didn't give him a chance to say more. "Don't pretend to be surprised to see me. It won't work."

He glanced at the broken shoe in her hand, then reached down and picked up its missing heel. "Why didn't you simply ring the doorbell?"

"You don't get the same satisfaction out of pushing a button."

"But I liked those shoes." He examined the heel as if checking to see if it could be repaired.

"Here. Have the rest of it." She threw the rest of the shoe at him.

He ducked quickly, and it sailed over his shoulder and clattered across the floor. When he went after it, Kitty stalked into the studio a bit unelegantly wearing only one shoe. She stopped on the Saltillo tile and slipped off the other shoe.

"You like them so much, take both of them." She tossed the second shoe at him, but without the force of the first.

"I didn't expect you home so early. It's barely eleven o'clock." He retrieved the second shoe as well and set them on a side table. "Where did you leave Mr. Chocolate?"

"We had an argument, as if you didn't know." She hurled the accusation.

"Don't tell me the engagement's off? Nope, it must not be," Sebastian said, answering the question himself and gesturing to her left hand. "I see you're still wearing the headlight."

"No, it isn't off. Yet."

"I hope you don't want a glass of champagne. I opened the only bottle I had, to toast your engagement."

"I wouldn't drink any of your champagne if you had it. This is all your fault."

"My fault?" He feigned innocence. "What did I do now?"

"Don't pull that act with me," she warned. "You know exactly what you did. You set out to deliberately undermine my relationship with Marcel."

"How could I do that? I met him for the first time tonight," he reminded her in an infuriatingly reasonable voice.

"Maybe you did," Kitty conceded, then gathered back up her anger. "But you're smart and quick. You can think faster on your feet than anyone I know. And you're an absolute master of sabotage."

"You give me much more credit than I deserve. I want you to be happy. If Mr. Chocolate can do that, then great."

"But you don't think he can. That's the point," she retorted.

"It isn't important what I think. Do you think he can?"

The instant he turned the question back on her, all her high anger crumbled, making room for the doubts and questions to resurface. "I don't know, Sebastian. I honestly don't know," she replied in a hopeless murmur.

"I'll tell you what—why don't we sit on the sofa and you can tell me all about it." His hand curved itself along her arm and steered her toward the sofa with light pressure.

Without objection, Kitty allowed him to guide her to the sofa, upholstered in a geometric fabric that echoed Zuni design. Flames curled over the logs in the corner fireplace, called a kiva. Before she sat down on the plush cushions, Sebastian slipped off her shawl and draped it over a corner of the sofa back. She sank onto the cushion and curled her stockinged legs under her.

Sebastian crossed to the kiva and added another chunk of wood to the fire, then reached for the iron poker to lever the split log atop the fire.

"Where do you want to start?" he asked, his back turned to her. "The beginning would probably be a good place."

"It began in the bathroom," she retorted with a ghost of

her former anger, "when Marcel walked in and found you there. That was difficult enough to explain. Then you had to go and bring up my trio of failed marriages."

"You *are* a three-time loser." He strolled over to the sofa and sat down on the opposite end.

"I'm well aware of that. The trouble is" —she paused and sighed in discouragement—"Marcel wasn't."

"I thought you handled it rather well. It really is common knowledge here in Santa Fe. It wasn't as though you were deliberately keeping it a secret from him."

"I honestly wasn't. But . . . I think it seemed that way to him."

"Grilled you about them, did he?" Sebastian guessed.

"Naturally he asked," Kitty began, then threw up her hands in annoyance. "Why am I trying to make him sound good? Yes, he grilled me about them. And I really got the third degree over you. Quite honestly, I could understand why he did ask. I didn't like it, but I understood. If the situation was reversed, I'd probably do the same thing."

"I hear a 'but.' " Sebastian cocked his head at an inquiring angle.

She flashed him an irritated glance. "Something tells me you already know what it is. You certainly made a point of raising the issue after you so gallantly toasted us."

"What point is that?"

"About the gallery."

His head moved in a sagely nod. "I thought so."

"Marcel didn't say it in so many words, but he wants me to sell it."

"And you don't want to."

"Of course I don't. Why should I? I don't expect him to give up his work when we're married. Why should I give up mine?"

"You could always open up a gallery in Brussels," Sebastian suggested.

"According to Marcel, I'll be much too busy entertaining

his friends and family, being a wife, and accompanying him on his business trips. And he believes it's definitely wrong for the mother of his children to work at anything, period. We aren't even married yet and he's already talking about children."

"I always thought you wanted a passel of little ones."

"I do, but I don't plan on becoming a baby factory right away. I'd like to be married awhile first."

"What about that biological clock ticking away?"

"That sound you hear is a time bomb about to explode." Reacting to her own inner confusion and agitation over it, Kitty rose to her feet and walked to the corner fireplace. "I was so happy until tonight. Suddenly everything is a mess, thanks to you."

"I didn't make the mess. If I'm guilty of anything, it's of opening your eyes to it."

"As I recall, you were never to blame for anything. It was always my fault," she said with a hint of bitterness in her voice.

"I believe the official term was 'irreconcilable differences.' It covers a host of sins on both sides." His mouth twisted in a wry smile of remembrance.

Turning from the flames, Kitty frowned curiously. "Why did we break up? What went wrong?"

"We did."

"Which tells me absolutely nothing." She shook her head in disgust. "I probably got fed up with your enigmatic answers that sound so profound and say nothing."

"No, I'm serious." With unhurried ease, Sebastian stood up and wandered over to the fireplace. "I think you and I stopped trying. It's hard enough for two individuals to live together in harmony, but we also worked together. Maybe we expected too much."

"Maybe we did." She felt a sadness at the thought, and a kind of emptiness, too.

"So, how did you leave things with Mr. Chocolate?"

"Up in the air, I guess." She lifted her shoulders in a vague shrug, then admitted, "I walked out on him."

"That was a bit on the childish side, don't you think?" His smile was lightly teasing, but his eyes were warm with gentleness.

"Probably. But it was either walk out and cool off, or throw his ring in his face."

"That bad, huh?"

"That bad." Kitty nodded in confirmation. "He never seemed to hear anything I said. If he just would have listened," Kitty murmured, her shoulders sagging in defeat. "Maybe it is inevitable that I have to sell the gallery. I realize that it will be extremely difficult to run it from a distance, and I can't count on finding someone to manage it who will care about it as much as I do. Maybe I will find married life to be as busy and fulfilling as my work. I don't know. But Marcel talks as though this all needs to be set in motion now, before we're married. Why can't it be something I ease into gradually?"

"Have you told him that?" Sebastian dipped his head to get a better look at her downturned face.

"More or less."

"Which means it was less rather than more."

"It was hard to get a word in," she said in her own defense. "He was too busy planning my life."

"Something tells me he doesn't know you very well," Sebastian murmured wryly. "So, what's the next move?"

She moved her head from side to side in a gesture of uncertainty. "I don't know. I probably should call him—to apologize for walking out like that, if nothing else. But he's staying at the Ridgedales'. You know how nosy Mavis is. I hate the thought of her listening in on even one side of our conversation."

"There's always tomorrow morning."

"Marcel's flying back to Brussels in the morning. His mother is ill."

"Oops."

"I know. My timing is lousy," Kitty admitted. "Even worse, he wanted me to go with him. That's why he came early to pick me up."

"And you refused to go, of course."

"How could I? In the first place, I can't take off at the drop of a hat. Who would open the gallery in the morning? And there's the exhibit coming up. There are a thousand things that have to be done in the next two weeks. Besides, even though he said his mother isn't seriously ill, I think it's a poor time to meet my future in-laws."

"It sort of makes you wonder if his mother took sick before or after she found out he was engaged."

Her gaze narrowed on him. "What are you saying?"

Sebastian asked instead, "How old is Mr. Chocolate?"

"Thirty-eight. Why?"

"Is this his first marriage?"

"As a matter of fact, it is. But that's not so unusual. European males tend to marry later in life. That doesn't mean he's a mama's boy."

Stepping back, Sebastian raised his hands. "I never said he was."

"No, you just hinted at it. Broadly."

"It is a possibility, though."

"You're doing it again." Kitty pressed her lips together in a grim and angry line.

"Doing what?"

"Putting doubts in my mind, making me suspicious of my mother-in-law before I've even met her. Why don't you come right out and admit you don't want me to marry Marcel?"

"All right, I don't."

Her mouth dropped open. She hadn't actually expected him to admit it, and certainly not with such aplomb. "I thought you wanted me to be happy."

"I do. Just not with Mr. Chocolate."

"Will you stop calling him that?"

"Maybe you can become a taster for the family business. Sample all the new products, or work on the quality control end."

"It is impossible to talk to you," Kitty declared angrily.

"But you love chocolate."

"As a treat, yes. But I certainly have no desire to make it my life's work." In disgust, she turned back toward the fire. "Why am I even talking to you?"

"Because you know I'll listen."

Kitty was forced to concede that was true. Sebastian didn't necessarily agree with her all the time, but he always listened. Which made it easy for her to return to the heart of the problem.

"I really do love Marcel." Yet saying the words only made her situation seem more confusing.

"As Tina would say, 'What's love got to do with it?' " Sebastian countered.

"It should have everything to do with it," Kitty stated forcefully.

"Maybe." But he was clearly unconvinced.

In some disconnected way, his reply raised another question. "Tell me something," she began, eyeing him intently. "A minute ago, you admitted you didn't want me to marry Marcel, but you never said why."

"Are you sure you want to know?"

"I wouldn't have asked otherwise."

"Okay." He nodded in acceptance. "It's very simple, really. I don't want to go through the trouble of finding another dealer to represent my paintings."

"That is the most selfish thing I have ever heard," Kitty huffed. "And you claim you want me to be happy."

"I do," Sebastian replied easily, giving no indication that he considered it to be contradictory.

"You want me to be happy so long as it isn't at your expense," she retorted in annoyance. "You certainly wouldn't have any trouble finding someone reputable to represent you. As successful as you've become, they'll be standing in line to take my place."

"But I don't want the hassle of all the meetings that go along with deciding which one to pick, not to mention the strangeness of working with someone new. We've been together too long, and I don't have any desire to change horses. Besides, you know me—I'd be just as happy selling my paintings on a street corner. That's how we met, in case you've forgotten."

"I hadn't."

The memory of that day was as vivid as if it had happened yesterday. As an art major and ardent fan of works by Georgia O'Keeffe, she had come to Santa Fe during spring break to view the O'Keeffe paintings on display at a local museum. She had also planned to make a side trip to O'Keeffe's former home and studio about an hour northwest of Santa Fe.

Late one sunny morning as she walked along a street, she had spotted a half-dozen paintings propped against the side of an adobe wall, with more standing in a plastic crate. Idly curious, she had stopped to look. Mixed in with some still-life works that showed good technique but trite subject matter were a series of New Mexican landscapes and Santa Fe streetscapes that completely captivated her.

There had been, however, no sign of the artist. Each painting had a price tag attached to it, with none selling for above fifty dollars.

A hand-lettered sign with a directional arrow had instructed buyers to deposit their money in a metal cash box with a slit in its lid that was chained and padlocked to a lamppost. To her utter astonishment, Kitty had realized that this fool of an artist was selling his paintings on the honor system.

At that moment, a middle-aged couple had strolled by, paused to look at the paintings, assumed Kitty was the artist, and begun asking her questions. To this day she still couldn't say why she hadn't disabused them from that notion, but she hadn't.

Before they left, she had managed to sell them one of the Santa Fe street scenes. Buoyed by that success, Kitty had lingered. By late afternoon, she had sold a total of eight paintings, including one of the dull still lifes to a woman who bought it because the colors in it matched her living room.

Concerned that the cash box contained over four hundred dollars and curious about the artist who had signed the paintings as S. Cole, Kitty had waited, certain that S. Cole would show up sooner or later.

But she certainly hadn't expected him to be the tall, blond hunk of a man who had ultimately shown up. By then she had already fallen in love with his paintings. It had been an easy step from there to fall in love with him.

"Why?"

Lost in her memory of that day, Kitty didn't follow his question. "Why what?"

"Why did you want to know my reasons for not wanting you to marry Mr. Chocolate?"

"Just curious." She shrugged, finding it hard to return to the present. "I thought it might be something personal. I should have known it would be business."

"Would it have made any difference?"

"What?"

"If my reason were personal."

"Of course not. I'll do what I want to do regardless," Kitty asserted.

"You always do."

Something in his tone made her bristle. "And what's wrong with that?"

Sebastian took a step back in mock retreat, an eyebrow shooting up. "My, we are testy. I thought you might have cooled down a little."

"I have," Kitty snapped, then caught herself. "Almost,

anyway." A kind of despair swept over her again. "How do I make such a mess of things?"

"You simply have a natural talent for it, I guess." His smile took any sting from his words. "I have an idea."

"What?" Kitty was leery of any idea coming from him.

"Since I don't have any champagne to offer you, how about some hot cocoa?"

Kitty smiled in bemusement. "Hot chocolate, the ultimate comfort drink. Why not?"

She trailed along behind him as Sebastian headed for the small galley kitchen tucked in a corner of the studio. "Which kind do you want?" Sebastian asked over his shoulder. "The instant kind that comes in a packet or the real McCoy?"

"I should ask for the real thing, but I'll settle for the instant," she replied, not really caring.

"That's not like you." He opened a cupboard door and took a tin of cocoa off the shelf.

"What isn't?" She wandered over to the French doors that opened off the kitchen onto the rear courtyard.

"Settling for second best. Your motto has always been 'first class or forget it.' "

"I suppose." Beyond the door's glass panes, Kitty could see her spacious adobe home, its earth-colored walls subtly lit by strategically placed landscape lights around the courtyard. "I really should go home, just in case Marcel calls." She released a heavy and troubled sigh. "But what would I say to him?"

"I suppose it would be too much to hope that you might say 'Get lost, Mr. Chocolate,' " he said amid the rattle of the utensil drawer opening and the clank of a metal pan on the stove top.

"You'd like that, wouldn't you?" Kitty grumbled.

"More than you know," Sebastian replied. "Would you get me the jug of milk from the fridge? I need to keep stirring this."

As she stepped to the refrigerator, she noticed him standing at the stove, stirring something in a pan with a wooden spoon. "What are you doing?" She frowned curiously.

"Making cocoa—from scratch."

She stood there with the refrigerator door open, staring at him in amazement. "I didn't know you knew how."

"It can't be that hard. The directions are right on the can." He nodded to it, then glanced her way. "The milk," he said in a prompting voice.

Reminded of her task, Kitty took the plastic container of milk from the refrigerator and carried it to the small counter space next to the stove. "Bachelorhood has clearly made you domestic."

"Think so, hmm?" he murmured idly.

"I've certainly never known you to cook before."

"Making hot chocolate doesn't count as cooking. Which reminds me, did you know that chocolate was strictly a drink when it was first introduced?"

"Quite honestly, I didn't. I'm not sure I even care." Kitty watched as he stirred the bubbling syruplike mixture in the pan.

"As a connoisseur of chocolate, you should," Sebastian informed her. "Columbus was actually the first to bring it back from the New World. Nobody liked his version of it, though."

"Really," she murmured, intrigued that he should know that.

"Yes, really. It seems the Aztec were the first to grind cocoa beans and use the powder to make a drink. They mixed it with chilies, cinnamon, and cloves, and cornmeal—the four Cs, I call it."

"It doesn't sound very appetizing."

"I don't think it was. The word 'chocolate' is derived from the Aztec word *'xocolatl,'* which literally translates to 'bitter water.' "

"It sounds worse than bitter." The mere thought of the combination was enough for Kitty to make a face.

"It was drunk by the Aztec, supposedly out of golden goblets, and only by men. They considered it to be an aphrodisiac." He poured out some milk and added it to the dark syrupy mixture. "Naturally cocoa beans became highly prized and were eventually used as currency. In fact, ten beans could buy the company of a lady for the evening." Sebastian wagged his eyebrows in mock lechery.

"How do you know all this?" Kitty marveled.

"I've been boning up."

"Why?"

"To impress you, of course. You're the chocolate maven."

"Hardly." Kitty scoffed at the notion. "I simply like it."

"A lot," he added, while continuing to stir the mixture, waiting for it to heat. "For your information, Cortez was the one who added sugar and vanilla to the brew, finally making it palatable. But it was years, not until the mid-eighteen hundreds, that a solid form of chocolate was marketed—by the Cadbury company, if I'm not mistaken."

"You are an absolute mine of knowledge," Kitty teased half seriously.

"Impressed?"

"Very."

"Wait until you taste my hot cocoa." Using a wooden spoon, Sebastian let a few drops fall on the inside of his wrist, then gasped. "Ouch, that's hot."

"I think it might be ready," Kitty suggested dryly, then shouldered him out of the way. "You'd better let me pour before you accidentally burn your fingers and can't paint."

"See what I mean?" he said. "Who else would worry about me like that?"

"I'm sure you'll find someone." After transferring the two mugs to the sink, Kitty filled them with steaming chocolate from the pan. She passed one to Sebastian, then took a tentative sip from the other.

Sebastian watched her. "What do you think?"

"It's delicious, but much too hot to drink."

"While it's cooling, do you want to take a look at my latest? I finished it about an hour ago."

Kitty was quick to take him up on his offer. "I'd love to."

Sebastian was notorious for not allowing anyone to see a painting while it was in progress. It had nearly driven her crazy while they were married. Over the years, she had learned never to venture into his work space without a specific invitation, or risk his wrath. In that way, and that way only, he fit the description of a temperamental artist, complete with tantrums.

Moving into the heart of the studio, Sebastian crossed directly to an easel and turned it to show her the painting propped on it. She breathed in sharply at this first glimpse of a streetscape. At the same time she inhaled the familiar smells of oil paints and thinner.

The painting was an intriguing depiction of all that was Santa Fe: A stretch of adobe wall with its strange blend of pink and ochre tones set the scene. Placed slightly off center was an old wooden door painted a Southwestern teal green. A niche by the door was done in Spanish-influenced tiles. Next to the front stoop was a geranium in full flower growing out of a large pot, decorated with Pueblo Indian designs. Propped against the stoop was an old skull from a cow. Most striking of all was the dappled shade on the wall.

"It's stunning," she murmured. "The sense of depth you managed to convey is amazing, simply by showing a few paloverde leaves in the upper corner and letting the intricate shadow pattern on the adobe show the rest of the tree. It's almost eerie, the three-dimensional effect you've achieved. How on earth did you do it?"

"It wasn't that difficult. I simply kept the leaves in the foreground in sharp focus and fuzzed the edges of everything else to create the illusion of depth."

"However you achieved it, it worked," Kitty declared. "But the painting itself addresses so completely the blending of cultures in Santa Fe. You have the influence of Spain in the tiles, the Mexican adobe, and the Pueblo pottery. And the cow skull is a personification of the Old West. As for the geranium, you couldn't have chosen a better flower to denote all things American—and even Old World. And I don't think there's a color more closely associated with the new Southwest than that sun-faded shade of teal green. But I like best your reference to the desert with the depiction of the paloverde tree. It's so much more original than the usual prickly pear or saguaro cactus."

"Most people won't recognize it. It'll be just another leafy tree to them." Sebastian's voice held a faint trace of irritation.

"That's their loss. There will be plenty of others who will appreciate it." If necessary, it would be a detail she would point out to them. "Have you titled it yet?"

"I've been mulling over a couple different ones—either 'A Place in the Shade', or 'In the Shade of Santa Fe.' What do you think?"

Kitty considered the choices. "Both would work, but I like the last one best, because everything in the painting shows shades of Santa Fe."

"I don't know. It almost sounds too commercial to me," Sebastian replied.

Kitty shook her head. "I don't think so. After all, it is Santa Fe you've painted. And wonderfully, too."

"I guess that means you like it." His sideways glance was warmly teasing.

"Like it?" The verb choice was much too tame for her. "I absolutely love it."

It was completely natural to slide an arm around his waist, a gesture that fell somewhere between a congratulatory hug and a shared joy in his accomplishment. His own reaction seemed equally natural when he hooked an arm around her to rest his hand on her waist.

"Thanks." He dipped his head toward hers.

A split second later, his mouth moved onto hers with tunneling warmth. Kitty was surprised by how right it felt and how easy it was to kiss him back.

The kiss itself lasted a little longer than the span of a heartbeat before he lifted his head an inch, his moist breath mingling with hers.

"You taste of chocolate," he murmured.

"So do you," she whispered back, her pulse unexpectedly racing a little.

She wanted to blame it on her delight with the new painting. But something told her the cause was something a bit more intimate, rooted somewhere in the physical attraction that still existed between them.

Chapter Four

"I have an idea." His half-lidded gaze traveled over her face in a visual caress.

"What's that?" Kitty knew she should pull away, create some space between them, but she was strangely reluctant to end this moment.

"Let's go sit on the sofa and see how the painting looks from there."

It was an old routine they had once shared that Kitty found as easy to slip into as an old shoe, one that offered comfort and a perfect fit.

"All right."

With arms linking each other at the waist, they moved together toward the sofa. Then Sebastian pulled away with an ambiguous, "Go ahead. I'll be right there."

"Where are you going?" She frowned curiously when he circled around the sofa and headed toward the front door.

"To set the mood. There are too many lights on." He flipped off all the switches in the main area except one to a directional lamp aimed directly at the completed canvas.

"Perfect," Kitty announced in approval, then lowered herself onto the sofa's plush cushions, careful not to spill her cocoa.

"It is, isn't it?"

Before joining her, Sebastian crossed to the kiva and added another chunk of wood to the dying fire. With the poker, he stirred it to life until the golden glow from the new flames reached the sofa.

He retrieved his mug of cocoa from the side table, took a quick drink from it, then made his way to the sofa and folded his long frame to sit down next to her, draping one arm along the sofa back behind her head.

"Better drink your cocoa," he advised. "It's just the right temperature now."

Obediently, Kitty took a sip. "Mmm, it does taste good."

"Not bad at all, even if I do say so myself," he agreed after sipping his own.

"You know, if anything, the painting actually looks better from a distance," she remarked after studying it for a minute. "It seems to increase the illusion of depth."

"It does, doesn't it?"

Some wayward impulse prompted Kitty to lift her cup in a toasting fashion. "To another stunning work by S. Cole." She clunked her mug against his and drank down a full swallow. "Good job."

"Thank you."

She settled deeper against the cushions, conscious of the brush of his thigh against hers, but oddly comfortable with the contact. "I'm glad you didn't have any champagne. Hot chocolate is much better." She idly swirled the last half inch of it in her cup. "The taste is somehow soothing."

"That's due to a chemical called theobromine that occurs naturally in cocoa. It's an antidepressant that lifts the spirits."

"More research," Kitty guessed.

"Yup. And, in addition to theobromine, chocolate also contains potassium, magnesium, and vitamin A."

"Stop," she protested with amusement. "I don't need an analysis. It's enough that I feel more content."

"Content" was the word that perfectly described her mood at the moment. And the quiet setting promoted the feeling with the lights turned down, a fire softly crackling in the corner fireplace, and a beautiful piece of art bathed in light. Background music was the only thing lacking.

"Just a minute." Sebastian leaned forward and set his empty mug on the mission-style coffee table.

"Where are you going?" For an instant, Kitty thought he had read her mind and intended to put on some music.

"Nowhere." Sebastian sat back and instructed, "Tilt your head forward a sec."

"Why?" she asked, but did as he said. She felt his fingers on her hair and the sudden loosening of its smooth French twist as he removed a securing pin.

"What are you doing?" She reached back to stop him.

"Taking your hair down. It can't be comfortable leaning against the knot it's in."

"It isn't a knot. It's a twist." Try as she might, Kitty couldn't repair the damage as quickly as he could pluck out another pin.

"Look at it this way," Sebastian reasoned. "You'll be taking your hair down before the night's over anyway. Now you won't have to."

He didn't stop until her hair tumbled about her shoulders. "But I didn't want it down yet." It made her feel oddly vulnerable to have it falling loose.

"Too bad," he replied, and ran his fingers through her hair, combing it into a semblance of order. "You have beautiful hair." He lifted a few strands and let them slide off his fingers. "Sleek and soft, like satin against the skin."

"Thank you." But the words came out as stiff and self-conscious as she felt.

"You hardly ever wear your hair down. How come?"

"I prefer it up. It's much easier to manage that way." Kitty refused to pull away from his toying fingers. It seemed too much of an admission that she was somehow affected by his touch.

"And you like being in control."

"As a matter of fact, I do," Kitty admitted easily. "I couldn't successfully run my own business otherwise."

"You know what?"

"What?" She darted him a wary glance as he bent closer to her.

"Your hair smells like strawberries."

"It's the shampoo I use."

"Strawberries and chocolate, now there's a delicious combination."

Only inches separated them. Without warning, he closed the distance and claimed her lips in a drugging kiss. The potency of it scrambled her wits and her pulse. She couldn't think, only feel the persuasive power of it.

Her own response came much too naturally and much too eagerly. Frightened by it, she pressed a hand to his chest, intending to push him away. But the instant she felt the hard muscled wall and the hypnotic beat of his heart beneath her hand, any sense of urgency to break off the kiss faded.

He rolled his mouth around her lips, teasing them apart, then murmured against them, "A kiss like that can become addictive."

Kitty managed to pull together enough of her scattered wits to turn her face away. "That's enough, Sebastian." But her voice was all breathy and shaky, without conviction.

"Why?" Deprived of her lips, he simply began nuzzling her highly sensitive ear, igniting a storm of exquisite shudders.

"Because." She knew there was a reason; she simply couldn't think of it, not with Sebastian nibbling at her earlobe like that. It had always been her weakest point, and the surest way to turn her on.

"That's no reason," Sebastian replied, and licked at the shell of her ear with the tip of his tongue.

Swallowing back a moan of pure desire, Kitty hunched a shoulder against her neck, trying to block his sensuous invasion. "I'll . . . I'll spill my cocoa."

"That's easily handled." Seemingly all in one motion, he planted a firm kiss on her lips, took the cup from her hand, and set it on the low table.

Kitty barely had time to draw a breath before he was back, once more giving her his undivided attention. Too much of it and too thoroughly. Worse, she was enjoying it.

Gathering together the scattered threads of resistance, Kitty managed to push him back and twist her head to the side, creating a small space between them.

"Will you stop trying to seduce me?" she said in quick protest.

"And here I thought I was being so subtle." He automatically switched his attention to the curve of her throat.

Kitty slid her fingers into his hair, then forgot why. "Sebastian, I'm engaged to Marcel." She managed to remember that much.

"Maybe you are and maybe you aren't. It sounded to me like it was all up in the air."

"I haven't decided that," she insisted a bit breathlessly.

"I think you have." His mouth moved around the edges of her lips, tantalizing them with the promise of his kiss.

"Well, I haven't." As if of their own volition, her lips sought contact with his.

As his mouth locked onto them, Kitty recognized the contradiction between her words and action, but she couldn't seem to do anything about it. It was difficult to care when the heat of his kiss satisfied so many of her building needs.

"Funny you should say that," he murmured, lifting his head fractionally. "That's not the message I'm getting."

"I know, but . . ."

"Sh." A second after he made the soothing sound, he began a tactile exploration along the bare ridge of her shoulder, nibbling and licking her there.

It was a full second before it hit Kitty that her shoulder shouldn't be bare. The lace dress should be covering it. Simultaneously with that thought, she felt the looseness of the material along her back and the tight constriction of the sleeves binding her arms against her sides.

"You unfastened my dress," she accused in shock.

"You didn't plan on sleeping in it, did you?" When he raised his head to look at her, the firelight's dim glow kept most of his face in shadow. But there was sufficient light for her to see that his eyes were three-quarter lidded and dark with desire.

It was a sight that took her breath away because Kitty knew her own reflected the same thing.

"Of course I wasn't going to sleep in it."

"Then I'm saving you some time." His fingers inched the sleeves lower on her arms, making it impossible for Kitty to lift her hands high enough to push it back in place.

While she could still muster both the strength and the will, Kitty ducked away from him and scrambled off the sofa. Dangerously weak-kneed, she hurriedly tugged the lacy material higher with fingers that trembled.

"Kitty," his voice coaxed while his hand slid onto the flat of her stomach, evoking new flutters of desire.

"Stop it, Sebastian. You're not playing fair." Kitty weakly pushed at his hand.

"When has love ever been fair?" He rolled to his feet directly beside her, his hands already moving to gather her back into his embrace.

She wedged her arms between them, needing to avoid contact with his hard male length for her own sake.

"This isn't about love. It's about sex," she insisted, half in anger. "You've always known which buttons to push."

"You pushed mine a long time ago," Sebastian murmured as he nuzzled her neck, "and ruined me for any other woman."

"Do you honestly expect me to believe that?" Kitty sputtered at the outrageous lie. "I've seen the parade of shapely bimbos that have filed past my house to this studio. What about that blonde who was draped all over you at the last showing?"

"Cecilia." He nipped at her earlobe while the pressure of his hands arched her hips closer to him.

"Yes, sexy Cecilia, that's one," Kitty recalled even as her pulse skittered in reaction to his evocative nibblings. "What about her?"

"I never said I didn't try to find someone." He lazily dragged his mouth across her cheek to the corner of her lips. "But no one did to me what you do."

"You're just saying that," she insisted, needing desperately to convince herself of that.

"Am I?" He tugged his shirt open and flattened her hand against his chest. She felt the furnacelike heat of his skin and the hard thudding of his heart somewhere beneath it, beating in the same rapid rhythm as her own. "What about the men I've watched go through your life? All those husbands of yours."

"Two. There were only two." Somehow or other, any thought of Marcel had slipped completely from her mind.

"Be honest. Did any of them make you ache like this?" His hands glided over her back and hips, their roaming caress creating more havoc with her senses.

It was becoming more and more difficult to hold on to any rational thought. "You . . . You were always good in bed," Kitty said in defense of her own weakening resistance to him.

"Good sex requires two participants. What we shared was special. Unique."

"But it's over." She needed to remind herself of that, but saying the words didn't seem to help.

"Not for me. And not for you either, or you wouldn't still be standing here."

"No." She tried to deny it, but she also knew it was true. "This is wrong, Sebastian."

"Then why does it feel so right?"

She had no answer for that as he claimed her lips in a hard and all-too-quick kiss. "Do you remember the first time we made love?" He took another moist bite of them.

"Yes." The word came out on a trembling breath.

"I'd brought you back to my apartment to look at more of my paintings." His hands, like his mouth, were never still, always moving to provoke and evoke. "It was cold that spring night. I added another log to the fire to take some of the chill off. Remember?"

Unable to find her voice, Kitty simply nodded, her memory of that night and what came next as sharp as his own.

"As I walked back to you, I took off my shirt, wadded it up, and threw it in a corner."

He stepped back from her long enough to peel off his shirt and give it a toss. But in those few seconds, when she was deprived of the warmth of his body heat and the stimulating touch of his hands, she felt horribly lost.

Then he was close again, his hand cupping the underside of her jaw, tilting her head up, his thumb stroking the high curve of her cheek.

"Do you remember what I said to you?" Sebastian asked.

The words were branded in her memory. Kitty whispered them, "I want to make love with you."

" 'Yes,' you said," he recalled, "and the word trembled from you like the aspens in a breeze." His voice was low and husky with desire, just as it had been that long-ago night. "I took you by the hand." His fingers closed around hers, their grip warm and firm but without command. "And I led you over by the fire."

He backed away from the sofa, drawing her with him as

he skirted the coffee table and continued to the gray-and-black Navajo rug in front of the kiva. There he halted and kissed her with seductive languor.

When his mouth rolled off hers, his breathing was rough and uneven. "You wore a dress that night, too."

He took her lips again, devouring them with tonguing insistency. At the same time, his hands went low on her hips and glided upward, pushing the lace of her dress ahead of them until the hem was nearly to her waist.

The past and present merged into one as Kitty automatically raised her arms, allowing him to pull the dress over her head. It flew in a white arc to the floor near a stack of blank canvases propped against the wall. Then the darkening heat of his gaze claimed her as it swept down her body.

"You're beautiful." His voice shook, thrilling her anew.

Kitty spread her hands over his naked chest, the golden glow of the firelight revealing each ripple of muscle. "So are you," she murmured.

In a mirror of the past, her hands moved to unfasten his pants while his fingers deftly unhooked her bra. Both items ended up in a pile on the floor, forgotten as his hands moved onto her breasts, feeling them swell to fill them. Then his hands slid lower to the elastic waist of her pantyhose, leaving his lips to make a more intimate exploration of the peaky nipples he had aroused.

With almost agonizing slowness, he worked her pantyhose down her stomach and hips to her thighs, then lower still to her knees and calves. His mouth followed every inch of the way until Kitty was a quivering mass of need.

First one foot slipped free from the sheer hose, then the other. Without invitation, Kitty sank to the floor, her arms reaching to gather him against her and assuage this physical ache.

They twisted together in a tangle of arms and legs and hot, greedy kisses. She cried with exquisite relief when he finally filled her. After that it was all glorious pleasure as they made love to each other, for each other, and with each other.

All loose and liquid limbed, she lay in his arms, tiny aftershocks still trembling through her, her breathing slowly returning to normal. This feeling of utter completeness was one she had forgotten somehow.

"You are still incredibly beautiful." Sebastian gently tucked a wayward strand of hair behind her ear.

She made a small sound of acknowledgment, then admitted, "I know I feel beautifully exhausted. I don't think I could move if I had to."

"And you don't have to." He folded her deeper into the circle of his arms and rubbed his cheek against the side of her head. "As far as I'm concerned, you're right where you belong."

"That's good to know." She closed her eyes in sublime contentment, without the energy to think past this moment. For now, it was enough.

It was her last conscious thought until a harsh light probed at her closed eyelids. Kitty turned her head away from it and buried her face deeper in a dark, warm corner.

"Sorry, kitten," Sebastian's familiar voice vibrated beside her, thick with sleep. "I don't think that will work. I forgot to pull the shade down when I carried you into bed. That's the problem with this room. The window faces the east. Every morning the sun plows through it and hits you right between the eyes."

"Sun?" Groggily, Kitty lifted her head and peered through slitted eyelids toward the offending light. "You mean—it's morning?" The sun's in-reaching rays struck the stone in her engagement ring and bounced off it in a shower of sparkling colors.

Two separate things hit Kitty at the same time. She was wearing Marcel's ring and she was in bed with Sebastian.

How could she have done such a thing?

As much as she wanted to plead ignorance, Kitty remembered much too clearly that little trip down memory lane she'd taken last night—all except the being-carried-to-bed part. A little voice in her head told her that Sebastian had known all along just where that little stroll would lead.

"You dirty rotten sneak." Kitty scrambled away from him, grabbing at the top sheet to bunch it around her. "You did it on purpose, didn't you?"

"What are you talking about?" Frowning in confusion, Sebastian threw up a hand to block the glare of the sunlight. "I wouldn't have left the shade up on purpose. You know I don't like to get up early. What time is it anyway?"

"Who cares what time it is?" she declared angrily and gave the sheet a hard tug to pull it free from the foot of the bed. "I should never have come here last night," she muttered, mostly to herself. "I should have known you would pull some cheap, rotten stunt like this."

"What the hell are you talking about?"

"Don't give me that innocent look. It may have worked last night, but it won't work now." Kitty fought to wrap the loose folds of the sheet around her.

"Talk about getting up on the wrong side of the bed," Sebastian muttered, eying her with a hopeless shake of his head.

"I shouldn't even be in this bed and you know it. I'm engaged to Marcel. Remember." When she tapped her engagement ring, the sheet slipped.

"I didn't forget." His frown cleared away, its place taken by the beginnings of a smile and a knowing twinkle in his eyes.

"You knew I had argued with him. You knew it and you deliberately took advantage of it," Kitty accused.

"I don't recall hearing any objections." Sebastian's smile widened, as if he found the entire conversation amusing.

"I made plenty of objections. You simply ignored them."

Kitty impatiently pushed the hair out of her eyes and looked about the room. "What did you do with my clothes?"

"They're probably still scattered around the studio."

"You loved saying that, didn't you?" The little smirk on his face was almost enough to make her want to walk over there and slap it off him. But Kitty wasn't about to get within ten feet of him again.

Intent on retrieving her clothes and getting out of there, Kitty set off toward the studio's main section.

Within two strides, she stepped on a trailing corner of the sheet and had to grab hold of the foot post to keep from falling face first on the floor.

"That robe I borrowed from you is hanging in the closet. It might be safer to put that on to get your clothes," Sebastian suggested dryly. "Otherwise you're going to break your nose, and it's much too pretty."

"Never you mind about my nose." Just the same, Kitty wadded up the length of sheet and stalked over to the closet.

After a first glance failed to locate the robe among his other clothes, Sebastian called from across the room, "It's on the hook behind the door."

Sure enough, that's where it was. Kitty snatched it off the hook, slipped her arms through the sleeves, and let the sheet fall to the floor, then stepped free of its surrounding pile. Hastily tying the ends of the terry-cloth sash around her waist, she turned back toward the door. To her irritation, Sebastian was out of bed and zipping up a pair of paint-spattered work chinos.

"I don't suppose I can talk you into putting on some coffee," he said with that infuriating smile still in place.

"Good guess," Kitty snapped, and crossed to the door with quick, angry strides.

Sebastian trailed after her at a much less hurried pace, then split away to head to the galley kitchen while Kitty began to search for her clothes. Ignoring the sounds coming from the kitchen, she retrieved her dress from the rack of blank canvases. She found her hose draped over the handle of the fireplace poker. Her shawl was still lying across the back of the sofa. After locating the obvious articles, the search began in earnest.

Sebastian wandered over to watch. "Want some juice?"

"No." Finding nothing more on top of the room's few pieces of furniture, Kitty got down on her hands and knees to look under them.

"The coffee should be done in a couple of minutes. Want me to pour you a cup?"

"No." She wanted to find her clothes and leave, but she wasn't about to ask for Sebastian's help in the search.

"Are you sure? It might improve your disposition."

"If you fell off the face of the earth, that would improve my disposition." Spying something under the sofa, Kitty reached a hand beneath it and pulled out her nude silk panties. She tucked them in with the wadded-up dress and hose bundled in her arm.

"My, we are in a foul mood this morning."

"I wonder whose fault that is," Kitty grumbled.

"Considering that you and I are the only ones here, it must be one of us."

"I'll give you another clue," Kitty retorted. "It isn't me."

"That narrows the field considerably, doesn't it?" Sebastian replied with a smile as the aroma of freshly brewed coffee drifted from the kitchen.

"Considerably." It was awkward crawling around on the floor while holding her clothes, but Kitty wasn't about to put them down anywhere. Knowing Sebastian, she was convinced he'd probably steal them and hold them hostage. "Where is my bra?" she demanded in frustration. "I can't find it."

"It's bound to be lying around here somewhere."

"That's a lot of help." She clambered to her feet to scan the area again.

"Smells like the coffee's done. Are you sure you wouldn't like a cup?"

"Positive." Kitty circled the area again, checking behind canvases and under sofa pillows.

"Would you like some hot chocolate instead? I'll be happy to fix you a cup," Sebastian offered.

"Not on your life," she flashed. "If it wasn't for you and your hot chocolate, I wouldn't still be here this morning!"

"At least it's not my fault anymore."

"It's all your fault." Kitty looked around his work area, first high, then low. "I should have known I couldn't trust you."

"Of course you can."

Incensed that he had the gall to make such a claim, Kitty spun around to glare at him, the missing brassiere temporarily forgotten. "No, I can't. I came to you last night as a friend. You knew I was upset over my argument with Marcel. You took advantage of me."

"If there's one person in this world least likely to be taken advantage of, it's you," Sebastian observed dryly and raised his coffee cup to take a sip from it.

"That isn't true." Pushed by the need to confront him, she crossed to the small kitchen area. "You caught me at a weak moment, when I was upset and confused. Did you try to comfort me? No, you fed me hot chocolate, spun tales about it being an aphrodisiac, kissed my neck, and lured me down memory lane."

"Sins, every one of them." He lowered his head in mock contrition, giving it a shake. "I should be ashamed of myself."

"Would you stop making a joke out of everything?" Kitty protested, furious with him. "I am trying to be serious."

"That's ninety percent of your problem, kitten. You're too serious."

"And you treat everything lightly."

"Not everything."

"Ha!" Kitty scoffed. "You don't even take your work seriously. If I hadn't come along, you'd still be selling your paintings on a street corner. You said so yourself."

"True. But that doesn't mean I'm not serious about my painting, because I am. It's just a question of ambition. And, heaven knows, you have enough of that for both of us."

"Is there anything wrong with that?" she challenged.

"Only when it gets in the way of life and living."

"And my work doesn't," Kitty asserted. "For your information, I have a life. The proof of that is right here on my finger." She shifted the bundle of clothes to her opposite arm and displayed her engagement ring. "If I were all work and no play the way you try to make me sound, I wouldn't have had any free time to date Marcel, let alone become engaged to him."

"We're back to Mr. Chocolate, are we?"

"We've never left him."

"I beg to differ," Sebastian said. "As I recall, you did last night before you showed up at my door."

"I didn't leave him. We were arguing, and I simply walked out before I lost my temper and said something that I would regret."

"So you came here and unleashed it on me." His lazy smile revealed just how little he had been affected by it.

"You deserved it after the trouble you caused," Kitty muttered, controlling her temper with the greatest of difficulty.

"I caused it?" Sebastian drew his head back in mock innocence. "Why are you blaming me? You're the one who argued with him."

"We went over all that last night," she reminded him. "You're not going to bait me into going over it again."

"Too bad." His mouth twisted in a smile of feigned regret. "Considering the way our conversation last night ended, it could have been a wonderful way to start the day."

Furious beyond words, Kitty growled a sound of absolute exasperation and spun away to resume her search for the missing brassiere. Before she could take a step, the doorbell chimed.

Its ring was like an alarm bell going off. Gripped by a sudden sense of panic, Kitty froze in her tracks.

Chapter Five

"Who in the world could that be?" Sebastian frowned and started toward the door.

"Wait." Kitty grabbed his arm to stop him. "What time is it?"

"I don't know."

She glanced frantically around the studio. "Don't you have a clock somewhere?" She glanced at the sunlight streaming through the French doors, but she had no idea how to tell the time of the day from the angle of the sun.

"You know how I hate them," Sebastian chided. "Why? What difference does it make?"

"Because if it's past eight-thirty, it could be Harve wondering why I haven't shown up to open the gallery this morning. If it's him, don't let him in, whatever you do." Kitty briefly toyed with the idea of making a dash for the bedroom, but if Harve happened to look in the front window, he would see her.

"Why not? He's found you here before," Sebastian reminded her.

"Not in the morning," Kitty hissed as she backed deeper into the galley kitchen, aware that its area couldn't be seen from the doorway. "And certainly not with me in a robe. You know exactly what he'll surmise from that."

"It would be true, wouldn't it?" Sebastian countered, smiling at her predicament.

"That's none of his business," she whispered angrily as the doorbell chimed again, then repeated its summons insistently. "Go. Get rid of him."

When Sebastian moved to the door, Kitty shrank into a corner, trying to make herself as small as possible. Silently she scolded herself for taking the time to gather up her clothes; she should have left Sebastian's studio the minute she got up.

The snap of the dead bolt was followed by the click of the door latch. But it wasn't Harve's voice that Kitty heard next.

"Monsieur Cole." It was Marcel who spoke, and her heart jumped into her throat and lodged there. "I am concerned for Kitty."

"Kitty?" Sebastian repeated, and she knew he was positively gloating inside.

"Is it possible that you would know whether she arrived safely home last night?" Marcel inquired.

"Had an argument with her, did you?" Sebastian asked instead. "Not over anything important, I hope."

"Mere trifling matters."

Trifling? His outrageous choice of adjective was almost enough to make Kitty charge to the door and confront Marcel. Only the thought that Sebastian would get way too much enjoyment out of such a scene prevented her from doing just that.

"Walked out on you, did she?" Sebastian said, as if he already didn't know that.

"Have you seen Kitty?" There was a note of suspicion in Marcel's question, enough to heighten the sense of panic Kitty felt.

"Isn't she at home?" Sebastian countered.

"She did not answer the door."

"What time is it? Maybe she's already left to open the gallery," Sebastian suggested.

"Not at this hour, surely," Marcel protested. "It is only half past seven o'clock."

"That early? I—"

"What is this?" Marcel demanded suddenly.

To her horror, Kitty saw Sebastian being forced to back up and open the door wider. A clear indication that Marcel had stepped inside. She flattened herself against the corner, her heart pounding like a mad thing.

"This is Kitty's shoe." Marcel's announcement bordered on an accusation, and Kitty realized that Marcel had noticed the pumps Sebastian had set on the catchall table by the door.

"Does she have a pair of heels like these?" Sebastian asked, again deftly avoiding both a confirmation and a bold-faced lie.

That's when Kitty spotted her missing bra. It dangled from the back of the sofa, a strap precariously hooked over the rounded corner of its back. It was clearly within plain sight of the door. Marcel was bound to see it; it was only a matter of when.

For now the open door blocked her from view. But if Marcel stepped past it, she could easily be seen. Kitty glanced frantically around, searching for a better hiding place. Her widely swinging gaze screeched to a stop on the French doors that opened onto the back courtyard.

Did she dare try to reach them? There was only the smallest chance she could escape detection if she remained where she was. But if she could manage to slip outside, unseen, she was home free.

"There is a lady's brassiere hanging off your sofa," Marcel declared in a tone of voice that insisted on explanation.

With fingers figuratively crossed that Marcel would be

sufficiently distracted by the sight of the lacy undergarment not to notice her, Kitty tiptoed as quickly and quietly as she could across the Saltillo-tiled floor to the French doors.

"So it is," Sebastian confirmed from the front door area as Kitty fumbled ever so briefly with the dead bolt lock. The latch made the smallest *snicking* sound, but Sebastian's voice covered it. "I had company last night. She must have forgotten to take it with her."

Not a single hinge creaked to give Kitty away. She opened the French door no farther than necessary and slipped outside. Immediately she darted to the left, not bothering to close the door behind her.

Any second she expected to hear a cry of discovery from Marcel. But none came. The minute she reached the security of the exterior adobe wall, Kitty halted to lean against it and drink in a shaky gulp of air.

Now, if she could just make it to the house without being seen.

But she soon realized that was impossible. There was a taxicab sitting in the driveway. Any approach to the house would be seen either by the driver or Marcel.

She debated her next move. She could remain where she was until Marcel left, or—Kitty froze, stricken by the realization that waiting for Marcel to leave wasn't a viable option. Her evening bag was on the coffee table. Sebastian might be able to convince Marcel that two women could have the same pair of shoes. But an evening bag, too? That would be too much of a coincidence.

If Marcel noticed the evening bag, Kitty was certain he would take a closer look. When he did, he would find her driver's license and a credit card inside, along with the usual lipstick, compact, and mascara. Her escape from the studio would have been for nothing.

Kitty knew she had to do something before Marcel discovered she had been in the studio last night. She knew of only one way to accomplish that.

Hastily, she stashed her bundle of clothes under an ancient lilac bush that grew next to the corner of the building. She peeked around its branches to make sure Marcel hadn't stepped back outside. But all was clear. After double-checking the sash's knot, Kitty took a deep, galvanizing breath and dashed from behind the bush toward the studio door, choosing an angle that might convince Marcel she had come from the house.

Marcel stood just inside the doorway. Kitty had a glimpse of Sebastian's bare chest just beyond him, his body positioned in such a way to prevent Marcel from gaining further entrance to the studio.

"Marcel." She didn't have to fake the breathlessness in her cry.

He swung around with a start, a look of utter relief lighting his whole face. "Kitty!"

His arms opened to greet her. She was swept into them just outside the door. Automatically Kitty wrapped her own arms around him while he pressed kisses against her hair and murmured little endearments in French.

A guilty conscience kept her from responding to his embrace—that and the sight of Sebastian leaning a naked shoulder against the doorjamb, an amused smile edging the corners of his mouth.

"Kitty, Kitty, Kitty," Marcel murmured in a mixture of relief and joy as he drew back and framed her face in his hands. "You are all right, *non*?" He ran his gaze over her face in rapid assessment. "I had fear that you came to harm."

"I'm fine," she assured him.

"Where have you been?" The look of worry reentered his aquiline features.

"I . . . I just woke up." Kitty stalled, trying to gain enough time to come up with an explanation that might satisfy him.

With a frown, Marcel glanced past her toward the house, then brought his probing gaze back to hers. "But I rang the bell to your door many, many times, and you did not answer it."

"I should have warned you," Sebastian inserted. "Kitty sleeps very soundly. A bomb would have to go off outside her window before she'd wake up. Even then, I'm not sure she would."

There was some truth in that, but not enough for Kitty to feel comfortable fielding more questions from Marcel. The certainty of that came with his next query.

"Why did you not answer the telephone? I rang you a hundred times after you left the restaurant."

"I wasn't ready to talk to you last night." Which was the truth as far as it went. Attempting to take the offensive Kitty asked, "What are you doing here?"

"When you did not answer the door, I had worry that you suffered a mishap and did not arrive home last night. I came here to speak with Monsieur Cole in the event he was aware of your return."

Sebastian spoke up, "I was just suggesting that he might check with the hospitals or contact the police to see whether you might have been involved in some accident on your way home."

"I see," Kitty murmured hesitantly, then explained, "Actually I was wondering what you were doing here because you had told me that you were flying back to Brussels early this morning."

"Ah." Marcel nodded in new understanding. "I postponed my departure. I could not leave when I was so concerned for your well-being."

"I'm glad you didn't leave today." At least Kitty knew she should be glad. But she felt so much nervous turmoil inside that she had trouble identifying any other emotion.

"We have much that we must discuss," Marcel began.

"Indeed we do," Kitty rushed, and darted a lightning glance at Sebastian, who was unabashedly eavesdropping. "But not here." She tucked a hand under his arm. "Let's go to the house. I'll put some coffee on and we can talk."

Before she could lead Marcel away, Sebastian inquired lazily, "Did you bring your key with you?"

"My key?" She gave him a blank look.

Sebastian nodded toward the house. "I can see from here that the door is closed. It locks automatically when you shut it. Remember?"

That's when it hit her that, as always, she had locked the house when she left with Marcel last night. Without a key, she couldn't get back in. And her key ring was in her evening bag on Sebastian's coffee table.

Thinking fast, Kitty said, "Do you still have that spare key I left with you?"

"Yes—"

"I'll get it." She pressed a detaining hand on Marcel's arm. "Wait here." She moved quickly toward the door, anxious that he wouldn't follow her inside.

"Do you remember where it is?" Sebastian shifted to the side, giving her room to pass.

"As long as you haven't moved it someplace else."

"I haven't."

"Good."

Kitty slipped inside and hurried straight to the coffee table, resisting the impulse to snatch her bra off the corner of the sofa.

Her evening bag lay exactly where she'd left it. She opened it, took out the ring of keys, and snapped it shut. With her fingers wrapped around the keys to silence their jingle, Kitty rushed back outside, straight to Marcel.

"All set," she declared with false brightness. Her smile faltered when she observed the hint of sternness in his expression. "Is something wrong?" she asked, worried that he had somehow seen through her charade.

"You do not wear slippers." His glance cut to her bare feet.

Kitty almost laughed aloud with relief, but a response

such as that would have been inappropriate. "I was in such a hurry I guess I forgot to put any on. Shall we?" As subtly as possible, she urged him toward the house.

Marcel stood his ground a moment longer and nodded to Sebastian. "I regret that I troubled you needlessly."

"Oh, it was no trouble," Sebastian assured him, then let his glance slide pointedly to Kitty. "In fact, it was all pleasure."

Inwardly she did a slow burn over Sebastian's parting shot as she ushered Marcel across the courtyard to her home's rear entrance. When she stepped forward to unlock the door, Marcel took the keys from her.

"Allow me," he said with typical courtesy, then inserted the key and unlocked the door, giving it a slight inward push.

He stepped back, motioning for Kitty to precede him into the house. She had barely set foot inside when he asked, "Why does this artist have a key to your house?"

"Someone had to let the maid in to clean when I vacationed in Cancun this past winter. Since Sebastian lives on the grounds, he was an obvious choice."

Actually that was true; Kitty had left a spare house key with him on that occasion, but she'd also gotten it back when she returned from the trip. But it was another one of those half-truths that pricked her conscience.

"That is another thing I wish to discuss with you," Marcel stated.

At that instant, Kitty knew she was much too tense, and the feeling of dancing around eggshells was much too strong for her to talk to Marcel right now. She needed a respite from it, however brief.

"There is much we need to discuss," she told him. "But it can wait a few more minutes. I'm such a mess." She pushed a smoothing hand over her loose hair in emphasis. "I'd really like to freshen up and slip into some clothes first. I won't be long."

Giving Marcel no opportunity to object, Kitty hurried

from the kitchen. The instant she reached the safety of her bedroom, she leaned against the closed door, tipped her head back to stare at the high-beamed ceiling and took a deep, calming breath.

A part of her wished she could stay in the room and never come out, but the rational side knew that was impossible. Pushing away from the door, she headed to the closet. Aware that dallying over a choice of clothes would accomplish little, Kitty quickly selected a pair of hunter green slacks and a cotton sweater in a coordinating apple green.

In five minutes flat, she walked out of the bedroom, fully clothed, a minimum of makeup applied and her long hair pulled back in its usual sleek bun. She decided there was some truth in the old saying that a woman's clothes were her armor. She certainly had more confidence in her ability to handle things.

Marcel had not ventured from the kitchen. He stood by the French doors in the small breakfast nook, staring in the direction of the studio. His hands were buried deep in the pockets of his trousers, his jacket pushed aside, and a heavy frown darkened his expression.

"I told you I wouldn't be long," Kitty said by way of an announcement of her return.

He dragged his gaze away from the view with a trace of reluctance that had little frissons of alarm shooting through Kitty. Had he seen something? For the life of her, she couldn't think what it might be.

Kitty hurried into her carefully rehearsed speech. "Before anything else is said, I want to apologize, Marcel, for walking out on you like that last night. It was—"

He didn't give her a chance to finish it. "It would be best for you to inform Monsieur Cole that he must move somewhere else."

Dumbfounded, Kitty stared. "I beg your pardon."

"I said, it—"

This time she cut him off. "I heard what you said." She

simply couldn't believe that he'd actually said it. "But I'm afraid that what you suggest is impossible. According to the terms of our divorce settlement, I got the house and Sebastian received the studio. I can't order him to move out. I have no right."

"Then we must find a different place for you to live until we are married," Marcel stated.

He suspected something about last night. Kitty was certain of it. Some of the inner panic started to return.

"Whatever for?" She forced a smile of confusion. "This arrangement has worked for years. Sebastian lives there and I live here."

"But it is not right that you should live so closely to him."

Worried that she was back on shaky ground, Kitty attempted an amused protest. "Surely you aren't jealous of him, Marcel."

"Mais non." His denial was quick and smooth, completely without question, which in itself was a bit deflating. "I simply do not wish my fiancée to associate so closely with his kind."

"His kind?" Kitty seized on the phrase, then challenged, "Exactly what do you mean by that?"

He gave her a look of mild exasperation. "It is known to all, Kitty, that such people are self-absorbed and self-indulgent, which leads them to loose ways of living."

Outraged by his blanket condemnation of an entire profession, she said furiously, "That is the most ignorant statement I have ever heard. For every artist you can show me who's into drugs and alcohol and wild parties, I can show you fifty who are honest and caring, hardworking people with families to support and a mortgage to pay."

Turning haughty, Marcel declared, "Please do not attempt to convince me that Monsieur Cole is one of these. Last night he entertained a woman in his studio. I saw with my own eyes this morning the articles of her lingerie flung about the room in wild abandon."

That nagging sense of guilt resurfaced to steal some of the heat from her indignation.

"His private life is no concern of mine," Kitty insisted in a show of indifference.

"But your life is a concern of mine, now that we are to be married. And I should think it would be a concern to you. This is what I attempted to explain to you last night, when you objected so strongly to selling your gallery. But you refused to listen to me."

"Try again," Kitty stated, her anger cooling, dropping to an icy level.

"It is quite simple, really," he began with a trace of impatience. "Even you must see that running a gallery of necessity brings you in frequent contact with such people. It would not be acceptable to continue such associations after we are married."

Kitty cocked her head to one side. "Acceptable to whom? You? Your friends? Your family?"

Sensing the hint of disdain in her words, Marcel drew himself up to his full height. "Is it wrong to value the good reputation of the Boulanger name?"

"That is the most supercilious question I have ever heard," Kitty snapped.

But before she could denounce him for being the snob that he was, the doorbell rang. For the first time in as many days, she sincerely hoped it was Sebastian. Right now, nothing would delight her more than to inform Marcel that she was the abandoned woman who had spent the night with Sebastian.

A smile of anticipated pleasure was on her lips when she opened the back door. To her eternal disappointment, the cabdriver stood outside, a heavyset man of Mexican descent.

"Por favor." He swept off his billed cap and held it in front of his barrel-round stomach. "Does the señor still wish for me to wait for him?"

"That won't be necessary. He's ready to go." Leaving the

door open wide, Kitty turned back to Marcel. "It's your taxi driver. I informed him that you'll be leaving now."

His jaw dropped. Kitty found his initial loss for words quite satisfying.

Recovering, Marcel managed to sputter, "But . . . We have still to talk."

"As far as I'm concerned, everything's been said." Kitty walked over to usher him to the door. "And you have a plane to catch. Here"—she paused to tug the diamond off her finger—"take this with you."

When she offered it to him, Marcel simply stared at her in shock. She had to actually open his hand and press the ring into his palm.

Even then he didn't appear to believe her. "You return my ring? I do not understand."

"That doesn't surprise me in the least."

"But—"

Kitty could see him frantically searching for words. "It must be obvious that I wouldn't make a suitable wife for you. And the thought of marrying a bigoted snob like you makes me sick."

In an indignant huff, he opened his mouth to object. Kitty didn't give him a chance to speak as she bodily pushed him out the door.

"Good-bye, Mr. Chocolate. Knowing you has been very enlightening and bittersweet," she added, unable to resist the analogy. "More bitter than sweet, actually, rather like your chocolate."

Marcel reacted instantly to that criticism. "Boulanger chocolate is of the finest quality."

"It's a pity the same can't be said about the family who makes it."

Across the courtyard, Kitty noticed that Sebastian was now standing outside the opened French doors to the kitchen area. As before, he was dressed in his work chinos, a cup of coffee in his hand, still without shirt or shoes.

"As much as I would enjoy trading insults with you, I really need to excuse myself." Her smile was all saccharine. "You see, I left some things at Sebastian's last night that I really need to pick up."

"Last night?" As understanding dawned, Marcel's expression turned thunderous.

"Yes, last night," Kitty repeated happily, then taunted, "I hope you don't expect me to draw you a picture. Sebastian's the artist, not me."

With that, she walked away from him, this time for good and without a single regret.

Chapter Six

The courtyard echoed with the sound of Marcel's hard-striding footsteps as he stalked to the idling taxi trailed by the slower-walking cabdriver. It was a sound that Kitty rather liked, and one that was punctuated by the creak of hinges and the metallic slam of the vehicle door.

Without so much as a backward glance, she walked directly to the gnarled lilac bush that towered by the corner of the studio. She was conscious of Sebastian watching her while she retrieved the bundle of clothes from beneath its lower branches.

"Mr. Chocolate didn't stay long," Sebastian observed when she emerged from behind the bush.

"There was no reason for him to stay." Kitty brushed a leaf off her shoulder.

"I see he took his ring with him." He used the coffee mug to gesture toward her bare ring finger.

"I insisted on it," she replied, then added quickly, "But don't start thinking you had anything to do with that decision. Because you didn't. There were simply too many important issues that Marcel and I couldn't agree on." Out in the street, the taxi backfired and rumbled away. Staring after it, Kitty couldn't resist adding a parting shot, one laced with thinly veiled sarcasm. "And I wasn't about to change just to be worthy of being his wife."

"I'm not trying to start another fight by saying this," Sebastian remarked, "but he is the one who wasn't worthy of you."

Everything softened inside her at the unexpected compliment. Kitty flashed him a warm smile. "Thank you."

"For what? It's the truth."

"I know, but it's still nice to hear someone else say it."

"Even me?" Sebastian teased.

"Even you," Kitty replied, then paused thoughtfully. "You know something else? I really didn't like his chocolate all that well, either."

"I can guarantee it couldn't be as good as my hot chocolate."

She eyed him with irritation. "I should have known you wouldn't be able to resist making a reference of some sort to last night. Let's just forget about it, shall we? As far as I'm concerned, it was all a big mistake."

"I think you're a little mixed up. Getting engaged to Mr. Chocolate was the mistake."

"That was a mistake, all right. And I'm not going to compound it by getting baited into a long, fruitless discussion with you. So if you don't mind"—Kitty moved toward the open door—"I'll just get my things and leave."

"Help yourself." With a swing of the cup, Sebastian invited her inside the studio.

As she approached the French doors, she felt a sudden nervous fluttering in her stomach. Kitty hesitated briefly before crossing the threshold. When she stepped into the studio's kitchen area, her heart began to beat a little faster. She felt exactly like a criminal returning to the scene of the crime, as all her senses heightened.

Without looking, Kitty knew the minute Sebastian followed her inside, even though his bare feet made no sound at all on the tiled floor. His presence made the spacious studio seem much smaller and more intimate. Or maybe it was the sight of her silk and lace brassiere still hooked on a back corner of the sofa, combined with her own vivid recollections of last night's events.

"Would you like a cup of coffee?" Sebastian's question was accompanied by the faint sound of the glass coffee carafe scraping across its flat burner, an indication that he was refilling his own cup.

"No, thank you." Kitty snatched the bra off the sofa corner and stuffed it in with her other bundled garments.

"Are you sure? It's—"

"I'm positive." As she circled the sofa to the coffee table, Kitty was careful not to glance in the direction of the kiva and the Navajo-style rug on the floor in front of it.

"Suit yourself," Sebastian said with a shrug in his voice. "Do you know something that amazes me?"

"No, but I'm sure that you're going to tell me." Kitty was deliberately curt, inwardly aware it was a defense mechanism. It bothered her that she felt a need for it.

"It's the way you run straight here every time you break off a relationship with some guy."

"That's ridiculous." She scooped up her evening bag, the last of the items she'd left.

"Is it?" Sebastian countered. "Look at this morning. You barely gave Mr. Chocolate a chance to climb in his cab before you made a beeline over here."

"I'm here to collect my things. There's nothing strange about that," Kitty insisted, and automatically glanced around, double-checking to make certain nothing else of hers was lying about.

"What about all the other times?" he persisted.

"Actually, I've never given it any thought. And there haven't been that many 'other times,'" Kitty retorted.

"But why come here? An ex is usually the last person you would want to tell."

"We are far from being enemies, Sebastian." She threw him a look of mild exasperation.

"But we aren't exactly friends, either," he pointed out. "There's always a subtle tension running between us. Why do you suppose that is?"

"I have no idea." It wasn't something Kitty wanted to discuss, and certainly not now. She moved toward the open French door, eager to leave now that she had retrieved all her things.

Sebastian stood by the kitchen counter, one hip propped against it. "Did you tell Mr. Chocolate you were with me last night?"

"It's really none of your business whether I told him or not."

Kitty wished that she had left by the front door. It would have been a much shorter route, and one that wouldn't have taken her past Sebastian. But she was committed to her path. If she changed directions now, Sebastian might suspect her reluctance to be anywhere close to him.

"I'm afraid it is my business," he informed her with a hint of a smile. "You know how these Europeans can be. He might decide to challenge me to a duel, and I'd like to know whether or not I should admit you were here."

"He knows. Okay?" she retorted with impatience, quickening her steps to reach the door.

"I'll bet that made him mad." Sebastian didn't move an inch as she swept past him.

"He was furious. Does that make you happy?" She threw the last over her shoulder, then opened the door, safety only two feet away.

"You're a lot more trusting than I thought you would be."

His odd statement brought her up short. On the edge of the threshold, Kitty swung back, curious but wary. "What do you mean by that?"

"I thought for sure you'd check your evening bag and

make sure I didn't take anything before you left." He continued to stand there, idly leaning against the counter.

"What would you take? There's nothing in it of any value except a credit card. Why would you want that?" As illogical as it seemed, Kitty knew Sebastian had taken something. Otherwise he wouldn't be drawing her attention to it now.

"I never said I took anything."

But that knowing gleam in his eye advised that she had better look. Kitty stepped over to the small breakfast table, deposited her wadded clothing on top of it, and unhooked the clasp on the slim bag. A quick check of the contents revealed nothing was missing. But there was something sparkling at the very bottom. She reached inside and pulled out a small solitaire ring—at least, it was small compared to the multicarat engagement ring Marcel had given her.

"Find something?" Sebastian wandered over to look.

Dumbfounded, Kitty dragged her gaze from the ring to his face. Staring in confusion, she murmured, "It's . . . It's my old ring. The one you gave me."

"So it is." He nodded in a fake show of confirmation, then met her eyes, a smile tugging at one corner of his mouth. "As I recall, you had a suggestion for what I could do with it when you gave it back to me. But I thought better of it."

"But what's it doing in my bag? Why did you put it there?" That was the part she didn't understand.

"It's very simple, really." He took the ring from her unresisting fingers, then reached for her left hand. "You seem to be determined to have some man's ring on your finger. I decided it might as well be mine."

As he started to slip the ring on her finger, Kitty jerked her hand away, pain slashing through her like a knife, bringing hot tears to her eyes.

"Everything's just one big joke to you," she lashed out angrily. "I'm sure you think this is funny. But it isn't. It's cruel and heartless and mean."

"This isn't a joke," Sebastian replied. "I'm dead serious."

"And pigs fly, too," Kitty retorted, resisting when he attempted to draw her hand from behind her back.

"I don't know about pigs. I only know about you and me," he continued in that irritatingly reasonable tone. "Since you seem so eager to marry somebody, it might as well be me again."

"That's ridiculous," she said, her voice choking up. She tried to convince herself it was strictly from the depth of her outrage.

"Why is it ridiculous?" Sebastian countered, and pushed the ring onto her finger despite her attempts to stop him. "After all, it's better the devil you know than the Mr. Chocolate you don't."

"Will you stop this, Sebastian! I am not laughing," Kitty tugged at the ring, trying to pull it off. "If this is some twisted attempt to make me feel better about breaking things off with Marcel, it isn't working."

Sebastian trapped her face in his hands and forced her to look him squarely in the eye. "Be quiet for two seconds and listen. I want to marry you again. I don't know how much plainer I can say it."

For the first time Kitty suspected that he really meant it. Suddenly her thoughts were all in a turmoil. "But . . . It wouldn't work." She said it as much to convince herself as him. "We tried it before and—"

"So? We'll try it again." A soft light warmed his eyes and his easy smile was unconcerned.

"You're crazy," Kitty declared, more tempted by the thought than she wanted him to know. "Have you forgotten the way we argued all the time?"

"Not about important things," he replied.

"That isn't true." She was stunned that he could have forgotten their many stormy scenes.

"Think back," Sebastian countered. "Ninety percent of all our arguments were about trivial things—like the proper way a tube of toothpaste should be squeezed. The only time we fought about anything major was when we let our business differences interfere with our marriage."

"Business differences?" Kitty repeated incredulously. "We don't have any business differences."

"Not anymore, now that you've finally stopped trying to promote me and settled for pushing my paintings."

"I never—" But she had. It all came back in a rush. The endless fights over his refusal to attend his own showings or to do any kind of publicity to promote his work. "It used to infuriate me the way you made fun of everything I tried to do to see that you received the recognition you deserved as an artist."

"And you took it personally," Sebastian concluded.

"Yes."

"I'm sorry for that." He pushed back a wayward strand of hair, a loving quality in his touch.

"So am I." Everything smoothed out inside her.

"So what's your answer?"

"My answer?" For a second, Kitty didn't follow him.

"Are you going to marry me or not? After last night, you can't deny the fire's just as hot as it always was."

"I think both of us are crazy," she said instead.

"Why?"

"You for asking and me for accepting."

His mouth moved onto hers even as she rose to meet it. It was a kiss full of promise and passion, a pledge one to the other. For Kitty it was exactly like coming home.